PROJECT VOYAGER

VERN & SUSAN NORDMAN

BLUE FORGE PRESS

Port Orchard, Washington

Project Voyager
Copyright 2020
By Vern Nordman and Susan Nordman

First Print Edition November 2020
First eBook Edition December 2020

ISBN 978-1-59092-984-1

For information about film, reprint or other subsidiary rights, contact blueforgegroup@gmail.com

This is a work of fiction. Names, characters, locations, and all other story elements are the product of the authors' imaginations and are used fictitiously. Any resemblance to actual persons, living or dead, or other elements in real life, is purely coincidental.

Blue Forge Press is the print division of the volunteer-run, federal 501(c)3 nonprofit company, Blue Forge Group, founded in 1989 and dedicated to bringing light to the shadows and voice to the silence. We strive to empower storytellers across all walks of life with our four divisions: Blue Forge Press, Blue Forge Films, Blue Forge Gaming, and Blue Forge Records. Find out more at www.BlueForgeGroup.org

Blue Forge Press
7419 Ebbert Drive Southeast
Port Orchard, Washington 98367
blueforgepress@gmail.com
360-550-2071 ph.txt

*To anyone who has ever dreamed
of the possibilities of life
beyond our solar system.*

ACKNOWLEDGMENTS

Thanks to Neil deGrasse Tyson, Stephen Hawking, Carl Sagan, Albert Einstein, and all scientists dedicated to understanding our world and the space that surrounds it. While we never interviewed you for *Project Voyager*, we did watch a lot of your documentaries.

ALSO BY VERN NORDMAN

Uncle Sam, My Sailor, and Me:
Experiences on the Lighter Side of a Long Military Life

ALSO BY SUSAN NORDMAN

Psions of Janus: Ascension (Book 1)

PROJECT VOYAGER

Vern & Susan
NORDMAN

CHAPTER 1

"**D**amn it, Sam, you cranky bitch. Don't you freeze up on me now!"

"John!"

"Huh! What?" I asked innocently.

"John, if you are going to swear at a piece of unfeeling, uncaring, imamate machinery, at least try to not do it over an open mic."

"Oh! Sorry, Luv."

That was Dr. Alexandria Cummings, PhD telling me to behave myself. On the job, she's Dr. Cummings and the Director of Operations for Project Voyager and my boss. Off the job, she's just Alex, still my boss, but also my ever-loving spouse.

Physically, Alex was three hundred miles away, not as the crow flies, but as the asteroid plummets because she was three hundred miles straight down. Her plush office was in a big hangar on a huge airfield just outside of a hot and dusty town smack-dab in the middle of the California desert in a place called Sand Flea City... and that's all I have to say about that.

Alex's office was so up-graded it practically hummed. She had enough super-duper, super modern and super expensive communication systems at her fingertips that she was able to monitor all of Project Voyager's activities and still keep me on the straight and narrow even though I was in orbit and she wasn't.

Alex was right, of course. She usually is; I shouldn't swear at Sam. Short for Samantha, this version was actually Sam II. The original Sam was the female voice of a Global Positioning System unit that I had owned many years ago that just annoyed the hell out of me with her constant—RECALCULATING! My current Sam didn't recalculate, but at odd and unpredictable times she would decide to seize up and just stop working which wasn't very helpful when you're sitting in a plastic ball in the void of space.

My current Sam is a construction robot designed to build things in the cold, unforgiving vacuum of outer space. I guess she isn't much to look at, but there is nothing else like her and her sisters in the world... either above or below. She, I always think of her as a she, is just a clear, super strong ball made of some top secret, ultra-grade plastic-like material, about eight feet in diameter with four mechanical arms, an unpredictable solar power pack, (also top secret) and an environmental system that provides a shirtsleeve environment inside the ball and lets me work in space without a space suit.

She does, however, have two major faults. The first is her storage pouches that are normally filled with the tools of our trade because they are located at extremely inconvenient places on the outside of her well-endowed middle. The second is the control panel. The operator, that's me, sits inside the ball and has to use this control panel to manipulate the mechanical arms to get at the tools in the pouch on the outside of the ball. The pouch, again located around her middle, is perfectly positioned where I can't see it. Like anything that should be simple, this was designed by idiots who would never actually use it and therefore was made as complicated as it could possibly be.

Sam II earned her nickname because just like my old, and not so faithful GPS, this current piece of machinery could be just as frustrating. And of course, Alex is correct—not in that I shouldn't swear at an inanimate piece of machinery, but because Sam is *my* piece of machinery and as cranky and obstinate as she is, I love her. Sam and I have an understanding and I know for a scientific fact that if I didn't curse her a blue streak once in a while, she'd feel unloved and quit on me. She occasionally quits on me anyway, but that's just Sam letting me know she cares. What I shouldn't do is swear over an open mic. Bad, John... very bad!

By the way, my name is John, John Marshal.

Yes! *That* John Marshal. The one who got blamed for the spectacular rocket explosion on the launch pad at Kennedy a few years ago. Of course, when the big bang went off, none of the senior engineers, politicians, administrators, presidential appointees or anyone else involved in that particular fiasco were going to take the rap. The shit and the stink rolled downhill until it landed on the junior engineer of the project—me!

It wasn't my fault. Really!

Due to weather, high tides caused by rising sea levels, parts not delivered on time, crappy parts that were delivered but were unusable and a dozen other reasons, the scheduled rocket launch had been postponed seventeen times over a period of four months. The senior engineers, politicians and administrators who were now denying responsibility were the same ones who decided that after each postponement, it would be too inconvenient to cover the rocket while it stood outside in the weather or too expensive to move it back inside. No matter how many times they were told protecting their precious rocket would be less costly in the long run, the Powers That Be refused to listen and actually demanded we leave the darn thing on the launching pad until showtime. Dumb! And as a result, there it sat for four months exposed to the heat, wind, rain... and birds.

Stupid birds.

Full of naïve honesty, little junior engineer me, told them several times and in no uncertain terms that it wasn't a good idea to leave the big rocket outside. It was, after all, an expensive and delicate machine that wouldn't take kindly to the elements.

The PTBs didn't listen and just patted me on the head and told me to run along. Having about as much authority as a freshman at a senior dance, I had no choice but to obey.

Being young and dumb, I insisted that it should be re-inspected nose to tailfins before it launched and naturally assumed that suggestion was a no-brainer when, in not so many words, they in effect said, "Go away, boy, you bother me."

The inspections obviously never happened because in addition to all the problems sitting out in the weather could possibly cause any piece of machinery let alone a space rocket, a bunch of birds, (seagulls, I think) had taken up residence in one or more of the exposed nozzles. When launch day finally came, the 3—2—1—IGNITION! was followed by an Earth-shattering kaboom that didn't do the seagulls or my career any favors.

After that well publicized fiasco, the only reason I got this job on Project Voyager was because of Alex. She's one super smart lady! She's not only an expert in cybernetics, but also telecommunications and half a dozen other fields—the only dumb thing she ever did was hook up with me. I, on the other hand, definitely married up.

Now, as a graduate engineer, I'm not exactly moron material. I'd saved all my money when I was in the Army and taken advantage of every government education program that I could get my hands on in order to earn my Engineering Degree. But after being thrown under the bus in what was being called the 'Rocket Incident', my prospects of any future engineering employment had been reduced to approximately zero.

After driving a forklift at a local warehouse for a couple of years, my prospects looked to remain zero until Alex pulled a few strings.

During this dismal time, my second and much more important job was as Alex's chauffeur... air chauffeur that is. I had been in love with flying ever since I was a kid and I had held my single and twin-engine licenses for years. So, whenever Alex was hired to give a lecture or to consult on something, we would just jump into our little old single engine puddle-jumper (which we affectionately called PJ), and I would fly her to wherever she needed to go. It saved her the airport hassle while I got to sit in on some interesting meetings and lectures, meet some interesting (and not so interesting) people and enjoy a free meal now and then.

A side benefit of flying Alex around was that while we were in the air, we got to look down and enjoy Mother Earth from above—although lately there wasn't much left to enjoy. It seemed that since the world started warming up, we mostly tracked the damage that the latest hurricane (fifteen named hurricanes last year) had caused. Of course, hurricane coverage was on all the Vid newscasts, but it wasn't until you saw it for yourself, and from above, that you began to realize how deeply in trouble Mother Earth was.

Florida and the entire Southeast Coast of the US was especially taking a licking. Miami alone had an inch of water covering the streets even at low tide. Another thing we noticed in our trips up and down the East Coast was a lack of shipping of all kinds from the big container ships right down to the smaller fishing boats. It was obvious that fewer sailors were venturing out upon the briny deep and who could blame them? Storms were increasing in both strength and numbers; A mariner could set sail on a beautiful, warm sunny day when suddenly a completely unpredicted and unpredictable storm would blow up seemingly out of nowhere. The Vid was full of news reports of ships lost at sea and fishing boats that failed to return to port.

A direct result of the falloff in the shipping industry we couldn't help notice was the lack of *stuff* available in the stores. All kinds of stuff from food and clothing to household and big-ticket items were becoming increasingly scarce on store shelves and the cost of the items that were available had gone up—way, way up.

The Vid said that the huge international shipping companies were spending billions on their port facilities to combat rising sea levels and keep international shipping moving, but from what we could see from the air, it seemed a futile exercise. Although the President and most of the local politicians denied it, even environmental novices like Alex and me could see that the coastlines were shifting. After a major storm, many inland areas remained flooded.

But I guess like most everyone else, we didn't give it too much thought, either. Beyond observing and commenting and complaining about shortages and rising prices, we were just kind of drifting along. Alex was writing a book, (something about cybernetics that I didn't understand a word of), taking an occasional consulting job and giving lectures.

It was sometime in here when Alex received one of those life altering phone calls. A huge multi-national conglomerate called Visions Unlimited was considering her for a position as Project Manager for their Project Voyager exploratory probe to Mars and would she be willing to come to Los Angles this coming Friday for an interview?

You bet she would!

At the time we were living in Florida. Seeing as her interview was only two days away, and Visions Unlimited was providing first-class airline tickets *plus* door to door limo service, she flew out commercial. When she returned after an entire weekend of grilling interviews and cross-examinations, she greeted me with, "Well, my love, we have jobs."

"We?" I said, too stunned to process her words clearly. "As in both of us?"

"As is both of us," she smiled... rather smugly too, I thought. "I told them we were a package deal. If they wanted me, they'd have to hire you, too."

After the 'Incident' they must have really wanted her! In order to make their Project Manager happy, Visions Unlimited offered me a job as an operator for one of their newly invented Space Construction Robots, the machines that were going to launch their space construction industry and build their space craft—in space.

I said, "Wait? What? You signed me up to work in space. As in *outer* space?"

"Of course not! You won't be in outer space," Alex laughed.

I can't tell you how relieved I was to hear that!

"You'll only be three hundred miles above the Earth which is not even a fraction of the way to the moon, which technically still counts as inner space. Sounds interesting, don't you think?"

"Well, yes! No! I don't know? It's all kind of, you know... sudden. Space?"

"To help your thought process, my love, they are offering me a quarter of a million a year to manage this thing they call Project Voyager and they are offering you a hundred and fifty thousand a year to operate one of their robots."

That actually did help my thought process... a lot. "I'll take it!"

Alex and I then hit the internet to see what we could find out about our jobs and our new employers. There wasn't much on either. Unlike many of the modern-day companies constantly on the Vid and internet bragging about some new gadget they might have put on the market or about how wonderful they are, Visions Unlimited tended to keep quiet; However, despite this extraordinarily low profile, they still managed to make billions.

On Project Voyager, there was even less information. The only thing we were able to find was a single press release about an exploratory mission to Mars.

We did mange to find out that the Visions Unlimited Corporate Offices were in Los Angles and it made me think of them as an octopus with tentacles stretching out in all directions. In some ways, they're sort of like a think tank, but they were also in control many manufacturing companies; However, no one seemed to know exactly what companies or research institutions VU (we pronounced it "view") actually owned or directed, what projects they were working on or even who all the Directors of VU were. The internet did say that some guy named Harrison was the Chairman.

From my perspective, they seemed to be one of those background companies that you never hear about until they suddenly brought a new product or innovation to the market and, whenever they did, it always seemed to be a blockbuster. The speculation was that they have teams of scientists under contract secretly working on their various projects all over the world, but nobody really knew for sure.

One name that kept floating to the top in our internet searches as being on Visions research team was a Professor Gustave Gutman. Now, even we had heard of Gutman. His was a name that almost everyone in the world had heard of, but someone no one really knew anything about. The Man of Mystery was a German or Hungarian or Pole—somewhere in that part of the world—who was a professor of something or other who had been around for years expounding wild and unproven theories about energy drives, fusion, anti-matter and who knows what all. I guess that most scientists and the world in general had written him off as a quack, but after seeing his name connected to some *really* smart guys like the ones employed by VU, I wasn't as quick to discount him as a nut case.

My own pet theory was that Gutman was a modern-day Count Dracul who had a bunch of aging, gray bearded, middle European scientists imprisoned in the dungeons of his medieval castle somewhere in Transylvania chained to their work stations inventing doomsday devices to end the world. Just a thought.

Meanwhile, Visions Unlimited just went quietly ahead making billions on their inventions and products.

This particular brain child, Voyager, was touted as a manned survey mission to Mars whose purpose was to investigate the possibility of establishing a colony. Their plan wasn't to place this colony on the surface of the planet as other private companies and NASA were envisioning, but in caves and caverns underground where they could create an Earth-type environment. My guess was that once they did that, they would then go into the real estate business—one of their more ambitious attempts to make a buck in outer space.

They certainly weren't the first people to dabble into the space business. As there were already half a dozen companies, billionaires or groups of billionaires not to mention the government already exploring various aspects of the space business, I guess that you could call Visions the interstellar Johnnie-Come-Latelies.

It all sounded pretty nutty to me.

All we really knew was that Project Voyager was going to be based out in the California desert on an airfield near a town called Sand Flea City which didn't sound very promising and looked even less attractive when we looked it up. Despite this, Alex and I signed on anyway.

Seeing as the VU Board of Directors seemed pretty anxious to get Project Voyager under way, Alex took the car and headed west while I packed up our stuff, got it loaded on the moving van and followed her out in PJ.

That was quite a flight! It took me almost a month of dodging weather to get from Florida to the California Desert.

First, I had to go North all the way up to Pennsylvania to get out of the way of yet another hurricane that was bearing down on the Florida Panhandle. I landed at a little field just west of Pittsburgh and after I taxied in, shut down and arranged for servicing, I was asked if I wanted dinner and shelter here at the airfield. That's when I got my first real taste of how things were going weather-wise in this part of the country. Constant wind and rain and one tornado after another made traveling even the five miles into town for a meal and a motel iffy.

So, the folks who ran this little airstrip were making an extra buck, actually a lot of extra bucks, providing food and a bed to transients like me.

Then once I got started west, I was grounded twice—once in Ohio and once in Arkansas waiting out tornado alerts. Yeah, I had to fly north from Florida to Pennsylvania in order to fly back south to Arkansas! Someone on the Vid said that the United States used to get twelve or fourteen hundred tornados a year and now it was close to three thousand. I felt like I was flying around the pieces of a jigsaw puzzle!

What you really couldn't get from the Vid was how extensive the flooding in the mid-west was. When I was finally heading in the right direction, it seemed to me that every river, stream, brook or little creek was out of its banks. Towns were flooded and roads looked like dash lines as they rose in and out of the water. Farmland was under water as far as I could see. I'm no agricultural expert, but it seemed to me that it was going to be a very lean harvest this year. When I flew over the Mississippi River, it reminded me of the floods back in the nineties. It looked like the Amazon in the wet season.

After wandering around the mid-west dodging tornados for a couple of weeks, I finally made it into Texas and a whole new set of weather problems as vast grassfires raged over West Texas and New Mexico. Fires can create their own air turbulence, especially for a little guy like PJ, so I wasn't dumb enough to try to fly through them. As they were just too extensive to fly around, I was stuck on the ground again.

I was stuck on the ground for three days, but no sooner did I get back into the air when I was grounded again waiting out a huge sand storm. Haboobs the locals called them, which always amused me, but this was no laughing matter. Dust storms could bring a plane down in no time.

As a result, it was almost a month after Alex had left Florida that I finally flew up to Sand Flea Airfield. Now that was a whole experience in itself and I will never forget the sight! I guess with a name like Sand Flea, I was expecting to see a small hard surface landing strip with a couple of old hangars sitting out in the cactus, but that mental vision was about as far from reality as you could get. Sand Flea Airfield was enormous.

As I flew in from the east, practically all I could see from horizon to horizon was an industrial complex with a single east/west runway in the middle that was at least two miles long and three or four football fields wide. There were acres of hard surface parking aprons and big... really big... hangars stretching off to the north and south on both sides of the runway. On past the flight line I could see manufacturing type buildings and warehouses of all kinds.

This place was huge! I even overflew a rocket launch pad and I saw another one off to the south. If I wasn't mistaken, there was an electrical power plant in the southern industrial area.

I wondered what the hell I was flying into. I really wondered when I made my initial tower call identifying myself and PJ and requested landing instructions and was told to just go ahead and land.

Beg pardon?

They said again that I was clear to land.

Ah! As a new guy, could I get a little info?

I could hear laughter in the background as they gave me the weather, field elevation, wind (there wasn't any) bug advisory—clear (what the hell was that all about?) temperature (122 degrees), traffic (there wasn't any). And then they told me again to just go ahead and land.

By this time, I was more than a little confused. Air traffic control is usually a little more formal than that. But, okay.

As I overflew the field, I could see the town, Sand Flea City, off to the north maybe four or five miles away. My first impression was that it was a pretty good size town, maybe twenty-five or thirty thousand people. There was one east/ west highway cutting through the north edge of town which disappeared into the shimmering heat in both directions. A smaller road wound into the hills to the north, but all of the other roads out of town, including a four-lane divided boulevard, went south to the airfield.

Making my approach, I could also see that there were practically no airplanes on this giant airfield. There were a couple of cargo planes on the south side and a handful of executive type jets scattered around, but that was it and as far as I could see there was no commercial terminal. But as I flew to the west and turned around, I over flew an aircraft storage park. It looked like there were two or three dozen commercial jets just parked there in the desert. Some looked as if they'd been there for quite a while.

I landed right at the western end of this long, long runway. Hell, PJ was so small, I could have probably landed on a tennis court and the sight of my tiny little plane on this massive airstrip got a big laugh from the tower. The Tower radioed and asked where I was going. When I told them Visions Unlimited, they laughed again and said that at least I had picked the right end of the airfield and I wouldn't have to taxi the whole length of the field because I would probably run out of gas before I got there.

Comedians. Considering the amount of traffic here, I guess PJ and I were the only action they'd had today and they were making the most of it. Anyway, they directed me onto a taxi way and then onto acres... and acres... of concrete parking aprons towards a huge hangar on the north side of the runway. There were two more hangars beside it heading away from the runway all surrounded by the vast concrete wilderness.

The hangar doors didn't face the runway, but were on the side. As I taxied up, the doors opened and there was Alex standing right in the doorway waving a little flashlight around like a parking wand.

My wife, also the comedian. Alex directed me and little PJ into this giant hangar that was so huge, you could have parked a 747 in it with lots of room to spare. Alex kept backing up waving her little flashlight until poor little PJ was right in the center of this cavernous and completely empty hangar.

Alex thought that it was hilarious and I had to admit PJ did make quite a sight sitting all alone in the middle of this giant hangar.

Giving me a big welcoming kiss, Alex said, "Welcome to Voyager."

CHAPTER 2

Looking around the cavernous empty hangar and at the smug expression on Alex's happy face, it was obvious that she knew things that I didn't.

I said, "I don't mean to be picky, Luv, but unless Voyager is pushing the limits of stealth technology, I don't see anything that looks like a spaceship. In fact, the place looks a little like, well... empty."

Alex laughed and poked me in the ribs. "Of course, you don't see anything, you big oaf.

All this here on the ground at Sand Flea will be the support facility. You, my love, are going to build Voyager," and she pointed to the ceiling, or rather to what was above the ceiling, "up there."

Oh, yeah. I knew that.

Walking me over to one side of the hangar, Alex started filling me in on the local set-up. Even before there was such a thing as a Project Voyager the Visions Unlimited operating area consisted of buildings and hangars for something called the Starduster Program, but they had since acquired three more hangars for Voyager for a total of six and had now taken over a substantial chunk of real estate on the airfield.

"So, what and where is Starduster?" I asked.

Alex kind of frowned. "Starduster, my love, is a space shuttle. It's the breakthrough that everyone has been looking for, for fifty years: a shuttle that can fly under its own power from Earth right up into space and land on its own back on terra firma. The Starduster Program is located in the next three hangers over, but at the moment there aren't any Stardusters. The facility here at Sand Flea is being set up for sending paying customers on a day trip up into space and for the servicing and maintenance of the shuttles. The Stardusters themselves are being built at some plant up in Kansas. This hangar and the other two in this row belong to me, or rather to Voyager."

"Wow! Can they really do that? Just fly up into space?"

She frowned again. "Well, the big brains that VU have working for them say they can, but the program seems to be stalled in the manufacturing plant. But come on and I'll show you what I do have."

As we walked across the hangar, I saw two cars parked inside and asked, "That our car?"

"Yes. With the heat, wind, sand and bugs, everyone tries to stay inside, and we also try to keep vehicles inside as much as possible."

Alex led me through the door into a really plush suite of offices. The suite came complete with a reception area, a very decorative receptionist named Elizabeth (nice kid, never did know her last name), a couple of offices, a conference room and even a full bath with a shower and clothes closet. From her point of view, the most important item of her administrative set up was the multi-million-dollar communications package that Visions Unlimited had provided.

She was like a kid at Christmas. The very big desk was smooth and flat until she pressed a couple of buttons. When she did so, panels slid back and a computer and Vid screens rose up. With the press of another button, she could view or speak to any area in the three hangars, receive any Vid transmission that was broadcast world-wide or communicate with anyone anywhere. Alex said that once we were up and running, if that ever happened, surrounded by her Vid screens and computers she would be able to even monitor our progress or lack of it in space as well as deal with the Project's many vendors, contractors and manufactures.

"Very impressive, Luv. However, if you don't mind my saying so again, it does look a little empty around here. How many employees do you have for Project Voyager?"

"With your arrival, my love, we now have three."

"What?"

"Three!" Alex laughed. "You, me and Elizabeth." She seemed completely undaunted by the number.

"Ah! Pardon me for pointing this out, Luv, but that seems like a mighty thin workforce to build a space ship."

Alex laughed again. "Patience, my sweet, patience. I have plans! But first, let's enjoy my very expensive plush chairs, have some coffee and I'll give you a run down on the set up here at Sand Flea."

For someone who had only been here a couple of

weeks she was pretty clued in on the town and the major companies. "If Starduster ever becomes operational, it would be in competition with a couple of other companies here who are also trying to make a buck from the space tourism angle. The Wendover Group is one of them. It's a big outfit and they own the whole southern half of the airfield. Among other things, they have a real-life rocket launch pad about five miles further south."

"Yeah. I saw that one when I flew in," I said, pleased that I at least knew *something* about the area.

"Their main effort, though, seems to be the production of rockets—big heavy-lift rockets, but they have also produced a kind of space shuttle that will be carried into the upper atmosphere by another aircraft. Once it achieves a certain altitude, the shuttle will be released and fly up to touch the bottom of space. This will give their passengers a few minutes of weightlessness and a terrific view of Earth for a quarter of a million bucks a pop."

I whistled at the expense until I reminded myself that I was going to get paid for the same experience. Nice!

Alex continued, "Wendover is also exploring the possibility of establishing a colony on Mars. Another big company here is Pearson Enterprises. Pearson is working on rocket powered shuttles that could fly under their own power up to the lower regions of space and land under their own power back on Earth. Kind of like our Starduster, only without actually getting out into space. I don't think that they, or anyone else knows about Starduster and I think VU would like to keep it that way."

I nodded that I understood and took a sip of my coffee.

"Robertson Rockets owns most of the northeast side of the field, down the other end of the flight line from us, and they are also in the heavy lift rocket business. They have a launch pad off to the east."

"Yup! Saw that one too when I flew in," I said, doubly pleased with myself that I could at least locate the launch pads.

"I guess those are the major companies. Oh, there's also Nielsen Engineering who makes precision machine parts. They're a pretty big outfit, but not in the space business."

"What about air traffic?"

"Nothing commercial. The only traffic is private for the various companies—and the military, of course."

"Military?"

"Many, probably most of the companies here have government or military contracts of one kind or another, so military procurement people, engineers, etc. are popping in and out all the time."

"Impressive, Luv. How did you learn so much so quickly?"

"Oh, no secret. There's a loosely organized airfield management committee that meets every two weeks to discuss items of mutual interest: air traffic control, security, runway sweeping, stuff like that. They like to talk; I like to listen."

I thought that was very impressive. Alex had only been here a couple of weeks herself. In just one, two meetings at best, she'd absorbed just about everything she needed to know about our neighbors.

Alex's train of thought kind of wandered off to other organizations in other locations around the country that were engaged in space activities. In Texas, a company was building really heavy-lift rockets to boost large objects into orbit—for a fee, of course, and another group was also going to put a colony on Mars.

The US Government was still in the space game, but they seemed to be fifty years behind the private organizations in some areas and still seemed to be fixated on the Moon. The current administration didn't seem to be much interested in space outside of the military aspects of orbiting weapons and they were very suspicious of any and all civilian attempts to do anything in outer space.

Apparently, there were still other companies who were considering setting up whole industries in space. Their interests ranged all the way from mining to manufacturing and using the asteroid belt as a source for raw materials.

"Wow! Space mining. Is that even possible?" I asked, both intrigued and skeptical.

"Well, a lot of people with really deep pockets seem to think so."

Then she told me about VUs plans as much as she knew them. Apparently, the Visions Unlimited Board of Directors were pretty stingy with their information even with senior employees, but from what Alex could determine, while standing on the shoulders of all the space researchers who had come before, Visions Unlimited was going to carve out their own niche in space.

"Well, several niches," Alex said. "First, Visions Unlimited owns a space station."

That got my attention. "Really? A real space station?"

"Yup! A real space station like the International Space Station. They call their station 'Wisdom' and it has been quietly orbiting three hundred miles over our heads for a couple of years now. Wisdom is manned by VU scientists who do their work up in space and rotate back to Earth every three or four months or so. Of course, seeing as this isn't a government operation, Wisdom will conduct any test or experiment someone requests."

"For a fee of course," I smiled.

"But, of course! And, unlike the government, Visions Unlimited is more than breaking even on their space station. Apparently, we have been listening to Wisdom for a couple of years now and didn't even know it. The Wisdom science team always has at least one meteorologist on board to participate in global weather forecasting. From what I've found out using my magnificent new communications system and talking directly to their chief Meteorologist, Dr. Al Wilson, the Wisdom meteorologists also bombard the government and anyone else who wants to listen with information on Global Warming and Climate Change. In Wilson's opinion, the current administration seems to be the most anti-science bunch since the Inquisition; The current government just doesn't want to listen."

"Typical," I said rolling my eyes. It made me wonder how many storm-of-the-century events we could have in a single decade to get them to open theirs.

"Second, I told you about Starduster. They look kind of like the old space shuttles of the eighties and nineties, but without the necessity of the rocket boost and are capable of a powered landing."

Yeah. I could see the tourist potential. Instead of the five or six minutes of weightlessness at the bottom of space that Pearson and Wendover were offering, Visions space shuttle customers would fly right out of the Earth's atmosphere up into space and get a couple of weightless orbits of Earth for their $250,000.

Alex thought for a minute and said, "I have plans for Starduster."

I looked a question at her, but she just smiled and shook her head. "Later, my love. We'll see. The third thing is that VU is going to go the current Mars planners one better. Instead of a rocket landing on Mars, VU is going to build a spaceship that can travel to Mars and land under its own power.

"Forth, instead of building a spaceship on Earth that would require a rocket boost to get into space, VU is going to establish a whole new industry of space construction and actually build their spaceship in space. Visions Unlimited named this little flight of fantasy Project Voyager. And that, my love, is where you and I come in."

Right.

Alex had found us a very nice apartment in town not too far from the airfield; In fact, it was just off that big boulevard that I had spotted flying in. Among its other attractions, it had an over-sized air conditioning unit. With temperatures now hitting over 115 degrees every day for more than half the year—sometimes getting up around 125—we needed it. We even bought a big generator as a backup to keep us from melting when the power went off—as it often seemed to do these days.

Our apartment complex also had a swimming pool that was in an enclosed courtyard. With Global Warming pushing temperatures ever higher, the pool was too hot to swim in during the day but rather pleasant in the late evening or early morning. Kind of like a warm bathtub. The main attraction of the enclosed courtyard was that it provided some protection from the Haboobs, those really big, nasty, ugly dust storms, that were blowing up with alarming frequency.

The little courtyard also had some big fans set up, not so much for cooling but to help keep the bugs away. It seemed that as the temperature rose, the bug populations were also going up. Especially gnats. Little, tiny gnats each one hardly bigger than a spec, but they came in giant swarm clouds that we could see for miles. They didn't bite or sting, but they got into your eyes, your ears, mouth, and clothes. They could drive you mad.

I didn't get to hang around and enjoy the apartment and Alex's plush office for long before I was sent up north to some suburb of Chicago to a manufacturing plant called Ajax Industries. These were the people who had contracted to design and build the construction robots and as one of their pilots, there were things that I needed to know... apparently.

Most of what I got out of my trip was that for smart people, they were extremely dumb. It didn't take me long to really, *really* dislike these guys. One of the Visions Unlimited Directors must have owned or had a majority interest in Ajax because after I met them, I couldn't imagine any other reason that these inept knuckleheads would be given the contract.

It is, however, where I met Sam.

Sam and her eleven sisters were designed and put together by the so-called scientists and engineers at Ajax—a team of complete morons who were never going to have to operate them in space. Although no one had ever actually constructed anything in space outside of sticking together pre-fabricated space stations, the guys at Ajax who designed and built the robots clearly knew all that there was to know about space construction robots and building things in zero gravity.

If you didn't believe that they knew everything, just ask them.

For a while there, I was a lone voice in the wilderness of reason until help arrived in the form of three more newly hired construction robot operators: Jack Jackson (everyone called him JJ), Fred Thompson and Billy Wright. While I was accumulating an ulcer in Chicago, Alex had been busy and Project Voyager had now doubled in size. We now had six employees!

Fred, Billy and JJ quickly proved that they were good, practical, hard-headed engineers who took one look at the ongoing construction of the robots and wholeheartedly joined me in the fight. Sadly, though, it was hopeless as any practical suggestions that we, the future operators, made as to construction, function or design of the robots just rolled off the Ajax people like water off of a duck's back.

For example, the storage pouches that I mentioned for carrying tools and various bits of hardware. For some reason known only to them, the Ajax people had located the tool bag around the outer midsection of the ball while they put the control panel where the operator was going to sit against one of the inner walls. Obviously, having the tools out in space with the pilot protected inside the ball was a very good thing, but with that design it took a bit of yoga for the operator to twist around to see exactly what he is taking out of the pouches and putting back in.

We said, "It's a clear plexiglass ball."

We said, "You are in space. Zero G."

We said, "Why not put the operators console in the middle of the ball with a nice 360-degree view? Or, if you are going to insist on putting the console forward why not put the storage pouches forward where the operator can actually see them?"

We were wasting or breath. Not only does sound not carry in space, it didn't carry with these maroons, either. During the many months and years that we worked on Voyager, I don't know how many tools and other bits and pieces of hardware we lost control of due to Ajax's ingenious design of the robots. As hard as we tried to prevent it, stuff just sort of drifted away and went into orbit. If I had a way to collect our tools and all the other pieces of junk that are floating around up there, (over 35,000 someone estimated) I could probably open a hardware store somewhere and retire quite comfortably.

But I digress. With the aid of these construction robots, Voyager was going to be built in space.

Well, hopefully not *entirely* built in space.

It was evident that we couldn't influence the design and construction of the robots, but there was a possibility we could have some sway on the actual construction of Voyager. The construction robot operators (we started calling ourselves robot jockeys which then got shortened to RJs) might be able influence how much actual construction we would or could accomplish.

We could see where the Visions people were coming from: they were trying to create a new industry, a space construction industry. Maybe a good idea and maybe in the future it would work, but not with these robots. After all of us

RJs had a turn manipulating the robots four mechanical arms we came to a unanimous conclusion: the robots could handle and assemble large objects, but it would be impractical to actually try to manufacture anything.

I know that the VU Board didn't want to hear that. Alex didn't want to hear that. I don't know what kind of discussions went on, but Alex gave us the word that the original plan would go forward, but every effort would be made to manufacture components on Earth and send sections as large as possible up to orbit for assembly.

Okay, we'll take what we can get. In our opinion, the bigger the pieces, the better. If they sent us little pieces, it might take us forever, but we'd eventually get it done, but as they say, it's their money.

After I fiddled frustratingly around Ajax for a few weeks, I was sent to some old closed down Air Force Base near Big Spring, Texas that now had several rocket pads. With the Atlantic Ocean steadily rising, the costal launch sites were all but useless and launch facilities were being moved inland. Also, with the current administration diverting funding away from space programs, everyone who had been associated with government space programs and could find another job with civilian industry was bailing out (pun intended). A team of technicians (I thought I recognized some of them from Kennedy), gave me some basic training in the wearing of a space suit for working EVA maneuvers in the vacuum of space. Not that I would ever need it, they said. Both Wisdom and the robots had atmosphere and were shirt sleeve environments, so I would probably never have to wear a space suit.

The lying dogs.

During the next weeks, months and years, I and the

other robot jockeys became the world's leading experts in maneuvering and working in free space.

When it was time to actually start launching stuff into orbit, the Powers That Be decided that the first item that was needed up at Wisdom was a construction robot.

Why?

I have no idea, but as I was designated as the lead operator, Sam and I would be the first ones to fly up to Wisdom.

It wasn't an honor. I guess after the *Rocket Incident,* I was considered the most expendable. I knew some of those guys were from Kennedy!

Alex insisted that she knew nothing about this.

Well, in those early days of Project Voyager, we didn't actually fly up into orbit. The Starduster space shuttles that VU was developing were still not ready—almost, they said.

I noticed they said "almost" a lot.

Their solution was to stick Sam and me on top of a big-ass rocket. After a massive explosion that shook apart every atom in my body, my stomach got sucked down into my lower intestine as they literally threw us into space. I was never so scared in my life! I think that the Project might have made a little extra money on the side by selling the recording of my terrified screams to Hollywood.

For some reason, it didn't seem to bother Sam.

When we arrived in orbit, we found that Wisdom was just a regular looking run of the mill space station made from a collection of pre-assembled modules that had been boosted up into space and then stuck together. The only thing that made this space station different from the International Space Station was the fact that it wasn't operated by NASA or any other government agency. This was a private enterprise.

To this day, I still have no idea how Visions Unlimited got hold of a space station and managed to get it launched, assembled and operational without it being all over the Vid. Like the ISS, a rotating team of scientists cycled in and out, did various experiments, wrote reports, made weather observations and so on.

For me, of course, Wisdom's main function was as a base to build the Voyager spacecraft that was going to explore Mars.

Well, not quite.

It wasn't until I actually got up to Wisdom that I found out what the Visions Unlimited Board of Directors really planned to do with Voyager. A secret that was so well guarded that only a handful of people in the entire world knew it. As there was no way they could hide the fact that we were building a spaceship in space without every astronomer and school kid with a telescope knowing, Wisdom announced the station was going to be used as a base to build a space vehicle to go to Mars.

True as far as it went. Voyager *was* going to Mars—but the secret was that it wasn't going to stop at Mars.

What Visions Unlimited envisioned with Voyager was not only a get-away from Earth vehicle, it was a get-away from the Solar System vehicle. An honest-to-goodness, hand-across-my-heart spaceship designed to go to another world... a world orbiting around another sun in another star system.

Effing awesome.

CHAPTER 9

After my heart stopping departure from Earth on the top of the big-ass rocket, I drifted up to Wisdom in my old-fashioned space capsule. I had no control over anything and seeing as everything was automated, I just sat back and watched as the capsule docked at one of the entry ports—Wisdom had three. (I don't know why there were three docks, but it turned out to be a good thing.) It was a weird feeling just being a spectator while the computer lined the capsule up to one of the docks, floated it in and secured it. Then a crane-like grapple reached out, opened the cargo bin, and extracted Sam.

I was relieved when Sam was taken over to another one of the entry ports and attached to Wisdom. With that setup, I could enter Sam from Wisdom without having to go out into space. The Ajax people had said I wouldn't have to, but I didn't trust them.

When everything was sealed and I floated out of the

dock into the station I must have bounced off of every hard surface in sight. Floating in zero gravity is a kick, but it does take practice.

I certainly had mixed feelings when I first arrived at Wisdom ready to start working on Voyager. First and foremost I thought that the Visions Unlimited people were bat-shit crazy to think that we could actually build a spaceship up here in space and bat-shit crazier to think that a spaceship, with two dozen passengers no less, could travel to a planet in another star system, carry out an exploration of undetermined duration and return to Earth.

I may not be the brightest bulb in the chandelier, but I did know that space is kind of like 'BIG' and stars, planets and such things are kind of like really, really far apart. On top of that, if I remembered anything from school it was Einstein who said that you can't travel faster than the speed of light, which is about 186,000 miles a second, and who am I to argue with Einstein?

That's also what all the other scientists with all the fancy letters before and after their names said and I found no reason not to believe them, either. So, even if we *could* travel at light speed (which we can't and aren't anywhere close to achieving) it would still take four years to get to our closest star and maybe hundreds if not thousands of years to get from Earth to a star system with an Earthlike planet.

I presumed that once Voyager with its team of explorers arrived at the planet, wherever it was, it would then take just as many years to get back to Earth—and that's not counting the time that it took to actually explore the new world.

It was crazy but in my little brain, there wasn't really

any conflict. One side said, "These guys are crazy!" but that side was completely overwhelmed by the other side that said, "One-hundred and fifty thousand bucks a year!"

I was convinced that, even if we did manage to put it all together, it would never get any farther away from Earth than Wisdom was right now. But what the hey! The cash that Visions Unlimited was shelling out for this venture was fantastic and if they wanted to pay me a hundred and fifty thousand bucks a year to fly around up here operating Sam just to put their nutty idea together, I was definitely their man.

Yup, no conflict for me, anyway.

Yet in another side of my tiny little brain, I knew that the Directors of Visions Unlimited were no dummies. Seeking enlightenment, I went to my primary source of information— Alex—and asked her what made VU think that they could travel to another planet? Or rather, send other people to explore another planet? And why would they go to the expense of doing it?

After reminding me for the umpteenth time that traveling to anywhere except Mars was a deep dark secret, Alex filled in the blank spaces in my little brain. The concept of Voyager, she told me, started with three completely unrelated events.

The first was Global Warming, or to use its more accurate term: Climate Change. The Directors of Visions Unlimited are very intelligent people who didn't get where they were by ignoring facts; And the obvious facts were that if the human race continued to follow their current trends in carbon production, resource exploitation and over population, the Earth's life support system was going to collapse, or to be more accurate, it was already collapsing. They determined that if the human race was going to survive it either had to change its ways or it needed to find another home. The Directors of VU were also smart enough to know that human beings were too stupid to change their ways. It seemed obvious to them that people weren't going to stop destroying the only home they had ever known. So, in the next hundred years or so, maybe sooner, Earth was not going to be a very pleasant place to live, if humans could live here at all.

Others had been keen observers of the obvious also and that was why several private corporations at Sand Flea like Wendover, Robertson and a few others were working on Mars, Moon and even orbital habitat projects.

The second reason that made VU think that Project Voyager was viable was the work or at least pronouncements of the mysterious professor, Gustave Gutman, who claimed to have invented something he called 'the Gutman Drive'. This drive, Alex said, was a power source for engines of all kinds that, among other things, could also power a starship at nearly the speed of light.

Yeah, right! But for some reason, the Board of Directors at Visions Unlimited believed him.

The third item or event was the launching of a new space telescope. A telescope that was ten times more powerful than any of the existing telescopes, either on the ground or in space, whose positioning was much farther away from Earth than any of the telescopes it replaced. With this expanded capability, a whole new world of space exploration suddenly opened up and a million new Gee-Whiz space stories and unbelievably beautiful pictures of what was out there filled the media outlets every day.

The story that seemed to capture everyone's attention was the discovery of what looked to be an Earth-type planet in a star system that was only, *only* mind you, twenty light years from Earth. The as yet unnamed planet, amusingly nicknamed Planet X, was right in our own back yard—just a hop, skip and a hyper-jump away... so to speak.

The Visions Unlimited people believed they could build a spaceship and with the Gutman Drive travel to this planet would only, *only* again mind you, take them twenty years.

Sure, they could.

Of course, the talk shows were full of uneducated opinions about Planet X, but the truth of the matter was that no one knew what the flora and fauna of the planet was really like or if it even *had* flora and fauna. The astronomers said that Planet X was the fourth planet from its star, which also didn't have a name, just a string of numbers. Seeing as no one could remember or say the numbers the same way every time, someone started calling the star Sol II, then someone else called it Sol II and now everyone on Earth was calling it Sol II.

The only things that the scientists would say for sure was that Sol II was a little bigger and brighter than our Sun and that the orbit of Planet X was, supposedly, in the just right, not too hot, not too cold Goldilocks habitable zone.

And that's about all that anyone really knew for sure. Everything else was pure speculation. The fact that Planet X was in the Goldilocks Zone still didn't mean that it *was* habitable. Was there life? Higher life forms? Intelligent life? They didn't even know if Planet X had the little things a human prefers—like dry land, potable water... *air!*

With Voyager the Directors of Visions Unlimited were

not only thinking big, they were also thinking long term. If the newly discovered planet was habitable and Voyager got there first and claimed it, VU would own the only real estate that humans could migrate to when Planet Earth's life support system finally collapsed. And if Gutman's drive system worked, they would also own the only taxi service capable of getting human beings from here to there.

Now that's long-range thinking.

But first things first… they had to check it out and Visions Unlimited was investing billions to finance Voyager. This gang of would be Columbuses (actually the Board of Directors at VU were the Queen Isabella's—the intrepid space saps onboard Voyager were going to be Columbus) were going to answer all the questions about Planet X and then come back to Earth and report to our grandchildren.

With all that in mind, I vowed to do my best to build Voyager (but I thought that the whole idea was bat-shit crazy!)

Wisdom had a staff of scientists who were not a part of the Voyager Project but who were employees of Visions Unlimited. Nice guys and gals, always willing to cooperate and educate dummies like me. Life sure would have been much harder without them.

During our meet and greet, the scientists working in Wisdom just happened to mention that one reason that they were glad to see me was that they had a solar panel that had broken loose. Seeing as they really didn't want climb into a space suit, go outside into free space and fix it *and* seeing as I was here with Sam would, I take care of that little thing?

Sure! Why not? I didn't know what else I was going to do.

But (there is always a but), when I crawled into Sam, cranked her up, and tried to manipulate the arms, they were stuck tighter than a banker's wallet. No matter how I pushed and pulled at the controls the arms would not move.

Naturally, I called Alex who then called Ajax and the three-way conversation was pretty unproductive. The engineers on the ground at Ajax were having fits. The robot's arms, they told me, were the simplest of devices.

I knew that.

All the operator had to do was stick his hand into a sleeve on the control panel and move his arms and fingers which would then move the mechanical arms.

I knew that too.

How could I possibly get this wrong?

They concluded, in no uncertain terms, that it must be my fault.

Of course, it was. After *the incident* everything was John Marshal's fault.

Boy! Once you get a rep!

So, here I was, the first RJ up to the space station with a shiny new construction robot and my robot had broken arms. Sam flew around just fine, but her arms were frozen solid.

Everyone on the ground was yelling at me to do this—I did this.

Nothing.

Do that—I did that, too.

Nothing.

Finally, I got to have a quiet, long distance conversation with Alex. We went over all the steps leading up to the launch and tried to think of anything that could have possibly affected Sam.

Nothing.

On a side note, Alex was also very apologetic about my trip up into space saying that she knew nothing about the manner in which I was launched up to Wisdom. She said that until two days ago she didn't even know that VU had a launch base in Texas and had no idea why they would want a construction robot up at the space station this early in the game. Alex told me to just hang in there and that tomorrow she was going to fly to Los Angles for a meeting with the VU Board of Directors to get, as she said, "a few items straightened out," and after the meeting, if we still had jobs, she would see what she could do about getting Sam fixed.

I guess the meeting went well because when she called me after she got back to Sand Flea, Alex had complete control of anything and everything that had to do with Voyager. There would be no more micro-managing or going around her from the VU Board. The meeting apparently went so well that Alex was also now the Director of the Starduster Space Shuttle Program *and* responsible for the management of Wisdom!

Boy, that must be quite a meeting! I would have loved to have been there for that little tête-à-tête.

Meanwhile, there was my little problem. I still couldn't get Sam's arms to work and I did promise the science guys that I would fix their panel, so I suited up and went out into space and did that thing.

I knew the people at Ajax were lying dogs!

A couple of days after her Los Angeles trip, Alex went up to the Kansas aircraft plant that was building the four Stardusters and she said that they had a meeting of the minds.

Yeah! Right! I'm sure that when Alex left, the management team, whose heads didn't roll, had no doubt as to who their boss was and what was expected.

From Kansas, Alex then travelled to the Ajax plant in Illinois to see if she could determine the cause of Sam's problem. When she called a couple of days later, I couldn't tell if she was laughing or crying. She had found out what the problem with Sam was; It *wasn't* my fault and it would not occur in any of the other robots.

Well, that was great, but in the meantime, I still had a very big problem.

What had happened was that some overzealous factory hand at Ajax (who had probably been named employee of the month for his brilliance) had given all the joints in all the robot arms an extra dose of grease so they would move freely. That worked great on Earth, but in the cold, cold dark of space, the grease had literally frozen Sam's arms solid.

Ha! I knew it wasn't my fault.

The robots on Earth could be cleaned up easy enough, but my poor Sam was sitting outside the space station in the cold and lonely void with no way to bring her inside to warm her up and clean her even if there had been room for her. The only answer the ground folks had was for me to suit up in the spacesuit that they said I would *never* use and go outside and clean the frozen grease out of every knuckle and joint.

With four arms and twenty fingers that's a lot of knuckles and joints. And "clean" was also a concept the Ajax guys hadn't thought through. I had to chip and chisel the frozen grease out of every moving surface which took me two miserable weeks. This, of course, set the work that I was supposed to be doing, that no one could define, also back two weeks and that was somehow my fault, too.

Geez!

Another thing that Alex didn't tell me about her trip until later was that she was just a few miles south of Chicago visiting Ajax the day a giant tornado wacked the downtown Chicago business area. This monster was so huge it was off the scale and was the first twister ever to be labeled an EF5+! It knocked down every wood or brick and mortar building in its path and took out every pane of glass in the downtown Chicago area. I'd heard it had killed around three thousand people mostly due to flying glass, injured several thousand more and caused over four billion dollars of damage.

That tornado was part of what was labeled the great once in a century (and how many of those were we having lately) tornado swarm that moved over the northern great plains and southern Canada. Dr. Al Wilson, who was on rotation as the senior meteorologist on the space stations science staff, said that there were over four hundred tornados that touched down within a twenty-four-hour period in North and South Dakota, Iowa, Minnesota, Wisconsin and Illinois.

The biggest one of course was the EF5+ that hit Chicago and there was my Alex somewhere just a few miles south. Even though I didn't learn about it until long after the fact, I was still belatedly terrified for her. Alex, however had just been annoyed. She said that she didn't really know what was happening at the time and the worst part of the ordeal was sheltering in place for six hours with the nit-wits at Ajax.

That's my girl!

But now that it was over and Sam was operational, I asked her what she'd like us to do. Good question. Without plans or even materials, there wasn't really anything that I *could* do, but the VU Board of Directors obviously wanted *something* to happen. They were paying a lot of money for this and didn't like their RJs and robots sitting idle and somehow that was all my fault, too.

Like I said, Wisdom had three entry ports and the only reason I could think of at the moment was because they wanted to be bigger and better than the International Space Station who only had one. We were about three hundred miles up and the ISS was a little over two hundred a fifty, so we could see it below us a couple of times a day. From what I could tell, one docking port seemed to be enough for them. Anyway, since Wisdom had three and Sam was only tethered to one of them, VU said why not use the other two?

With that decision, up came JJ Jackson and Fred Thompson with their robots who also got to experience the thrilling ride on top of the big-ass rocket. Alex was going to argue with VU that without materials, there wasn't much we could accomplish, but later realized that with two more RJs and their robots in space, the Board would at least feel as if progress was being made.

One item the guys brought with them was the first set of blueprints for Voyager that I had ever seen. Once we rolled them out, we got the shock of our lives!

To keep up their going to Mars fiction, Visions Unlimited had released a couple of crude sketches and drawings of Voyager to the public. This public version looked like the rocket ships from the old fifties and sixties sci-fi movies—a real Twentieth Century Buck Rogers rocket that would fly to Mars and land on its tail.

The plans of Voyager that we were looking at was

about as far from a rocket as you could get. Instead of a rocket it looked more like a 747. A 747 with stubby delta wings. According to these plans, Voyager would not only travel through space, it would fly into the atmosphere of Planet X like a shuttle, and land horizontally like a jump jet. There was also a section in the fuselage for Cryogenic Pods where the passengers would snooze the trip away in suspended animation.

This thing was far out, but we were young and dumb, brash and fearless engineers. It might take us a while, but once they sent us the pieces, we were confident that we would be able to build it.

Of course, despite all their promises, the Visions Board of Directors were pressuring Alex to have us get started on the ship right away. That's when we—or rather Alex—pointed out to them a couple of problems that, in their eagerness to achieve the impossible they had overlooked.

1) The Project had twelve construction robots, but in Wisdom's current configuration there were only three docking ports and because of this, we could only send three robots into orbit at a time. And, 2) it would probably be nice to have some kind of a docking and maintenance facility for the robots and not just keep them permanently stuck out in space attached to the outside of Wisdom.

That's true. The robots were temperamental beasts and it seemed that one or more of them were always out of service for one reason or another, the most common reason being the drive system. The drive systems were solar powered which solved the fuel problem, but Ajax couldn't have made them more complicated and harder to access if they tried. It was almost impossible to work on them out in space in a clumsy space suit.

The Directors grudgingly had to agree with Alex and we were ordered to begin building a Robot Maintenance and Storage Facility.

But first we had to have a major squabble with the engineers at Ajax.

Did I mention that I really, really dislike those guys?

We had our ideas about what the maintenance shop should look like and how it should function. Of course, the guys at Ajax who had never been into space and wouldn't listen to us on the building of the robots weren't going to listen to us now. Our plans were rejected and they submitted a totally different plan.

But, unlike the building of the robots, we now had a secret weapon—Alex. Once she slapped them up the side of the head a couple of times, we got the go ahead to do it our way.

And our way didn't intend for the maintenance facility to be a separate structure in orbit next to Wisdom—we made it a *part* of Wisdom. By confiscating one of the docking ports, we built it out away from Wisdom piece by piece in three sections with each section housing four robots along with its own maintenance bay and space dock. From each section, four construction robots could pop right out into space and go to work. When all four robots were in, they kind of lined up on one side of the maintenance bay like the metal balls in an old pin-ball machine.

When we finished the first section and had a spot for our fourth man, Billy Wright came up. Now with four of us working, things started moving right along; In fact, we got so efficient, we kept getting ahead of the available material.

When the second section was finished, four more robots and their operators came up.

We dubbed our maintenance shed Robbie's Robot Roost. We named it after Robbie the Robot the robot in the old movie and TV shows. We shortened the name to R3 (which in our opinion was one better than R2). Seeing as we kind of pulled the design out of our lower regions, R3 didn't turn out too badly. It had twelve robot parking stalls in three sub-sections of four robots each and each four-robot section had its own air lock where robots can be launched directly into space. R3 also had room for all the tools, work benches, testing equipment, etc. that we needed.

If we had to, we could strip a robot right down to the nuts and bolts… and I had to. The very first thing I did once R3 was up and running was to give Sam four new arms.

The only thing we couldn't give R3 was gravity, but at least it was a shirt-sleeve environment just like the space station.

We were very pleased with ourselves, but we had overlooked one rather important item—us.

CHAPTER 4

Once we started building R3, and our work force grew as more and more robot jockeys came up to work on Voyager, we had two problems—namely eating and sleeping.

We couldn't do much about the first. Not only was eating in space a challenge in itself as we were floating in one direction while our food was drifting off in another, but we were forced to use the term "food" rather loosely. What we ate was freeze-dried stuff and some kind of military rations called MREs. I had been told that it stood for Meals Ready to Eat, but I was pretty sure the acronym meant Meals Rejected by Everyone. I didn't like them when I was in the Army and in my expert opinion, they hadn't improved any.

But as problematic as our diet was, that wasn't our main problem. Our main problem was the fact that we had overpopulated our habitat. We had built a great facility for the storage and maintenance of the robots, but we neglected to provide living accommodations for us robot jockeys. At the moment, we were sharing space in Wisdom with the science staff already stationed there. That had been all fine and dandy when I was the only intruder up on the station, but it was becoming an increasing challenge as more RJs were blasted into orbit. As the work on R3 progressed, it was bad enough when there were at first seven then eight of us all crammed into the station. Once we started on the second section of R3 and four more jockeys joined us, space was at a premium with the twelve of us bumping into to one another. It would only get worse by the time the third section was done and we had a total of sixteen people up in space as Wisdom only had four bunks! With that many people trying to find time to get some shut-eye, hot-bunking could only go so far.

Of course, the Directors, probably through brilliant advice from Ajax, had a simple solution for our little accommodation problem: we RJs should move in with the robots as there would be plenty of room for all of us.

Room to work, yes; A place to sleep? Not in this universe!

Needless to say, we were not thrilled with their solution, but this time, not even Alex could come up with an alternative. Not too subtle in our grumbling, this time we had no choice and resigned ourselves to learning how to sleep on a metal bench in zero gravity. It's a good thing we put mesh cages around the work benches to keep the tools from floating away as it kept us from floating away, too.

In spite of our sleeping arrangements, we were still pretty proud of ourselves. It had taken us only four months to build Robbie's Robot Roost, the first construction job ever completed in space. And did we get any credit for it?

Of course not!

All Visions Unlimited wanted to know was where their spaceship was.

Picky! Picky!

But still, we had learned a lot, most of which only reinforced our original opinion that building from scratch in space wasn't worth the effort. Though neither Alex nor Visions Unlimited had asked for it, we wrote up a big report on the experience. They probably liked our conclusion even less: if VU had designs on establishing a permanent construction facility in space—forget about it! In our opinion it was dangerous, unwieldy and very expensive.

Also, in our opinion, the best way to continue forward would be to build the biggest components for whatever project they had in mind down on Earth, boost them up to orbit and then let us assemble them in space.

But that was another problem for another day. With the completion of R3, we twelve RJs and our construction robots were ready to start building Voyager. This we learned came with another and potentially bigger problem: The United States Government.

Now that R3 was finished and Wisdom was a much bigger satellite, everyone on Earth with a telescope had taken notice and Visions Unlimited had been bombarded with questions. Everyone from the Junior Congressman from Podunk Nowhere to the President had called VU wanting to know what we were up to. Well, I should say the Vice President was interested. The President didn't say much, but then he never did.

Everyone wanted to know what was going on and what was VU constructing in outer space. To their credit the

VU Board took the pressure off of Alex and sent some of their members and experts to make the rounds in Washington to tell the White House and every suit in Congress who would listen about R3 and the space construction of their Mars Mission… and how it would ultimately benefit companies in their home districts.

Visions Unlimited knew their target audience well and probably spreading a little cash and a few contracts around certainly didn't hurt their position. Except for a few of the talking heads and conspiracy theorists who insisted that we were building everything from a high-tech security prison to a terrorist launch pad for orbiting missiles, it all eventually settled down.

I had to hand it to the Board; They were so successful in their disinformation campaign that Sand Flea wasn't even mentioned.

While all that commotion was going on, we pulled out the Voyager Plans and got ready to go to work.

From nose to tail, Voyager had five sections: the cockpit (or what VU grandly called the Command Section), the Cryogenic Section that would house the Cryogenic Pods where the intrepid explorers would be sleeping for twenty years, a section for supplies, another for all the equipment they thought the survey team might need when they arrived at Planet X (excuse me, *Mars*), and the last section for the propulsion unit that would house Gutman's engines— whatever they were.

To make the shipping of pieces of Voyager into orbit and its construction in space smoother, it had been decided long ago that we would build Voyager section by section.

Now that we had the plans, we wondered where we

should begin. Even though there were plans available for the engine section, Alex decided to leave construction of the engine housings until we actually saw some engines. Because Voyager was as much aircraft as space craft, she also managed to convinced the VU Board to contract the Command Section out to one of the large aircraft manufactures and the word was that that section was nearly ready.

Looking at the designs, I decided to add the Command Section to my list of Nutty Ideas that people had come up with for Voyager. I don't mean to be a wise guy, but Alex also said that the Big Brains planned to have two or three people awake in this Command Section throughout the trip to handle any emergencies whatever they might be. I wasn't sure what emergencies they had in mind to handle, but even if one came up, what was the crew supposed to do about it? If Voyager was going to be moving very, very fast through a vacuum at nearly the speed of light, it wasn't like they could really get out and fix a flat.

Whatever. That was going to be someone else's problem. I only had to build the darn thing. Seeing as how the Command Section was being built offsite and the Engine Section would be left for later, that left us with Cryogenics, Supply or Equipment to choose from.

We immediately pitched for the Cryogenic Section to be built next; In fact, we were insistent on it. Alex knew we were up to something, but just raised an eyebrow and went about the business of getting us what we needed. After a call to VU, she told us that one of the Board members was a pioneer in the science of cryogenics and both the Cryogenic Section for Voyager and the individual pods were being manufactured in one of his plants in San Diego. Contracts went out to all three heavy launch facilities in Texas and Arizona and pieces of the cryo section started arriving.

Yeah, I had to add cryogenics to the long list of things that I know nothing about. As I understand it, you lie down in a specially constructed pod, get hooked up to some kind of fluids and gasses and you just go to sleep. The weird thing was that no matter how long you have been in cryogenic stasis in Earth time, when you woke up you wouldn't have aged. It truly was suspended animation.

Again, whatever. I didn't need to know how they worked; I just had to build the section that carried them.

Based on what we learned from building R3, we hijacked another of Wisdoms ports and started building the Cryogenic Section of Voyager out from there. Naturally, that activity caused another flurry of excitement in Washington, but I was too busy to follow the Vids and keep up with it. I only heard about it in bits and pieces from Alex and the Vid and didn't really care what part of the latest Conspiracy Theory we were now a part of.

Everything was a learning experience these days and one of my biggest lessons was discovering that building the Cryogenic Section wasn't easy. For some reason, it was much more complicated than just throwing together the metal container we'd built for our maintenance shed. Apparently, the pieces of the Cryogenic Section could only fit together a certain way. To further complicate matters, they were being sent up by three different rocket boost companies from three different locations so they came up higgledy-piggledy. Sometimes it would take us several hours just to figure out that the two parts we had, that the folks on the ground said fit together, didn't.

Nevertheless, we pressed on and four months later the first section of Voyager was complete. Thrilled at our latest accomplishment, I called Alex and told her to send up twelve of the actual cryogenic pods and we would install them.

"Why just twelve?" she wanted to know.

"You'll see," I said with a smug grin.

I know she wondered what the hell we were up to. Once the Cryogenic Section was fully complete, it would have twenty-four individual pods—a row of twelve on each side of the hull, so why did we only want twelve? To her credit, Alex decided not to argue and up the pods came. We were even more thrilled when they arrived and the cryo-beds were just about what we expected. Each one looked like a seven-foot-long padded torpedo with a full-length plastic folding top. The cryogenic units were individually packed in multiple layers of insulation with very stern instructions NOT to open them until they were ready to be hooked up.

Yeah! Right!

We opened those suckers the moment they arrived. We built the frames to hold the twelve we requested and, after unpacking the pods and bolting them down, we moved in. After months of first hot bunking it in the space station and then living in a machine shop—we had a dormitory!

At first, I thought it was going to be a bit creepy sleeping in a cryo pod that looked like space-age coffin, but I got over it quickly. Whatever the kooky vibes, it sure beat the hell out of trying to sleep in R3.

We got to ride our proud wave for exactly one night. Well rested from our pods, we woke up the next morning only for Alex to point out that we were now using all three of Wisdom's docking ports. Where, she wanted to know, were we going to put the next section of Voyager?

Well, crap! We hadn't really thought about that. With the main port left open to move supplies in and out and R3 and the Cryo Section in the other two, Wisdom was all out of holes.

Alex, of course, had thought ahead which is why she's the boss.

She called up the Board of Directors and told them that we'd run out of ports.

Naturally, they went nuts and told her to have us just detach something from one of them.

Alex told them that she was very sorry, but that wasn't an option. We can't detach the Cryogenics Section or R3 out into free space without everything floating away.

They really went nuts.

Then Alex told the Directors that it would be impossible for us to start building the rest of the ship until we built some kind of space dock to actually build the Voyager in.

They really, *really* went nuts.

But Alex calmly explained that even in ancient times, no one ever built a ship before they first built the shipyard.

Begrudgingly, they conceded that Alex was right.

Personally, I couldn't blame the guys who were financing this operation for blowing several gaskets. They were going through money like water going over Niagara Falls. Billions of dollars. Still a drop in the bucket when you are talking about space, but it was still a hell of a lot of money.

Anyway, we, or rather Alex, figured out what we needed for a space dock and the pieces came up boosted into orbit by rockets at great expense. Upon their arrival, we built a kind of long circular cage for a graving dock and another for a storage yard for all our bits and pieces to keep them from floating away until we needed them. Once that was complete, we detached our dormitory, put it inside our 'dock' and attached the whole thing to Wisdom.

Finally, everything was in place and we were ready to get cracking on the rest of Voyager.

No matter what, Voyager would never look like the spaceships that I remembered seeing in the old Star Trek or Star Wars movies. The Enterprise and the Millennium Falcon, those were like... cool. Voyager was more like a 747 with stubby wings. Just a long tube to hold a couple dozen sleeping homo sapiens in cryogenic pods along with their gear and supplies for a twenty-year journey—one way.

By this time the Project Directors must have been really exasperated with us because after almost a year of work, the only part of Voyager that was completed was the shell for Cryogenic Section with twelve Cryogenic Pods partially installed. To our credit, we did have a space station (which we didn't build) a machine shop for the construction robots, a shipyard (space yard?) and a dormitory of sorts. It might not have been the progress they were hoping for, but it was still progress.

That was when the first Starduster appeared. A real space shuttle that could take off from Earth and fly right out of Earth's atmosphere into space and back again. Take that, Captain Kirk!

After Alex's big LA meeting all those many months ago, she had control of the Starduster shuttle program, too. I'm not sure exactly what happened on that side of the house, but before Alex got hold of Starduster, the program seemed to be an endless string of delays. Just about a year after my lady took over, the first Starduster was operational and flew into Sand Flea. The scientists who worked in Wisdom were ecstatic—no more rides in a tin can on top of the big rocket and landing out in the desert or, even worse, out in the ocean. With the Starduster, we now had regular taxi service to and from Wisdom.

All I could think of when I saw a Starduster for the first time was that it looked a lot like the old NASA space shuttles of the eighties and nineties only a bit smaller, about three quarters size. Each shuttle had a two-man crew deck, an environmental cabin that could seat ten passengers and a non-environmental storage compartment aft with full length clam shell doors. Starduster couldn't carry really large items, but it could transport about ten thousand pounds of small stuff.

When all four Stardusters were ready and the first one showed up at Sand Flea, that led to another difference of opinion between Alex and the Directors. Alex wanted to use them to get stuff up to us; The Directors, or at least some of them, wanted to use the shuttles to off-set some of their losses by making money on the space tourist trade.

I will take full credit for the brilliant compromise that was implemented. I suggested why not do both? All we had to do was load up the ass end of the shuttle with our stuff, load ten paying passengers in the front and make a stop at Wisdom part of the tourist trip.

It seemed to work. There had already been a half dozen well-heeled space travelers making the trip. It was too bad that the world was going to pot climate wise; UVs

Starduster flights would have made millions.

We were working on the sections for equipment and storage when Alex changed her mind on the engine section. Even though we didn't have a clue to what the engines looked like or how they actually worked, she decided we could get going on the Engine Section. We didn't care. What section we actually worked on depended entirely on what was sent up, so it was all the same to us.

Alex worked her lovely derriere off. With various parts of Voyager being manufactured by several companies in multiple locations, not only around the United States but around the world, keeping everything flowing up to us in some kind of proper order was a Herculean exercise and Alex was really earning her money. To add to her headaches, in addition to using the three widely separated space launch facilities to lift the larger pieces, she was also using the Stardusters at Sand Flea Airport to shuttle any of the smaller items that would fit into their cargo bays.

Occasionally, large items that could only go up by rocket would be sent to Sand Flea by mistake and they would have to then be re-shipped to one of the rocket bases. Smaller pieces that could be carried by the shuttles would be sent to one of the rocket bases and Alex would have to decide if it was more cost (and time) effective to send them up by rocket or ship them back to Sand Flea.

To add to Alex's problems, the increasingly worsening worldwide weather would sometimes scramble her carefully planned flow schedules. Monumental rainstorms, flash flooding, tornados and hurricanes were now so commonplace around the country and around the world that the media outlets rarely reported them as they just weren't newsworthy anymore; However, when two truckloads of robot fittings from Ajax were lost in a flash flood coming down from Illinois and another truck containing connections for the cryogenic pods was burned in a raging brush fire coming up from San Diego, the Directors at Visions really began to take notice.

Despite of all those problems on the ground, with twelve robots working (or usually working as one or more was always down due to some problem or another), we were building faster than the ground folks could get the materials up to us. The Stardusters hustled their little mechanical butts off flying people and parts up and down, but they were machines, too. It wasn't very long before one or more of them was out of commission for maintenance.

And always there was the lingering question of Voyager's engines. In addition to Gutman's main engines, Voyager was programed to have eight other engines for vertical landing and take-off as there was the real probably that there would be no runways on Planet X. I did wonder if those engines would still be operational after a twenty-year trip in space and then coming down through atmosphere, but that wasn't my problem. Those engines were available and all I had to do was install them when they were sent up.

Which I did. These were Gutman engines but they were not THE mysterious Gutman Engines that were going to drive Voyager through space. I was betting that they would just be something that's sealed in a metal box, but I really didn't have a clue. All I knew was that the people who were paying the bills were convinced that Gutman's invention would drive Voyager through space at somewhere near the speed of light. That sounded pretty fast to me, but even I knew that when you're talking about going to the stars, it was

Model "T" speed.

I wished them all the luck in the world, but I still thought they were bat-shit crazy.

Fortunately, the arrival of the Starduster shuttles solved another major problem: getting us Robot Jockeys out of Zero G and down to Earth on a regular basis.

Alex had argued with the Directors for months to get us on some kind of rotational schedule back to Earth to counteract the effects of weightlessness. The science guys who occupied the space station with us swapped off every three or four months, but no such provisions had been made for the people on the construction side of the house. We just kept working, one day blending into another as we floated around putting Voyager together.

Of course, before Starduster, moving people in and out of Wisdom could only be done the old-fashioned way using the rockets—very cumbersome and very expensive. That and the fact that they didn't want to slow down the work were the Directors main arguments against a rotational program.

But Alex was worried about us... well, me anyway I hoped, and she fought hard for us.

She submitted a proposal to VU to hire more RJs. The Directors turned her down.

She made another proposal to rotate us down to Earth in shifts like the Wisdom people.

No dice.

To put it mildly, Alex was pissed.

My Alex is one smart lady. If the Directors weren't going to listen to her on what was essentially a medical problem, she would find someone with medical credentials that they *would* listen to. She wrote up another proposal and convinced the Directors that because of the steadily increasing numbers of people working for VU at Sand Flea, the Project needed to have its own medical team and she knew just the people.

That one got approved.

Alex went local.

John and Nancy Watson ran a medical office/clinic/ infirmary in Sand Flea City only a mile or so from the airfield and they had been practicing medicine in local area for nearly a quarter of a century. They knew everyone in town and were loved by all. Ever since Voyager had set up shop at Sand Flea Airport, project members had been going to Doc John and Doc Nancy with their bumps and bruises, colds and flus. It didn't take too much convincing for either the Directors or the Watsons for them to come on board the Voyager Project full time—especially since it would not interfere with the Watson's regular practice.

A good deal all around.

What Alex knew and the Directors didn't, was that in addition to being a great doctor, Doc Watson (John) was a space nut who had made an extensive study of the effects of weightlessness on the human body and now he had real bodies to play with. Doc was convinced that being in Zero G over extended periods was a bad thing as far as human physiology was concerned and through Alex, he made his views quite clear to the Directors.

Being badgered by the double team of Alex and the Watsons on one side along with our Stardusters eliminating the cost of the large expense of a rocket boost, it finally got through to the big boys at VU that we needed to come down.

However, Alex and the Watsons did it, it worked and a rotational schedule for all of us working on Voyager was set up. We'd spend eight weeks up in space and one week down on the ground.

After more than a year in space, I was ready.

CHAPTER 5

I couldn't believe it. I was back on the ground... Earth... good old Terra-Firma. After fourteen months and two days of floating around in Zero G working on Voyager, my feet were on finally back on solid ground.

Well almost.

As the Starduster descended and entered Earth's atmosphere, my weight seemed to increase more and more and by the time we landed, I thought gravity was going to pull me down right through the shuttle's padded airline seat and straight to the center of the Earth.

The accepted wisdom in both the medical and scientific communities is that extended periods of weightlessness are not good for the human body and, buddy, I believe it. While I don't know what it does to the internal organs, I can speak for the muscles which were now so flabby I felt like a hacky-sack. I was as weak as a kitten.

The Starduster taxied right into one of the hangars and as we slipped in through the open hangar door, we passed through floor to ceiling strips of plastic before the doors closed behind us. A part of my brain wondered what that was all about, but I was too tired and too dozy to focus my mind enough to ask. I was far more aware that there was a hell of lot more people running around than there was the last time I was here. Only fifteen or sixteen months ago, Voyager had three employees consisting of me, Alex and Elizabeth and now there were dozens including a bunch of kids.

Once we came to a stop, I was more than grateful when two big guys came on board, picked me up and carried me off. I literally wouldn't have been able to move without them. Even better, I was no sooner off the shuttle when Alex bounded to my side and planted a kiss on me that made my toenails curl. Wow! It was good to be home.

Fortunately, with Doc John and his knowledge of how zero gravity affects the body, and the other robot jockeys that had come down before us, these big guys knew what to expect and they didn't set us down until JJ and I were plunked into the plush chairs in Alex's office.

A prisoner in my own body, I could only smile weakly when a middle-aged lady who introduced herself as Nancy Watson wrapped a cuff around my arm and took my pulse. While she was busy with my vitals, her husband Doctor John Watson hovered in the background.

"Drink this fruit juice," Nancy said before adding unnecessarily, "and don't move around too much."

Don't worry. I could barely move at all let alone too much.

In the other chair, JJ looked even worse than I felt. At well over six feet, JJ was a big man and must weigh around

220—all muscle of which he had none left. The soft spoken, gentle giant was the type who rarely spoke, but when he did, it was usually wise to listen. The poor guy wasn't saying much now as his complexion was positively green and he looked like a big bean-bag chair that had just collapsed.

The Docs seemed anxious to get us over to their little infirmary for a thorough examination. Seeing as I had been the first robot jockey sent up into space and the last one down, I had been the longest in space which made me their number one test subject; An honor that I could do without.

But despite this, Alex seemed reluctant to let us go. She was seated at her massive desk behind her multitude of computer screens, but every few minutes she would bounce up and ask if I was okay and did, I need anything. Finally, Doc John took her firmly by the arm, walked her around to her desk to her giant swivel chair and told her to stay there. Though her mouth silently opened and closed like a cod fish gulping for air, she obeyed.

After a few more minutes chatting in Alex's office about incidentals like weightlessness and the weather, Doc Nancy finally put her medical foot down and cut the conversation short. My transport team came back and we were out the door.

In all this time, my feet still hadn't touched the ground.

To my surprise, the big guys loaded me onto a gurney and we left by an ambulance that was parked in the hangar. It was only a couple of miles to the Watson's office/infirmary, but I guess cars just wouldn't do. JJ and I were strapped down onto our gurneys in the ambulance as if we were going cross-country. While I thought that was a bit much, I was too tired to argue.

I had a random thought that, due to the heat, one didn't go outside if one could help it which reminded me to ask about the plastic strips.

"Bugs," one of the big guys said. "It helps to keep out the bugs. And the Bug Brigade takes care of the ones that get in."

"The what?"

"The Bug Brigade, the little kids. Dr. Cummings directed that everyone here at Voyager had to have a job. To give the little kids something to do when they weren't in school and to make them feel a part of all this, Ms. Cummings organized the Bug Brigade. Their job is to kill every bug in all six hangars. The kids take it seriously and are pretty good at it too."

I laughed. Alex never misses a trick.

The short whirlwind trip that followed would probably have felt a lot smoother if I hadn't been strapped to a gurney in the back of an ambulance and weighing a ton. Once we got off the airfield, it was just five-minute ride to John and Nancy's medical facility, but every corner made me feel like I was going to tip over. Of course, that never happened, but when they opened the doors of the ambulance, I got my first real taste of what Global Warming was all about. It was the first time that I had actually been outside since I had blasted off in the big ass rocket over a year ago and the heat hit me like a blacksmith's hammer. Fortunately, we were only outside for a moment before we were blissfully inside in the air conditioning again.

We got some rather startled looks from the two patients waiting in the office as we sailed through the Watson's waiting room on our gurneys. The big guys pushing the gurneys went straight into an examination room where Doc John proceeded to drain me of fluids, replaced them with new ones and checked me over for everything in the Medical Book.

I didn't hang around. I vaguely remember the gurney being pushed into a hospital room, being slid off the gurney onto a bed and I think there was something about being hooked up to a dozen bottles containing who knows what. Beyond that, I have no idea. I was in dreamland for the remainder of whatever else John and Nancy did to satisfy their medical curiosity.

When I woke up the sun, was shining. Surprisingly, I felt really good; Still a little weak, but pretty good. And hungry! I guessed that whatever juice the Docs had pumped into me and a good night's sleep must have worked.

The door to my room cracked open and Nancy stuck her head in. Giving me a big grin, she said, "Well, it's about time you woke up."

Returning her smile, I said, "Come on, Ms. Watson, everyone should get to sleep late in the morning once in a while."

She laughed. "Technically, I'm an MD, same as John, but around here, I don't go for titles—Nancy will do just fine. But to get you up to speed, it's two thirty in the afternoon and morning was a long time ago. If you feel like getting up it's okay, but take it slow and easy."

Deciding that I would like to stand and actually place my feet on firmly on solid ground, Nancy scooted to my bedside and helped me up. It didn't go well. The moment I was officially vertical to the floor, my legs folded like a collapsible beach chair. Ruefully, I thought this must be how a sailor must feel when he comes ashore after a long stretch at sea. Trying again, I managed to wobble myself erect again and maintain it without Nancy's support.

The door cracked open again and Doc John stuck his head in. Giving me a steading hand, he walked me down the hall to the examination room where he gave me another very thorough examination. The verdict was that he thought that I would live and that Alex would be over in a few minutes. Fine by me. To kill the time, I practiced my walking by wandering around the waiting room. There was only one person there and I commented to Doc that business seemed slow.

Doc shrugged. "Nah, it's just a slow day. Business comes and goes which was one reason I was happy to get the Voyager contract."

"Don't the locals love you anymore?" I asked.

"Oh! I guess they still love me, or Nancy anyway," Doc laughed. "The truth is that most of the big companies followed Voyager's example and have their own clinics now. Another reason is that a lot of people are just drifting away from the Sand Flea area."

"Why is that?" I wanted to know. It was sad how much had changed in the year I was gone.

Doc thought a moment and then shrugged. "I guess it's mostly because they are tired of fighting the desert—the heat, the wind, the sand, the flies. It seems to get worse every day and there's no break. Then there's the food shortages."

Whoa! I hadn't heard that one. "People can't get food?"

"Well they're not starving—yet, but as you know, Sand Flea's a bit off the beaten track. Some food items have become hard or even impossible to get. Seafood was the first to go. First the price went up... way up, then any kind of seafood from shellfish on up, fresh or frozen, just sort of disappeared from the store shelves. Unless they're seasonal or local, fresh fruits and vegetables are also hard to get. According to the Vid, in some parts of the country any truck carrying food, especially fresh food of any kind, is liable to be high-jacked. Beef is still available, but you will have to mortgage your house to buy a steak."

"Wow! I didn't realize that. So, where are the people going?"

"I don't know and I doubt most of them do, either. Big cities, probably. These days, densely populated places get the supplies before our less populated rural areas."

"Well I wish them luck," I said shaking my head. "From what I've seen from space, what you're seeing out here in the desert is probably just the tip of the iceberg to use a very bad metaphor. All over the world thousands maybe tens of thousands of people are on the move and it looks like there is no place to go. One place is as bad as another."

I went on, "If people here are trying to get away from the heat and the bugs, elsewhere they're trying to get away from the rising seas or intense storms and somewhere else it's fire, flood or drought. The scientists up at Wisdom tell us that Earth is in serious trouble and there's every indication that Global Climate Change is accelerating. Things are only going to get worse, my friend. A lot worse".

"Do you know Dr. Al Wilson?" I asked.

Shaking his head, Doc frowned as he thought. "Name's familiar, but no I don't think I've met him."

"He's the Chief Meteorologist up on Wisdom. Nice guy."

"Right! That's where I heard the name. For some reason, since Nancy and I have become Voyager, Wisdom and Stardusters' official doctors, we haven't been able to catch him for a physical. Doctors always make the worst patients and it doesn't matter what our specialty's in."

"Yup! That sounds like Al," I said as we laughed in agreement. "But really, he's a great guy and really knows his stuff. He's always willing to take the time to explain to us RJs just what we are seeing down here on Earth and in his opinion, it's not good. You're right; Climate Change is accelerating. Al says that all the global models that the major weather services around the world are currently using for weather forecasting aren't accurate because changes are happening so fast. Things that the experts thought would take centuries to occur are now happening in decades and even less."

"Interesting. Outside of giving him a physical I would like to talk to him."

"I'll tell him that you're not really Frankenstein and to get his butt over here."

"Thanks."

We both looked up as Alex bounded through the door. Giving me an anxious look, she said, "I parked right out front. Are you okay?"

"Just fine, Luv," I smiled. "Let's go."

But Doc wasn't quite finished. "Remember, John, I want you back here tomorrow morning."

Yeah! Yeah! He probably would have tracked me down with bloodhounds if I missed that appointment.

It was wonderful just being with Alex. We hadn't seen each other in over a year and we spent the afternoon and evening making up for lost time. I might have been weak, but I wasn't that weak.

The next day I showed up right on time at the clinic. If I had known Doc was going to test, poke and probe me almost literally all day, I might not have been so willing, but I sat there like a good boy and finally in late afternoon Alex came to collect me.

After spending just about all day with Doc, I was more than little a bit hungry, so I was surprised when Alex drove back onto the airfield and said we were having dinner at the Visions Unlimited/Voyager/Starduster Cafeteria. My surprised rivaled my hunger as we drove onto the airfield and I noticed that there were guards and a gate at the entrance. What was once a four-lane open boulevard had now been reduced to two lanes with one going in and the other going out. Before I could ask about the change, we were through and quickly came up to another guarded gate. Alex stopped and a very serious guard gave us a close look before waving us on.

With a smile, Alex looked over at me and said, "Only one more gate to go, my love."

The last gate and fence were around the VU area. My Army brain started to kick at the triple security. Wow! What the hell had been going on down here?

But the changes kept coming. When we drove in through Alex's garage door in the hangar door, I began to see just how busy my lady had been since I had last been here. Over the past year she had worked tirelessly to move everything inside the hangars and away from the weather. As we walked across the big hangar Alex began pointing out what she called "her improvements." This was Hangar 1 and housed food service, billeting and the school. The next hangar over in this row of three, the one that my Starduster had taxied into yesterday, was Hangar 2 and contained the Starduster tourist operations. Hangar 3 was used for supply and storage and was the last in the row.

On the opposite side of the complex from us across a fairly large expanse of concrete were the three hangars that Alex had inherited when she acquired Starduster. Hangar 4 housed the motor pool and what automotive repair equipment she had, and Hangars 5 and 6, was for Starduster parking and maintenance.

Alex had also built enclosed steel and concrete walkways between each of the hangers in each row and between hangars 3 and 6 so personnel could get from hangar to hanger and side to side without going outside in the heat and the bugs.

Alex led me over to the cafeteria which was built into what would have been the offices and machine shops on the side of the original hangar. Alex's suite of offices was on the other side. Service was buffet style and at Alex's direction we picked up trays and went through a serving line that I could see was backed by a full kitchen. The food was good if basic: meat, salad, potatoes, veggies, even desert. After my year in orbit it was wonderful. It sure beat MRE's and, best yet, it didn't try to float off my plate, either. Yay, Earth!

Looking around, I noticed the dining area covered a large section of the hangar floor and consisted of very sturdy looking, card-table size metal tables and chairs that could be easily moved around to accommodate any size group. There were probably twenty or thirty people already seated including a dozen or so kids.

Bless her, Alex didn't say anything and just sat quietly

while I took it all in. When I noticed the hangar was divided by what looked to be seven or eight-foot-high plastic, movable panels, she said, "Billeting is on the other side of the panels, men on one side women on the other with individual cubicles for families. His and hers toilets and showers are on this side of the hangar in the shop space past the kitchen. A couple of ladies and young girls volunteered to take care of sheets and towels. We have a deal with a local laundry, but there are washing machines and dryers in the back for individual use."

I was more than a little awed by what she'd accomplished in a relatively short period of time. "I noticed that we have grown some from three employees."

She laughed. "About a hundred and thirty at last count, but most of our people still live in town. I made this billeting area available free of charge to any of our employees and their families if they get tired of the commute and trying to get essentials in Sand Flea. At a guess, I would say that about half of our people live here now, but I expect it will grow."

I nodded. "By the way, that was pretty impressive security we came through."

"Yes. The first and second rings are funded and operated by the airfield committee. Whatever security arrangements an individual company like us wants to make beyond that is up to them. Chet takes care of that for me."

"Who?"

"Chet Barton. I hired him to be our security chief. He's good people; You'll like him."

It just so happened that while we were eating Barton came in and Alex waved him over to our table. He was a big guy, about JJs size, middle aged in his late forties or early fifties with hair cut short and going gray around the temples. I found out later that he had put a hitch in Uncle Sam's Special Forces. When he got out, he went to work as a Deputy Sheriff.

Alex was right and I took to him right away. He was a tough, no-nonsense cop, but with a wicked sense of humor that I appreciated.

After introductions he seemed impressed with the mysterious Robot Jockeys who worked in space. Well, if you looked at it that way... before my head got too swollen Alex told him to tell me about the security arrangements.

Chet Barton not only knew his stuff, but it seemed that he also knew how to take the best advantage of *other* people's stuff. For example, due to the increasing number of transients who seemed to be wandering through Sand Flea City, the airfield administrators had thrown a security fence around the entire perimeter of the airfield and reinforced it with roving patrols and overhead surveillance with drones. Chet had relieved VU of the requirement of providing warm bodies for the security patrols by furnishing drones for perimeter surveillance.

As I had noticed driving in, there was now security on every gate onto the airfield. Chet thought that it would probably be better to close more gates, but at the moment that wasn't practical because several thousand people had to get to work in the many companies on the airfield every day.

The airfield management committee had also set up inner secure areas around the flight line, hangar and storage facilities on both sides of the runway (that was the second gate that Alex and I had driven through) and every major company who was operating on Sand Flea had made their own security arrangements.

Chet had established a security perimeter around the Voyager/Starduster hangars that he said was at the moment mostly concertina wire, but was gradually being thickened with concrete barriers. When he was finished the only entrance into the VU complex for vehicles and personnel would be located on the northeast corner of VUs area and, if he could block off a few hundred yards of parking apron, there would be a single aircraft gate into the VU area.

Before I could express how impressed I was, Chet went on to say he had hired and trained a force of fifty deputies, (well, he called them deputies), who were mostly middle-aged guys, all of whom were either ex-military or law enforcement and all of them personally recruited by him. He ran three eight-hour shifts with eight or nine deputies on duty at any one time and the rest on call no farther away than the hangar. Chet had moved all of his people and their families into Hanger 1 weeks ago.

But wait! There's more. In addition to his deputies, every able-bodied resident of Hangar 1 over the age of sixteen was expected to have a weapon, be proficient in its use (the airfield committee had built an indoor range on the far side of the runway) and be ready to stand to when needed.

It took me a moment in the silence that followed to see that he was finally finished.

Wow! Alex sure picked a winner when she latched onto Chet Barton. I had spent four years in the Army, but I would have never thought about half the things that Chet came up with. Before we left the table, Chet discovered that I had military experience and I was recruited (or rather drafted) to be a deputy when I was dirt side.

While Chet and I were chatting, Alex looked up and

said, "Oh good, there's Dot. I wanted you to meet her."

Waiving Dot over Chet said, "Yes, let me introduce you to the Mrs."

While Dorothy Barton was what I would describe as a very substantial matron, she was also a force of nature. She had to have been close to six feet tall and solid. Though she was around 175 to 180 pounds, not an ounce of it was fat. Dot was just a big woman, fiftyish with gray hair and a huge smile. She moved through the small crowd like a battleship cruising through a fleet of sampans. She evidently knew everyone and there was a chorus of "Hi, Dot!" from all sides. Three children at one table were waving enthusiastically and yelling "Hi, Mrs. Barton!"

Dot went through the line chatting with everyone and came over to the table. After the introductions she said, "So you're one of the famous Robot Jockeys that all my students want to emulate?"

Once more, my ego swelled.

"Well, I must say that you don't look like all that much."

Ego shrinks. If you think that Chet Barton had a wicked sense of humor you haven't lived until you've been skewered by Dot.

I asked, "Students? Where do you teach?"

She gave me look that I am sure was reserved for the not-too-bright members of the class and pointed over to the far corner of the hanger. "Right there. We now have two teachers and fifteen students in seven grades. You will come and give a talk."

Drafted once again, I answered the only way I could. "Yes, Ma'am."

Alex knows who to recruit.

CHAPTER 6

Later in the evening, Alex and I were back at our apartment complex curled up in a big comfy lounge chair by the pool with a tall, cool adult beverage and about six fans blowing on us. The fans weren't helping much; They just seemed to blow the hot air around without doing anything to relieve the scorching heat, but they were keeping the bugs away.

Giving me a lazy look as she poked the ice down to the bottom of her glass, Alex asked, "So, what are we going to do now?"

I said, "Well, I don't know. I am a bit tired."

"Not that, you big oaf!" Alex laughed and poked me in the chest. "I mean after Voyager."

Honestly, I hadn't given it a thought. The last fourteen months had been consumed with putting the pieces of a giant metal puzzle together and there hadn't been room in my tiny little brain for what came next.

Alex said, "Well, you'd better start thinking about it. It won't be much longer before we're unemployed again."

As always, my lady was right. One way or another, in a few months to maybe a year, the Voyager space craft would be completed... or not depending on if the mysterious Gutman engines ever materialized... and Project Voyager was going to come to an end. The ship was about half finished now. Well, half with the pieces we had; Everything that we could do up till now had done. We still hadn't seen anything that looked like an engine or a Command Section for that matter, but Alex said they'd be along soon. In six months to a year, Voyager was either going to head off into the void or become a permanent piece of orbiting space junk. Whatever happened, we were going to be out of work—not that that really bothered us. Whether she flew to the stars or not, thanks to Voyager, we were almost millionaires. On the other hand, what good was money if there was nothing to spend it on?

I didn't have to be a genius of Alex's caliber to understand that what was on her mind wasn't so much what we were going to do, but where we were going to live. Al was right about the fact that the world's climate was going to change, was changing, so much that large chunks of the planet would be uninhabitable by humans. The nearly continuous storms, droughts and fires had already proved that. Populations in the regions where people could still exist were already beginning to fight over food, water and anything else they had left.

Before I went up into space, I had heard about Global Warming, the Greenhouse Effect, Climate Change or whatever the term-du-jour was. Heard about it all my life. While I can't say I was ever a denier, I have to admit that I hadn't given it much thought, either. Well, not until I'd flown from Florida to Sand Flea and I had to go north and south across the country to avoid the storms when I needed to be flying east to west. It's hard to deny floods exist when the river is sweeping through your back yard.

Scientists had been warning the world about all this for more decades than anyone could keep track of and I believed them, but until recently, I guess I just never really thought about it. I couldn't stop thinking about it now. Al was now preaching to the choir when he said that pumping shitloads of carbon into the atmosphere was a very bad thing—right along with dumping our crap into the oceans, lakes, rivers and any other body of water we could find. Unrestricted population growth wasn't helping the situation, either.

My flight across the country had been an eye-opener, but once I got up in space and had an opportunity to look down and really see what was happening down on Planet Earth, I was scared. From hundreds of miles in space, I could literally see clouds of pollution hovering over the major cities.

Yet there were people who continued to deny what was happening all around us. People who couldn't step outside their door without facial masks protecting them from the toxins still wouldn't believe it. Hard-core deniers, members of the Flat Earth Society and anti-vaxers who refused their shots; People who didn't believe we were actually living and working up in space.

But there were others; Powerful people employed by politicians and the fossil fuel industries who gave them a voice and twisted science for them to latch on to. People who looked out of their airconditioned offices at the populations collapsing in the 120-degree heat while peddling their theories that there wasn't any such thing as Global Warming.

In addition to the heat most places of the world were blanketed by a stinky haze. What people were breathing was no longer air but a noxious aerosol cocktail of fumes from the burning of fossil fuels, exhaust of a bazillion cars and the smoke from the wildfires blazing throughout the world. This mix also added to our atmosphere an increase of toxic heavy metals, radiation and thousands of other harmful chemicals. Painful respiratory diseases, airborne mercury poisoning, asthma and cancers were spiking to epidemic proportions all over the globe. Every year, millions of deaths have been directly attributed to air pollution.

Then there were the storms. A simple shower was a rarity as most rain pelted the earth with monsoon force causing flash floods that washed out whole towns. The northern areas and higher elevations still received their rain as snow, but in the last decade alone, it seemed that every snowstorm piled up several feet of the white stuff. Everything was extreme; Hurricanes moved coastlines and tornados flattened towns. They didn't just knock down several houses, they completely destroyed whole cities like, most recently, Chicago. Everyone who still wanted to live in Tornado Alley was digging in—as far underground as they could get. Hobbit holes were becoming increasingly popular.

And that was if the area was lucky enough to receive any precipitation. Out here in the desert, we not only had to deal with the heat and bugs on a daily basis, but also the sandstorms—the Haboobs. I used to get a kick out of saying that word, but it was no longer funny. When one of them blew though, and they blew through often, all outside activities ceased.

So where were Alex and I going to live? As far as Alex was concerned, it most certainly wouldn't be here. If she never saw another tumbleweed or dust cloud again, she would be a happy lady. On the other hand, she was creating a pretty sweet set up here at Sand Flea complete with secure shelter, power, water, security, food... the Visions Unlimited area was an oasis within an oasis.

This was not going to be an easy decision.

We had already ruled out anything to do with living by the oceans especially the East Coast. We had flown up and down the eastern seaboard enough times to know that. Al said that seventy percent of the world's population lived within fifty miles of the ocean and from Wisdom it looked like at least half of those populations were leaving their coastal homes to go somewhere else. The glaciers were melting so fast that the oceans had risen three feet in the last one hundred years and were still rising. I never thought three feet sounded like much, but it was enough that most of the coastal cities had some kind of flooding problem. Of course, the coastal cities and towns didn't just disappear under water, but their water fronts were becoming unusable. Homes and buildings that were located along the shore were now standing in water even at low tide. Every country that had a coastline had a New Venice these days. Alex and I used to laugh at people in Miami Beach who were still living in multi-story condo buildings that were sitting in three feet of water.

Not so funny now.

"What about an island?" Alex asked. "A nice tropical

island where we could watch the sunsets drinking mai tais?"

"As awesome as it would be, Luv, island dwelling is also out."

"Yeah, you're right," Alex sighed. "If coastal cities are becoming inundated, low lying islands are practically disappearing. I saw on the Vid that some islands in the South Pacific have been submerged completely, their entire populations forced to move. The problem was that there wasn't anywhere they can move to. Other nations aren't too happy to take in island refugees."

I snorted. "I can just picture how that scenario went. Imagine you're the president of some inland highland nation. You get a knock on your door and are greeted with 'Hi! I'm the Prime Minister of Swamp Island and my country just became part of the Pacific Ocean. Could I and a couple thousand of my neighbors come live with you?' Can't see how that would go over well."

"I'm sure it wouldn't." Alex agreed. "On larger islands with some high ground in the interior, the costal population is moving inland—if there is room to squeeze in. That, of course, brings up new problems with what they're going to eat. When the water rose, their coastal ports and towns were gone along with much of their coastal farming areas and their fish and food production went with it. They also lost their oceanic trade when the ports shut down."

We fell silent as we thought about the dying oceans. They were changing, getting warmer and becoming more acidic. The once brilliantly colorful coral reefs were bleached skeletons and unable to support life. As a quarter of all marine life depends on the reefs, the entire oceanic food chain that half the world's population depended on as a primary source of protein was collapsing.

Climate change hadn't been a catastrophe for every species. The jellyfish, for example, were loving it. When I was up in Wisdom or working on Voyager, on some days when the light was right, I could see massive clouds of jellyfish that measured hundreds of miles across. The swarms were large enough to see in orbit and more than one ship went down as the gelatinous masses clogged up their engines and a storm finished them off.

Another big thing that banished any thought of living on or near a coastline were the hurricanes. After watching the Atlantic shore get pounded by a Category 4 or 5 with three more hurricanes close on its heels... yeah, we didn't even consider it an option.

We were no closer to choosing where we were going to live the following morning as we briefly tossed around ideas of either the mid-west or the great plains. The first was nixed when I reminded Alex of the flooding that I had witnessed when I flew out in PJ a year and a half ago. In addition to the rain, as the oceans rose many of the rivers were backing up, spreading out, flooding areas miles away from their normal water courses, so if we lived in the interior that would be a consideration.

All Alex had to say was "tornado" and the great plains was dropped even quicker. Drought ridden for nearly a decade, the grasslands were so parched they were nothing but a tinderbox of fuel for more and bigger fires.

Our options were becoming severely limited.

"What about New England?" Alex suggested.

"It's a possibility," I conceded with a sigh. "They get their share of winter blizzards and it's hot and muggy in the summer, but it can't be anything like the saunas in the south."

Even in the best of times, every area had its problems; We just wanted someplace that was ideal *most* of the time and we were running out of options. Even the west coast and the mountains had their share of fires and floods... and earthquakes. The Southwestern United States had been in drought conditions for years. Any fire that started there was a flaming maelstrom driven by Haboobs and Santa Ana Winds. Once a blaze got going, it was nigh unstoppable. And what acreage wasn't engulfed by the fires were finished off by the killing heat. The climate was shifting the ecosystems as vast forests of the Rockies and the Cascades were being devoured by armies of insects moving north with the warming temperatures. Entire mountain ranges were drying out and the western skies were full of smoky clouds.

We had dozens of questions and no answers. Alex and I had worked ourselves into such a gloom that we decided to crank up PJ and go up to Vegas the next day to cheer ourselves up.

The next morning while Alex worked at her big desk clearing up a few items, I sat out in the reception area chatting with Elizabeth and enjoying a cup of her really good coffee. If there was one thing that I missed working in space it was coffee.

Elizabeth was one in a million. The first hire of Project Voyager, she was Alex's girl Friday. She screened Alex's calls, managed her calendar and guarded the gates. It also seemed that she knew everybody and everything that had happened and sometimes what was *going* to happening on Sand Flea. She was better than a newspaper.

There was no commercial air traffic in and out of Sand

Flea, but somehow Elizabeth managed to keep track of all the private company traffic that came in and out of our area. If Alex, or anyone else in VU, wanted or needed to fly somewhere, she could usually fix it.

As we waited, I noticed how much Elizabeth's reception area had changed as a group of well-dressed people oozing of pomp and privilege flooded into Elizabeth's reception area. With a winning smile, Elizabeth welcomed them to the Starduster Space Tour.

A few of our Voyager people followed in behind them and began serving them drinks. I realized that Elizabeth's reception area had been turned into a waiting lounge to pamper these wealthy tourists before a Starduster took them into orbit. Alex even had a model of the flight up to Wisdom made. It was a globe with a spiral wire representing the flight leading up to a model of Wisdom and the whole thing stood about four feet high. A few of them asked me questions and I used the model while describing my job of building the ship that would take human colonists to Mars. I thought that the whole thing was all pretty hokey, but the paying customers seemed to love it.

As they sat in the plush chairs drinking champagne and waited for the announcement that the shuttle was ready for boarding, I resisted the urge to warn them against drinking too many liquids. These people had probably never flown commercial in their entire lives and would probably take offense if I explained how bathrooms worked without the benefits of gravity. Better let them figure that one out for themselves.

After a while, Elizabeth ushered them out and we resumed our conversation as if nothing had happened until

Alex rushed from her office and told her to turn on the Vid. She quickly punched a button on her counsel and a big screen in the corner came to life. For a minute we couldn't make sense out of what we were seeing—a road block on a rural road with a bunch of people with guns, but then we kind of caught up with what the reporter was describing. Some little town up in the Appalachian Hills (I didn't catch the name) had announced that "seeing as local, state and the federal government could no longer provide us basic services and security, we're declaring ourselves an independent sovereign state."

The three of us just looked at each other with a "what the hell?" expression on our faces until Alex broke our stunned silence. "They're scared," she reasoned. "No electricity, running out of food, forest fires to the east and south, temperatures well over a hundred every day and a federal government run by coal and oil executives that deny that it's even happening. Those people are going to do what tough independent people always do: rely on themselves. Probably not a smart way to do it, but I can see where they are coming from."

I couldn't even think of a response one way or the other.

With a sigh, Alex could only shake her head. With another sigh, she turned to me and said, "Well, come on, my love. If we are going to go to Vegas we had better get going."

Walking through the covered walkway into Hangar 2, Alex saw a couple of people working at a bench on the side. Leading me to them, she introduced me to Phil Reston, her Chief of Starduster Operations.

"Don't let her modesty fool you," Phil said giving me a

hearty handshake. "Alex is the Chief, I'm just a mechanic."

"That's not true," Alex protested. "I'd be lost without Phil. He knows these Stardusters inside out."

With the eagerness of a schoolboy, I asked, "Do you have a flight training program? I'd love to get checked out."

"You fly?" Phil asked, his eyes lighting up with the comradery in meeting a fellow pilot.

"Yup! Single and twin. Little PJ that I see you have tucked away over there in the corner is my baby."

"Nice machine," he said before shuffling his feet. "Uh, I hope you don't mind, but I didn't think that it was good to just leave her sitting there, so I've taken her up a couple of times. Come and see me the next time you're down and we'll see what we can do about getting you checked out in the shuttles although after flying a sweet little machine like— what did you call her?"

Alex said, "PJ, for puddle jumper."

Reston laughed. "Well, after flying a smooth aircraft like your PJ, you probably won't enjoy pushing a pig like Starduster around the sky."

Straight-up guy, Ruston. I liked him. I liked him even more when I saw that he had taken good care of PJ. After throwing our bags in the back, I couldn't help but spend a minute or two (maybe three) just sitting in the cockpit and running my hands over the switches and dials. Well, I hadn't seen her in almost a year and a half, so it was a very emotional reunion.

Remembering my first experience with the comedians in air traffic control, I called the tower and asked for traffic info and wind direction, and then just took off from the parking apron. No one even noticed, so that at least hadn't changed. Other things, we found out, had.

Vegas just wasn't Vegas.

From the moment we got within sight of the city, the entire valley looked like a huge, dirty fog bank. The upper floors of the tallest casinos pierced through the gritty layer, but everything else was obscured in the sepia haze. We were sorely tempted to just give it up and go home.

There was no other air traffic so we flew right in. As we taxied in, we could see three or four people excitedly waving their wands as they tried to compete with each other to get our attention. What the… ?

Hangar space. They all had hangar space for rent and wanted to make sure we gave them their business. We picked one that looked like it had a covered walkway to the terminal. Cost an arm and a leg, but we weren't about leave PJ out in the smoggy heat.

The terminal was practically empty. Alex pointed to a row of empty slot machines with only one player—a little old lady with a walker. Perfect. At least we knew we were in the right place. For a moment there I thought I was in Tokyo or some other Asian city because everyone I saw was wearing those white gauze face masks. When we stepped out of the terminal to get a cab we knew why as we nearly choked on the fog bank made up of smoke from industrial discharges, cars, and both forest and grass fires.

And it was hot! Our home in the desert was hot, but this was different. Without a breath of air, it was like being in a sauna and in just the few minutes it took to get into a cab, the sweat was already pouring off me.

"It's hot," I said. Keen observer of the obvious, that's me.

"Yup! It's 118 degrees today," the cabbie cheerfully informed us as if it were something to be proud of. "Last week it hit 122, but you get used to it."

Yeah! Right! Even with the taxi's air-conditioner going full blast, there was no way I even wanted to get used to it.

The cabbie said, "Where to?"

We hadn't really thought about that. I said, "We don't have any reservations. Do you know where we could get in?"

He laughed and said, "Look around; The town is half empty. You can probably stay anywhere you want."

He was right. While there were people on the street, there weren't very many and not anywhere near the crowds that you would usually see roaming up and down the strip. And everyone that we could see was wearing those gauze face masks.

Over the years we had been to Vegas a few times and had stayed at other casinos, but had never been to Caesars. Not having a real plan, we decided to go there, but as we drove up, Alex's voice was full of disappointment. "The fountains are off."

"Where?" I asked.

"The Bellagio," she said pointing. Sure enough, the fountains were not only off, their basins were bone dry.

"It's because of the water shortages," our driver said and went on to explain that the water features are off all over town. "From what I hear, Lake Mead is down as much as twenty-five feet."

"Why turn them off?" I asked. "I thought most of them were closed systems."

"Public Relations. The hotels and casinos didn't want people mad at them for using water which has been strictly rationed for months. You'll see when you get into the hotel."

He was right again. We got into Caesars with no problem at all; In fact, we could have taken almost any room in the place... and dirt cheap, too. We checked into one of the big suites that usually go for a few thousand a night for a couple hundred bucks and were told that if we were on an extended stay, they'd knock even more off. It was a lot more room than we needed, but as they say, we did it because we could.

But no amount of money was going to buy us water. The taps were dry and there was a big bottle of water mounted over the sink. We were informed that that was our ration for the day and was for washing hands, brushing teeth, etc. If we used it up, we were out of luck until housekeeping came around tomorrow. There was also a timer on the shower that worked with our room key card. One five-minute shot per occupant.

I guess to soften the blow there was plenty of booze in the refrigerator and cabinets.

Alex and I went down to the casino and gave the slots a whirl. We didn't win anything, so we went to dinner. Though Caesar's had several dining rooms, only two were open: the buffet and the Homestead Steak House—all the rest were closed.

We opted for the steak house and surprise, surprise... no line at all. The place was half empty and quiet. It seemed like everyone was whispering and the waiters were tip-toeing around. Kind of spooky. Alex went for the prime rib, but I had my taste buds set for surf and turf.

Fuhgeddaboudit.

The waiter apologetically informed us that while steak

was available, lobsters were not. Apparently, while I was off-world, the lobster industry had collapsed and the crawly crustations were not available *at any price*. Our waiter said that with the warming waters off the Northeast coast, the lobsters had just disappeared.

So, I had a steak and Alex did the prime rib. The meal was very good, but at $250 for dinner for two, it sure wasn't cheap. After renting out the hangar for PJ, I was going to have to hock a kidney on the black market if we stayed much longer.

It was a sad and dismal evening. Trying hard to put a good face on it and cheer each other up, we went into the lounge for a drink and catch the floor show. It didn't help. The room was less than half full with people who, just like us, wanted to get away from whatever misery was plaguing them at home by trying hard to have a good time.

It wasn't working.

This was a little bubble in a world that was falling apart. The jokes fell flat; The laughter was forced. While the band was fine and the singer was pretty good, everybody seemed to be pre-occupied and no one was really listening.

During normal times we would have gone out for a walk to enjoy the evening and people watch, but with the heat and smog outside, we never gave it a thought.

We checked out early the next morning and flew back to Sand Flea.

CHAPTER 7

After what seemed like a whirlwind week on the ground, I was back up in space again where time couldn't seem to make up its mind. When the Command Section was lifted into orbit and we were finally able to join all five sections of Voyager together time flew by.

Once we had all the pieces, it took another two months, but when we were done, for the first time Voyager looked like a real spaceship. We still had a lot of work to do on the inside to make the cockpit operational and hook up the cryo-pods, but that would require specialists, so all that remained for us to complete on the exterior was cosmetic. She would be the first Earth ship to leave our system and, by golly, we RJs were going to make sure she represented us properly.

After that, time began to drag. It was like racing through the desert at 75 mph and suddenly having to putter through a small town at the break neck speed of 25. I got into the groove of being busy, so once the workflow stopped, I was bored out of my gourde.

Fortunately, we now had the Stardusters. While we were marking time waiting for the aeronautical and cryogenic specialists (and waiting for Gutman's phantom engines) to show up, we RJs started to spend more time on the ground. Most of the guys took off for other parts but I took that opportunity to make Chet happy and filled my training squares as a security deputy. And to make me happy I managed to talk Phil Reston into formalizing the training program so I could become a qualified Starduster pilot.

That was pretty awesome, but once the specialists arrived, it was back to business and back up to Voyager. The guys who were going to make our spaceship operational were a great bunch and we got along. They not only didn't turn up their noses at the MREs, they didn't even blink when we showed them the cryogenic pods that they were going to sleep in and they went right to work.

Like I said: great guys and once they made themselves at home, time sped up once more as we got busy again. That's when we had our first major accident with the construction robots.

One of the aeronautical specialists, Tom Burwell, was with me in Sam as we worked on an exterior portion of the Drive Section while another RJ, Bob Harrison, a cocky young engineer from Brooklyn was in another robot working up near Voyager's Command Section. Bob had been with us from the beginning and although I always thought he was a kind of smart-aleck, wise-cracking kid. I couldn't help liking him.

"What was that?" I asked reflexively as I caught a flash

out of the corner of my eye.

"What was what?" Tom said, not taking his eyes off what he was doing. I had no idea what he did, some specialist thing.

"Nothing," I said. "I guess just one of the windows catching the sun."

That happened a lot up here in orbit as we caught a sunrise every ninety minutes. I didn't think anything more about it until Al paged me.

"John! John! Get up to the nose. I think we just lost Bob!"

It took Tom and me a few painful minutes to safely finish extracting Sam's claws from the Drive Section and by the time we got to the nose, all we saw were tiny pieces of Bob's robot slowly drifting apart. I was stunned. This was the only major accident we'd had in the two years we'd been working on Project Voyager, but that was small consolation for the loss of a good friend and co-worker. The worst part was that we had no idea what had happened; His robot just seemed to have blown up. We held a funeral but we never found enough remains to put into a box. Not even a small box.

Of course, Alex shut everything to do with the robots down while we investigated and tried to figure out what happened.

We never did, so as we cautiously got back to work, I wondered if Sam was secretly planning to kill me.

The only good news was that the explosion only caused minimal damage to the Command Section which we repaired.

Bob, however, wasn't our only casualty. A couple of weeks later we lost two more of our RJs, but not to accidents related to the construction of Voyager.

Stan Smith had an invalided mother who lived in a nursing home in the Phoenix area that was experiencing short term power blackouts. With the possibility of no air-conditioning and the temperature hitting 130 degrees on some days, Stan was really worried. He told us that he was going to Phoenix to see if there was anything he could do, but when he didn't return, Alex had Chet investigate. Sadly, Chet reported that Stan had flown into Phoenix and rented a car, but he never arrived at his mother's. Somewhere between the airport and the nursing home, Stan had been caught in a flash flood and had drowned.

Charlie Pitt just up and quit. He'd been with us from the beginning too. On his down time he travelled regularly to his family in Florida. With a third of the state going downhill fast as it disappeared in the rising ocean, Charlie decided he was needed there and called Alex to resign.

Morale was low as we licked the wounds of our losses. Down to eleven robots and nine jockeys and only busy during the times the specialists needed us to ferry them to the exterior of Voyager, JJ, Billy, Fred, me and the rest of the RJs were usually idle and bored. Without anything better to do, we hung out with Al in Wisdom's Met capsule to watch the changing climate do a number on the planet.

The latest disaster was called Hurricane Harriet and we watched as it swept across the Atlantic and obliterated Puerto Rico before it slammed full force into southern Florida. Harriet was a monster; She was so big that Al and the other weather guys weren't sure how to measure it. As best as they could figure, her wind speeds were close to 225 miles an hour when Harriet made landfall and the storm surge was over twenty feet high. The news reports said that there wasn't a window left in downtown Miami area and every wood or brick and mortar building was destroyed.

What was most shocking, after Harriet passed, the water that had flooded the land from the storm surge didn't recede and, in Al's opinion, it wasn't going to recede... ever. From what we could see through the telescopes the entire coastline in the Miami area had permanently shifted west anywhere from a hundred yards to a quarter of a mile. While we couldn't see it from three hundred miles up, the news reports on the Vid said that at high tide the hotels, condos and commercial skyscrapers of Miami and Miami Beach were now standing in anywhere from two to twenty feet of water.

And that wasn't the end of Harriet. After hitting Miami and the east coast of Florida, the super hurricane continued to roar west across the Florida Peninsula before turning north and driving up the west coast hitting the Florida panhandle just east of Pensacola. Of course, all we could see were the massive cloud bands nearly six hundred miles across and Harriet's eye, perfectly formed and intact over a hundred miles inland.

When the storm finally passed and we could see the ground again, even we meteorological morons could see how extensive and wide-spread the damage was. Both the east and west coasts of the sunshine state looked, well, shrunken. It was as if Florida had been a giant balloon deflated by Harriet.

Anything left of the coastal towns and villages were swimming in several feet of water while the bays and harbors were unrecognizable. The entire length of the Florida Keys had been completely erased. The news Vids estimated that the death toll could be well over a million... I wondered if they ever found out for sure.

But before I could wrap my mind around it, Al began tracking Jason. A hurricane just as big as Harriet that followed the almost exact same track. What little survived of Puerto Rico, Jason finished off. Rescue agencies estimated that out of a population of over three million, only about two hundred thousand survived and they were scattered across the island without food or water and with hardly a structure left in which to shelter. The death toll was still rising.

But Jason didn't stop with Puerto Rico. After gathering strength over the warm waters of the Atlantic Ocean, Jason also hit Florida just south of Miami and, just like Harriet, went on to cross what was left of the southern peninsula. This was where the two storms differed as Harriet had taken an immediate turn north up the western Florida coast while Jason went out into the Gulf of Mexico. Picking up more energy from the warm Gulf waters, Jason made landfall just west of Mobile, Alabama before proceeding to devastate the state.

I couldn't believe what I was seeing once I could see the United States again. South Florida from the tip of the peninsula to the northern edge of the Everglades was just... gone. Key West and the rest of the Florida Keys had completely vanished from the map. It was as if a giant had taken a bite out of the southern peninsula. Where there was once green, there was now nothing but blue water.

Every Gulf coast state from Florida to Texas had been affected by Harriet and Jason, their shorelines shifting inland as much as half a mile to two miles depending on how high they were above sea level or how close to the surface their water table was. The only structures that survived were made of steel and concrete and, like Miami, most of them were now standing in tide water.

Despite Jason's ferocity, the only piece of good news was the multi-billion-dollar dike and levy system that had been built around New Orleans held. Al said that the bayous and marshlands also helped by absorbing much of the hurricane's energy and the natural topography in combination with the dike had saved the city from major flooding; However, a big hunk of the Mississippi Delta was now permanently under water. Al predicted that with the changed coast, if New Orleans were ever hit again by storms the size of Harriet or Jason, the surges would probably wash right over the city.

And the United States wasn't the worst hit around the world. While Harriet was pounding Florida, a huge cyclone was roaring across the Indian Ocean, churning up the Bay of Bengal and smashing into the Northeast coast of India and the South Coast of Bangladesh. Like Florida, when it was over, the water didn't recede; The southern third of the vast Ganges-Brahmaputra Delta and the Sundarbans, was gone. The news feeds estimated that as many as three million people had lived in the Sundarbans before the cyclone and as many as a million may have lost their lives.

It was estimated that a million people were lost in the cyclone, but the final count would never be known. Once the storm passed, the millions of shell-shocked survivors didn't stop to count their dead, but began moving north from the delta into the interior of Bangladesh, but there really wasn't any place for them to go. Bangladesh, already one of the most overcrowded countries in the world, couldn't absorb that many people and they wouldn't be receiving any help from neighboring India who had closed their common border and reinforced it with steel, concrete… and soldiers with guns.

And these were just the snapshots of Earth that we could see from three hundred miles up—hundreds more climate disasters large and small were playing out all over the world. There were multiple storm systems mixed with toxic industrial smog and the smoke from a thousand major fires. From space, it was hard to clearly make out anything on the ground through the billows of smog, smoke and cloud. But between the news feeds that we received from a dozen satellites and AL's patient explanations, it was clear that Mother Earth was dying.

I was relieved to get a call from Alex, her voice a ray of sunshine after the storms. "Hello, Luv."

"I love you, too… business."

Her curtness got my attention. "Yes, boss."

"I just received a question from the Visions Unlimited Board of Directors. Would it be possible to put more Cryogenic Pods into the Cryo Section of Voyager?"

"I don't know. Never thought about it."

"Well, why don't you and your gang of merry men stop pestering Al and go check it out?"

"Yes, boss," I said again while trying not to scratch my curiosity itch by blurting out the thousand questions springing to mind. "Any hurry?"

"I don't know, but I'd say yes," Alex said, her brow furrowing in concern. "As I said I got a call from the Board and they seemed pretty anxious about something when they asked about increasing the number of pods, so try to give me an answer as soon as you can."

After assuring her we'd look into it, I hung up and

looked at the puzzled faces around me. What the hell?

We wasted no time digging out the blueprints and some tape measures before heading out to Cryogenic Section of Voyager. Built according to Project Voyager specifications, the twenty-four pods in two rows of twelve filled the chamber.

After a fair amount of bumbling around, we called Alex with our answer: unless they wanted to make the Cryogenic Section bigger, we could add twenty-two by offsetting the existing pods and double bunking them thereby increasing pod capacity to forty-six. As we assumed the colonists would be thawed out on Planet X, we also calculated room to build a kind of service platform with stairs so they'd be able to exit the pods in gravity.

As Alex thanked us and rang off, JJ, Fred, Billy and I just looked at each other and wondered what the heck this was all about. This was going to be a big survey crew! We really wondered when Alex called back about a half hour later. The Board wasn't happy with our answer; They wanted more pods added.

I could only shrug as VU demanded the impossible. "Well, Luv, we looked at it from every angle we could, but it looks like forty-six is the limit."

"Okay," Alex frowned, but then brightened as something occurred to her. "Listen, I'm going to send a Starduster up tomorrow. I want you, JJ, Fred and Billy on it and bring whatever plans you have with you when you come down."

What the hell was going on? While Voyager wasn't complete, we were nearing the finish line and now they wanted to change things up? Voyager was all but finished.

From the Command Section at one end to the Drive Section at the other, a three hundred-foot-long silver tube with stubby delta wings lay there in space.

It even had landing gear. That had been a big argument with Ajax (who else?) over whether we should put wheels or skids on it. Skids won as the counter-argument was that there probably weren't too many long, hard surface runways on Planet X. Us dumb engineers had pointed out that we'd already installed engines for a vertical landing, so why would they need wheels. They didn't want to hear it but in the end the skids were subsequently added.

Another redesign came in for the Command Section. The cockpit had seats for a pilot and co-pilot, but after yet another argument with Ajax (I really didn't like those guys!), we were instructed to install four more seats for whatever crew members were required to be awake while everyone else slept. I wondered why they put in so many seats as it seemed to me that if you had too many people awake you would definitely run out of food and water.

Eventually, I assumed another control panel would be installed for the Gutman Drive, but these mysterious engines still hadn't appeared let alone installed. Until that happened, Voyager sure wasn't going anywhere no matter how well we put her together.

And with or without engines, it wasn't going to leave Earth if they kept changing things. Something was up with the cryo pods, but I had no idea what and Alex wasn't saying.

The shuttle showed up bringing back two of our RJs and four Wisdom scientists after their rotation down on the ground. The RJs were Paul Mahoney and Tony Simmons, our two "wild child's". If anyone was going to end up broke after

Voyager, it would be these two. Whenever they hit the ground, they headed to Las Vegas. They were never late for their flight back into space, but on more than one occasion, the hungover hooligans cut it mighty close.

On the way down in the Starduster JJ asked, "Do you now if there are any apartments available where you and Alex live?"

"Sure," I said surprised. Since we had started our rotations down to Earth, all I knew about what JJ did when he was dirt-side was that he flew to Los Angles every time he was on the ground. "With half the population pulling out of Sand Flea City, there are several apartments empty. Why? Are you going to rent one?"

"Yeah, I'm thinking about getting a place in the area. Somewhere close to the airfield or maybe even in Alex's dormitory in the hangar."

"I thought you went to LA?"

"I do, but LA's getting pretty rough. It's getting hotter, the smog is terrible and it's getting harder and harder to buy basic supplies. Electricity's becoming more and more unreliable; Cops aren't doing anything to enforce the law and the street gangs are growing bolder. I want to bring my wife out to Sand Flea."

Dumbstruck, I almost fell out of my seat. In the almost two years that we had worked together, I never even knew that he was married. Now there's a guy who doesn't talk much!

Before I could get any more information out of him about the mysterious wife our Starduster landed and taxied toward Project Voyager's secure area. Dumbstruck again, I couldn't believe how much the place had changed since my last trip just a few weeks ago. Security was everywhere! VU's entire parking ramp and hangar area was now surrounded with piles of razor wire and concrete with armed guards stationed in well protected bunkers. Apparently, Chet had completed his security perimeter. There was even a gate across the taxiway that was closed behind us after we passed through. The Starduster didn't stop on the ramp, but taxied through the plastic curtain into a hangar.

Before we were able to disembark, someone stuck their head in and said that Ms. Cummings wanted the construction crew in her office pronto, but the moment we climbed out of the shuttle we were lost. The last time I was dirtside the Stardusters taxied into Hangar 2, the operational hangar for the tourist's flights but this didn't look like 2. The guy who had stuck his head in the door pointed us toward a door, said goodbye and headed off in another direction.

We went through the door into the closed and air-conditioned walkway which linked this hangar with another where two shuttles were parked. We were still lost. Finally, we saw a mechanic working on one of the shuttles and asked where Alex's office was and were told it was in the next row of hangars over.

At last I had some idea of where I was. Instead of taxing into hangar 2 we had come into 5. We walked through the above ground tunnel into the supply hangar and managed to stumble on through 2 which no longer looked like 2 and finally into Alex's outer office… which was empty. Not even the extremely capable receptionist Elizabeth was there.

"Is that you, John?" Alex called through her open office door.

"Uh, yeah," I answered, bewildered with it all.

"Good!" Alex said not wasting any time with pleasantries. "You and the boys get in here and grab a chair. I'll be with you in a minute."

When we entered, all I could see of Alex was the top of her head behind computer screens, counsels, telephones and I don't know what all. As she finished the rather animated discussion that she was having with someone, she came around to my side of her command center and gave me a quick kiss before perching herself on the edge of her desk. We hiked our chairs around facing her and leaned in. This was going to be good.

"Alex, what the hell is going on?" I asked.

"All in due time, my sweet," she smiled at me before addressing everyone. "First, let me tell you that when I reported your conclusions that you could add twenty-two more cryo pods, the Directors seemed more than a little disappointed and pressed me to see if we couldn't install more than forty-six. To make a rather long conversation short, they were very unhappy about the numbers and they want to see me in the VU main headquarters in Los Angles day after tomorrow, on Friday."

Alex paused for either effect or to curb her frustration, I wasn't sure which, before she continued. "So, as my beloved husband says, what the hell is going on?"

She paused again as if expecting an answer. She wasn't going to get it from me. I was already lost which is why I asked and from their expressions, JJ and Fred were just as clueless.

Billy, however, sat back and steepled his hands under his chin in Alex's classic pose as he quietly processed Alex's question. With a sly grin he said, "Voyager has a new mission."

Alex beamed and smiled at him like a teacher smiles when her prize pupil comes through with the right answer. "I always knew that you were a bright boy. Would you care to expand on that, Dr. Wright?"

Doctor Wright? Billy has a PhD? Why am I always the last one to know anything?

"Well," Billy said slowly as he began his mental processing aloud for the benefit of the class. "Twenty-four people for the exploratory mission would have been just about right, so why add more? And if adding twenty-two isn't enough, the only reason that I can think of is that Voyager has now morphed from an exploratory ship to a colony ship. Voyager could actually be going to Mars now in order to start a colony, but my guess is that it's still going to Planet X and, if the planet can support human life, it's not coming back."

Stunned, I looked between Billy and Alex and was even more astonished at her expression which said that Billy was spot on in his assessment. But Billy wasn't finished.

"The reason for their agitation is that not only are forty-six people not enough to start a new civilization, it probably won't accommodate all the people that the VU Directors want to get away from Earth."

Alex's grim expression told us that Billy was right again. "Understand, the Directors haven't told me anything about this, but what you just said are my thoughts exactly. I am almost 100% sure that that's what the Directors are going to be asking when we show up in Los Angles and that leaves us with some work to do. In the next day and a half, we—as in you—need to determine if turning Voyager into a colony ship is even possible."

Billy frowned. "Personally, I don't think that it will be

possible unless Voyager can carry enough people to make a human colony sustainable. Right off hand, I have no idea exactly how many people that would be... a couple of hundred at least."

"Exactly," Alex nodded. "So, gentlemen your mission if you choose to except it, and you do, is to see how we can fit more passengers into Voyager. I have collected every blueprint, study, file, equipment and supply load inventory that I could find and they are all on the table in the conference room next door. Nobody knows more about Voyager than you four, so in the next day and a half you are going to figure out if we can get more people on board and if not, why not. I need you to have a presentation ready for the Directors if I call on you. There are coffee and soft drinks on the side board. I'll see you for dinner. Now, go," and she waved her hands to shoo us out of her office.

"Oh, and one more thing," Alex added as we stood up. "No one outside of the five of us knows anything about this and I would like to keep it that way."

That's my Alex, the original Action Figure. Wonder Woman.

As we headed for the conference room Alex asked JJ, "Is Cathy still in LA?"

Good gravy, even Alex knew JJ was married. Even knew her name. Geeze!

"Yeah," he answered. "But I was thinking of bringing her over here."

"I think that that would be a good idea. By the way, has she graduated? What's her degree in again?"

"Yeah, about six months ago," JJ said proudly. "She's a Registered Dietitian working at Good Samaritan."

Alex got that gleam in her eye that indicated the hatching of a plan. "I look forward to meeting her and I'll book a separate room for you two."

I asked, "Are you doing the travel arraignments too? What happened to Elizabeth? I noticed she wasn't out front."

"Elizabeth resigned a couple of weeks ago."

I was sorry to hear that; She was a sharp kid. "What happened?"

"Oh, nothing here. She was worried about her mother. She lives alone and with the food, water and security situations going downhill all around the country, Elizabeth just felt that she had to go back to Ohio and take care of her."

"That's too bad. I suppose there was no chance of getting her mother out here."

Alex smiled and shook her head. "Not a chance. I tried but her mother moved into the house she is living in as a bride fifty odd years ago. Her husband, Elizabeth's father, passed away a few years ago so all her life and memories are in that house and wild horses couldn't drag her out of it. Elizabeth was their only child and she felt that she just had to go. Now, *you* go and get to work! I'll collect you for dinner."

CHAPTER 8

J, Fred, Billy and I trooped into the Conference Room. As we sat around the big conference table, we just looked at each other still trying to wrap our minds around this new concept: a colony of human beings on Planet X!

For the many months that I had been up in space building Voyager I still thought that the idea of an exploratory mission to Planet X was nothing more than a fantasy... an expensive, nutty fantasy. Now I was looking at the reality of Voyager as a vehicle to transport human beings to another planet to establish a colony. What did Alex and Billy say, a couple hundred people? Would even a couple of hundred be enough to maintain a population?

Was this new concept even nuttier than the survey mission or could it really be done, I wondered? I mean, even if we could transport colonists to Planet X, could they really survive and prosper?

It was as these ideas were chasing each other around in my head that suddenly everything changed for me. I don't know how it happened, but as I sat there thinking about it, I morphed from a hired hand who was just doing a job for money and thinking that the whole idea of Voyager was nuts into a true believer—that we really could put a human colony on another planet. In an instant, I wanted to do all I could to make that happen, not because it was my job and they were paying me big bucks, but because I *wanted* it to happen.

My newfound enthusiasm slid down the embankment of discouragement as we worked late into the afternoon and weren't any farther along. We crunched the numbers on paper and played with Alex's desk top model and the big break away floor model of Voyager. No matter what we did to the math and the models, Voyager stubbornly remained the same size. Forty-six people were all we could cram into Cryogenic Section of Voyager and as little as I knew about genetics I was sure that a colony that size would be practically dead on arrival.

Where we were really stuck was that we couldn't just expand the Cryogenics Section in order to fit another hundred and fifty people in without messing up the ship's aerodynamics. Once Voyager got to Planet X, it was still going to have to land, so making the ship longer wasn't an option.

We briefly tossed around the idea of making the supply and equipment sections smaller in order to expand the Cryogenics Section, but we then tossed that idea out. No matter how large the colony ended up being, they would still need as many supplies as they could take with them. Supplies for a short survey mission was one thing—clothing, shelter, food, water and equipment for a couple hundred humans while they got themselves established on Planet X was something else.

Of course, there was always the possibility that there was intelligent life on Planet X, civilizations and such things and survival supplies wouldn't be necessary. But I wouldn't want to bet the farm on that. And if there was intelligent life where were they on the evolutionary scale? Assuming that the inhabitants of Planet X had progressed beyond fire, they might only have stone tools. Metal would be better putting them into maybe a mediaeval range. But where ever they were the indigenous might not be willing to share.

And then again, Planet X might be a barren rock. If there weren't any neighbors to borrow a cup of flour from, our colonists better make sure they bring what they need with them. While we didn't have a clue what a couple hundred colonists might need, reducing either the Supply or Equipment sections wasn't going to be an option.

It was very disheartening. As far as we could see, to make this colony thing work we'd need a half dozen Voyagers!

Alex came and collected us for dinner around 1700. She didn't even ask us how we were coming along; I guess our faces told her all that she needed to know.

When I reminded Alex that Fred, JJ and Billy would need a motel for the two days that we were here, she explained that that wouldn't be necessary there was plenty of room here in her billeting area. Taking us out through another door and into the hangar, I saw that the dormitory had grown and now had several dozen rows of beds.

"That's a lot of beds," I said. "What happened?"

"Several things," Alex explained. "Between the Voyager personnel and the Starduster people, Visions

Unlimited now has about a hundred and seventy-five people working here at the airfield. Most of them aren't locals and when they were hired by the Voyager/Starduster Project, several of them brought their families with them to Sand Flea and, like us, they rented houses and apartments in town. That was fine for a while, but with the heat, the weather getting worse and the electrical power becoming more and more unreliable, living out in the city was at best damn uncomfortable and could sometimes even be deadly. With civil disorder on the rise and law and order breaking down, their safety became a huge consideration—it's just too dangerous to live anywhere else. So, when the last motel closed down a few weeks ago, I expanded the dormitory into Hangar 2 and made accommodations available to any of the employees who wanted to live here... free. Those cubicles on the end are for couples and families and that one is ours."

"What happened to our apartment?" I asked.

"Well..." Alex shifted uncomfortably. "I didn't want to tell you before because I knew that you would get all protective and worried, but it was broken into and ransacked."

"Good God!" I exclaimed. "And you didn't tell me. Where were you?" The moment my terror verbally erupted, I knew she was right again. I was scared to death over something that was already over and that I wouldn't have had any control over even if I had been here.

Alex smiled reassuringly. "Fortunately, it happened in the afternoon and I was here. I didn't even know about it until I went home around six. The police were still there, or what's left of the police. It was awful. From what the police told me group of probably a dozen wandering thugs just swept in and took over the place. Mr. Jorgenson, the manager was killed and that nice older couple that lived across the courtyard from us were so badly beaten that the Docs don't think that they'll survive."

I was stunned. "Is the Watson's office and infirmary ok?"

"Oh yes, but it's not where it used to be. I moved their whole set up, infirmary and all onto the airfield over a month ago. They're now over in Hangar 4. This is now Hanger 1, by the way. Your shuttle parked in what's now Hangar 5. Until you get reacquainted with the new layout, four, five and six are across the way."

"Yeah, we caught that as we came in," I said glumly, my mind still on the break in. To try and lighten the mood, I gave her a mock scowl. "You gotta stop changing things around. I'm like a rat in a maze that keeps getting bigger and you keep moving the cheese."

"Well, then, let me continue with the new and improved tour," Alex smiled and pointed in the direction of the hangars across the concrete. "I gave up the couple of buildings that VU had further on down the flight line. Everything that VU owns and that I am responsible for is now in these six hangars. Chet says it makes security a little easier if we're not so spread out."

I was still trying to process all that as we went through the buffet line. Alex didn't say anything, but she didn't seem entirely satisfied with her meal. After a few weeks on freeze dry dinners trying to float away from me, I personally thought dinner was great. We pulled a couple of tables together and while we sat there it seemed that everyone who worked for Voyager or Starduster dropped by to say hello. The RJs were introduced to Chet and Dot. Dot looked the boys over and said that she didn't see much improvement and she still wasn't impressed while reminding me that I was still supposed to give a talk to the kids.

Phil also came by and while I was talking to him, I was introduced to Alice Smith and Pedro Gonzales. Alice managed the supplies which were now in Hangar 3 while Pedro ran the motor pool which was located along with the infirmary in Hangar 4. Pedro had the hangar floor while the Docs had what used to be the offices and shops along the side.

After dinner we went back to the Conference Room and continued our very unproductive evening. Sometime around ten, Alex finally ran us off to bed.

If there was anything that I liked more about being dirtside other than being with Alex it was being able to take a long, hot shower. On the same side of the Hangar 1 as the cafeteria, there were huge his and hers bathrooms and shower rooms. My fingers were prunes before I blissfully decided I was clean.

The next morning, the guys and I were back in the Conference Room, but sadly, nothing had changed. The plans hadn't stretched overnight, the models hadn't gotten any bigger.

By noon, after going over the same arguments, the engineering humma-humma and drinking several gallons of coffee all morning, we only knew two things: there was no way we could pack more than forty-six cryo pods into the existing cryo section and we couldn't alter the current shape and size of Voyager—at least, not without screwing up the aerodynamics which would be vital when we brought Voyager back into an atmosphere for landing on the planet's surface.

In short, we were screwed. If VU wanted more people to go, we were going to have to build a bigger ship or another ship or ships.

After we had run the numbers a dozen more times and come up with the same answer, we decided that we would go to lunch and then prepare the very sad and negative briefing for Alex that afternoon. While we were sitting having our very glum lunch, Billy Wright suddenly sat bolt upright.

"No!" he exclaimed, as if explaining to a first-grader for the fiftieth time that two plus two doesn't equal five. "Boy, are we dumb. We can do this thing."

"Billy," I said, sympathetically. "I fully understand your frustration."

"No, I mean we can really do this thing. I'll explain when we get back to the conference room and I'll show you."

No amount of prodding could get him to explain further. So eager to learn his epiphany, we cut lunch short and crowded around Billy the moment we got back into the conference room.

"Think about it," he said, his eyes gleaming with excitement. "What are we doing now? I mean building Voyager. We build the components for Voyager on Earth, boost them up into space and build a ship to fly through space to another planet and land. But Voyager only has to be aerodynamic for its final trip down to Planet X."

Our expressions showed that we didn't get it. "Billy," I said, "I'm the dim bulb in our chandelier, but keep going."

"Okay, look at how aerodynamic Wisdom is... meaning it isn't. Why couldn't we just add more sections on to Voyager here in space and then do the whole construction thing in reverse when we get to Planet X? We can add anything we want to Voyager, fly her to Planet X, and take her apart again in space before we land?"

We all looked at each other. Why not? Voyager is a spaceship, after all and aerodynamics only matter in an atmosphere.

Now I was excited! "Yeah, we could make another cryo section and just strap it on to the outside."

Billy did me one better. "We can do more than that. Why not make an even bigger cryo section seeing as we have a three hundred-foot-long tube to attach it to?"

JJ shook his head. "Not quite. You still have to consider the tail assembly."

"We could strap it on the side."

"Why just one?" asked Fred.

"What do you mean?" asked Billy.

"We could make two or maybe even three cryogenic cylinders and strap them to the side of Voyager." Then Fred continued, "But remember while you're considering this construction or deconstruction of Voyager in orbit around Planet X, to make it work we would have to bring some or all of the robots. I think to make it really work we'd have to attach R3 to Voyager as well."

We all looked at each other as we realized that not only was Fred right, but at the implications of what that would mean. We, or at least some of us, would have to go. If we made this proposal, we would be committing, if not ourselves, at least some RJs on a nonrefundable one way space cruise.

Did I want to go? Would Alex want to go?

I had no idea.

In the end we decided that we would lay out the possibility and see who went and who stayed later. By the time Alex came and collected us for dinner, we were feeling pretty good. We had a plan and most of a presentation. During dinner she noticed our high spirts, but we weren't talking. As our boss, she had ways to make us talk. With a sly smile, said that she would like to see what we had at 2000 because tomorrow morning Visions Unlimited was sending one of their executive jets and we were going to be heading for LA.

We were ready! We cleaned up the conference room and when Alex came in, we sat her at the head of the table with a big Vid screen in the middle of the table that was connected to our phones. Fred Thompson was a pretty fair artist so we just photographed his line drawings of the new Voyager for the presentation.

Billy gave the briefing while the rest of us sat quietly imitating junior executives.

"Ms. Cummings, you tasked us to investigate the possibility of increasing the number of humans that could be transported to Planet X on the Voyager space craft. The information that we were given was that the original flight profile remains, i.e. Voyager crosses space to Planet X, enters Planet X's atmosphere and lands under its own power. Given these restrictions we have concluded that for many reasons the number of cryogenic pods for human beings in Voyager cannot be increased past forty-six."

Alex kind of sighed.

"However," Billy continued, "the number of humans on board could be increased by six—the number of seats in the Command Section. That would be forty-six in stasis and a six-person command crew who would be awake. However, we do not recommend this option due to the amount of supplies that would be consumed by six people during a twenty-year journey."

Billy paused and Alex's shoulders started to slump as he went on.

"The only other possibility that we can see of increasing the number of passengers would be to increase the length of the cryogenic section. As Voyager itself cannot be lengthened due to aerodynamic considerations, any stretching of the cryogenics section would be at the expense of the supply and/or the equipment sections. Naturally, we do not recommend this option, either. As Voyager was originally designed to support twenty-four humans, if we add twenty-two more passengers the mission will now have to support double that amount. It is our opinion that adding even more people by decreasing the amount of space available for supplies would reduce the mission's chance of success even further."

I watched as Alex dejectedly sagged her shoulders a bit more. I have to admit, I was rather enjoying this as Billy played it with just the right amount of hesitation before he went on.

"However, we think that with an alteration of Voyagers basic design and flight profile, we think we can increase her carrying capacity of human beings by six hundred."

"What!?" Alex exclaimed almost jumping out of her chair. "Six *hundred*? How?"

Billy couldn't help share his grin with us as he explained, "Our basic problem with adding more passengers was doing it without changing Voyagers size and shape to keep her aerodynamic. But as long as Voyager is *in* space, those considerations didn't exist. Instead of looking at Voyager as an airplane, we needed to look at her like we would look at Wisdom. What we propose is that we add on three new sections. Two of these would be cryogenic cylinders each holding three hundred individual cryogenic pods and the third section would be a two hundred and fifty-foot-long cylinder for the supplies and equipment that a colony of over six hundred people would need."

As Alex nodded at the wisdom of that, Billy continued. "We have the capability to accomplish all of this. We can build the new Voyager here in space and when we get to Planet X dismantle her in space by stripping Voyager down to its original configuration for atmospheric entry."

Billy paused.

"But?" Alex prompted sensing there was more.

"But… and this is a big but… none of this is going to work without the Stardusters."

Alex nodded. "And the Stardusters aren't going to be viable unless they could be retrofitted to land and take off vertically."

"Exactly," Billy confirmed. "If this option is adopted, it would require the use of some or preferably all of the Starduster shuttles as they would be required for ferrying the colonists down to the planet before we could dismantle Voyager. In addition, once we're on the ground, the Stardusters would provide the additional advantage of moving around on the planet."

Alex didn't even blink at that. She just smiled and nodded her head. That really surprised me. I thought that the fact that the Stardusters could only land on a runway, and a fairly long runway at that, would be a show stopper.

Alex nodded to Billy to go on, so he started showing Fred's line drawings of the cryogenics cylinder on the Vid screen. Once again, Alex was blown away. Though it was similar to the cryo section that was already a part of Voyager, Fred's image was three times longer and quite a bit wider. In the original section, the individual cryogenic pods were in two rows of twelve; Our proposed section would have two rows of fifty stacked three deep—one hundred and fifty on a side, three hundred in a cylinder and we proposed the construction of two cylinders.

The next slide showed the current Voyager with a cryogenic section mounted on each side. To me it looked like the booster rocket with the two fuel tanks attached that NASA used to use to lift the original shuttles into space.

The next slide showed Voyager with the two cryogenic sections attached to the sides and a third section which was a little shorter about two hundred and fifty feet in length mounted on top of Voyager in front of the vertical stabilizer. Billy explained that this was for equipment and supply storage.

The final slide showed the complete Voyager with yet another section mounted on its underside and four Starduster shuttles mounted under the wings.

Alex pointed to the section and asked, "What's that?"

"That," Billy replied. "is R3. We would have to have some robots to dismantle Voyager when we got to Planet X, so we thought, 'Why not bring them all and the maintenance shed, too?'"

"Boys this is wonderful!" Alex beamed before noticing my frowny face. "Problems, John?"

I had been chosen to be 'Devil's Advocate'. "Problems

by the score, Luv. We looked at this very quickly and from an engineering view point. We are pretty sure that everything Billy gave you is possible. But there are many buts."

"Let's have 'em."

"The Stardusters, for one."

Alex shook her head and laughed. "It's funny how things seem to work out. When the Stardusters were first designed, a vertical lift capability was considered and then for a number of reasons, mostly money, it was rejected. However, by the time vertical lift was rejected production was already far enough along that the mounts, but not the engines, were installed. I'll have to talk to the experts, but it looks to me that if we go forward with this proposal, we just need to find the engines and install them."

Wow! Well, that was less of an issue then I expected. "Next are the robot jockeys and Starduster drivers. We will have to have operators for both and I have no idea who would be willing to volunteer. I, for one, am not sure that I want to go. Certainly not without you.".

I looked a question at her, but she just smiled and waved me to go on.

"We're pretty sure that we can put all this stuff together—if we get the stuff. I have no idea how long it would take to manufacture six hundred Cryogenic pods and the two three-hundred-foot-long sections to install them in. The equipment and supply section isn't as complicated as the cryo pods, but it would have to be built by someone somewhere."

Sensing there was still more, Alex nodded for me to continue. "Also, given the current uncertainties of the transportation system and the increasing weather problems, can the bits and pieces be shipped to us here or to the rocket bases? And to be honest the more that can be done on Earth the better. That means more rocket lifts will be required. Are there enough heavy lift rockets available to lift the big pieces into orbit?

"And finally," I concluded with a slight sigh, "as it has been pointed out many times before, Voyager has no engines."

My nay-saying didn't faze Alex a bit. She just smiled and said, "All noted. Good work boys. Now before we knock off for the night let me emphasize the major issue. Outside of the Stardusters themselves, none of this works without you and the Starduster pilots at the other end. That's something that each of you and all the other RJs and pilots will have to decide for yourselves—but not right now and not tonight. It's not an easy question so consider it carefully: do you want to leave Earth forever and travel to Planet X?"

Alex paused as she looked at each of us before dismissing us with a very pleased smile. "Now, go! Get some sleep and don't miss the flight to LA tomorrow morning."

JJ, Fred and Billy trooped out leaving me and Alex alone in the empty conference room. Without saying a word, we just sat there just looking at each other. Then we both smiled.

It was settled. We were going!

CHAPTER 9

I had never flown in one of these really posh executive jets before. I mean, this flying cocktail lounge had everything—a wet bar, seats that reclined so far back they were practically beds, Vid screens and a stewardess and a steward whose sole purpose during the trip was to ensure I was happy. Oh, yeah. I was *very* happy.

Once we got underway, I went up front and got a quick tour of all the dials and gages, but seeing as they weren't going to let me fly this magnificent machine I went back and snuggled into one of the posh chairs and went to sleep. It seemed like a short flight, but that was probably because I slept the whole way.

That was where the luxury ended. When we landed in Los Angles, we apparently didn't rate the passenger tube into the concourse, but stepped right off the plane and out onto the tarmac... the steaming, melting tarmac. Instantly drenched in sweat, I couldn't breathe because of the fumes. It was like Las Vegas only twice as bad. The air, to use the term loosely, was worse than fog or smog. It was like trying to breathe smoke laced with soot, toxic heavy metals, radiation and who knew what other chemicals.

Fortunately, VU was on the ball and a van pulled up right next to our airplane. I had a taste of what was coming when our driver stepped out not wearing a gauze mask but a full military gas mask. He couldn't believe we were unmasked and handed us all gauze masks as he quickly loaded us into the van. The blissfully air-conditioned van.

His cheerful chat of "It's not so bad today, you should have seen it last week," and "It's not so hot today, day before yesterday it was 123," didn't go over too well. I guess we were spoiled. When we were working in space, we kept all our environments on the comfortably warm shirt sleeve side and on the ground at the Project Voyager Compound, we lived inside our nice, air-conditioned hangars.

But it wasn't just here in LA. From what I had gathered on the Vids, temperatures in the equatorial zones were averaging 125 to 130 degrees for more than half the year while in the temperate zones' temperatures were reaching 115 to 125—occasionally even higher. According to Al Wilson this was a three-degree average increase in just the last year alone! When you combined that with the thickening air pollution, living outside was just impossible. That's why as we drove toward the hotel, I was surprised to see hundreds of people sitting outside on the steps of their apartment blocks. Most of them wearing gas masks.

"What gives?" I asked the driver.

"No electricity," he explained. "The morons that run

the power grid can't keep the juice coming, so they turn it off periodically. Without AC, it's probably ten or fifteen-degrees hotter inside those buildings than it is outside. The people that live in those apartment blocks have a choice: stay inside and cook or come outside and choke.

"How about food and water?" I asked.

"Well, for water it's pretty bad: bottled water only. You'll see when you get to the Hilton—no water coming out of the taps."

"Yeah," I said. "That's the way it was in Vegas, too. A bottle of water over the sink and timed showers. How about you?"

"Well I don't spread it around, but I live out in the valley and I have a well. So far so good."

"How about food?"

He shrugged. "Hit or miss. For fresh veggies most of the markets have some produce, but it's strictly seasonal and not in the quantities they used to have. The farms out in the valley that have access to water are still getting the occasional crop in. But with the breakdown in the worldwide transportation system, the only fresh stuff that's available in super markets is grown locally. As soon as it hits the shelves, it's gone in a heartbeat. Most farmers have stopped shipping out of state or even to the big stores closer at hand and are selling their stuff at local farmers markets or roadside stands at astronomical prices."

There wasn't anything for me to say, so I just sat back in my sticky, wet shirt, watched as the hot air seemed to warp around the people fanning themselves for any kind of cool breeze and thought about what Al had said when we were up at Wisdom.

Before the world started going to pot, almost everything that was produced or manufactured around the world was transported across the oceans to markets or distribution points in giant metal containers that were loaded on 50,000 container ships each carrying thousands of these containers. But that system was all but gone now. The containers of raw materials that manufacturers were still able to produce were expected to be delivered by road or rails to the ports, but the trucks and trains were having a hard time getting through to the coastal areas. All over the world floods were washing out the roads and extreme heat was warping the rail lines. On top of all that, there were local bandits ready to ambush and steal supplies.

If any of the containers did make it to a port, there was a good chance they might not make it onto a ship as many of the shipping ports were under attack by the oceans. With the rising waters, many of the large container ships sometimes couldn't dock and if they could the cranes that did the loading might be inoperable because they were standing in tide water. All the low-lying port areas were at risk and if they were under water, not only could the trains and trucks not get in, but the longshoremen couldn't, either.

The final nail in the international transportation system's coffin was that *if* a container ship did get loaded *and* the ship made it to sea, many were being lost in the increasing number of violent hurricanes, cyclones and typhoons that were raging around the oceans of the world.

As we continued driving through LA, I saw several store fronts that looked damaged. A few even carried the scorched scars of arson burns

"Gangs," our chauffeur said. "It's not bad in this part

of town, but in some of areas there is a small riot almost every night. It's the heat and the lack of basic necessities. It makes people crazy."

Pulling into the Hilton, I couldn't help think that if our driver didn't think this was bad, what were the other areas of LA like?

As we were unloading our bags a miniature tornado hit us—in the form of Cathy Jackson, the human dynamo. Gleefully, she swirled out of the front door of the hotel and slammed full force into JJ.

I swear if she was five feet tall and weighed more than a hundred pounds, I'll eat a Starduster! Cathy was all smiles, bubbling laughter and of course we all took to her right away. We couldn't help it! Even though she looked like everyone's little sister, we soon learned that Cathy Jackson was a very smart, very tough, no nonsense lady.

Apparently, JJ did talk sometimes... well, at least to Cathy. She said that she'd heard so much about us and was happy to finally meet all of us. Cathy did seem to be a little in awe of Alex, especially when Alex told her that she would like her to come to our suite for a chat as soon as she and JJ got settled.

That request went out to everyone though. Alex informed us that VU was sending a car for us at 1330 for our 1400 meeting with the Board of Directors of Visions Unlimited and she wanted to speak to everyone in our suite before we left for the meeting.

When JJ and Cathy came in, Alex took the tiny woman off to one of the other rooms "for some girl talk" she said. While they were gone, JJ and I settled in to see what was on the Vid. The usual crap—game shows, sit coms, daytime drama. I hadn't watched daytime Vid in years, but it seemed to me that everything was old and dated. We switched over to a news channel and kind of wished we hadn't. It seemed like the news around Planet Earth was just disaster after disaster.

In Central America, Civil Wars were raging in both Guatemala and Honduras while South America had one in Venezuela and another in Bolivia. The federal governments had all but disappeared and gangs were taking over. In view after view bodies on the streets were so commonplace that they were not even being removed never mind investigated.

Thousands of refugees trying to escape from the brutal fighting in Central America were now pouring into Mexico and trying to cross the border into the United States. The situation had been escalating to where our military had been deployed along the southern border and the administration was considering using deadly force.

We hadn't reached that point yet, but other nations had.

On the other side of the Atlantic five small boats so overloaded with desperate people they could barely stay afloat had been fired on crossing the Mediterranean Sea. I didn't catch what countries they were fleeing from or which country they were hoping to get to but it didn't matter; They were all dead.

In Asia, whole populations were dying from starvation or dehydration as nations fought over territory and resources.

Adding to the refugees' misery, heat and rain had either killed off massive populations of birds and bats or had driven them away to seek their own refuge in cooler climates. Without them, insect populations were exploding as were the inevitable diseases of Malaria, West Nile, Zika and Dengue

Fever. People who fell by the way were abandoned when their families had no choice but to move on.

The scenes on the Vid resembled the worst horrors of World War II.

JJ and I were relieved when Alex and Cathy joined us again. A few minutes later, Billy and Fred turned up and Alex gave us the game plan for the meeting with the VU Board of Directors. She said that she didn't know exactly how the meeting would go, but she would run it from our side and we should just follow her lead; However, she wanted Billy to be ready to give his pitch and I should be ready with my Devil's Advocate. Alex made it clear that if she called on me, I was not to pull any punches.

Then Alex turned to Cathy and told her that she was going too and would be introduced as Alex's Executive Assistant. I don't think Cathy was pleased because she just kind of squeaked.

"Don't worry, you'll be fine," Alex smiled. "Just find a chair against the wall, bring a pad of paper and take lots of notes."

"Okay," Cathy squeaked again.

Our ride to the VU meeting was in the same the van with the same overly happy driver. I wasn't sure what to make of that. With Cathy, there were six of us… well, five and a half counting Cathy. We could have fit into a limo and I was a little put out that we weren't given one. Oh well, another time.

The offices of Visions Unlimited weren't far from the Hilton. After about ten minutes, we pulled up to a typical office building and were shown into a typical air-conditioned conference room. Inside the room, the atmosphere was decidedly cool and I don't mean the heat. We took our seats at one end of a very long conference table while the VU Board of Directors gathered at the other end and proceeded to stare down the length of the table at us. There were nine men and three women, mostly middle-aged with two of the gentlemen who looked to be well into their seventies. I looked them over and it wasn't hard to gauge the mood. This group of powerful executives was nervous, uncertain, pissed off and maybe even a little scared.

The waiting game continued at both ends of the table until one of the VU members, Harrison, finally said, "Well, Ms. Cummings?"

Alex snapped back, "Well what? You summoned me and per your request, I'm here with my staff. What do you wish to discuss?"

I almost busted out laughing. That knocked them back on their heels. If they thought that they were going to intimidate Alexandria Cummings they definitely had forgotten their previous meeting when she got complete control of both their Voyager and Starduster programs. They kind of looked at each other and Harrison said that the reason for the meeting was that they, the Board of Directors, weren't satisfied with the conclusion that only twenty-two additional individuals could be added to Voyagers compliment.

Alex glared down the table and said, "Why? If the original plan of twenty-four individuals was sufficient for the survey mission why is forty-six now not enough?"

The Directors looked at each other again and Harrison started to say something about the board wasn't required to give reasons... blah, blah, blah until Alex cut him off.

Giving them a smile, Alex said, "Director Harrison, Ladies and Gentlemen, let's be honest with one another. I believe—we believe—that you are now looking to expand Voyager's original mission and view it not as only a survey ship to explore Planet X, but as a possible colony vessel as well."

There was dead silence. The board members all looked at each other. Clearing his throat, Harrison asked, "What brings you to that conclusion."

"Because we're not idiots. But I would also like to point out that forty-six people, make it fifty counting the command crew, won't be enough to establish a sustainable colony assuming that Planet X is even habitable."

That brought sputtering indignation from the other end of the table! Trust my Alex to call them all morons without ever saying so.

Alex nodded at their reaction. "That's what I thought. You see what's happening here on Earth and your intelligent enough to see that it's only going to get worse, so you are grasping at a chance to possibly give, maybe not yourselves, but some of your younger family members a chance at a better life. I understand that, but I am not only saddened but offended that you have not shared those thoughts and concerns with me and considered us in your plans for Voyager. To be blunt, have you given any thought to us? Even if Voyager is viable as a colony vessel, have you allocated any spaces to the people who have actually built Voyager who might also want to take a chance on a new planet?"

More silence. The Directors looked at each other and finally back to Harrison. He sighed. "You are quite right, Dr. Cummings, we are scared and on behalf of the Board, I apologize. But with only fifty spaces available, I guess the question of who stays and who goes is moot."

Alex smiled. "There might be a way if we can agree to

work together and maximize all our resources."

That got their attention!

With the entire Board hanging on her every word, Alex continued, "When you asked if we could increase the passenger carrying capacity, we took it literally. My engineers," and she waved her hand at us, "looked at Voyager as she is with the one Cryogenic Section and concluded that only twenty-two cryo pods could be added. Naturally, we thought about extending Voyager to add another cryo section of the same size, effectively increasing cryo capacity. Unfortunately, this solution proved impractical due to the aerodynamics required of Voyager when she enters an atmosphere."

I have to admit, I was enjoying watching their shoulders slump as Alex continued to point out what couldn't be done. Serves them right!

"However," Alex said, "when my staff got to thinking outside the box, or outside the ship if you will, they believe that there is a possibility Voyager can be re-configured. This new design would allow Voyager to carry as many as six hundred and fifty individuals. But to achieve this it will require the full cooperation of both ends of the table. Are you interested?"

They exploded. Hell, yes, they were interested like a drowning man who has just been thrown a life line.

Alex turned to Billy and said, "Dr. Wright if you please."

Billy introduced himself with his full credentials: Dr. William Wright, graduate of Embry-Riddle Aeronautical University, PhD in Engineering, Georgia Tech. Blah! Blah! Hell, even I was impressed and I've known him for a while now.

When they could no longer dispute his expertise, Billy hooked up his phone to the giant Vid screen and gave them the same briefing that we had given Alex back in her conference room at Sand Flea complete with Fred's hand drawn graphics.

When he finished the Directors, all started to talk to each other at once and, after a short while, Harrison asked Alex if she thought that we could really do it. Alex smiled giving me my cue to begin.

Not having as many letters and credentials, my introduction was much shorter than Billy's.

I explained to the Board that from the time we first conceived of this plan, Dr. Cummings had me stand aside and play the role of Devil's Advocate. My explicit instructions were to find as many faults, problems and stumbling blocks as I could and to poke as many holes in the plan as possible. My conclusion was that, while there were enough holes to make the plan resemble a piece of Swiss Cheese, it was technically possible. There were several problems, but the ones that I foresaw were solvable; However, the solutions rested mainly with them, the Board of Directors.

At a nod for me to continue, I began listing them.

"First and foremost are the Stardusters. Assuming that there will be no runways on Planet X the Stardusters will require a vertical lift capability. So, the question is, do the vertical lift engines exist and if so, can they be installed?"

The Directors all turned toward one of their members who just smiled and slipped the knife in a little further. "If the Board will recall, installing the vertical engines is what I proposed from the beginning." He turned to Alex and said, "Just send the Stardusters up to Kansas and it will be done."

Wow! Well, that was easy, I thought and pressed on.

"Next, the cryogenic pods for the sleeping colonists. The new Voyager will require six hundred and forty-six and as of right now, we have twenty-four. Are six hundred plus cryogenic pods available and if not, can they be made available in a reasonable period of time?"

The Directors all looked at a small older gentleman who had been sitting quietly taking it all in. He introduced himself as Joshua Simmons which was a name that even I recognized as being heralded as the father of cryogenics. With a little smile, Simmons shrugged and said that he didn't know, but if at all possible, it would be done. He went on to say that there were a hundred completed pods available at one of his manufacturing facilities and these could be shipped to us anytime we wanted them. For the other five hundred, he just wasn't sure until he had talked with his experts.

Alex thanked him and said that unless there was a security problem where the hundred pods were currently being held, she would prefer that he kept them there until we had the Cryogenic Cylinders to install them in. However, if he did have security problem, by all means ship them and we would store them at Sand Flea. She nodded at me to continue.

I smiled and said that that was a great lead in because my next item was the two three-hundred-foot-long cylinders that the six hundred individual pods were going to be mounted in. These were not just two, round, three-hundred-foot-long hunks of metal; They each had to have the special fittings for three hundred cryogenic pods. In addition, the current cryogenic section that was in Voyager would have to be retro fitted to hold twenty-two more cylinders—if they still wanted them and the work of installing all the pods would have to be done in space.

That led to a brief discussion and they nodded at me to continue.

"We'll need another cylinder for equipment and supplies which will be mounted on top of Voyager, so we were looking at a cylinder probably about two hundred and fifty feet long. Now, we aren't equipment experts, so we don't know if a two hundred and fifty-foot cylinder will be big enough."

"Duly noted, Mr. Marshal. Next?"

I had to admit, I was really impressed with the Board. From their uncertainty at the beginning of the meeting they were now showing the qualities that made VU the powerhouse that it was. "Yes, sir. There are dozens of other small items and I'm sure many more will turn up, but last on my list of show stoppers is the heavy lift rocket capability that will be required to get pre-assembled sections up to Voyager. We control the shuttles and anything that we can lift in them we will, but we do not control the rockets that operate from other locations. Our success will absolutely depend on heavy lift."

"Also noted," Harrison said, "and thank you very much. Do you have anything else to add?"

I glanced at Alex and at her nod, told them that one area that we really lacked current information about was exactly what Voyager should carry to establish the colony. "Should we bring regular camping gear, state of the art survival equipment, outdoor clothing? Anything else that would ensure the colony's survival? I guess what I'm saying is, if you have any contacts along those lines, we'd sure like to get in touch with them."

To my surprise this brought a general chuckle from

the Directors and they turned to a petit woman who said, "Mr. Marshal, have you ever heard of Grant Foster?"

Well, hell yeah! Anybody with access to a Vid screen knew Grant Foster, the outdoorsman's outdoorsman. From what I'd heard, Foster had climbed every mountain in the world worth climbing, led expeditions into just about every remote corner of Earth, written a few books, had a Vid show and I think he even held a couple of patents on outdoor equipment.

"Wow!" I said. "That guy knows everything. Do you think you could put us in touch with him?"

That brought a genuine laugh from the other Directors.

"Young man," the woman smiled, "Grant Foster is my son-in-law and I am certain that when I tell him about this little adventure, wild elephants couldn't keep him away."

Harrison looked down the table at Alex and said, "Dr. Cummings, on behalf of the Board please accept our thanks and again our apologies. At this time, I think that it would be more productive to break up into smaller discussion groups, but before we do that, do have anything to add?"

"Thank you, Director Harrison. Before we break up, I would like to be clear on personnel. If all goes as planned, we will be able to carry six hundred and fifty people. I propose that you, the Board, nominate three hundred and Project Voyager nominate three hundred and these six hundred would be in stasis in the two auxiliary cryogenic cylinders. I would also propose that if Planet X proves uninhabitable, they would never be awakened until we returned to Earth. The remaining fifty are what I call the Command Team. These are the people with specialized skills who will operate Voyager during the journey, conduct the evaluation of the planet and establish our initial base of operations. I will be solely responsible for the composition of the Command Team. Is that agreeable?"

The Board huddled together around Harrison who said, "We are in agreement with one question: do you plan to include in your Command Team people from outside the Voyager Project?"

"Absolutely. I might end up a little heavy on the Voyager side as I will need my RJs, my shuttle drivers and security people, for example. But I will also need people like your Mr. Foster, Dr. Al Wilson who is a meteorologist currently working in Wisdom, botanists, geologists, entomologists, etc. We are currently thinking about having a crew of four actually awake at any one time, but we need to discuss this with medical doctors and Mr. Simmons' cryogenic specialists before we finalize anything."

But Alex wasn't finished. "One last thing just so we are clear. We have no idea what conditions we will find on the planet. Who knows? We could find an environment between not survivable to that of the Jurassic, or there may be civilizations anywhere from medieval to the modern. You are certainly free to nominate anyone you like for Voyager, but I urge you to consider people with useful skills. Skills not necessarily Twenty-First Century, but perhaps more like Sixteenth Century. We may need weavers, blacksmiths, carpenters, masons, sheep herders, farmers, millers. We will arrive at Planet X as Twenty-First Century humans, but our modern technology is fragile and we can only carry so many spare parts. Once our machines break or wear out , they will probably not be repairable until we can develop the machines to make the machines that make the parts to repair them. Weapons are a good example. Once the ammunition for our modern weapons is expended, they will nothing more than metal clubs."

Whether they'd thought about that or not, I couldn't see any sign of surprise.

Alex said, "Also, if you could, I would like you to consolidate your nominations and furnish me with a roster just so we know who is authorized when they show up at the gate. We can accept all nominees any time they want to come, but be sure that they understand that once they are inside the Project Voyager Compound, they are under what I would call military regulations. Quarters are assigned; Meals are served cafeteria style at set hours, take it or leave it. And everybody has a job. If we can utilize an existing skill, we will. If not, a job will be assigned. We also have a school for grades one through twelve and a fledgling apprentice program for the older teens."

Harrison said, "That sounds excellent, Dr. Cummings and before we break up into smaller groups, I have a question for Mr. Marshal."

"Yes sir?"

"How long do you think it will take to finish Voyager?"

I was ready for that one as we had been kicking it around for a couples of days. "Understand, Director Harrison, this guesstimate is with all the ifs, but we figure that once the bits and pieces start flowing to us, and if they keep coming on a regular schedule, we can put Voyager together in a year."

That pleased the Dickens out of the Board, so I made my security pitch. "And one more thing, ladies and gentlemen: secrecy is essential. When you are screening your potential colonists, please be as discreet as possible. As you probably know, once the Administration got interested in space, Voyager and every other private company dabbling in space had to submit what started out as a quarterly report and is now a monthly report to Washington on our progress. As far as the Government knows, Voyager is a survey ship to Mars. If word of what we actually plan to do gets out to the Government or to the general public, it could result in a Government takeover or even a stampede at the gates which could get really, really ugly."

"Noted Mr. Marshal and thank you."

"One more thing, sir. On behalf of my colleagues here, we're sure tired of calling it 'Planet X'. Does our new home have a name?"

Harrison smiled and said, "As a matter of fact, we propose to call it Sanctuary."

Everyone at both ends of the table looked at each other and smiled.

Sanctuary!

Cool.

CHAPTER 10

It was surreal. Only a few hours ago we were a bunch of employees highly skeptical of Voyager's proposed survey trip to a totally unknown planet and now we were enthusiastic participants—colonists to Sanctuary. That the planet now had a name made a huge difference. Sanctuary!

The work groups were a great success. We lowly worker-bees from the desert kind of moved up the table and the high and mighty Directors of one of the largest and most successful corporations in the world kind of moved down and we all sort of merged in the middle. Soon little groups spontaneously formed, the I-Pads and scratch pads were out and we were working on problems as if we had been colleagues for years.

JJ and Billy headed for Simmons and the result of their discussion was that Simmons would immediately send twenty-two cryogenic pods so we could finish the cryogenic section in

Voyager. Simmons's people would hold the remainder of the pods until we were ready for them.

Fred huddled with four Directors to talk about vertical lift motors and Gutman's engines for the main drive while a guy named Johnson or Johnstone spoke to Alex about the possibility of using a cargo airplane's fuselage for the supply and equipment capsule. Sure, why not?

I sat down next to Louise Carson, the lady who said she was Grant Foster's Mother-in-Law. Lou was a kick! After just a couple of phone calls, Grant and his wife Maryanne, who was Lou's daughter, agreed to join Lou in coming out to Sand Flea in a couple of weeks for the fifty-cent tour. Lou said that Maryanne was just as adventure crazy as Grant and she was sure that both of them would want to be included in the mission.

After setting up a few more trips and conferences, the meeting finally broke up. We were a very happy group as we sat around the dinner table at the Hilton. Even happier when everyone made their own decision clear: we were all going. Only three days ago I thought VU was bat-shit crazy and now I was one of the crazies. Wild.

While we were laughing and chattering at dinner, Cathy, who had been sitting quietly taking it all in, spoke up. "I have a question. It seems that all our planning for Sanctuary is that the it will be a primitive planet and we'll need tons of supplies and equipment to survive. What if we encounter an intelligent civilization or has anyone thought about that?"

We all looked at each other.

Alex, however, gave her a reassuring smile. "That is a good question, Cathy, and I have considered the possibility. I think that if we do encounter a civilization at any level only one of three things can happen: they either accept us, tell us to go home or kill us."

"Ooh, Luv, that's cold," I said. "But you're also right. I also think that you have omitted a fourth possibility."

Alex cocked an eyebrow at me and I went on. "What if they tell us to leave and we choose not to go? What if we choose to fight for a piece of the planet?"

Alex frowned as I reminded them that our track record as a species wasn't good. There were countless examples right here on our own planet… in our own country… and it hadn't fared well for the indigenous.

Cathy shuddered. "I don't think I would like that."

"Well, neither would I, but what if the choice is to fight or spend twenty years in cryo to come back to who knows what back here?"

Alex said, "They would wipe us out."

"Maybe," I acknowledged with a shrug, "but that depends on the level of civilized society we encounter. We're few in numbers, but we would have superior fire power over anything up to say a hundred years ago. But then again, we also have a limited amount of weaponry. Once our bullets are gone, even cavemen would have the advantage over us."

What a party-pooper I am. Everyone retreated into their own thoughts and we all drifted off to bed soon after. Bright and early the next morning, our same van with the same smiling driver was waiting for us in front of the Hilton. We followed the same route back to the airport only this time I noticed that there was no one outside sitting on the steps and curbs.

"Power's back on. Everybody's back inside where it's cool," he told us. Then for the first time, I saw him frown and heard him mutter to himself, "One of these days the power won't come back and that will be the end of Los Angles."

No one spoke for the rest of the trip.

When we got to the airport, the executive jet with the same aircrew was waiting for us. They seemed anxious to get going and hustled us into the plane and quickly got us strapped down so they could take off. I asked one of the pilots what was up and he said that a big storm was moving in and if we hurried, they thought we could make into Sand Flea before it hit. We managed to get airborne okay, but it was like riding a roller coaster until we got over the mountains. Even then, I couldn't see anything except the swirling red grit of a massive Haboob.

We landed at Sand Flea just as the wind started to pick up and as we deplaned and the jet pulled out of the hangar, we could see the wall of sand heading for us. Alex tried to get the air crew to leave their plane in the hangar and stay with us until the storm passed, but they declined. Just off the runway the plane disappeared into swirling blackness.

They were never seen or heard from again.

Unable to stop them from leaving, we headed for the dining hall. After we went through the line and sat down, Cathy remarked that it was wonderful having some fresh fruit and vegetables as they just couldn't get them in LA.

Alex laughed so I said, "Yeah, Luv, how do you manage that?"

Laughing again, Alex said, "Let me tell you it's one of those serendipitous things that just happen. Shortly after I came out here to Sand Flea, I was shopping in a local market and I just *happened* to comment to the produce manager how *impressed* I was with the quality of the fresh veggies. He smiled, thanked me and told me that they had an exclusive deal with a local supplier, a little farming co-op at a place called Junction which is about fifty miles north of Sand Flea.

"Well, a week or so later when I was in the store, I was introduced to a big old Swedish farmer named Sorenson who just *happened* to be one of the representatives of the Junction Co-op. Shortly after that, the market closed, so I called Sorenson and we made a deal. Now we, Visions Unlimited, just *happen* to have the exclusive deal."

We all laughed and patted her on the back.

Sobering a little, Alex turned to Cathy and said, "Well, now that you have officially joined us, we will have to find you a job."

Hesitantly, Cathy lowered her eyes and said, "Ms. Cummings, from what I have seen in the last couple of days, I don't think I would be a very good Administrative Assistant."

"Neither do I," Alex laughed. "I have something else in mind. As a nutritionist, outside of the quality of the fresh veggies, what do you think about the food here?"

Clearly not wanting to badmouth anyone, Cathy hedged, "Well, overall, it's not bad and very well prepared."

She wasn't getting out of it that easy! We all just stared at her until she squirmed and added sheepishly, "It is kind of heavy on the fats and starches and some of the items don't complement each other very well. But really, it's not bad."

"My thoughts exactly," Alex smiled. "Edible doesn't necessarily mean it's good, or good for you. At the moment, our food service is all run by volunteers. They work very hard and their hearts are in the right place, but I need someone to get it organized, take care of the fresh produce, prepare the menus and handle the expansion when the new colonists start to arrive. Want the job?"

Cathy gave Alex another meek squeak, but her eyes were shiny with enthusiasm. "I'll try."

"Good!" Alex exclaimed with a decisive nod of her head. "You just come with me, and you too, JJ, and I'll show you around."

Taking her by the elbow, Alex led Cathy into the kitchen and introduced all one hundred pounds of her to the volunteer staff as their new boss.

"And by the way, this hulk next to her is her husband and he would probably not take it very kindly if you gave her any crap."

That got a big laugh. Everyone knew that JJ was as scary as the average Teddy Bear. But as it turned out, Cathy Jackson didn't need any help. Despite her bashful hesitancy when it came to food, she knew her business. Better still, she knew how to lead. In a matter of moments, Cathy had the entire kitchen staff under her charms and soon she was everywhere smoothing out the menus and juggling the shifts. She even made a trip up to Junction to meet the farmers. From what I heard, she charmed them, too.

Satisfied, Alex crossed food service off her list of things to worry about. Well, almost. There was the time we got hi-jacked. Well, our produce truck got hi-jacked. I was up at Voyager at the time, but I heard the embellished story several times, once while I was still in orbit and three times after I got dirtside before I could sit down with Alex and she could tell me what really happened.

The story went that soon after Cathy took over, she worked out a delivery system where a couple of times a week a truck would show up from Junction to bring Cathy her fresh stuff. Then one day, the produce truck didn't arrive and Alex received, of all things, a ransom call. The hi-jackers had our truck and we could have it back for $50,000.

Alex called Chet who said he had just the man to see about retrieving the truck, his senior deputy Link Lincoln. His given name was Bartolomeu which he hated. I guess he hated Bart, too, because everyone called him Link.

The situation was explained to Link who merely nodded while he took the bag of ransom money that Alex was willing to pay, and headed toward the motor pool. Apparently, we were getting quite a motor pool which already included a couple of Army Humvees, a SWAT van, a gasoline tanker and a half dozen police cars.

Calmly as you please, Link just climbed into one of the police cars and headed up the road. Alex wondered if he shouldn't take some deputies with him, or a posse... or the army.

With no more concern as if he'd been asked to pick up the dry cleaning, he shrugged and said, "No thanks, Ms. Cummings. I'll be fine."

That was it. Off he went all alone to deal with hijackers and retrieve a stolen truck. Alex didn't hear anything until late afternoon when Link came driving in with his police car followed by the regular drivers from the co-op driving their truck still full of produce. Link turned the truck over to Cathy, gave Alex back the $50,000 and started to walk away.

I couldn't believe it. "Well, wait! What happened?"

Alex laughed and shook her head because she still couldn't believe, either. "Well Link just shrugged and said not much, they just talked a bit. He said they were just a bunch of young people, street kids mostly from the City; Scared about what's happening in the world, scared about not having any place to live, scared about being hungry. So, he hired them to guard the road for us. But get this: then he took them up to Junction and Junction also hired them for three meals a day and a warm place to sleep to guard the farms and keep the roads open around there. From us they get a paycheck and from Junction they get room and board. To cap it all off, Link said, 'By the way, Ms. Cummings, I invited them down here for a meet and greet and to work out the details for a permanent arrangement.' And then he walked away like it was just another day at the office."

Yeah, that sounded like Link. It was a great story without the embellishments.

Having a bit of time on my hands, I went to speak to Dot on when would be a good time to keep my promise and speak to the kids. By this time, the true nature of our mission was still under wraps, but word of a possible "expanded mission to Mars" was spreading fast and the cafeteria was buzzing with questions and speculation. To make sure we understood what the private page was versus the public one, we went in search of Alex. When we found her, she was sitting at one of the cafeteria tables trying, without much success, to answer a hundred questions at once.

Dot shooed everyone away and told Alex about the little talk we were planning for the kids. Never one to miss an opportunity, Alex thought that was a great idea and told me to hunt up Billy before meeting her and Dot in her office.

By the time I showed up with Billy, the two women already had a plan. Word went out that the next day right after lunch, everyone who was interested and wasn't engaged in something vital would gather in the cafeteria for a "Project Voyager Update". As we didn't have a recreation hall or an auditorium, the cafeteria was packed and the Colony Mission to Mars was officially launched.

Alex did the introductions and explained that Voyager was now a colony ship, told them about the trip in cryogenic hibernation and what we might expect to find on Mars and how colonists were going to establish a habitat in the caverns before reassuring them that anyone who was interested in joining the colony should make an appointment to see her privately. It was during these private meetings that Alex planned to swear those potential colonists to secrecy when she told them that Voyager would be going to Sanctuary and not Mars.

To all those packed in the cafeteria, Alex also emphasized that anyone who elected to stay would be welcome to all the facilities and supplies here at Sand Flea when the "Mars" mission departed. As there was still plenty of time, no one had to make up their minds right now, but please, please keep it quiet. We didn't want anyone outside of the Project to know that Voyager was now a colony ship. As far as the outside world knew we were still building a survey ship to go to Mars and it was best to keep it that way.

The kids loved being in on the secret and whispered excitedly together while Alex introduced me and I gave my presentation of the history of the project up to now starting with the construction robots. Seeing as that was going to be the original show for the kids, I had all of Dot's class sitting at the tables right up in front and used the small model of Voyager that sat on Alex's desk and the larger one from the Conference Room as very effective visual aids. I hoped that

Sam wouldn't be offended—she was just a tennis ball in my presentation.

Though everyone was leaning in to listen, I mainly spoke directly to the kids while I gave them the full run down of how we moved stuff around in space, how we built R3, our dormitory… everything right up to where we stood now. After answering their questions, many of which were quite insightful, I turned the presentation over to Billy who explained how the new Voyager would look and how we would travel through space.

There's nothing like playing to a receptive house! The crowd went wild and two hours later we were still playing with the models and answering questions. Probably the best result of our big production was when three older teens approached us and asked if there was an apprentice program for robot jockeys.

Ah, not until two seconds ago there wasn't, but there sure was now!

Tommy, Dwight and Kevin were our first three apprentices, but they weren't our only new recruits to Project Voyager. We had also acquired a chef—André.

How André came to be among us at Project Voyager was quite a story. I guess that indirectly, it was a result of our being in a "waiting for parts" holding pattern that we occasionally found ourselves in. Two of our young robot jockeys, Paul Mahoney and Tony Simmons, didn't have anything to do up in space, so they were spending their time on the ground and, seeing as they were rich due to VU's generous salary, a lot of their dirtside time was spent in Las Vegas.

That's where these two would be playboys met André.

André was the quintessential Frenchman. He looked, talked and acted like a stereotype from an old black and white movie: a little on the short side in a kind of roly-poly way with one of those little French pencil mustaches. English was definitely his second language, maybe even his third, and he spoke it with an accent that was stereotypically thick. His thick round cheeks were a constant rosé because he never once stopped smiling. André bounced around like a chattering rubber ball, loving everything and everybody. In his professional life, he was a chef and from what I have seen (and eaten whenever I am on the ground) a hell of a good one!

Despite that, André had a hard time keeping a job because of two small quintessentially stereotypical problems the French have endured. André likes to cook with wine... a lot of wine. Sometimes the wine even makes it into the food. Most of the time, the wine makes it into André. His second problem was that he loved the ladies. Not being a lady myself, I didn't quite see the attraction, but they seemed to love André right back. The fact that a particular lady might be someone else's lady was a trifle that concerned André not at all.

Our French chef's favorite hangout was an up-scale night club in one of the big Las Vegas casinos that just happened to be the preferred watering hole that Tony and Paul went to regularly. After meeting André, they were happy to keep him supplied with vino. As he seemed to know every woman in Vegas, the playboys were able to share in the Frenchman's riches.

The way I understood it, Tony and Paul weren't present the evening that André and a tall blond lady became quite enamored with each other and decided to make a night of it. Well, it seems that one of the more unsavory members of the Vegas mob scene thought that this particular woman was his personal property. When he got wind of the previous night's activity, Johnny-Two-Thumbs went looking for André.

Apparently, the next day the unsavory character was still looking for him when our two robot jockeys turned up at the night club. Of course, everyone at the club knew that they were Andre's friends and quickly clued Paul and Tony in as to what was going on. When André walked in, they decided that it was their duty to rescue him.

André, of course, was completely oblivious to the fact that he needed to be rescued, but after a few glasses of wine and several people insisting he'd better make himself scarce, André finally got the message. Needless to say, he was petrified.

Not to worry! Our two RJs, who by this time were also pretty well sloshed, were on the job.

After several retellings of the account that became more embellished each time, they left the club just in time with Johnny hot on their heels. The three drunks had to think fast on where they could hide their pal. In a flash of supernova inspiration that should have sobered them immediately, they hit on the perfect place and flew André from Las Vegas to Sand Flea. Once there, however, they reasoned (to use the term loosely) that the hangers weren't safe enough for a permanent hideout, so they stuffed André into a spacesuit and hid him away in one of the Stardusters cargo bays.

It was quite a scene when the shuttle arrived up at Wisdom! Paul and Tony popped in through our docking collar, quickly floated into R3 and grabbed a robot in order to retrieve their friend.

By the time Alex heard about it and was about to throw all three of them off Wisdom, the Starduster had already returned to Earth. André was in orbit until the next shuttle showed up. Once the yelling and general confusion settled down, André just bounced around Wisdom, R3, and the dormitory curious about everything and charming everyone.

Then the gourmet discovered we were eating MREs and freeze-dried stuff. Not only do they taste as bad as their names implied, but are bloody hard to eat floating around in zero gravity. The first thing he wanted to know was what the *merde* we were eating and then how do we eat it. We explained that you just pull the tab and it heats up on its own, but he had to be careful or it would be floating around the room.

"Non, monsieur. How can you eat this?"

Suddenly, André was in his element and a short time later, he floated something he "just whipped up from your supplies" over to us.

As far as I was concerned, after that meal, André was in! Not only was he the only guy I ever knew to use a space shuttle as a get-away-car and hide out in a space station, but he'd somehow figured out how to make even an MRE taste good.

Of course, André couldn't stay up at Wisdom. The next day, I had no choice but to put him on the arriving shuttle only this time, he could ride in the cabin. Lucky, the inebriated fools had the presence of mind to put him in a spacesuit so he survived coming up in the cargo bay!

I also sent Tony and Paul down to explain all this to

Alex. That must have been an epic meeting and I wish I had been there. Alex told me later that on one hand she was furious at these two knuckleheads while on the other hand, she was trying hard to keep from cracking up. Tony and Paul had been petrified that she was going to have them drawn and quartered… or pulled apart by wild horses.

André, however, was André. "Oh, Madam Cummings, these are fine boys. Everything is fine. I will fix you a fine dinner."

Alex said that she had to throw them out of her office before she did burst out laughing!

What to do with André was a problem unto itself as Alex didn't want to turn him loose to blab what he had seen at Voyager.

"It's no problem, Madam. I am chef—I cook for you!"

So, Alex sent him to the kitchen to make himself useful which presented her with yet *another* problem: Cathy! I am told that that first meeting was also epic: burgundy and butter meets humus and kale. In addition to both of them having rather strong opinions about food—what constitutes good food, the preparation of food, how much wine needed to be used to enjoy the food—they were both animated talkers of the wind milling arms variety. Anyone within five yards in any direction was in mortal danger.

But they worked it out. André kind of controlled the kitchen while Cathy did all the ordering and made up the menus: healthy meals with a French flair. It sure worked out well for the rest of us. We never had it so good!

CHAPTER II

There really is a Professor Gustave Gutman. I was beginning to wonder.

While waiting for the first pieces of the "Great Voyager Expansion Project" to arrive, I was spending a few days on the ground trying to make myself useful.

When the call came in Alex was in her office speaking to Lou Carson while I was sitting in the Conference Room with Grant and Maryanne Foster who were now officially on Alex's staff. We were working on equipment and supply lists for the stuff that we thought we would need on Sanctuary and the order we should pack it so what we needed immediately would be on top when we actually arrived on the new planet. Seeing as Grant and Maryanne's immediate need list started with camping and survival equipment and my list started with guns and ammunition, it was, shall we say, a lively discussion.

That was when Alex stuck her head in the door and

said she had just received a call from Sand Flea's outer security gate. A man who identified himself as Professor Gustave Gutman had shown up at the gate and said that he was with Visions Unlimited. Alex wanted me to go out to the gate and sort it out. As Lou had already met him once, she offered to come along.

Rather than go outside in the heat and bugs, we traversed through all the hangars and through the long connecting walkway to get over to our motor pool in Hanger 4.

When we walked in, I waved my arm grandly and said, "Take your pick." pointing to our collection of Humvees, SWAT vehicles and assorted police cars.

With a wicked grim, Lou pointed to a State Police cruiser. "I always wanted one of those."

We jumped in and I asked, "Lights and siren?"

It was a stupid question.

We roared off on our four-hundred-yard jaunt to the main gate, lights flashing and siren wailing all the while giggling like a couple of little kids. Lou was laughing even harder when we got to the gate only this time, she was laughing at me. The rat didn't warn me that the first sight of Herr Professor Gustave Gutman was a jaw-dropper and my jaw was officially dropped.

"Is that him?" I was stunned.

"Sure is!"

I was speechless. Gustave Gutman is a caricature, make no mistake. If I had been told to draw a picture of a middle aged, middle European male out of the 1930s or 40s, it would look like him. No more than 5'5" or 6", the uber skinny Gutman weighed maybe one hundred and twenty pounds soaking wet. He has a hollow pinched in face with glasses as thick as Coke bottle bottoms. To make himself look even scrawnier, he was wearing of all things... a brown, wool, double-breasted suit that might have been fashionable over a hundred years ago and the suit was at least one size too big for him. To complete the picture, he had a full head of snow-white hair that stuck out in all directions.

I was so flustered Lou had to remind me to turn off the lights and siren.

When I walked up to the gate, Gutman was jammed into the guard post with a half dozen of the company guards chattering away in some unintelligible mixture of, I think, English, German and Polish.

"Professor Gutman?" I asked.

Proudly thumping himself on his skinny chest, he lit up like a Tannenbaum at Weihnachten. "Ja, Ja! Gutman."

I introduced myself before turning to Lou. "Professor, you remember Ms. Carson?"

"Ja, Ja! Frau Carson. Visions Unlimited." And I swear he kissed the back of her hand... much to her delight.

Lou asked him how he got here and he said by taxi. Long drive. Very bad, water, flood, wind, big storm, very bad. I turned to the guards and they told me that he was in the back seat of an unmarked Junker of a car that just drove up to the gate, dropped him off, turned around and drove away. Clearly not it a taxi, it must have been one of those rides share things.

Tuning back to Gutman, I asked where he came from. That got a long and unintelligible answer that I guessed was supposed to be English, but wasn't.

"No, professor," I clarified. "Where did the car pick you up?"

"Oh! From rocket base. Big rocket base. Ja, Ja! Very good."

He had to be kidding! There were only three rocket bases that I knew of, one was down near Tucson, Arizona and the other two were in Texas. If he was telling us that he rode a few hundred miles in an Uber I'll bet VU was going to flip when they got that bill. And who the hell was the guy that drove him all the way here through the wind and water and the "very bad" storm only to just turn around and go home? I want someone with Cajones like that on my team. Too late now; Mr. Uber was long gone.

Ok! Why were you at the rocket base?

"Deliver engines," he answered, thumping himself on the chest again. "Gutman engine. Ja, Ja! Very good."

"Do you mean the main engines for Voyager?"

"Ja, Ja!"

Wow and double wow! I have got to get this guy over to Alex ASAP. Looking around, I asked him where his bags were.

"No bags. Bags all blown away in wind. Very bad. Ja! Very bad."

That must have been some trip! I would have loved to hear the whole story, but I probably wouldn't have understood a word of it.

We put the delightfully strange little man in the front of the police car so he could play with the lights and siren, then whisked Herr Professor Gutman off to the VU compound and into Alex's office. We all had a million questions and, of course, we were all asking them at once. Alex shut us up and took over.

It was tough talking to Gutman. In addition to the

English, German, Polish jargon that he was speaking, he just couldn't sit still for a minute. He reminded me of a sandpiper or one of those other shore birds running in and out of the tideline, bouncing up and down and constantly on the move.

Alex finally got him a cup of coffee (which got a "ja, ja coffee good!") before sitting him down in one of the big easy chairs and planting herself in front of him so he couldn't get up without knocking her over. But even when he was sitting down, his bird-like head kept bobbing up and down.

"Professor Gutman..." Alex began.

"Ja, Ja! Gutman."

Alex couldn't help her grin; None of us could. Trying again, Alex finally understood which rocket base he'd been at before asking if he was going to stay and help us get the engines installed.

"Ja, Ja! Gutman install engines."

Well, that was a relief! As far as I knew the professor and his minions that he had locked away in the dungeons of his Transylvanian castle were the only ones who knew anything about them.

Then Alex asked him if he was going to stay with us until we launched and possibly make the journey to Sanctuary?

"No, Nien! Gutman install engines then Gutman go home."

Ha! I knew it! Back to the castle and the dungeons.

After speaking, or trying to speak, with him further, Alex said she would get the engines scheduled for delivery to Voyager. In the meantime, why didn't I take the Professor over to billeting and get him a place to sleep while he was here.

In other words—out—and let me get back to work.

Lest I risk my busy wife's wrath, I prudently took Gutman into the dormitory in Hangar 1. We found the two ladies that, with a flock of young helpers, ran the bed assignments and took care of the sheets and towels. They were all agog when I introduced Gutman.

Yes! This was *the* Professor Gustave Gutman who had invented the engines for Voyager. They were all impressed and while the younger gals thought the hand kissing was kind of creepy the older ladies loved it.

Gutman was a rock star! They were so impressed with the professor, they moved around some of the dividers to create his own private little space before making his bed for him with nice, fresh linens.

But they weren't done yet. As the laundry was also one of the many things that they took care of, they continued the royal treatment and promised Gutman that they'd have his suit cleaned and pressed once he changed clothes.

We had a row of eight or nine washers and dryers for general use, but the big stuff, like sheets and towels went out to a local laundry—apparently, the last one in town that was still in operation. I guess that if it wasn't for the Voyager contract, the guy that ran it would have been long gone too. He was great and even picked up and delivered, though the ladies didn't know how much longer the service would last. With the number of transients flowing through and around Sand Flea City steadily increasing, getting in and out of the gates to the airfield was becoming harder.

As we were out in the middle of the desert, I couldn't help but wonder where all these people were coming from and how they were getting here.

But apart from his laundry service, what this guy was really making money on was embroidered name tags.

Alex had decided on standardized clothing for the passengers on Voyager—the one-piece coverall flight suits that the Navy and Air Force pilots wore. Durable and easy to take care of, everyone seemed to be wearing them now whether they planned to make the trip or not.

The current height of fashion, the coveralls came in an array of colors: blue or green... until Alice Smith our supply chief ran out of blue and green. Each flight suit had a Velcro strip over the left shirt pocket that the military aircrew members used for name tags with their flight wings. Naturally, the Voyager and Starduster crews jumped right on this and soon everyone not only had their own embroidered name patch, but in place of the military wings a symbol above their name designated what team they belonged to.

I think the Starduster pilots started it. One day they were sporting their name tags with a design of some kind of shuttle with big angel wings. Not to be out done, the shuttle mechanics came up with a crossed wrench design. Then Chet's deputies introduced a crossed rifle patch and the race was on! Suddenly, everyone had a name tag along with some kind of specialists' symbol. One of the RJs came up with a design that had a ball with four arms. I thought that if you weren't part of the Voyager Project you wouldn't have any idea what it represented, it kind of looked like a mutant pumpkin to me.

Our laundry guy was making a fortune!

Gutman told the ladies that he didn't have any other clothes. ""Ja! Ja! All blown away!"

The ladies thought that this was terrible, so I was

immediately ordered to take him over to supply and rectify this shameful situation like it was all my fault.

However, before I could get him out the door, Gutman heard the kids in the partitioned off schoolhouse in the back of the hangar. We walked over and stuck our heads in so he could see what was going on.

Ja! Ja! School. Good.

Dot looked up and saw us so we had to come all the way in. When I introduced Gutman to Dot and he kissed the back of her hand, the kids squealed with laughter. But they were really impressed when I told them that he was the man who invented the engines that were going to take us to Mars.

The kids giggled. Yeah, yeah! Mars survey. Nudge, nudge, wink, wink.

The kids had a million questions for the Professor, but Dot ran us off saying that she would set up a Gutman Lecture for another day. She did, too. That was a riot! Herr Professor Gutman explaining in his mixture of English, German and Polish the principles of the Gutman drive, that no one in the world outside of Gutman understood, to a bunch of space happy school kids.

Once free of the kids, we ran into Doc John and once Doc found out that Gutman was *the* Gutman he got off on his favorite soapbox—how were humans going to fare after twenty years of weightlessness. Gutman seemed puzzled for a moment then he launched into an unintelligible English, German, Polish arm waving tirade the gist of which was that Voyager would have gravity

What? Doc and I tried to slow him down and we finally realized what he was saying. Once Voyager got close to light speed, we would have gravity. Wow! Wow! How could that be? I had no idea and when we started to question him and why hadn't we heard about this before he started to back track. It turns out that this was just his understanding based on Einstein's theory.

So, we went back over to Alex's office and reported this new wonderful revelation. Of course, Alex knew all about the possibility and it was still just a possibility and why wasn't I taking care of Gutman?

Geez!

When I finally got Gutman into our supply hangar, he was immediately distracted by... everything. At least here, I couldn't blame him as there was much to be distracted by. The hangar floor was covered with piles of stuff. All kinds of stuff: tools in one pile, tents in another along with even more piles of sleeping bags, pots and pans, collapsible boats, archery equipment—more stuff than we could ever fit into Voyager! But Alex's philosophy was to get everything and anything that anyone thought that they would want or need and we would sort it out later. She even bought the entire inventory of a local home improvement store that was going out of business. What we didn't take on Voyager would be left for those who weren't planning to make the trip.

I would guess that more than half the people were like Gutman—working hard to make Voyager a success, but planning taking their chances on Earth after we were gone.

In among our solar powered generators, Gutman spotted one that was powered by one of his very own Gutman motors. I don't know where Alex found that one. There probably weren't a half dozen of them in the whole world. But the professor was delighted!

Ja! Ja! Gutman! Good.

Then he stopped, looked around and asked me how we were going to explain all this equipment as part of a survey mission to Mars when the government inspectors came around. I don't think that he really believed me when I told him that we hadn't had any government agencies asking about our work outside of Alex's monthly reports.

"Nien," he shook his head gravely. "Government always interferes. Take over!"

I told him that as anti-science as the current knuckleheads in Washington were, we could tell them that we were going camping on the surface of Mars and they would probably buy it. That got a Ja, ja chuckle out of him.

I *finally* got him over to clothing section and fitted into a flight suit. He is such a shrimp that we had to go to the smaller ladies' sizes. After we added socks, underwear and a set of toiletry items, it was back over to billeting where he took a shower, changed into his new duds and sent his wool suit off to the cleaners.

It was now just about time for dinner so I took him over to the cafeteria and I introduced the professor to Cathy and André. Where the tiny Gutman had to reach up to kiss Dot Barton's hand, he wasn't much bigger than Cathy and only needed to give her a slight bow to place his greeting on her delicate hand. Then after introductions he and André were off in their own lively conversation that was totally unintelligible to the rest of us. German—Polish English meets French. English punctuated with lots hand waving.

During the meal, it seemed that everyone in Project Voyager dropped by the table to meet The Professor. Gutman was loving it, bouncing up and down out of his chair like a rubber ball again and again, and everything was Ja! Ja! Good.

I began to wonder about him when he was introduced to Chet and Link.

"Ja! Ja! Policemen! Good! Very good!"

A group of Starduster pilots and mechanics came in and after dinner it was off to one of the space shuttle hangars for the full tour.

Gutman may be a little on the comical side in appearance and actions, but it was soon obvious that he was one smart strudel. The engines that were used for vertical take-offs and landings had been installed and were, of course, his but he had never seen Stardusters solar-powered main engines. Within a few minutes you would have thought that he had invented the things.

He was interested in everything. He was in the engines, he was in the cockpit, he was checking out how the cargo bay operated. What part of the shuttle was Earth atmosphere and what was open to space? What about weightlessness? After about three hours, I called a halt and said that we would give the Professor a ride up to Voyager tomorrow.

Once I got Gutman bedded down for the night, I wandered over to Alex's office to chase her off to bed and said hello to her new secretary, Rita. She was one of Pedro Gonzales many children and a damn good secretary. Among the many things she naturally took care of without needing to be asked, she screened Alex's calls so everything that she knew her boss didn't want to deal with immediately went straight to voicemail.

Alex was going through her messages when I walked in. Waving me to a chair, she said, "Listen to this."

A voice that was pure 'Yankee' said "Hello! My name is

Brian Anders. I heard about your little Mars project and I wondered if you could use a blacksmith?" He left a phone number and hung up.

Alex said, "What do you think about that? How did he hear about us and just what did he hear?"

"I don't know, but he would be handy to have if he's the right kind of blacksmith."

Clearly more concerned with a possible leak than the man's credentials, Alex's expression told me that we weren't on the same track with the call. "What do you mean?"

I shrugged. "Well, I don't know anything about blacksmithing, but if he is a guy who only uses modern methods, I don't see how we can use him. But if he's one of these throwback guys who knows how to smith the way they did a few hundred years ago, he would be invaluable to Voyager."

Alex nodded, thoughtfully.

We were having our coffee in her office when she called Mr. Anders back the next morning.

"Anders Forge." I had to strain to hear over a dull roar in the background. Is that what a furnace sounds like?

"Mr. Anders?"

"Yup."

"This is Alexandria Cummings from Project Voyager."

"Yup." Not one to mince words, this Mr. Anders.

"You called about possibly joining the Voyager Project."

"Yup."

I started to crack up. To say that Brian Anders is a taciturn, yes/no kind of guy would be giving just plain taciturn a bad name. Alex pressed on.

"Mr. Anders, where we are going, there will probably not be any modern facilities available. Are you familiar with smithing methods and techniques that were employed say a couple of hundred years ago?"

"Yup.

"Have you used these techniques?"

"Yup."

"Tell me, what do produce?"

"Medieval stuff mostly. Armor, Swords, Knives."

For the first time, we got past a yup. From the gleam in Alex's eye, she was now very interested in him. "Well, Mr. Anders, I would like to talk to you in person. I can send you a plane ticket if you would be willing to come down here for an interview. By the way where are you?"

"Upstate New York."

"OK! Let me have a mail or e-mail address and I'll send you a ticket."

"Don't bother. I'll manage." And he just hung up!

Flabbergasted, Alex and I just looked at each other. Finally, I said, "One thing's for sure, Luv, this guy isn't going to make the debate team."

Alex asked, "Did I or did I not just hire a blacksmith?"

"Beats the hell out of me, Luv!"

A couple of weeks went by and I had all but forgotten about Mr. Anders when out of the blue Alex got a call from the outer security gate saying that there was a guy named Anders out here with a truck full of junk who said he had an appointment. It took Alex a few moments, but she finally put the pieces together and said to send him in.

When they finally got Brian into Alex's office, it was quite a meeting. I was up a Voyager at the time, so all I know is what Alex told me.

Apparently, just from what he had seen between the gates and Alex's plush office, Brian was impressed... and Alex was equally impressed by him. He came across as just an old working country boy. Blue jeans flannel shirt, quiet, not very tall, about six feet, but built like a steel post. When you see him working with his shirt off, you know he is solid. Brian had muscles, his muscles had muscles... His ears even had muscles!

But Brian was also smart. Very, very smart.

So, what was in the truck? Apparently, he had brought his entire forge with him: bellows, anvil, tools even a few hundred pounds of working scrap.

We had a blacksmith.

CHAPTER 12

Our plans to take Gutman up to Voyager the next day were wiped out by the weather. I guess we human beings are really slow learners. These days everything that you did on Planet Earth depended on the weather. Of course, we had to plan for the heat and the bugs on a daily basis, but a big sand storm would shut down all outside activities especially flying.

We watched in real time while we were having breakfast as Al Wilson's Vid prediction of a large Haboob came true. Even as he was speaking, we could hear the wind and feel the initial sand-filled blasts hitting the hangar. Once Gutman understood that we wouldn't be going anywhere until this sandstorm blew itself out, he decided that he would like to go and see if he could make himself useful on the Stardusters.

I'll say this for Herr Professor Gustave Gutman, he was

never dead weight. Interested and knowledgeable in almost everything, he was always ready to roll up his sleeves and pitch in.

As we were getting ready to head for the shuttles, the billeting ladies bounced over to the table all excited. There on a hangar all cleaned and pressed was Gutman's brown suit, but along with it they handed him one of the Velcro name tag patches with his name and Starduster wings on it. The professor was so delighted, he completely ignored his oversized wool garment, immediately slapped the patch onto his flight suit and strutted around the table while pointing to it with a, "Ja! Ja! Gutman."

The professor was "in" and it seemed that everyone loved him. As we walked through the hangars, everyone wanted to say hello and wish him a good morning… and of course he wanted to stop and talk to everybody, see what they were doing, see how they were getting along. And, of course, everything was punctuated with his perpetual Ja! Ja! Good! Good!

At the supply hangar, Gutman asked what was going to be done with the supplies that were going to be left behind when Voyager departed and I told him about Alex's plan for the "stay behinds" as they had started calling themselves. Alex was going to leave them everything we didn't take with us—food, supplies, vehicles, weapons, the buildings… everything. The stay behinds already had themselves organized as a community and were planning a mayor/council type of government. Chet and Dot Barton had also decided that they were going to stay at Sand Flea and, although there hadn't been an election yet, it was a certainty that Dot would be the Mayor and Chet the Chief of Police.

I wished that Chet and Dot were going with us. Not only were they competent in everything they did, they were just great people. To my dismay, they said that seeing as they were in their fifties and had no children, they had decided to leave the colony for the younger generation. Too bad, but at least the stay behinds would be in good hands.

We were delayed from the shuttles once again when Gutman spotted the stack of storage containers with names neatly printed on them and wanted to know what they were for.

"Some of these contain professional supplies and equipment," I explained. "Things like carpenters' tools, farm implements or weapons. They'll be bulk stored in either the supply cylinders, the shuttle bays of the space shuttles or in R3. The rest of the storage containers we call foot lockers. Each individual has one and it contains his or her personal items—clothing, toiletries, photographs, mementos, things like that."

Gutman liked that Alex had issued everyone individual footlockers. Each came complete with three flight suits, two coats (a heavy one for winter and a light one for summer), a summer hat, a winter hat, gloves, ten sets of underwear and socks, a toilet kit, and two pair of shoes. The standard issue took up about eighty-five to ninety percent of space in the foot locker leaving the rest for personal items and mementos. We were, after all, leaving Earth forever and Alex made sure that everyone making the trip had room for any sentimental objects they might wish to bring even if it was just an extra pair of long johns. As long as it fit in the locker, it was okay.

In my own locker I had thought about taking a couple of bottles of booze, but eventually opted for extra ammo.

With Chet electing not to go, Link Lincoln, his second in command, was the obvious choice for our Chief of Security. Along with being a robot jockey and a Stardust pilot, I was also a member of Link's security team, so tucked away somewhere in storage was my rifle and five thousand rounds of ammunition. I figured that, not only would a little more ammo in my personal gear not hurt, but I wouldn't be dry, boozewize, for long. Throughout human history, the first thing we human beings did anywhere in any civilization was figure out how to ferment anything edible into adult beverages.

When we finally left the supply hangar, I took Gutman through the connecting above ground tunnel to Hangar 6. Gutman didn't much care for the tunnel, but then, who did? With the Haboob still raging outside, the passage was not only dark from the lack of sunlight, but loud and shaky from being power blasted by the wind. I couldn't blame Gutman for his trepidation as I felt a bit claustrophobic myself. Once free of the oppressive passage and in the Starduster maintenance area, everything else was immediately forgotten and the professor went right to work.

Gutman was especially impressed with the apprentice mechanics who were working on the Stardusters. Of course, all the young people associated with Project Voyager were learning one trade or another including the five we had up in space learning how to be robot jockeys. In addition to our original three young men, we had added Jennifer and Betty, two very capable young ladies, to the program. I was glad to have them and more than willing to train them, but I kind of thought that it was a poor career choice. I kept my concerns to myself, but I couldn't help wonder what our five apprentice

RJs were going to do when we got to Sanctuary. Once we took Voyager apart and everyone moved down permanently onto the planet, there wouldn't be any robots for them to jockey.

I didn't have any answers and resigned myself that something would present itself. In the meantime, I was grateful to have them.

When we walked into the Starduster maintenance area everything suddenly... stopped. Like we were suddenly in a sci-fi movie, all activity just froze as if the evil antagonist pushed a button and stopped time. After about ten seconds, time resumed in a flurry of noise and motion as *everyone*, mechanics and apprentices alike, wanted to be introduced to The Master. The feeling seemed to be mutual for Gutman. For such a bouncy and distracted guy, he showed endless patience explaining to his fans how something worked or how to repair it.

It took three days for the storm to blow itself out. Although that particular Haboob was pretty intense, it was relatively short in duration compared to some others which had lasted for six or seven days. Once it was over, we had to spend another day cleaning up all the sand and debris that had blown in. Alex always insisted that after every storm no one would resume regular operations until every grain of sand was removed from the outside of the Visions Unlimited area. She was a tough boss, but as always, she was right. After experiencing a couple of Haboobs, it was easy to see how the Sphinx and the Pyramids got buried.

Then, of course, after we cleaned up our own area, we helped the airbase sweep up the runways and taxiways by attaching plows to the front of the ATVs. Even with everyone working, it took all day to remove the sand, so it wasn't until the next day that we were finally able to load Gutman into a Starduster and head up to Wisdom and Voyager.

Herr Professor... I couldn't help but love him. We buckled him into a window seat so he would have an excellent view, but he wouldn't stay put. The moment we were airborne, he was up moving around the cabin looking out every single window the shuttle had to offer and even invaded the cockpit to make sure he didn't miss anything from the pilot's perspective. Then he would come back and sit down before bouncing up to do the same thing all over again. Once we flew up into the lower regions of space and weightlessness kicked in, he was in hog heaven.

"Wunderbar!" he exclaimed with all the delight of a kid being told that unicorns are real. "Never been weightless before. Ja! Ja!"

Several times I tried to buckle him into his seat, but he was having none of it, so I finally gave up. It was hard to catch him anyway floating around on the ceiling and bouncing off of everyone and everything with many a Ja, Ja and Good, Good. After a while we just sat there and just kind of passed him around overhead.

When the shuttle docked with Wisdom, Gutman wanted to get aboard in a hurry so he could see the robots unloading the shuttle bay. We couldn't slow him down and in no time at all he collided with everyone present. The only way to stop him was to keep a firm hold and guide him to where we thought he wanted to go.

The Professor was having the time of his life and we all got caught up in the game. I guess weightlessness was the greatest thing since sliced strudel. After the novelty wore off,

Gutman wanted to sit down with Al and get his perspective on what was happening on planet Earth. This was a presentation that Al had given many times before both to us working in and around Voyager and Wisdom and to the world at large during his weather forecasts.

As Wisdom made its orbit around Earth, Al gave the Professor the full load of how rapidly the planet was changing. Climate shifts that in the past had been gradual, historically taking thousands of years, were happing now in a matter of decades. Every year was hotter than the year before. The rising temperatures were causing longer periods of drought in the naturally dry areas and resulting in more frequent wildfires that ravaged these already struggling regions. But in direct contrast, the normally wet areas were getting even wetter. Widespread flooding was increasing due to the increase in the number, duration and intensity of storms all over the world. Along with the increasing storms and the growing deserts, the glaciers were melting and the oceans were continuing to rise. All the climate scientists that Al had talked to predicted that all of these natural disasters would continue for decades to come as global temperatures continued to rise.

Looking like a punctured balloon, Gutman sadly asked, "Then we all die?"

"No, not everything," Al reassured him. "In my opinion Earth isn't going to die in the sense that all life will be extinguished. Many species will disappear and some are already going extinct, but others like the insects were thriving. Life will go on, but whether or not that life includes human beings... that's solely up to us."

I'd heard Al's opinion before. Humans are certainly

intelligent enough to survive, but whether we're smart enough to stop overpopulating the Earth, destroying our environment and killing each other was an open question that he couldn't answer.

To drive his point home, Al directed Gutman's attention to the windows and telescopes pointed down at the only home mankind had ever known and we watched as Australia, New Zealand and the Southern Ocean slowly orbited below us. Australia was so covered in smoke it looked like the whole country was on fire from coast to coast. The Vid had reported that hundreds of towns, villages, hamlets and stations had already been destroyed, hundreds of thousands of people had been forced to flee while hundreds if not thousands more had died.

The fires Down Under had been raging for so long now that a permanent smoke cloud not only covered the continent, but extended a thousand miles east to New Zealand. This smoke cloud was so full of toxic chemicals that gas masks were mandatory for any outside activity. The drought-fueled fires had been smoldering for seven years and showed no signs of ending. In Al's opinion, Australia was going to burn until there was nothing left to burn.

Even the Great Barrier Reef had been burned; Nothing was left but a lifeless scar decaying under waters too warm for the polyps to survive. The castles of thousands of marine species were ransacked, bleached white and abandoned to crumble in their ruin.

"Look at this!" Al directed the professor's attention to the Antarctica and the Southern Oceans before putting up some comparative photos to show how much of the sea ice had disappeared. "Look how much the ice and glaciers have receded. Even the krill is gone!"

"Krill?" Gutman asked.

"Krill are small shrimp like creatures about the size of your little finger."

"Oh! Ja, ja! Krill! That is bad?"

"Very bad, I'm afraid. Just about everything in the Southern Oceans eat krill. The phytoplankton and algae the krill eat grow on the underside of the ice and there isn't enough ice left to support the species. Without the plankton, the krill are dying and as a result, all the marine animals that feed on the krill are also starving. There used to be a trillion tons of krill in the Southern Ocean in colonies so large we could see them from space... and now there's practically nothing! The penguins, seals, even the whales are dying off and it's all because of climate change."

"Ja, is bad," Gutman said softly. "Climate change, people... Nien."

In the Pacific, a typhoon was bearing down on the Philippines. Al told Gutman that the Islands had already been hit by more than twenty typhoons in the last few years. Manilla was already a ghost town and mostly under water due to rising sea levels. If this latest typhoon followed its projected track and hit the city, it would probably finish the Philippines off as a functioning nation. More than half of its hundreds of islands were already under water while the others hardly had a multi-story structure remaining. Inter-island communication and travel was practically non-existent.

I guess just about the same could be said for all the islands and island nations of the Central and South Pacific. Rising sea levels and more intense storms were submerging entire islands forcing people to either abandon their island homes altogether or move inland to higher ground—if it existed—and try to establish towns and villages on the revised coastline. Even Japan with their massive flood control systems were losing the fight. Tokyo, Nagoya and other great Japanese coastal cities were flooding on a regular basis.

With the vast blue waters of the Pacific stretching endlessly below us, it was difficult to see from space, that the oceans were dead—with our carbon emissions and overfishing, we had killed it. We had destroyed the main source of food for a quarter of the world's population and eliminated the main source of income for three-quarters of a billion people. These same people who for generations had made their living from the sea were now moving inland abandoning ancient homes and villages. Anything too close to the shore was being consumed by the rising waters, so these fishermen were leaving their prized possessions—their boats—rusting and rotting in the tide.

When the commercial fisheries collapsed and the maritime nations of the world became more and more desperate for food and income, the Nations of the World scrapped all marine mammal protections and now the great whales, seals, walruses, anything with meat on its bones were being hunted to extinction.

As Wisdom moved on, Al showed Gutman pictures of the disappearing Himalayan glaciers that fed the five great Asian rivers and provided fresh water to almost half of the world's population. At the moment, a lack of drinking water was not these people's immediate problem, though that was coming. Right now, massive torrents of frothing rapids from the rapidly vanishing glaciers were pouring down the mountainsides and into the lowlands while erratic monsoons added to the deluge. When the glaciers were gone, so would be their main source of fresh water. The millions who managed to survive the floods would soon be dying of thirst.

We knew that coastal cities like Hong Kong and Shanghai were drowning, but how the Chinese Government was handling the effects of Global Warming was a mystery. A year and a half ago, they had effectively severed all communications in and out of the country, kicked all the foreigners out and nationalized all industry and manufacturing. Ever since, no one really knew how conditions inside China actually were. The only thing we knew for sure was what we could observe. All along its long coastline, the Chinese had abandoned their container shipping facilities including the world's largest offshore container port at Shanghai.

Moving around the southern coasts of India, the cities of Surat, Calcutta and Bombay were becoming tidelands while the interior of the country was suffering from a multi-year drought. Despite all that, the government still found time to engage in a full-time war with Pakistan. The countries around the Persian Gulf had always been hot and dry, but were now just hotter and drier with maybe more sandstorms.

Al said, "That's one area we can't blame on the weather. Drought and famine don't seem to have any effect on the many wars, conflicts, rebellions, acts of terrorism. Family and tribal feuds have always seemed to be raging throughout the region."

Of all the continents, Climate Change seemed to be hitting Africa the hardest. The Sahara Desert was marching south rapidly absorbing the area that had previously been called Sub-Saharan Africa. Perhaps a quarter of the entire

African population didn't have a reliable source of clean, fresh drinking water and thousands were dying of thirst daily. Drought was ravaging the central and eastern areas and continuing torrential rains were drowning the west.

As domestic food supplies dwindled, people started to turn more and more to harvesting the native flora and fauna. The great herds of Wildebeest, Antelope and Impalas that once roamed the Savannah were all but gone with only a few scattered pockets remaining. With the loss of their prey, lions and cheetahs were also on the decline and there hadn't been a confirmed leopard sighting in eight years.

If the continent had been populated with countries with stable political establishments, the results of Climate Change probably wouldn't have been so severe, but Africa had been at war with itself for decades. Country against country, tribe against tribe, religion against religion—all with in an inability to cope even in the best of times.

The result was a human population of hundreds of millions on the move with nowhere to go, but that didn't stop the desperate people from trying. The mass movement was generally to the north although everyone knew that even if they made it to the shores of the Mediterranean Sea the countries of Europe were not allowing entry for any migrants. Many argued that that wasn't true, that there were quotas— that there was a *chance*. But they were wrong. The quota systems had collapsed years ago due to the sheer weight of numbers of people fleeing the mid-East and Africa. Now, not only were the European Union Countries not allowing migrants, but they had deployed the fleets of two dozen nations to the Mediterranean to ensure that migrants never reached the shores of Southern Europe.

But any chance was better than none and the waves of migrants kept crossing the wastes of the Sahara piling up on the northern coast of Africa. It was said that you could walk across the Sahara on the bones of migrants.

Of course, we couldn't see that from our perch and Al got back to the weather. The Northern Hemisphere was suffering from extreme heat, but even with increased storms and polluted air, it was still better off than most of the rest of the world. The length of the growing season was increasing across the United States, Central and Northern Europe and Russia and the average rainfall was increasing. But in that twisted paradox there was less water available for farming. The rains were coming in waves of deluge and drought. If a farmer could avoid a flood, keep himself from being blown away *and* had access to a reliable source of water like an aquifer, he might, just *might*, be able to get a crop in. But even so, there was less food being produced. If a farmer was lucky enough to succeed, it was becoming increasingly difficult to move agricultural products from farm to market.

But we knew that even in the West, the future wasn't looking bright. Wealthy coastal cities like London, Amsterdam, New York, and Miami were losing their battle with the ever-rising waters and Venice was gone. Well, the upper floors still stood above the waves, but with its ancient foundations crumbling away, the city was uninhabitable.

On a brighter note, the European and North American governments were still functioning and, although there were isolated flareups, law and order still mostly prevailed. Although, a gang took over a food distribution warehouse in Germany and declared it a separate country. That was exciting and I hadn't heard if it had been resolved yet.

It wasn't until Al pointed out two hurricanes that were forming in the Atlantic that I realized how much time had gotten away from us. We'd been watching the world turn almost all day and I didn't think we were going to stop until we were back looking at Australia. Of the Atlantic hurricanes, Al didn't think that either one of them would hit the North American mainland and that their current trajectory would turn them both north as they passed over the sunken reef that used to be the Bahamas. As far as we could see there were no major storms in the US, but Al said that that could change in a matter of hours.

"Why is that?" Gutman asked.

Al explained, "Among other things, it's the deviation of the Jet Stream. It used to circle the polar regions in a fairly constant circle, but now it resembles a sine wave."

The mathematical mind of the professor understood sine waves and nodded solemnly as Al continued. "At any time, a wave could dip as far south as the Gulf of Mexico, pulling the cold artic air with it. Inside the wave, the air is frigid while outside, it's unusually warm. These waves were rare in the past, but have been happening almost every year now. I've recorded snow in St. Louis in July and one hundred degrees in Minneapolis in January. Today's a hot one all over. It's 115 degrees in Washington, DC and 122 in Los Angles with an air quality index of unbreathable."

When Al finished Gutman sat there silently looking down at our increasingly dark cloud that covered blue green Earth. I patted him on the shoulder and said, "It's not a very pretty picture is it, Professor? And Al can only predict the weather. Who knows what human beings are going to do to each other as the world goes deeper and deeper into the crapper? Why don't you reconsider and come with us to Sanctuary?"

Gutman sighed. Shrugging his shoulders, he gave me a sad smile and said, "No, danke. Thank you, you are all very good, but Gutman go home. Gutman have, what you say in English, obligations. Ja! Obligations. Gutman go home."

Too bad; We really could have used him. Well, I hoped that things wouldn't get too bad for him in his Transylvanian Castle.

CHAPTER 13

Enough of this gloom and doom, professor," I said with a sigh as I pulled him away from the window. "Come on and we'll show you the good stuff."

Floating him over to another view port, I pointed to Voyager drifting in space in all her glory. Except for installing the engines, the three-hundred-foot-long gleaming tube with delta wings was complete. I described to Gutman that the first section was the cockpit, or Command Section while the next section down was the Cryogenics Section. It was also fully installed with its forty-six cryogenics pods and was just now waiting for the "away team". He didn't understand what that meant until I told him it was a nickname from the old Star Trek shows.

"Ja! Ja!" he exclaimed jubilantly. "They must not wear red shirts!"

I cracked up that the professor got our little joke. It

seemed that in the TV shows, the guys in red shirts *always* got lost or captured or crushed or drowned or eaten. I liked this guy. It was really too bad he wasn't coming with us!

Continuing with the visual tour, I told Gutman that the next section down was Supplies and whatever consumables we would use on the trip and in the initial exploration of Sanctuary. The last section was, of course, the Equipment Section. With the expansion of Voyager, the thinking was changing on the initial equipment. Rather than stow it all aboard Voyager we were now thinking of packing some of it into one of the Starduster cargo bays.

She was a beautiful sight—right out of the old science fiction movies, Voyager was all smooth and shiny and we Robot Jockeys were immensely proud of her. It was only a couple of years ago that where she sat was nothing but an empty hole in space. Of course, in the coming months we were going to destroy those beautiful lines by sticking things all over her like warts on a frog, but that was for the future. Right now, we swelled with pride as Gutman praised our efforts.

Then we took the Professor out through the tube and into Voyager itself. Gutman being Gutman was all over everything. We showed him where his engine controls would go and that got a Ja, Ja, Good. As it turned out, the Gutman Engine controls weren't much more that an off/on switch and a rheostat.

He didn't think much about the command crew having to be awake for a year or more monitoring Voyager's progress through space along with keeping an eye on their six hundred plus sleeping passengers. As I was going to be one of them, I had to admit it didn't do much for me, either.

When we took him back to our dormitory in the cryo section and showed him where he was going to sleep while he was with us, he seemed surprised. I don't quite know what he expected, but it definitely wasn't that. Not that it mattered. With as much as he floated around, I doubted he'd spend much time in the pod anyway.

After the Professor had enough of bouncing around inside Voyager, we went back through Wisdom and out through the other dock into R3. At least that impressed him and he gave us quite a few "Ja! Ja! Goods!" as he explored the line of robots, work benches and maintenance facility.

I then loaded Gutman into Sam and we went out into space for a fly-by around Voyager. The Professor was delighted; Looking at Voyager, looking at Wisdom, looking at Earth, but he was all business, too. He had me fly him back to where the engines were going to be installed, and after a close examination of the housing, he wanted me to get in as far as I could to shine the lights inside. I wasn't sure what he was after, so I showed him how to manipulate the lights. The excitable little man quietly muttered to himself as he scrutinized every connection of the inside of the housing.

Noticing his reflective frown, I asked him if there was a problem.

"Ja! Maybe. Not enough room. Would have been better if engines had been installed before housing."

Now you tell me. "Is this a show stopper? Will we have to dismantle the housing?"

"No, Nien. I don't think so." After another few moments of silence, he smiled. "Not to worry. Is OK. Gutman fix."

And that's all he would say, but I was worried.

With that, we went back in, parked Sam and floated back into Wisdom. Everyone was at our usual gathering place—around Al, chatting, looking at the weather down on Planet Earth.

Gutman said to Al, "You are going to Sanctuary?"

Al replied, "Sure, I wouldn't miss it. A chance to forecast weather on a new world even though it will be harder without all the bells and whistles."

Gutman got a funny look on his face and he asked Al what he meant.

"Well, Professor, I will only have equipment that we can find space for in Voyager."

"You not taking Wisdom?"

"No."

Gutman started sputtering like a fuse on a bottle rocket and bouncing up and down like a beach ball and waving his arms. To say that Herr Professor Gutman was agitated would be an understatement.

"But that is foolish," he sputtered. "You must take Wisdom!"

We all kind of smiled. Having never considered taking Wisdom with us to Sanctuary we just kind of brushed the suggestion off.

Gutman kept sputtering, "Look around. Look around. How can you not have all this at Sanctuary?"

Dumbstruck, we did look around: Al's weather station, scientific equipment of all kinds, computers, telescopes, cameras—a complete habitat in space. And then all hell broke loose with everyone talking at once.

Shortly after, I called Alex. "Hello, Luv."

"Hello yourself, my sweet," she said rubbing her eyes.

I'd forgotten it was the middle of the night in Sand Flea. "And to what do I owe this late-night call? How are things going with the Professor?"

"Well," I said, "it's actually the Professor I'm calling about."

"You haven't lost him, have you?" Alex asked, more alert with her sudden concern as if we'd let go of Gutman in a spacewalk and he was now circling the Earth in his own private orbit. "And what's all that noise in the background?"

"No, we haven't lost the Professor although it seemed that it was touch and go for a while. And that noise it is part of the reason I called."

"Well?" Alex wasn't ready to drop her guard. I had called in the middle of the night, after all, and that kind of news was rarely good.

"Well, basically Gutman has been telling us how stupid we are."

Alex laughed in relieved agreement, "I'm not surprised. What have we done now?"

"Not what we have done, Luv, but what we *haven't* done."

"OK, Mr. Mysterious, before I come up there and personally strangle you for stringing this out, what *haven't* we done?"

"We haven't planned to bring Wisdom with us to Sanctuary."

I don't often see my Alex at a loss for words. "Bring Wisdom... I never thought..."

"None of us did, Luv! That's what all the noise is about! That's the sound of a dozen people talking simultaneously... and loudly... about the possibilities and practicalities."

"Well, you sure know how to wake a girl up!" Alex exclaimed. "I'm numb. Could we do it? I mean, could we really take Wisdom aboard Voyager?"

"Aboard no." I was all business now. "There's not a chance it can fit, but it doesn't have to. As you know, Wisdom came up into space in sections and was then assembled. There's no practical reason we can't take it apart again, stick it somewhere on the outside of Voyager's hull with all the other junk and then reassemble it in orbit around Sanctuary. I think the main question isn't 'can we' but 'may we'. Alex, check me if I'm wrong, but Wisdom doesn't belong to us; I mean, it's not under your control as part of Project Voyager. Wisdom belongs to VU."

"You let me worry about Wisdom and VU," Alex said. Catching up to her racing mind, she started to think out loud. "Okay, first things first... I was going to tell you tomorrow but seeing as I'm up... . the first of Gutman's engines has been delivered to Rocket 1 and will be lifted up to you as soon as possible. Before that happens and while you boys have Gutman and are twiddling your thumbs waiting for it to arrive, I want you to start doing the engineering and work out a rough plan for the disassembly and the storage of Wisdom on Voyager. And while you're at it, get with Al and make a provisional plan for how we are going to make Wisdom gradually disappear without anyone on Earth noticing."

I never thought about that aspect, but Alex was right. If Wisdom suddenly went offline, people in high places would probably start asking embarrassing questions.

Alex smiled. "Don't worry, my sweet, we have plenty of time. We are not going anywhere for months yet, maybe years, so just get your merry men to look for anything that would be a show stopper and leave the fine details for later."

After telling Alex we were on it and we said out goodnights, I returned to the noisy crowd in the weather station to report. Everyone, including Gutman, calmed down; if Alex was on the case, all was well.

"Okay, gang, we've got work to do." I grinned. "While she didn't say it in so many words, there are three things she wants us to do. The first thing is, of course, installing the engines. The first one is at Rocket Base 1 and will be lifted ASAP baring any technical difficulties and bad weather."

Gutman thumped his skinny chest. "Ja! Ja! Gutman install engines."

I said, "Nien! Nien! Gutman will be in Sam with me directing the installation."

Gustave didn't care for that and started the fuse sputter again, but I didn't care. There was no way Gutman was going to be allowed into free space because I was afraid that I really would have to tell Alex we'd lost him. Billy Wright and Tony Simmons were the smallest of the RJs, so I asked them to volunteer to suit-up.

"Next," I continued, "is we Robot Jockeys need to survey Wisdom to see exactly how it was put together so we can actually take it apart when the time comes. We also need to give some preliminary thought as to where we can actually stow the pieces on Voyager's hull."

"On it," Billy said. "For some strange reason, I found a complete set of Wisdom's plans tucked away. I'll get them."

"That's great, Billy," I said. "The last item, that of hiding our departure from prying eyes, falls to you, Al, and the other scientists working in Wisdom. How many are there?"

"Four including me," Al answered. "Dan McIntire's an entomologist and Tyler West is a botanist. They're both scheduled to go Sanctuary with us."

"And the other one?"

"Dave Engle. He's one hundred percent on our side, but not planning on leaving Earth."

With that, we broke off into our respective tasks. Billy quickly returned with the plans of Wisdom he'd found and it took Al and his team less than a day to come up with a deception plan that could be implemented immediately.

Al pointed out that Wisdom's Meteorological input to the worldwide weather net was the only report that people expected on a regular basis. Everything else consisted of studies and experiments many of which lasted for months— even years—so if they quietly dropped off the net no one would notice. But seeing as we had plenty of time, they proposed that all experiments, studies etc. continue, periodic reports would be made and, in the future, only studies with a long duration would be accepted. Wisdom would remain connected to the worldwide weather information net right up to the moment that we departed Earth orbit.

It was both brilliant and simple! Better yet, Alex loved it.

Once that was settled, we spent the next several days floating around the rear end of Voyager with Gustave pointing out how every connection worked. He even sat down and made engineering schematics from memory of the engines and its connections. I was confident that the Professor would solve any technical difficulties that might arise.

But the major problem he couldn't overcome was the very small working area. We were used to working in space and slapping big pieces of metal together with unlimited elbow room, but installing the engines was going to be something completely different.

Five days later, Rocket 1 lifted the first of Gutman's Voyager engines and we went to work. With the robots, we maneuvered the engine into the housing and held it in place so the connections to Voyager could be made. That sounded easy, but as Gutman had said, there was no room to work. The problem was that the engine had to be really close to the housing and that left a space of only about six inches for Billy and Tony to work and they were working in free space in bulky space suits with fat mittens. On top of that, instead of being able to stand and do the job at eye level, they were forced to lie face down on the hull and reach down into the gap to make the connections while Sam, Gutman and I hovered overhead trying to shine some light into the hole. Whenever they tried to maneuver the tools in the little gap, they blocked the light and their view.

The entire process reinforced my belief that building things in space is not worth the effort. If we had done this on Earth with the aid of a proper hangar with a work stand, not to mention little things like gravity and air, it still wouldn't have been easy, but it would have been a hell of a lot easier.

Of course, we eventually got it done. Billy came up with the idea of borrowing some of those little telescoping mirrors that the Docs use to look into people's least desirable places. When the mirrors were properly positioned, Billy and Tony could finally see what they were doing, but even that was tricky. I had to carefully maneuver Sam so the mirrors wouldn't reflect Sam's lights, but also so Gutman could see.

So, I had three people yelling at me.

A tool dropped into the gap could take forever to winkle out, but unlike some aircraft manufacturers, we couldn't just leave it there. The alternative would have been to disconnect everything and pull the engine out.

Frustrating. Maddening. It took three and a half weeks to connect one engine—and there weren't that many connections. And our reward was that the second engine came up and we had to do the same thing all over again.

In the end it was done. The engines were installed and Gutman was anxious to get home.

We should have known better! Before they were going to let Gutman go, the Visions Unlimited Board of Directors insisted that there had to be an engine test... a big, well publicized engine test.

Gutman was pissed. I wasn't sure if it was because he couldn't go back to Transylvania right away or because he thought they didn't have faith in his engines.

But VU made a big deal of it and an engine test was scheduled. Once the Visions Unlimited Board of Directors and a whole gaggle of dignitaries started arriving, Gutman apparently changed his mind about holding a test and was strutting around thumping his skinny chest with a "Ja! Ja! Gutman Engines. Good!"

Alex tried in vain to convince the people arriving at Sand Flea that it was just an engine test and that there was nothing really to see. Wisdom and Voyager could only accommodate a handful of visitors and, even when they were on board, only a few people would actually be able to see anything.

They were having none of it. VU had been funding this thing for a couple of years and I guess that they just wanted to see the original Voyager before it flew away. But I thought they had lost their minds to allow all these other people to witness the test. What ever happened to secrecy?

This time, Alex had no choice but to bow to the inevitable. To make matters worse, she was notified by Harrison that there might be a couple of observers from Washington present. Not good, in my humble opinion.

About forty of the high and mighty made the trip to Sand Flea for the Project Voyager Engine Test. Alex and Phil had every square inch of available hangar space crammed with executive jets and a few more were scattered around the field in other companies' hangars. Of course, favor for favor some of the other companies' representatives were allowed to make the trip up to Wisdom too, which brought our total up to fifty.

Alex didn't even bother trying to sort out who was who in the pecking order. She sat everyone down in the cafeteria and told them that there were only three Stardusters available, each shuttle only carried ten people, once they were in space only twenty people could actually fit into Voyager and Wisdom and it was a three-hour round trip. Two shuttles would take the twenty to Wisdom and return, then all three would load up with the remaining thirty people who would have to view the engine test from the Stardusters.

Of course, the dignitaries who went up first and who were actually going to be in Wisdom or Voyager would be stuck up there in space until the shuttles took their passengers back down to Earth and came back for them.

No one seemed to care. They'd get to experience weightlessness while sitting in space. What had become an everyday experience to us was a great adventure for them.

Somehow, they sorted themselves out and the first two Starduster loads docked with Wisdom.

As the crowd started to squeeze into Wisdom, I spotted Lou Carson. I told her that unless she was going to be in the Voyager Command Section or right up against one of Wisdom's view-ports, she wasn't going to see anything. Leaning in like I was asking if she wanted to buy some contraband, I whispered, "Are you ready for another adventure?"

With a wicked grin, Lou asked, "Lights and siren?"

"Lights, no siren."

Lou laughed as I took her through the docking collar into R3. Grabbing hold of the port jamb to stop her forward momentum, she looked amazed at the work areas and row of robots.

"You guys built all this?" she asked, pushing her hair out of her face as it continued to float wildly around her without gravity to hold it in place. Ever the mechanic, I fixed the problem with a zip tie.

"Yup!" I said proudly. "Months ago—right down to the last bolt. This, however, is the warm up. Wait until you see Voyager."

I grabbed a couple of pillows and loaded Lou into Sam. Much to the betterment of my ego, she continued to be impressed with my achievements. "So, this is the famous Sam that I have heard so much about."

"She's my girl... when she isn't trying to kill me. I'd be lost without her. I'll try not to bounce you around too much; The construction robots weren't built for passengers. But Gutman spent the last two months sitting right where you are."

I dropped out of R3 into space and Lou gasped, "Ooh! I never dreamed…"

I did a slow flyby past Voyager and Lou was all Ooh and Aah. Voyager was quite a sight, but I figured we had plenty of time for sightseeing after the engine test. I positioned Sam where we would have the best view of the engines, Voyager, Wisdom and Earth before turning on the Vid so we were looking into the Command Section.

"See, Lou? You've got the best seat in the house."

I couldn't tell how many people were trying to cram into Voyager's Command Section. I could only see Harrison, Alex and Gutman. Harrison said a few words and looked like he was going to start the engines, but Gustave wasn't having any of that.

"Nien! Nien! Gutman!"

Lou couldn't help laugh as we watched the Professor literally slap Harrison's hand away before switching the engines on and slightly turning the rheostat.

I'm not exactly sure what I thought was going to happen, but I think I was expecting smoke and flames to shoot out of Voyager's back side. I definitely thought I'd see Voyager moving… maybe even quivering a little bit, but as far as I could see nothing happened. Voyager still sat there in space looking magnificent, but unmoving. We looked at the Vid and everyone in the Command Section was smiling and happy and declaring the test a success. Lou and I looked at each other and shook our heads. Apparently, we didn't have the best seats in the house because we definitely missed something.

To make up for it, we spent the next couple of hours flying around Wisdom and Voyager while Lou took in everything. She especially seemed to like looking down on Earth.

In an awed whisper, she said, "It still looks so beautiful from up here… all blue and clouds. You can't see all the problems."

Then we spent a half hour prowling around in R3 and Voyager. I'm not sure that she really believed me when I told her about our months of living in R3 before we built our "dormitory". At least Lou wasn't impressed with that part of the tour, neither sleeping in the workshop nor bunking in the cryogenic pods. She did get really thoughtful, though, when she realized that that's where Maryanne and Grant were going to sleep for twenty years.

It was hard to pry Lou away, but we managed to catch the last shuttle. I wanted to get back on the ground before Gutman left. He was going to ride back to Los Angles with the big boys from VU in their plush executive jet and I wanted to say goodbye and thank him for his help. I made it, but not by much. Just as we were taxing in, we had to wait while a small convoy of vehicles left our area and headed out the gate. I wondered what that was all about, but with all the excitement of everyone leaving, I forgot to ask.

We were just in time. I walked over with Lou and she gave me a big hug and thank you before she boarded her plane. Wonderful lady. I wondered if I would ever see her again.

From there, I went over to where Alex, Harrison, Gutman and a few others were chatting and shook the Professors hand. After thanking him yet again, I made my last pitch for him to join us.

He laughed. "Nien, Nien, John Marshal. You are very

good and Gutman enjoyed working with you very much. But Gutman must go home."

I took that as a high complement. Even Harrison seemed impressed.

"Well, good luck, Professor. I will miss you." There wasn't much else to say. Gutman and the VU Board loaded up, taxied out and took off.

The plane made it to LA okay and I heard that Gutman then boarded a flight to Berlin. As far as I know he made it; I'm sure that we would have heard if he didn't. I think about him now and then especially when I am benefiting from one of his marvelous inventions. They broke the mold after they made Herr Professor Gustave Gutman.

CHAPTER 14

With or without Professor Gutman, Project Voyager went on. The ball was in the manufactures' court so after the dignitaries left, I just stayed on the ground. While Alex and I were having dinner, I told her that even though there wasn't much to do on Voyager until we started getting some of the big pieces, I'd probably head back up tomorrow to work with the apprentices. That was when she dropped a small bomb on me. Chet Barton wanted me to become a permanent member of the security team and he wanted to move me up to assistant chief along with Link.

I was kind of shocked. "Why would Chet want me? I am just a part-timer on his security team and when would I find time to do it anyway?"

"That's exactly what I told him, but he likes your military background. He also likes you personally and thinks you'd be a good choice to back up Link when we get to

Sanctuary. If you're going to be dirtside for a few days, I think you should talk to him."

While I was still dithering on whether I should talk to Chet or quietly sneak back up to Voyager, Al Wilson decided the issue for us. The Vid chimed and his smiling face came on with a Haboob Advisory which predicted that a big storm he was monitoring would hit Sand Flea sometime after midnight and we should spend the rest of the day securing anything that was loose.

That settled that! And the thought of spending the next few days with Alex didn't break my heart. After we got everything secured, I spent the rest of the day with Chet talking about police work and kicking around various possible security arrangements once we were on Sanctuary.

Three nights later the storm was still howling and every few minutes the hangar would shake violently when an exceptionally strong blast of wind hit it. That didn't bother me, either; In fact, I barely noticed it snoozing away snug in Alex's arms. Well, I was until an ear-shattering siren split the air and a loud voice blared out of every speaker in all six hangars.

"Red alert. Red alert. All personnel report immediately, fully equipped, to your assigned emergency stations."

Far more used to the silence of space, the alert was in its second repeat before my fuzzy brain was able to focus on what was happening. My sluggish reaction wasn't echoed by the project people who lived permanently in Sand Flea who practiced this red alert stuff on a regular basis. Before I got my feet on the floor, Alex was up, dressed and out the door headed for her office which was also the Emergency

Command and Communications Center.

"Red alert. Red alert. All personnel report immediately, fully equipped to your assigned emergency stations."

"Yeah, yeah, I heard you!" I muttered at the disembodied voice.

I finally got my tiny brain in gear and remembered that I was not only dirtside, but I was also a member of Chet Barton's security force. After I managed to put all my gear on, what amazed me most was that my muddled brain actually remembered to pick up my rifle. Finally, I was ready and headed for my duty station which was the bunker at the southwest corner of Hangar 1. Though it was only about fifty feet from where I was sleeping, I was the last one to check in—much to the amusement of all present.

"So, what's going on?" I asked when the snickering died down.

No one had a clue. All I could see out through the plasto-glass was total blackness interspersed with brown streaks of horizontally blown sand and there wasn't much more to see when I looked out through the low light and infra-red telescopes. With that first class sand storm raging outside, we couldn't possibly be under attack. But then, if someone was out there, they could have walked up and tapped on the window and we would never have seen them.

With a shrug, we all dutifully manned our stations, such as they were.

About ten minutes later all the Vid screens lit up with Alex's no longer smiling face. "Ladies and gentlemen, first let me apologize for the early morning wake-up call and to thank you all for your prompt response."

That got another giggle from my bunker mates, but they were no longer amused when Alex continued.

"Let me also reassure you that, while we are not under attack, this was not a drill. About four hours ago our farming community up at Junction was assaulted by a force of about thirty to forty individuals wielding small arms and Molotov Cocktails. Six, maybe seven, of our people were killed, eleven were wounded and one is missing. I'm sorry, I know that many of you have friends up there, but at the moment I do not have a list of the casualties. I will post it as soon as I receive it."

Looking around at the array of grim faces, I knew that more than one of them were worried about the people they knew in Junction.

Alex went on. "As to the state of the co-op at Junction, I only know that our security force and the farmers drove the attackers off and that in addition to our casualties two buildings were burned. The attackers did get away with two truckloads of fresh produce that were scheduled to be on their way to us today. We will, of course, mount a rescue operation as soon as this damn sand stops blowing. You may resume normal activities, go back to sleep if you can. Thank you again and André and Cathy say breakfast will be ready in a few minutes. Lastly, would the Project Voyager staff and John Marshal please report to my office."

I could see why Alex wanted the staff, but I didn't know what I could contribute. I soon realized that this was Chet's not so subtle way of breaking me in.

Filing into the conference room with everyone else, I waited for Alex to take her place at the head of the table before I sat down. To her right sat Chet and Dot while Doc

Watson (Nancy) and Cathy Jackson took the open spaces on her left. Filling up the rest of the table was Phil Reston, who was Chief of shuttle operations and maintenance, Alice Smith our supply chief and Pedro Gonzales who ran our motor pool and maintenance... and me. Looking around, I felt as out of place as a freshman at the senior prom.

Alex was impressive, a CEO using the expertise of her staff to full advantage. Unfortunately, after giving us a more detailed outline of the attack, we still didn't know very much. "What I need from you is to see what we need to bring forth a rescue mission."

Doc Nancy didn't hesitate to be the first to chime in. "We'll need the ambulance and I can give you a tentative list of supplies and personnel."

Alex gave her a nod of acknowledgement.

Chet, of course, covered his tentative security arrangements. "Sixteen to twenty deputies, small arms and I'll defer final arrangements. I want to confer with John first."

I couldn't imagine what I had to offer. It must have shown on my face because Alex almost laughed when she caught my eye. Recovering, she asked, "Phil, what's our Starduster status?"

"Three operational," he told her.

"Excellent," Alex nodded again. "Pedro, how are we on vehicles?"

"Good, I can get you anything you want."

"Alice and Cathy, how are our supplies and rations?"

Alex smiled at their efficiency when Alice just told her to give her a list while Cathy recited her stocks as if she planned for this very crisis a week ago.

Around the table they went and not more than half an

hour later, Alex summed up. Tentatively, the relief operation would consist of two Stardusters, two armored Army Humvees, the ambulance, a four-person medical team, and a security force. "Ok," said Alex, "make your preliminary arrangements and we will meet back here at 1600 to finalize details. Thank you very much!"

When the meeting was adjourned, I fell in with Chet and we headed for his little office next to the bunker. Laughing, he said, "Your good lady runs a good meeting. Get the facts, assign tasks and get to work."

"You got that right," I said. "Now, what do you want me to do?"

"Nothing right now. Why don't you get us a cup of coffee and sit down while I make a couple of calls?"

Coffee was an excellent idea. When I got back, I sat by his desk and drank away the dust from the few remaining cobwebs in my head while Chet made his first call to Junction. At the moment, all was quiet. Since the raid, they had pushed patrols out ten miles in all directions and established a roadblock twenty miles down the road to the east. Chet told them that that was good and, in his opinion, the attack was a hit and run raid and whoever it was were just after the trucks with the food and they were probably long gone. He thought that Junction was probably secure and we would be up as soon as the damn Haboob slacked off.

His next call was to a couple of his deputies. He told them to each pick a seven-man team with a basic load out of weapons and supplies for a week and he would see Pedro for two armored Humvees. Chet wanted them to be ready as soon as the storm cleared and for them to plan on one team going up in a Starduster and the other in the hummers.

"That's a force of sixteen deputies counting you and me," Chet said when he hung up. "Unless whoever pulled of this raid is holed up fairly close by, I don't expect to see them. What do you think?'

I couldn't help laugh that Chet, of all people, wanted my opinion. "You know you are talking to a rank amateur when it comes to police work, but what you are describing sounds more like a military operation."

"It is; Any thoughts?"

"Well, one. What about Bobby and Kevin?" Bobby Burke and Kevin Young were our resident teen age computer nerds who were currently part of the Sand Flea Airfield's drone surveillance network. "If you could get them and a couple of their birds, it would give us some longer-range eyes."

"I never thought of them. Great idea." Chet immediately placed another phone call and we had our airborne surveillance team.

When we met back up in Alex's conference room, there wasn't much more news from Junction except that Alex had a confirmation of the dead and wounded. The community was pretty shook-up, but outside of needing medical assistance, they were OK. As expected, Alex had already approved all arrangements and almost everything needed was already on board the Stardusters and hummers.

"I don't like having to use the Stardusters," Alex frowned. "I want to keep the vertical lift capability secret but, in this case, we will make an exception." Turning to Phil, she said, "Normal runway take-offs and landings here at Sand Flea and don't mention the vertical capability at Junction unless someone comments on it. Just do it. If someone does mention it, take them aside and caution them. I think that that's about all we can do."

Nothing to do now but wait for the weather. That was one of the biggest troubles with this new climate of ours; There were more storms, stronger storms which lasted longer each time one raged through. As Al confirmed their frequency and intensity, it wasn't our imagination, either.

Twenty-two of us plus the Starduster crews were itching to get the show on the road and head north to relieve Junction, but the Haboob just wouldn't let up. As we waited, I noticed that it wasn't just us, but our whole community was anxious for the relief operation to get on the road. Everyone with any kind of a communication capability was bugging Al for information on when the storm was going to end and we could get going. What made it even more maddening was that the weather in Junction, a mere fifty miles north, was clear. Al tried to explain—again—that Junction was in the hill country and, tucked into the eastern flank of the Sierras, they didn't get haboobs. It was no use; They blamed the weatherman.

With a roving band of killers loose right in our own backyard, we were stuck at Sand Flea for another day and a half before the storm finally blew itself out, but the moment the weather broke, we were gone. Chet took one squad of deputies and the medical team and went off with the two Stardusters. I was placed with the other squad and the drone team and we drove up in the ambulance and two of the armored Army-style Humvees that we had. It only took us an hour and a half to get to Junction, but by the time we arrived, Chet and Doc Watson (John) had everything organized. They had found the individual who had been missing, dead, inside one of the burned buildings.

Taking me aside, Chet showed me the damage and reviewed the tentative plans and the enhanced security arrangements we'd made before leaving our compound at Sand Flea. His challenge now was getting the farmers and the security crew that Link had hired a couple of years ago focused on enhancing security at Junction. Seriously pissed over the attack, they wanted to go after somebody and Chet was having a hard time containing them.

Fortunately, they had waited for the storm to die out and for Chet to arrive before they took matters into their own hands. Even though the patrols were still out, Chet was pretty sure that there wasn't a threat within a ten-mile radius, but he wanted more information before he initiated any action. And what he needed to know most was if the gang was still in the area or if they'd possibly moved on to the east to the little town of Rawlings, the only other settlement in the area, a small hamlet about thirty or forty miles down the road.

"John, I need you to do a reconnaissance patrol out toward Rawlings," Chet said. "Take one of the Army vehicles and a few guys and check it out."

"Yes, sir!" I said, snapping to. At least that was something I understood. The moment he gave the order, I saw the locals from Junction nod at his decisive command. Good! There was no question in their eyes of who was in charge. Taking four deputies and one of the hummers, I headed twenty miles east to where the Junction people had set up their road block.

It was a pretty basic road block—two of the farmers had just driven a couple of pick-up trucks out and parked them across the road, but they were in a pretty good position. On the top of a slight rise, they had an unobstructed view to the east for about five miles. I got out my map and they began drawing me a rough sketch on it to fill in the gaps.

Both of them had been born and raised in Junction and what they didn't know about the local area wasn't worth knowing. According to them, the town of Rawlings was another fifteen miles down the road. We couldn't see the town from our position, but I was informed it was hardly more than a wide spot in the road with maybe two hundred permanent residents. The main east/west road that we were on ran through the center of town and on it was a general store with two gas pumps. The general store carried just about everything, mostly farm machinery, tools, groceries, but it also had a small lumber yard.

Next to the store was the only bank for fifty miles in any direction and across the street was a bar-come-restaurant that was the watering hole for all the cowboys and hired farm hands for miles around. Beyond that, they guessed there weren't more than two or three dozen houses in the whole town.

On their hand drawn map were two smaller streets, one to the north and the other to the south, which ran parallel to the main road with a few connecting streets. In addition to the houses, Rawlings had a school and two churches and that was about it. It didn't even have a Dairy Queen or a stop light. The farmers hadn't gone any closer to Rawlings than their road block so they didn't know how many people if any were still in town.

Okay, good! Now that I had a mental picture of Rawlings, I had to see if the town was occupied and by who. Relieving the farmers with two of Chet's deputies, I sent them and the hummer back to Junction with instructions to the hummer driver to return ASAP with the drone team and Jerry Smith. I didn't know many of Chet's deputies, but I knew Jerry had been a recon scout in the Army. It was only a forty-mile round trip back to Junction and the hummer was back in less than an hour with Jerry, Bobby and Kevin and their flying machines.

While Bobby and Kevin set up their equipment, I said, "Guys, I need to get a good look at a town that's about fifteen or twenty miles down the road, but I don't want the drone spotted. Can you do that?"

They were as excited as little puppy dogs wagging their tails.

"Yes, sir!" said Bobby. "We can absolutely do that and you can have a real-time picture on the monitor here."

"That's great, but how noticeable will the drone be to people on the ground?"

Kevin only smiled, flipped a couple of switches and lifted the drone up to the altitude they planned to fly over the town. Beautiful! No noise and even when I knew where to look, I couldn't see it.

The drone sailed out over the countryside and we all crowded around the monitor. There weren't many farms and ranches between Junction and Rawlings, but it looked like every one of them had been burned. Kevin wanted to know if I wanted a closer look; I told him that he probably didn't want to see what was down there and to keep going.

When the drone got to Rawlings, Kevin sent it around the perimeter of the little town and then right over the center. As it flew down the main street, we could see people moving around, several vehicles haphazardly parked along the curbs and there were roadblocks on the east/west road at each end of town. All the individuals and vehicles that we could see seemed to be clustered either around the general store and bar or around one of the larger houses to the north.

In the way the vehicles were dispersed, I didn't think that they were townspeople and that we had probably found our marauders. If there were any locals present, my guess was they were being held in the large house and the school.

I told the boys to look for the highjacked trucks and in no time, they found them. As there weren't many places to hide trucks of that size, they were parked in the narrow space between the general store and the bank. Then I had them send the drones on a wide sweep around the countryside. It was pretty grim; We didn't see a single human being and most of the farms and ranches were burned or partially burned.

Jerry and I looked at the map and reviewed what we knew. We were pretty sure that the bad guys were in town and that outside of their road blocks on the east and west edges of town there was no other security. Judging by what they had done at Junction they were vicious little bastards. What we didn't know was how many of them there were, how many civilians might still be alive and being held prisoner and where exactly any survivors might be held.

After Jerry and I had a quick conference, I called Chet and outlined what we planned to do: as soon as was dark, Jerry and I were going in on foot for a night recon. We also told Chet that we thought that it would be a good idea to bring up a couple of rocket launchers from the Flea for the roadblocks.

While Chet didn't sound too happy with our "night recon" plan, he didn't argue. After assuring us he'd think about the rocket launchers, he told us to watch our asses because he didn't want to have to explain anything to Alex.

Bobby and Kevin had done a great job, but as there wasn't much more they could do here, I sent them back to Junction in the hummer. The driver returned around dusk with another deputy, water and some rations. While Jerry and I waited, we went over the map again and formed a loose plan for our nighttime reconnaissance: a quick in and out to ascertain the status and location of the civilians, if any, determine the enemy's strength and, as Jerry pointed out, see if they had any weapons heavier than small arms.

We got a break in the weather, no moon and thick clouds. When darkness descended, we had the deputy driving the hummer take us down the road to within about five miles of the town where he could drop us off.

I told him to be back by dawn.

He said he would wait.

I liked him.

Slipping into the bush, we headed northeast figuring to come into town on the side where our two suspect buildings were, but as soon as we were off the road, Jerry just disappeared. One minute he was a little bit in front of me moving through the trees and brush and the next minute he was gone. I kept going and now and then I caught a glimpse of a fleeting shadow up ahead of me. I thought that I was a pretty good woodsman, but compared to Jerry Smith I was a lumbering rhinoceros. I swear that man could disappear in the middle of an empty basketball court.

There wasn't much to our recon. For all the attention these punks were paying to security, we could have probably just walked in with a clipboard and taken notes and they wouldn't have even noticed us. As we suspected, those who were left of the townspeople, around two dozen as best as we could determine, were locked in the schoolhouse. They were mostly men with a few kids and a couple of older women—all of them looked to be in pretty bad shape, beaten and starving. On the steps of the school were a couple of thugs who were evidently supposed to be guarding their prisoners, but were more interested in passing a bottle back and forth between them.

It didn't take much imagination to figure out where the rest of the women were. We moved over to the large house that we had located on the drone feed. These bastards were using it as their own little pleasure house. Mean sadistic pleasure. It was hard not to start exterminating that vermin immediately. I had to tell myself to cool it and that we would be back tomorrow.

Jerry drifted like a ghost toward main street to count noses and check for heavy weapons and I went to check the road block on the east side of town. Same as the other; Some cars and junk across the road, no sign of heavy weapons and two tattooed punks in leather jackets passing around their own bottle. These guys were so oblivious I didn't even bother to circle around outside of town to get to the south side. I just walked across the road and started checking out the houses. The ones that hadn't been burned were all empty, but I saw three bodies that had just been left where they fell when the punks killed them.

My little recon didn't take long and I waited in the shadows for Jerry. My heart almost stopped when a voice in my ear said, "Are we done?"

My ego felt a little better when we crept up on the deputy waiting in hummer and scared the crap out of him.

Leaving the road block in place, Jerry, the deputies and I went back to Junction. After breakfast everyone gathered around a big table and I spread out the map and made my report. When I got to the part about the prisoners and the women, they were ready to jump into the cars and head for Rawlings then and there. It took a while and all of Chet's persuasion and authority to get everyone settled down with a promise that retribution was coming and swiftly.

"Don't worry, everyone," Chet said dangerously. "We're going in tonight!"

CHAPTER 15

At midnight, one of the shuttles dropped me, Jerry, Doc John, one of his medical assistants and first squad north of the little hamlet of Rawlings—close to the town, but out of sight and sound. During the next four hours we worked our way into the northern part of town and proceeded to permanently silence the two sentries at the school house and the four lowlife scums who were at the pleasure house.

While my team was carefully moving through Rawlings, the second shuttle dropped the other squad and a two-man rocket team out beyond the road block on the east end of town and they worked their way into firing range. Once both of our squads were in position, we waited.

In the still, pre-dawn morning air, I heard the rumble of the two Humvees and a half dozen pick-up trucks carrying the farmers, security people and our two-man rocket team as Chet lead them openly down the road from Junction. He was making sure the caravan made plenty of noise, but was careful to stop well out of rifle range. Over the sound of Chet's engines, doors began slamming in town and the members of this miserable gang of punks started shouting as the alarm was raised. As we suspected, the hoodlums all rushed to the west roadblock to defend against whatever was coming down the road.

I couldn't see Chet and his farmers from where I was hiding, but I didn't really need to. The show opened with a high-pitched scream and then an explosion as a rocket blast hit the roadblock, completely blowing it apart. The continuing shockwave proceeded to shatter several windows in town.

The first blast was followed by a another one behind us as our second rocket team destroyed the roadblock on the other end of town. The second squad was on the move even before the rocket hit and lost no time in joining up with us. Between the two squads, there were fifteen of us hitting the remaining punks.

Slowly, we made our way through Rawlings, dispatching the marauders as we went. We were just about finished when we heard a frenzied cry coming from the direction of Chet's roadblock. Recognizing two of them as the farmers from Junction, I signaled my guys to hold their fire. It was clear that Chet couldn't hold them back any longer and the farmers had rushed in to take their revenge.

It didn't take long after that. Excluding the six we had dispatched coming into town, the final marauder count was thirteen dead, two wounded and thirty captured. Two of the farmers who'd rushed the town had also been wounded, so Doc Wilson moved them and the rest of the civilians into the schoolhouse. From there, Doc assessed everyone's injuries before the Stardusters were called in to evacuate them to either Junction or Sand Flea where he had better facilities.

That left the question of what to do with the prisoners. While Chet Barton is a hell of a good soldier, he is first and foremost a policeman and policemen have rules. Before we attacked, he insisted that anyone who wanted to surrender would be allowed to do so. Of course, as soon as the marauders faced someone who was actually able to fight back, those knuckle-dragging knee breakers quit. As a result, we had thirty punks on our hands. All of them clearly had previous arrest records and I was sure by their actions that any punishment they'd received in civilian courts up until now had probably been the equivalent of a wrist slap.

Not this time. Farmers and deputies alike—me too, for that matter—wanted to shoot them on the spot, but Chet wouldn't have it. He was right, of course, but it left us with a dilemma.

Taking Chet aside, I said, "Well, Captain, what *are* we going to do with them? There aren't any authorities to turn them over to, we don't have a jail, no one wants to spend their time guarding them and we all feel that it would be a waste of our resources to feed them."

Chet just gave me a smile that I would come to learn meant he was way ahead of us. I must have advertised that I trusted the Captain had something in mind because no one even hesitated when Chet ordered a group of the farmers to take their pick-ups and our hijacked trucks back to Junction. Once they were rambling down the dusty road, he had his deputies march the prisoners to the east roadblock at the other end of town.

"You don't deserve it," Chet said, "but I'm going to let

you go."

They sniggered; It was exactly what they expected would happen.

It wasn't what we expected. With a growl, we sputtered our protest as we wondered what the hell Chet was thinking.

Unconcerned that he might have a revolt on his hands, Chet just held his hand up and waited for us to quiet down. With another smile, he turned to the punks and said, "Empty your pockets... everything! Right here on the ground in front of me."

I'd never seen the color puce before, but I was given an excellent example as the face of one of the punks began to resemble a crab boiling in a pot. Clearly, he'd never been forced into a subordinate position before, and he didn't like it.

One of the deputies recognized the brewing trouble and clocked him with his rifle butt before he could draw breath to counter Chet's order. With the reminder that they were no longer in charge, Chet had a nice pile of knives, razors, brass knuckles and unidentified junk piled in front of him.

"Now, take off your shoes," Chet ordered.

That drew protests from all of them which gave the lead bruiser confidence that they had strength in their numbers. Snarling that he wouldn't do it, a knife that hadn't made it into the pile appeared in his hand as he advanced on Chet.

Chet shot him right between the eyes.

Immediately, a pile of boots and worn sneakers grew next to the contraband weapons.

"Now," Chet snarled, "as much as everyone here

would like to, we won't kill you. So, as long as you follow instructions, you can just walk out of here."

With their last reserves of false bravado laying at their feet with a bullet in his brain, our remaining prisoners nodded eagerly that they would comply with whatever Chet said. At his gesture, two deputies brought up a couple of cases of bottled water.

"Pick up the water and start walking that way," Chet pointed east down the road. "We will be right behind you. If you stop, you will be shot; If you turn around and try to come back this way, you will be shot; If you go off the road, you will be shot. Start walking!"

When they didn't move, Chet shot his pistol into the air. "Now!"

We cheered as they numbly began shuffling east just as the sun crested the horizon. I was told that the next town was about fifty miles down the road.

We kept pace behind the pack of vermin all day. Barefoot or sock-foot, they weren't moving very fast and they probably only made ten or twelve miles before dusk. I'll bet their feet were like raw hamburger. As night fell, Chet pulled the hummer back and we just watched them with one of the drones. Half crippled, they were too exhausted to be a problem.

The next morning, we saw that two of them had died during the night and almost half of the ones remaining could barely stand. Crawling was good enough for us and we marched them on. We followed them with the drones for two more days. By that time, half of them were lying by the side of the road and the other half were barely staggering.

I don't know what happened to them after that. Don't

care. We left them where they were and came home.

Apparently, Chet's solution to the marauders not only got back to Junction, but all the way to Sand Flea. Everyone seemed pleased with the results because we drove into Junction to a heartfelt, but brief hero's welcome.

After their scare, the farmers were taking security seriously. The two farms and the farmers' co-op that were clustered around the 'T' junction were being linked together and fortified. Everyone wanted to help and asked Chet to coordinate their defense. Chet was more than willing, and anything that he said he wanted from Sand Flea—either in men or materials—Alex promptly delivered. Even Brian the Blacksmith came up in his battered old truck with a couple of his apprentices to help.

There were only a handful of civilians left from Rawlings and, with everything that had happened to them… well, I guess the memories were just too painful for any of them to want to continue to live back there. Some of them moved into Junction while a couple of others tried to make a new life in the Flea, but most moved out. A few had family and friends in other parts of the country, but it seemed that most of them just left the area. I have no idea where they went.

As to what remained of Rawlings, we literally took it apart. We drove every truck we had available to the town and loaded them up with everything that we even possibly useable from the general store, the bar/restaurant and any of the houses that were still standing. Every stick of wood from the little lumber yard was loaded and some buildings were dismantled to salvage the wood. We even robbed the bank, not that there was much left after the punks were done.

Whatever was left of the town, we burned.

Junction, I discovered, wasn't an easy place to defend. Just as the name implied, it was a "T" junction where the north/south road that came from Sand Flea City met the road from Rawlings to the east and turned into a dirt track about five miles to the west. There were two farms at the intersection, one to the north of the 'T' and one on the southeast corner. Like all farms they were spread out with barns and out buildings. To make it more difficult, about two dozen farmers and ranchers around the area had formed a co-op and their storage buildings, grain drying hoppers and offices were on the southwest corner of the intersection.

The area covered by the farms and the co-op formed a triangle roughly four hundred yards on one side and five hundred on the other two. It was too big to build a fence around, so Chet and the farmers decided that the most practical option was a barbwire tangle around the perimeter. That way, all the livestock could be brought in and bunkers could be erected around the farm and co-op buildings themselves.

Personally, now that Rawlings was gone, I thought that their location was their best defense. There was nothing to the east for nearly a hundred miles and Sand Flea was another fifty miles to the south; The mountains to their west had only a dirt track that petered out after about twenty miles and there was nothing but rolling hills and farms to the north.

I hung around for a few days helping out where I could which was mostly building fences and bunkers. I wandered in and out of Brian's smithy quite a bit. The co-op had a blacksmith shop, but they hadn't had a real smith in a while. Brian was as happy as a clam on a sandy beach as he put the shop back together and caught up on all the work. He would get lost in his work, forgetting to eat or sleep. But that was Brian. We had gotten used to him down at Sand Flea, banging away at all hours of the day and night.

My first surprise came one day when I came into the forge to pick something up. The forge fires were growling away, but Brian was sitting on a bench eating a sandwich. Even more to my surprise, sitting next to him and holding a lunch basked was a very attractive blond and blue-eyed lady. Fortunately for them, they offered me a beer so I had an invitation to sit and chat, because I was going to get this story regardless.

That's how I was introduced to Helen Nordstrom, a widow in her late twenties who lived with her parents on a small dairy farm just north of Junction. She brought in milk every other day and helped with the canning when she could. Helen didn't expand on how she'd come to be widowed so early and I didn't ask, but a few weeks later, the grapevine told me that sad story. Only a few weeks after she'd gotten married, her husband had been gruesomely mangled by a piece of farm machinery. That had been six years ago and she had never re-married.

Anyway, Helen had taken Brian on as her own special project. She thought that Brian worked too hard and didn't take proper care of himself and when she was at Junction, she saw to it that he at least ate regularly and got some sleep.

To my delighted amusement, Brian, the confirmed bachelor in his late thirties who didn't care about anything except his work, sat there in a happy daze obediently munching his sandwich.

There was no doubt about it, Brian Anders was in love. I couldn't wait to tell Alex!

As it turned out, Brian wasn't the only one succumbing to Scandinavian charms. Kevin Young, one half of the Bobby/ Kevin drone team, had been tapped by Chet to stay up at Junction and use his drones to provide long range surveillance. Chet had taken one of the unused rooms in the co-op's storage shed as his office and Kevin set up shop in the loft right above him. I had to laugh when I saw his "command center." The loft had a big double door like the ones you see on the upper story of old barns and just inside the door, he had one of those plush looking easy chairs with the big arms. Kevin rigged his control panel and monitor so he could operate the controls and fly his drones in and out of the loft from his comfy chair.

Kevin also installed a repeater monitor on Chet's desk so if there was anything of particular interest, he would signal Chet by stomping on the floor... and Chet could then take a look. It was kind of humorous watching Kevin operate up to four drones at a time from his chair, but it was also impressive.

Kevin was the stereotypical computer nerd. While I don't know if he had a social life, I was fairly sure he never had a girlfriend. As a result, he was completely defenseless the day Olga discovered him.

Olga Sorenson, who really hated her name believing it to be too old fashioned, was the daughter of Ole and Helga Sorenson (well, one of their daughters—they had five as well as four sons) who owned the farm across the road from the co-op. I'm not sure where she ranked age-wise, but I think somewhere in the middle. Olga was eighteen, blond, blue eyed, perky and all smiles. The day that she breezed into Kevin's loft he was a goner.

I couldn't wait to get back to Sand Flea and tell Alex! It

wasn't often I had juicy pieces of gossip for her. As casually as I possibly could, I told Chet that if he didn't have anything special for me to do, I'd be heading home. I should have been forewarned of imminent disaster when he thought that was a great idea and, seeing as I was going that way, I could drive the last truckload of produce down to Sand Flea *and* since we were going to winter the truck in Pedro's hangar, we didn't need to send another car down to bring the Junction driver back.

I gave Chet a cheerful, "Sure! No problem," while internally wondering what could possibly go wrong this time. Chet clearly had forgotten he was speaking to John Marshal. The old Little Abner character Joe Btfsplk, (the bad luck jinx who had a perpetual rain cloud over his head and whose last name was pronounced by blowing a raspberry) would clearly have been inspired after me if not for the fact that Al Capp drew him decades before my parents were even born.

The next morning, I was off. No escort, just me, a medium sized truck full of veggies and a very pleasant late summer day. It was cool, probably in the high forties, but the sun was shining. It was all very nice until I came out of the low hills and actually started to get into outskirts of town and my phone rang. It was my girl.

"Hello, Luv," I said cheerfully until her serious tone clued me in that something was seriously wrong. It couldn't have been me... yet.

"Hello yourself, John. Chet said that you were bringing a truckload of veggies down today. Where are you?"

I told her and Alex said, "That's close enough. Pull over and stop."

What the... I turned into one of the side streets and

pulled over. "What's going on?"

"What's going on is that there are two to three hundred people crowded around the main gate raising hell and demanding food."

That was unusual. Sand Flea City was pretty far off the beaten path. Sometimes there were small groups of people drifting through Sand Flea, but they never went to the airfield.

"So, give them some food and send them on their way."

"That's what I told the knuckleheads on the council that runs the airfield, but they won't do it. Bunker mentality; Us against them. They're determined to keep the gates closed and defend the airfield with lethal force if anyone tries to break in."

"Call a meeting of the council and tell them," I said stating the obvious. Of course, that would have been the first thing Alex would have done.

"To late for that, my sweet, and the time for reason has passed," Alex sighed. "Besides that, I don't think that they would listen to me anyway."

"Why not? Isn't Voyager an important member of the airfield council?"

"A member yes, but maybe not so important. Compared to the Wendover Group that owns most of the south side or Pearson Enterprises who are all around us, we with our six hangars and a couple hundred people, are small potatoes. No, I'm afraid that this time, reason is not going to work. I told the council that you are out there bringing in a load of produce, but they are not going to open the gate until the mob disperses. So, you, my sweet, need to stay the hell away from here. If that crowd finds out that you have a truckload of food, they will tear it and probably you apart. Maybe you should go back to Junction."

We said our goodbyes and I started calling around to see who was actually manning the gate. The airfield authorities had called a full alert so there were several of our Voyager deputies present augmenting airfield security and I managed to get one of them on the phone. The guys told me that there was no chance of getting the airfield authorities to open the gates until the mob was gone. As far as they could see, that wasn't going to happen any time soon. Rubber bullets had already been fired and, if anything, the situation was getting uglier.

At least they knew I was out here. The Gate Commander was from airfield security and seemed like a reasonable guy and would open the gates as soon as he could; However, my best bet would probably be to return to Junction and come back in another day.

I know that the smart thing to do would be to listen to the advice of every single person I'd spoken with including my wife, but as they already knew, I wasn't very smart. I sat on the side of the road trying to figure out what to do next for the better part of an hour before I headed deeper into Sand Flea.

Before the world started going to pot, the Flea probably had a population of about twenty thousand, but as I drove in from the north to the airfield on the southern edge, I couldn't see a living soul. Cars and trucks were parked by the side of the road, but it looked like most of the houses were empty. It was like a creepy science fiction movie as if the people just vanished leaving all of their possessions behind. The noisy rumble of my truck would have woken the dead, but

I couldn't see anyone left in the silent ghost town.

I drove down the boulevard that ran past the apartment where we used to live. I stopped and walked out into the middle of the four-lane thoroughfare that went right into the airfield, but there was nothing. This place used to be busy with people driving in and out all the time—even our laundry guy made the trip a couple times a day.

Haboobs had deposited enough red dust over the pavement that I watched a tiny dust devil travel right down the center of the street. I almost laughed when I thought how much like Mars the place looked, but I didn't actually find it funny.

Getting back into my truck, I drove slowly down the boulevard, stopping while I was just out of sight of the gate. Shutting the motor off, I walked forward until I could see the airfield and a mob of at least two hundred people strong clamoring in front of the gates.

When we first moved here, the main entrance had been a four-lane boulevard with only a sign to tell you that you were actually on the airfield, but over the last couple of years that had changed. At first, there was a little gate house with a single guard, but that became a guarded entrance with a road gate and concrete barriers. Eventually, two of the lanes had been blocked off making a two-lane entrance instead of four.

In its present configuration, there was only one lane open with alternating one-way traffic in and out through a huge concrete structure that looked like the gate to a medieval castle with a wall twenty feet high that extended as far as I could see in both directions.

To make their bunker mentality even more bunkerish,

they had constructed four over-lapping barriers across the road in front of the gate, two on the left and two on the right so when anyone drove up to the gate, they had to weave through these things like a skier navigating a slalom course. As I hadn't driven off the airfield in over a year, this was all new to me and it looked like there wasn't much space between those barriers. From where I was sitting a little way up the road it looked like weaving around those barriers would be a tight for a car and I had this big produce truck.

By my estimates, the demonstration had been going on for about three hours now and the air field authorities were losing what little patience they had. When I saw them bring out the fire hoses, a dumb and totally unnecessary move in my opinion, I called my guys on the wall and told them where I was and that I would stay put until they gave me the go ahead that the coast was clear.

Just seconds later my phone rang. "Okay, you can come in now."

"Now? Are you sure? There are still people around the gate."

But they insisted, "No! No! It's okay. You can come in now."

That was when it should have dawned on me that we weren't thinking on the same wavelength. I had it in my mind that once they had dispersed the crowd, I'd slowly drive up to the barriers and carefully try to weave my way through them. They, however, were thinking I should approach the gates at speed and any protesters who got in my way they'd knock down with the water cannon.

They're the boss, I guess. Driving out of my parking spot, I headed for the gate just as a pressurized blast of water hit the mob knocking the closest ones flat and driving the rest back about twenty or thirty yards.

Now that I had my opening, I had no choice but to floor it as I headed for the opening gate. To my horror, I saw that the mob hadn't dispersed, but had just backed off from the water hoses. Fortunately, their attention was still on the hoses and no one in the crowd had noticed my big truck until I was almost to the barriers.

I was just starting to slow down to make my weave around the first barrier when one of the jets of water that was keeping the crowd back hit me right in the windshield. Instantly blinded I twisted the wheel to the right, hit the brakes and turned on the windshield wipers all at the same time. When I could see again, I was too close to the first barrier and going too fast. The mob had noticed me now so I couldn't stop. I also couldn't turn around.

I slid sideways into the first barrier. Then just as I was scraping the side of the truck around that barrier and was looking at the second one right in front of me, the water hit me again. I twisted the wheel to the left and the truck bounced sideways into the second barrier. When I could see again, there was a wall directly in front of me and a barrier to my right. Cranking the wheel back to the right, I bounced the left side of the truck into the third barrier, went around it and proceeded banging into the wall on my right. There were four barriers in all and with the help of my friends with the hoses, I hit every single one.

Once I managed to get my now mangled truck through the gate, I stopped. It was only a few hundred yards to the VU area, but I was shaking so badly, I didn't think I would make it. Climbing out of the cab, I sat down on the running board. The guards crowded around laughing and patting me on the back as if we had just accomplished some incredible feat.

"Thanks a lot, guys!" I scolded. "And don't you ever let me do that again."

My rebuke only made them laugh harder. As they drifted away chattering about the crazy man in the produce truck, it was like the *rocket incident* all over again. It wasn't my fault, but my name would be forever linked to this episode as well.

At least I got a huge welcome when I drove into the Voyager area. It seemed that everyone wanted to pat me on the back and shake my hand. If they only knew!

Well, everyone except Pedro congratulated me. He was the one who was going to have to repair the truck. I prudently made myself scarce when I saw him coming.

Alex was so mercurial about my *produce incident*. I wasn't sure if she was going to kiss me or slug me. Fortunately, she went for the kiss, but I determined that at the first opportunity I was going back up to Voyager. In orbit, I only had to contend with space and maybe Sam trying to kill me.

To end the day on a high note, I told Alex about the smitten Brian and Kevin. And naturally, just when I thought I had a juicy piece of gossip for Alex, she already knew about it. Of course, she did; Alex knows everything.

CHAPTER 16

Personally, I thought it would be a disaster when Visions Unlimited hired two different companies, one in Italy and the other in the United States, to build the Cryogenic Cylinders, but as it turned out, both companies sent Alex essentially the same production plan: the manufacturers would build the cylinders complete with all the internal fittings and connections that were required. In my opinion, that was fantastic and we were thrilled that our continued requests for big sections to be assembled in space were being heard.

But for every problem we solved, more seemed to arise. In the case of the cryogenic cylinders the first problem was that the three-hundred-foot-long, fifty-foot diameter tube that was being manufactured in Milan, Italy was too large to ship from the factory in Italy to a rocket launching base in the United States in anything except a big ocean going vessel and then by a really, really big truck to get it from the port to the launch site and the way the world was going, or had already gone, that wasn't going to happen. For the cryo cylinder that was being built in Italy, we had to deal with the worsening weather conditions in the Mediterranean Sea and the Atlantic Ocean *plus* the problems with the port handling facilities in both countries that may, or may not, still exist on the coasts of both Italy and the United States.

Despite all evidence to the contrary, no matter what the problem was, our government refused to acknowledge reality and continued to say that everything shipping wise was fine and dandy. Fake News and all that, designed to make the administration look bad. But eventually reality always wins and the reality was that as ships were sinking at sea and sea ports were sitting in tide water, things were neither fine nor dandy.

Deciding that ocean transport was out, the Italians were going to ship the Cryogenic Cylinders to the rocket facilities by air.

Which naturally came with its own host of problems, namely that there wasn't a cargo aircraft in the world that could accommodate a three-hundred foot metal cylinder so the Italian plant sliced their cylinder like a loaf of bread into twenty-five sections but the available airlines said, "so sorry— still to big." A full section of one of our cylinders, fifty feet across, was too big around. To make them fit, the plant cut their twenty-five slices in half again... right down the middle. Instead of twenty-five sections, Milan was now slicing and dicing our Cryogenics Section into fifty pieces.

Disappointing, but we could live with it.

Then the American shoe dropped. The San Diego plant

said they couldn't trust the roads any longer, so everything they built was going to be flown directly to the rocket bases to be lifted up to us. And surprise, surprise, San Diego's sections wouldn't fit in a cargo aircraft, either, so just to be on the safe side, they were also cutting their loaf in half.

Brilliant. Now we were going to get a hundred half sections from two different companies in two different countries on two different continents. Since we could practically guarantee they wouldn't be labeled or shipped in order, putting it together was going to be like assembling two giant three dimensional puzzles consisting of a hundred identical pieces in zero gravity.

And just to make life more interesting, we only had one three-hundred-foot-long space dock. Life was certainly not going to be dull in orbit.

Turns out, life certainly wasn't boring on the ground either when a tornado wiped out Rocket 2 leaving us with only Rocket 1 in Big Spring, Texas and Rocket 3 just outside of Tucson, Arizona available to send us the pieces. We couldn't wait to see how all that was going to work out.

Six months to the day after our life altering meeting with the Visions Unlimited Board of Directors that turned us from construction workers to colonists, Alex received a call from Milan that the Italian factory was ready to ship their first sections. Alex passed the word on to us and ten days later Rocket 1 sent up six of the half sections.

And low and behold, just as we expected, none of those pieces fit together. There wasn't a complete arch and not one of the half sections fit side to side.

So, we were still nowhere. All we could do was separate them into left and right sections and stow them in the space dock while we waited for more. A couple of days later, we got six more sections from Milan only to discover that matching up the half sections wasn't going to be fast or efficient. Our giant puzzle had fifty identical and unmarked pieces and the only way we could build it was through trial and error... lots of trial and even more error. The only good news was that we knew that they all went to the same cylinder. I would drive Sam to a half section, clamp onto it and then go to each of the other half sections in turn until I found a match, either side by side or to make a full round. With half a dozen other RJs doing the same thing with their construction robots, the work was slow, tedious and we kept getting into each other's way.

Despite the tragedy of losing Rocket 2, San Diego really came through by shipping six half sections to the launch site we called Rocket 3 that was located at an old Air Force Base just outside of Tucson, Arizona not four hundred miles away from their plant. Bless their corporate hearts, these pieces were all marked and appropriately labeled *and* fit nicely together giving us three full sections.

After that, we kind of expected big things out of the San Diego plant. They had built the cryogenic section and the individual pods for the original Voyager, so we figured that they had experience anyway. The bad news was that, although San Diego was fairly close to Rocket 3, Interstates 8 and 10 ran right along or close to the Mexican border and half of the highway incidents of hi-jacking, shootings and the like that were being reported in the country happened along the Mexican border. So, as long as the airlift held up, most of our future shipments from San Diego were still going to be flown to Rocket 3. Whatever! *Not my problem,* I thought. I just put 'em together.

And we, Project Voyager, were not alone.

Putting it bluntly, space was getting to be a premium commodity. With the world's environment going deeper and deeper into the crapper, Visions Unlimited wasn't the only company building spaceships or building habitats to live in space—or the moon or Mars. With all this frantic activity going on, it was starting to get down right crowded up here.

With so many companies building in space and only so many rockets available, rocket lift was becoming a limiting factor. But Alex had a plan. Ha! Alex always has a plan. She had VU buy Rocket 1 outright.

She'd been shipping the smaller items up to us on the Stardusters, but now was making a tidy profit by renting out the shuttles lift capabilities to other companies—two of them right at Sand Flea. I started to worry that our bits and pieces might get stuck in the queue at Sand Flea or some rocket base, but then decided that problem was for somebody else to develop an ulcer over. My job was to put together the pieces we did receive.

And so far, so good. For now, all we had to contend with was not mixing up the Italian with the American pieces which we did by putting them in opposite ends of our space dock. Eventually, we'd have to figure out what we were going to do when we had more pieces than our dock could hold, two three-hundred-foot cylinders in one three-hundred-foot space dock. But, at the moment we had another more immediate problem: Sam and her sisters.

The Ajax construction robots (that hadn't been all that well engineered to begin with) were getting worn out. Right from the beginning we'd had maintenance problems particularly with the solar drive and the mechanical arms. Even after we built R3, most of our repairs had been of the "remove and replace" variety. If a robot's arm had a bad joint, we would replace the whole arm—like during my frozen grease chipping experience when I first arrived up in space when I replaced all four of Sam's arms.

Because Sam is a unique piece of machinery and I couldn't just go over to Home Depot and buy new parts, Alex had negotiated a big contract with Ajax to keep us supplied with spares and as much as we didn't like working with Ajax, the one thing we didn't anticipate was that one day Ajax wouldn't be there for us to hate anymore.

Due to the increase in space construction, Ajax was doing their own booming business manufacturing space construction robots and selling them to several companies all over the world. Tragedy struck for all of us when the second EF5+ tornado to hit the Chicago area in three years not only took out the Ajax robotics facility, but also the spare parts storage warehouse that we all depended on to keep all the existing construction robots operational. In a matter of minutes, Ajax Industries had been obliterated. Though they planned to rebuild, it would be years before they'd be up and running again.

Alex had to scramble, along with everyone else who was now in the space construction business, to find other machine shops who were willing to re-tool to our special needs. She succeeded, but it sure wasn't easy. There were a couple of first-class engineering companies right here on Sand Flea Airfield, but they were either too busy with existing contracts or weren't willing to re-tool for what was really a small project. Alex then found a few relatively small machine shops around the country who were willing to build our stuff, especially for the money that Alex was offering; However, it seemed that as soon as one supplier was on line something would happen—weather, no supplies, no workers, fire, riot, some other company would offer more money—*something*. Alex would get everything all set up and the next thing she knew the company that she had been negotiating with would cancel the contract or be out of business, and Alex would have to go scrounging around for another machine shop all over again.

Up on Voyager, we did our part as best we could. While the robots had four arms, we decided that, so long as they had one working arm on each side, we were operational and could work short-handed—pun intended. I told Alex to buy all the spares she could and send them up... we'd find some place to put them. We even started saving broken pieces that maybe could be repaired.

R3 started to look like an indoor junkyard. Al took pleasure in reminding us that we didn't need all that junk because, once we arrived at Sanctuary, dismantled Voyager and moved everything down to the planet, there would be no more use for the construction robots. While he didn't say it, he was probably thinking there wouldn't be any more use for us pain-in-the-lower-regions robot jockeys either.

Well, I was thinking it, so why wouldn't he be as well? It was all probably true, but that was problem number 865 on the Not Today problem chart. Right now, all I could think about was fulfilling my end of our mission or there wouldn't be a Voyager to go to Sanctuary in the first place.

Looking at our handiwork as I helped Paul attach two of the San Diego sections together, I found it hard to believe it had been almost three years since Sam and I had first blasted up to Wisdom. I had to admit that I was getting tired working out in space every day. It was difficult trying to adjust my sleep/work schedule when I witnessed a dozen sunrises every twenty-four hours. At least, I could take breaks by hopping on a Starduster every once in a while, to go dirtside; However, that also meant I had to readjust to planet-side day and night *and* gravity every time. Still, that was where Alex was which made those annoyances easily ignored.

Thoughts of Alex made me feel better, but I think they made Sam jealous because she froze up on me... again. Fortunately, we were just finishing up, so Paul towed me into R3 and left me to my verbal robotic abuse while I tried to figure out what had caused Sam to quit this time.

I discovered it wasn't jealously.

The realization of what was wrong with my robot made my blood run as cold as if I'd just finished a spacewalk without my suit. Before I could fully wrap myself around my discovery, Al called and told me to come over to the weather pod because he wanted to show me something. I was never more grateful to have an excuse to get away from Sam, but Al knew something was wrong the moment I floated into his shop.

"Are you okay?" Al asked. "You look like you've just seen a ghost."

"I think I just did," I whispered. "Mine."

Giving me a water container, Al told me to take a deep drink before he asked me what I meant. Only when both my color and breathing had returned to some semblance of normal, did Al encourage me to continue.

"I was just out playing musical half sections with Paul

when Sam froze and Paul had to tow me in."

"That's nothing new," Al said cautiously while he studied my face for the cause of my alarm. "That happens all the time."

"That's true, but when I got her up on the rack and started looking her over, I found five holes, each one about the size of your thumbnail, right through the engine."

It was Al's turn to pale. "Wow! What caused that?"

"I don't know, Al, and that's what scares me. Some kind of space junk, I guess. The holes seem too neat to be a meteor, and five of them flying together?" I shook my head at how close I had come to death. "These things were going so fast that they went right through a solid metal casing and a motor and I never saw or felt anything. But the really scary thing is that if whatever it was that hit Sam had been a foot over, it would have gone right through the bubble and probably me."

"And Paul?" Al asked.

"Inside, he's OK" I answered, relieved that he was safe for the moment.

Stunned, Al and I just sat and looked at each other. I don't know about him, but I was thinking about the many ways space could kill you. In my attempt to shake off those unpleasant thoughts, I asked Al what it was that he wanted to show me.

Calling up a scope projection on his weather Vid, he said, "Take a look."

Wisdom was passing over the east coast of Africa. After all these months, Al had me pretty well educated on Earth's geography. "I think we're coming over Ethiopia, Somalia, Kenya... ," I said, "somewhere in that area, but I can't see the ground through the cloud cover."

"That cloud is what I wanted to show you."

"It does look kind of funny," I said, trying to catch onto what he was driving it at. "Is it some kind of weather phenomenon? It must be thousands of miles across, kind of grey and... weird! It just stops at the coasts. It doesn't go out to sea!"

Al nodded, his expression grim. "It's not a cloud. What you are looking at is doomsday. That, my friend, is a swarm of several billion locusts. These things are going to devour everything that grows from Central Africa to the coast of the Indian Ocean and from the source of the Nile north to Southern Egypt.

I was stunned as Al punched up more videos. One showed another swirling cloud of locusts further south over Madagascar while the next locust swarm he showed me covered all of Central South America.

"What does it mean?" I asked.

"It means, John, that within the next month or so, half a billion human beings are going to starve. As the planet becomes hotter and wetter, insects like these locusts, are going to keep multiplying into unimaginable numbers. As they increase, they are going to devour every source of food in their path."

"Can we do something about them?"

Al scoffed. "Not a chance! Humans have been fighting plagues of locusts for thousands of years and haven't won yet. And just imagine a swarm so large we can see it from space! No, my friend, what we're looking at is the beginning of a global famine. With the decline of food from the oceans, mankind is going to be in a fight for survival with the insects for anything that grows on land."

I couldn't wrap my mind around it. "Who's going to win?"

Al shrugged. "Well, the insects certainly have the numbers, but humans are pretty smart when we want to be. Plus, we have the birds and the lizards and other insect eating critters, so I don't think we will lose..."

"But?" I asked when Al trailed off.

"But it's going to be a different world. In this greenhouse world, there's going to be far fewer people.

"Do you really think so?"

"Absolutely. Mankind has fought wars with locusts for centuries. Basically, they're just grasshoppers, but when the conditions are right and their numbers increase, they undergo a metamorphose and change into locusts... a flying pestilence that will devour every scrap of food available until there is nothing for either species left to eat. You know this as well as I; It's why you were so quick to grab at the chance of a ride on Voyager."

I didn't like to admit it, but Al was right; Everything he said was true. The temperature had been going up for decades whether the vested interests and politicians wanted to admit or not. The oceans were changing—they were much warmer, more acidic. Many fish, bird and mammal populations that had once thrived in temperate climates couldn't adapt fast enough to keep up with the changes and had already died out. On the other hand, on land, insects in their billions could rapidly adapt and their populations were exploding.

Humans were a grey area. While I didn't know the exact numbers, what I knew from the Vid and what I'd witnessed from up here, hundreds of millions of people had already died in the last few years due to thirst, starvation, weather or conflict of one kind or another. A few years ago, the world population was over eight billion. What it was today I could only guess—maybe two-thirds of that. Maybe even less.

Al wasn't making me feel any better and, seeing as I probably wasn't going to get any sleep now I thought I might as well go out and work on Sam. I briefly wondered if I actually wanted to repair Sam and go back out into space only to be a target all over again, but then I rationalized that R3, Voyager or even Wisdom could be hit.

Since Sam was a smaller target, I went back to work

A couple of days later Alex called and said that she had good news. Good! I always like good news and I could use some right about now.

"Link made it to Rocket 1," she told me excitedly.

Individually I understood all those words, but put together in a sentence—nothing. Feeling like I hadn't studied for an important test, I said, "What's Link doing at Rocket 1?"

"He's got the Supply Cylinder."

As usual, I was lost. "Luv, what the hell are you talking about?"

"John, what's the matter with you? I'm talking about Link's trip up north to pick up the Supply Cylinder."

"We have a Supply Cylinder? That's great."

"John! Are you putting me on?"

"Luv, I think it's great that we have a Supply Cylinder where ever it came from, but I swear up until two minutes ago, I knew nothing about it. How big is it? How is it going to come up? When is it going to come up?"

"I can't believe you didn't know about our Supply

Cylinder. It's been in the works for months."

"So, give. Tell me the story," I said while privately swearing that, even if it turned out that I had been told, I wasn't going to admit it… ever.

"Well—are you sure you that didn't know that we had a Supply Cylinder?"

"Luv, all I remember about the possibility of a Supply Cylinder was that in the big LA meeting Director Johnson or Johnstone, whatever his name was, was talking to you about it."

"That's right! Well, it's Johnstone, Director Robert Johnstone, and he came through. He arranged for VU to buy just the fuselage of a big cargo plane and when I was notified that we had it, it was already cut into four sections, loaded onto four flatbed trailers and waiting for us to come and pick it up."

"Wow! Where was it?"

"Some big aircraft manufacturing plant north of Seattle."

"And Link got tapped for the job?"

"Yup! He pulled out of here the day we had Gutman's engine test."

"That I remember. I saw a bunch of cars and Humvees heading out the gate and with one thing and another I forgot to ask."

"Well, that was Link."

"Wait. What about the earthquake?" I remembered that the long-awaited Pacific Northwest earthquake had finally happened a couple of weeks ago.

"He was right in the middle of it. Apparently, and fortunately, neither Link, his people nor the vehicles suffered any harm."

"So, what's the story? I want some details!"

"You've got to be kidding... details from Link the stoic? But maybe we'll get lucky. I told him to keep a log, so maybe we'll learn a little more when he gets back, but don't hold your breath."

Nuts!

I wanted info. Well, whatever. At least we had a complete Supply Cylinder and if the heavy-lift rockets could get them up to us, we would only have four pieces to put together. I couldn't wait to tell the guys.

Of course, they already knew. How is it that I'm the one married to the project manager and I'm still the last one to know these things?

Four days later the first section of the Supply Cylinder came up and we attached it to the top of Voyager. The cryogenic cylinders were still coming up in little puzzle pieces, so the plan was to get them completely assembled and then attach the whole three-hundred-foot cylinder to Voyager.

Not so with the Supply Cylinder! The four sections went onto to Voyager as fast as they came up and before I rotated down to Sand Flea after my eight weeks, the completed supply cylinder was fully attached to the top of Voyager.

We hadn't completely neglected the two cryos, but we concentrated on supply. With the maintenance situation with the robots being what it was, we tried to keep six working on supply and whatever was leftover went to sorting puzzle pieces.

It wasn't really as bad as it sounded. Out of our eleven robots, we usually had eight or nine operational and although the two cryogenic cylinders looked like two separate collections of space junk at each end of the dock, there was method to our madness and the cryo cylinders were actually getting put together.

CHAPTER 17

When my turn finally came for my week dirtside, I was beat, worn out and just plain tired. I slept all the way down, hit the ground, kissed my sweetie and went to bed for a day and a half. Once I was fully rested, Doc Watson (John) tuckered me out all over again as he tested, poked, prodded and probed me for the better part of a day. He found holes that I didn't even know I had. His conclusion: I was tired. I kind of could have told him that, but after another good night's sleep, I finally felt a lot more human. Being with Alex sure didn't hurt.

To make Chet happy I spent some time on the rifle range and to make Phil happy I poked around the Stardust simulator. But most of my time I spent just sitting in one of the comfy chairs in Alex's office dozing on and off and listening to her conducting Voyager, Wisdom and Starduster business. It was a mystery to me how she could remember all that stuff.

Our evenings were usually spent at one of the tables in the cafeteria just talking with whomever happened to pass by. That's how everyone engaged in the various VU projects kept up on current events and probably why I, being three hundred miles straight up, was the last to know anything. Alex actually conducted a lot of business there.

While we were chatting, I suddenly remembered that I wanted talk to Link about his mission to fetch the Supply Cylinder and where was Link anyway?

Everyone smiled and Alex proceeded to tell me another story that everybody else knew. "Link and his posse of armored hummers have been dispatched to San Diego. After he returned from his northern adventure, Director Simmons called us with a problem. His San Diego plant was producing the Cryogenic Cylinder sections and individual pods, but they were having increasing problems transporting the finished products to Tucson and Rocket 3. The air freight company that he had been dealing with was going out of business, the railroad tracks were continually being torn up by the storms, and as a result, the trains weren't running. The only alternative was the Interstates. Simmons had the trucks, but due to the security situation, he couldn't get drivers."

"Ah," I smiled, "and you had Link take care of it. Well, he's doing a great job because the sections and pods have been coming up regularly. I didn't even know there was a problem. But, darn I really did want to talk to him about the trip to get the Supply Cylinder."

A little later after everyone had drifted away, Alex took my hand and said, "Come with me, my sweet, and I'll read you a story."

Leading me to her office, Alex took out a ledger from

one of her desk drawers and we sat down in the comfy chairs. "What have you got there?" I asked.

"This is Link's log book."

"You got him to write a log?" I scoffed. "Will the miracles of the universe never end?"

Alex grinned along with me. "You forget that, although Link doesn't talk much, he is a policeman and policemen write reports." She waved the ledger and smiled. "Before he left, I told him that I wanted a report, so sit back and listen."

Link's Log

Day 1. *Didn't get away from Sand Flea until 1330 due to all the dignitaries that were present for the engine tests. Got on the east/west road heading west, went only 33.5 miles when we hit a backup of cars which stretched ahead for as far as I could see. Couldn't raise anyone on the radio, but I could see a highway patrol car a little way ahead, so I walked up. Had a nice chat with a nice young fellow. Told me that the problem was that about 10 miles further ahead all four lanes of the highway had washed out. Department of transportation was working on it, but it was going to be several days before the road would be fully open again. In the meantime, they were bulldozing a single lane temporary road for one-way traffic which should be finished today or tomorrow.*

Walked back to the vehicles. There was no chance of turning around and going back to Sand Flea because there were now cars backed behind us for as far as I could see. Spent the night in the vehicles.

Day 2. *They started letting cars through this morning—about 20 cars at a time in alternate directions. Finally got* through at about 1500. Drove the last few miles to Tehachapi and called it a day. Decided to put a guard on the vehicles and a good thing, too. During the night, a couple of punks tried to break into one of the police cars, but when they saw us, they ran like scared rabbits. Decided that I would have a guard on the vehicles every night.

Day 3. Got a good start about 0800. Headed towards Bakersfield. No problems until we got to the outskirts where we heard police calls reporting that shots had been fired on the east/west road. By the police calls I couldn't tell exactly where the activity was happening. Called the highway patrol and asked them what the situation was. We were told that the incident was over and at the moment there was nothing happening right on the road and if we were going on through, we should be okay. Displayed the weapons anyway. Through Bakersfield about 1400. No problems.

Heading west from Bakersfield and looking out over the countryside, there was something wrong and I couldn't put my finger on it. Finally, one of the guys who had been a CHP deputy around here said there weren't any cows. There are dozens of feedlots along this stretch of highway and there should be thousands of cattle feeding in the stock holding pens just west of Bakersfield. He was right. All of the pens between Bakersfield and Interstate-5 were empty. Not a cow in sight.

Came up on the I-5 and not knowing what the gas and motel situation was further north and although it was still early, when we got to Interstate-5, I decided to stop for the night. Good facilities and we gassed up all the vehicles. Haven't had to use any of our gas yet.

Day 4. North on I-5. Hardly any traffic. Talked to highway patrol and they reported that the road was clear all the way to just south of Sacramento, but they said we might want to hold there because the rivers had flooded and merged around Sacramento and I-5 was closed.

I asked them if there was a good alternate route and they didn't have one. Stockton about 1700. Three tries before we found a motel that was still open. Sat for a day and a half just north of Stockton waiting for the water to clear.

Day 6. About 1000 got an all clear from the California Highway Patrol and we headed out and were north of Sacramento by noontime. We had clear sailing up to Redding, but we could see the glow of forest fires up ahead to the north, east and west. Wanted to talk with CHP before we went any further north. Luckily, we found an open motel and spent the night just north of Redding. A little after midnight a car load of punks drove into the motel parking lot, but after one look at our two well-armed deputies they turned around and headed out.

Day 7. After talking to CHP headed north again on I-5. CHP said that I-5 was clear but we could still see the fires north and east of us. Midafternoon got a fire caution from the highway patrol, so we didn't go farther than Weed.

Day 8. While we were having breakfast, I talked to Oregon State Police and they said that there was a big fire burning right around Siskiyou Summit. Planned to lay over a day in Weed.

Day 9. Woke up around 0400. Motel manager was running up and down the halls getting everyone up. Wind had shifted and was pushing the fire right into the eastern outskirts of Weed. Got everyone up and out of the motel and into the vehicles. Headed out of the west side of Weed and back onto the I-5 just as the fire began burning into town on the east side of Weed.

Headed north on I-5. No fires visible, but we could see some burned areas. Went over Siskiyou Summit a little after noon. Weather turned. Cold. Sleeting rain. We could see where the fire had been. Both sides of the road had been burned. Temperature dropped. It started snowing and the road immediately iced up.

Pulled over to chain up the vehicles. Got back on the road, but we couldn't move due to stalled traffic. Everybody was inching along and soon a few cars started to run out of gas. So, we filled up our jerry cans and started gassing everyone up. Made a lot of points that day. Night came and we were still not off the mountain. Stayed in the vehicles overnight. Cold.

Alex stopped and said, "I don't know if Link knows how many points he got. It was all over the Vid. Link and the deputies walking up and down the rows of cars gassing everyone up. The Vid reporters started calling them the Siskiyou Hero's or the Siskiyou Saints. They were gone before anyone really knew who they were."

"You know, I saw that on the Vid, but I didn't think anything about it. So that was Link and our guys."

Alex said, "Yup!" and went on.

Day 10. *As soon as the Highway Patrol opened up the highway, we started inching our way off the mountain. When we got to Medford, we unchained and had clear roads all the way to Salem. Called the Highway Patrol and they cautioned that due to the gang activity and food riots, it was not a good idea to use the Interstate through Portland, but to take the ring road around to the east. Which we did.*

Slow going with heavy traffic. No problems crossing the Columbia as the bridges were still up.

We got into Washington, but were stopped by the

Washington State Patrol who had closed the I-5 south of Chehalis due to flooding. I thought about taking an alternate route up around Mt. Rainier, but decided against it. We found a motel and waited two days for the floods to subside in Napavine just south of Chehalis.

Day 13. Got an all clear from the Washington State Patrol and headed out at 0800. Took us all day to get just past Tacoma and not quite up into Seattle due to highway construction, flooding and traffic. State Patrol cautioned against going through Seattle. Took ring road, I-405. We stayed the night just off the I-405. Not sure if we were in Renton or Tukwila.

Day 14. We were on the road at 0800, but with the traffic, it took us until early afternoon to get to the Boeing plant in Everett.

So, let me recap: It's taken us two weeks to drive from Sand Flea, California to Everett, Washington. Ten years ago, I did it in two DAYS!

There was some confusion at the Boeing gate when we showed up with our convoy of two Humvees, two California Highway Patrol cars and our fuel truck. But we finally got hold of the right guy and were let in where we proceeded to drive around the largest building I have ever seen. They drove us out to a huge apron on the airfield side of this huge aircraft manufacturing building and there were our four flatbed trailers all loaded up and ready to go. There were even four drivers! I thought we were going to have to drive them ourselves, but they were not only waiting for us, but were also ready to go.

Being it was now midafternoon, I decided to rest overnight and head out early the next morning. We left all the vehicles sitting on the apron. I figured that they were as secure there as anywhere else and just took one hummer and one patrol car to find a motel. As we drove off, I looked back at our convoy and realized we were going to stretch out for close to half a mile once we got out onto the road. For starters, I plan to go: police cruiser, flat bed, flat bed, hummer, gas truck, hummer, flat bed, flat bed, police cruiser.

Day 15. I was shaken out of bed at about 0400. Groggy from sleep and having never been in an earthquake before, it took me a moment to figure out what was happening. I managed to stuff my feet into my shoes and grab my jeans and a shirt as I ran outside to avoid the falling debris inside only to dodge the falling debris outside. The shaking lasted a full two minutes, but we all got out of the motel okay. Once it all stopped, I was amazed that the motel was still standing. It was then that I realized that it was cold and raining. I took a chance and went back into my room for the rest of my clothes and a coat.

Two of my deputies were qualified para-medics and all the rest had some medical training so we stayed at the motel and helped out as best we could for the next couple of days. Our paras set up a makeshift dispensary in one of the hummers. Called Boeing, vehicles reported to be OK. Spent the next couple of days helping out where we could, mostly search and rescue and traffic control. Got a big atta-boy from WSP.

Day 17. Talked to Highway Patrol and decided there wasn't anything more we could do with the earthquake relief. Drove back over to Boeing and checked out our vehicles. Fortunately, they were parked on the far side of the apron away from the buildings and away from the big aircraft construction hanger, so they had survived without any damage. The big building itself was not so lucky. One end was partially collapsed and I could see that at least one of the huge hangar doors was twisted. Apparently the tsunami that swept up the Strait of Juan de Fuca didn't reach to Boeing. Had a long talk with the highway patrol. With all of our large vehicles, would it be possible to go back through Seattle? That answer was a definite no. The earthquake had crumbled several of the old brick buildings onto the roads and an overpass had collapsed onto the I-5. No one was going through Seattle for a long time.

BUT the Space Needle was still standing!

I asked about the ring road that we had come up on through Belleview. No good, several bridges had collapsed onto the roadway. In WHP's opinion our best option would be to take Highway 2 east and over the Cascades. I was concerned that with our long convoy we'd block up the roads, but the patrol said it was probably our only option and to do it anyway.

We hit the road around 1100. Route 2 is mostly a two-lane road that goes over Stevens Pass. Checked with WHP weather. It was snowing in the passes, so we had to stop and chain up. Four flat-bed semi-trailer trucks, two Humvees, a fuel truck and two police cars, chaining up took about an hour. We drove on and then discovered that the earthquake had triggered a couple of avalanches. In a stroke of rare good fortune, work crews were already working on it and that only delayed us a couple of hours. We made it all the way to Wenatchee and stayed the night. No gas. Had to dip into our fuel truck.

Day 18. Good start. On the road by 0830. Kept heading south and joined up with Interstate-90. With this big convoy, I wanted to stay on the Interstates as much as possible. Rolled through eastern Washington and Idaho with no problems, but had to stop in Montana to chain up again. Heavy snow and we finally stopped in Missoula. Around 0200 guards chased off some would be vehicle prowlers.

Day 19. *0800. Good start. Snow was drifting on the shoulders, but the roads were clear. Made good time to Billings. We turned south staying on Route 90. About midafternoon, the snow started. Again. It kept getting heavier and heavier and was soon a blizzard. Got just over the border into Wyoming. I finally found a truck stop that was still operational, they even had gas, and enough room where I could park all the vehicles. It was snowing hard. I got all the guys inside and didn't even think about leaving a guard outside in a howling blizzard.*

Day 20. *0700. It was still snowing and blowing hard with three or four feet on the ground with eight to ten-foot drifts. We weren't going anywhere today or maybe for a few days. Sent a couple of the guys out to check the vehicles. When they came back, I was shocked when they told me that one of the police cars was gone. I couldn't believe it. I'll never know how someone got into it, started it up and drove off during a blizzard. If I ever caught him, I don't know if I would kill him or hire him. The blizzard kept us trapped for the rest of the day.*

Day 21. *The blizzard quit during the night and the plows got the roads cleared during the morning. We finally got under way around noon. It was a clear day and we didn't have any problems—in fact I don't think we saw more than a half dozen cars all day. Turned off the I-90 onto I-25 at Buffalo. It was midafternoon when we got to Casper, but seeing as the weather was decent, I decided to push on and we made Douglas.*

Day 22. *On the road at 0800; Clear and cold. Crossed into Colorado well before noon. Stopped for lunch around Fort Collins and contacted the Colorado State Police who advised me not to drive through Denver with our big convoy during the daytime due to traffic and that there was a danger of gang activity at night. They told me if I stopped at Lafayette and* waited until midnight, they'd give me a police escort to the other side of Denver. I couldn't pass that up!

Day 23. Right on time, the Colorado State Police showed up and we zipped right through Denver. We didn't usually drive at night, but we were already on the road so I decided to keep going. We went through Colorado Springs, Pueblo and Trinidad and crossed into New Mexico before the sun came up.

We stopped in Raton for a long leisurely breakfast where it started snowing... again. This left me with a dilemma on whether to stay on the Interstate or risk a smaller road in a snow storm. The I-25 was a much better road, but it would take us to Albuquerque and out of our way. I decided to risk State Route 87 which went in the direction we needed to go. It worked out okay. It was slow with the snow, but we kept on going.

Took the SR 87 into Texas and all the way to Amarillo. After such a long night and day, I stopped for the night planning to arrive in Big Spring the next day.

Day 24. We didn't make it. We were advised by the Texas Rangers there was a big grass fire just south of Lubbock. Seriously—a snow storm AND a grass fire!

Day 25. We got on the road around 0800, drove through the burned-out area and made it to Big Spring around 1400.

We turned over our four flat-bed trucks to Roberson Rockets, spent the night in Big Spring and with our two Humvees, our patrol car and our tanker and two new recruits for Voyager. Two of our Boeing drivers were married and were heading home but the other two, after listening to us for a couple of weeks, decided that they would throw in with us. I headed back to Sand Flea.

Day 26. Thought briefly about heading south on the I-20

to the I-10 to avoid the snow but would probably mean going through El Paso. A quick look at the Vid convinced me that that was a bad idea. The Vid was showing open warfare all along the border at El Paso with thousands of migrants pouring into the United States. Don't know where they thought they were going, every farm, ranch and town in southwest Texas was fortted up and armed. We'll stay on the Interstates going north and west and take a chance on the snow.

Day 27. Left Big Spring at 0800 and got stopped by a Texas Ranger roadblock just outside of Lubbock. Took some explaining, but I finally convinced them that we were all deputies from California and our armed convoy was on legitimate business. Couldn't blame them for being twitchy. Rangers are sitting on a Texas-sized powder keg that is going to blow. Took the I-27 to Amarillo and west onto the I-40 a little after noon. Started snowing. Made it almost to Albuquerque. Tried three motels before we found one that was still open. Three hundred bucks a room and no coffee. Another night time attempt on the vehicles. Deputies fired on. Returned fire killed one wounded two. None of our people hurt.

Day 28. Checked in with New Mexico State Police to report incident. No problem and got a road report. Interstates were about the only roads being plowed. Took a chance and didn't chain up. Little dodgy getting to the highway, but once we were back on the I- 40 we were OK. Slow going forty to forty-five miles an hour. Stopped at Flagstaff.

Day 29. On the road at 0800 and drove the rest of the way to Sand Flea. Had to wait until mob was cleared from the gate.

Alex finished and closed the ledger. We just looked at each other.

Wow!

CHAPTER 18

After that week on the ground, I got my second wind and felt great. Sam, with her brand-new motor was working just fine and the days started to fly by. The half sections were coming up from both Rockets 1 and 3 just about as fast as we could handle them and we were finishing segments large enough that we could start installing some of the individual pods. Hooking up the cryogenics for the pods required factory specialists, so we got the got the pods anchored down until those guys could make the trip into orbit. I bet they never expected that as a job perk when they got hired!

While we were putting the individual cryogenic pods in, Paul made a comment that brought us all up short. "We're working on these in zero gravity, but didn't Gutman say gravity would be restored when Voyager was in flight?"

"Yeah, that's what he said," I shrugged.

"So, what if someone needs to reach an upper pod on the trip?"

It was amazing how so simple a question could enact such a flurry of activity. After a globe spanning discussion between Alex at Sand Flea, Director Simmons in Los Angeles, a couple of his senior scientists in San Diego, a couple more scientists from the plants in Milan, Italy and a half dozen of us up here at Voyager, we decided to err on the side of caution. Since we believed Gutman's engines would carry us to Sanctuary, we also had to trust that the professor was right and that there would be gravity as we whizzed through space. We were given the go ahead and began construction on stairs and walkways to the upper tiers of individual pods.

Of course, it would have been better if that decision had been made while the cylinders were still in the factory, but we didn't tell them that. We just told them to send us the parts and some installation schematics and we'd get it done. We did, too, although it felt pretty weird building stairs when I was hanging upside down and backwards.

When my eight weeks were up were up, I was almost reluctant to go dirtside for a week... almost.

While I was waiting for the Starduster, I was floating at my favorite window in Wisdom where I could see it all. The original Voyager was complete and the Supply Cylinder—which was the first part of the expanded Voyager—had already been attached. When the Stardusters weren't doing anything else they were already bringing up supplies and equipment to be packed away for the trip to Sanctuary.

The Italian Job was about three-quarters finished and, now that Link and his merry men were on the case to ensure delivery to Rocket 3, the San Diego factory was catching up fast. My best guess was that, barring any delivery delays, we would be ready to attach the large Cryogenic Cylinders to Voyager in three or four months. We planned to attach them and provide a shirt sleeve environment inside before the cryogenic specialists went to work hooking up the individual pods.

R3 was still attached to Wisdom, but it would only be a couple days work to detach it and hook it up on the underside of Voyager. Wisdom was also still in one piece, but two of the five cylinders were packed with scientific instruments and cushioning material ready to be detached and mated up with Voyager. I am pretty proud of the cushioning material. Once we started packing up Wisdom's laboratories, we wanted to use any open space leftover for supplies, but the scientists were adamant that sharp or heavy objects would not be packed in the Wisdom Cylinders with their precious equipment. After a brief discussion, they were very happy with the brilliant "cushioning material" solution thought up by the even more brilliant robot jockey... John Marshal.

A few weeks ago, Alex had told me that she almost had a revolt on her hands when the ladies found out that, due to the bulk of certain products, Alex wasn't planning to include any toilet paper on the supply list. That's when I came up with my brilliant solution that kept both the ladies and the scientists happy. With a smile, I told her that TP wouldn't be a problem for us to pack.

Personally, I didn't know how far a couple hundred cases of toilet paper would go once we got to Sanctuary or even where we'd put it once we started unpacking Wisdom in orbit around our new home, but that was a bridge to cross in twenty years. Right now, Alex was happy, the ladies were happy and my scientists were happy. I did wonder what the ladies would have said if they knew what we normally used up here in space, but decided not to bring it up. For the moment, no one was unhappy with me and I wanted to enjoy it for as long as I could.

After returning to the ground, I spent a couple of days catching up on my usual routine of security requirements with Chet, my flight requirements with Phil and Doc's probing into orifices that I didn't even know I had. Once all the planet side people were happy with me once more, I was sitting in Alex's office catching up on dirtside events along with Chet, Dot and Phil when Alex took a Vid call. While we couldn't see the screen and were only privy to Alex's side of the conversation, what we did hear certainly got our attention.

"Good morning, Bill! And what is on your mind this fine day? You do… From Washington."

That got our attention!

"What are they looking at? Yes… Is it just you? No… Everyone… Okay…What? They were? Were they the same ones? Not sure… Okay, Bill. Thanks for the heads up. I owe you one… Right. Bye."

Alex didn't say anything for a minute or two, but just sat there with her hands steepled under her chin, her classic "don't bother me I'm thinking" pose. Then she kind of shook herself, looked out over her desk at four faces bursting with curiosity. With an apologetic smile she said, "Sorry, I was thinking."

"So, what gives, Luv?"

"I'm not sure," Alex frowned. "That was Bill Williamson. I don't know if any of you know him, but he's my counterpart at the Wendover Group across the runway. Good people; We get along. Anyway, this morning a team of eight people, three of them in uniform, who said that they were representing 'interested parties' in the administration flew into Sand Flea unannounced in a plane with Air Force markings. Without any warning they just turned up in his office and started asking questions."

Dot asked, "Questions about what?"

"Anything. Everything. They wanted to know what projects Wendover was engaged in and how far along they were. They also wanted to know if they had anything or were building anything in orbit around the Earth. Bill said that they were especially interested in the rocket launch pad that Wendover operates down to the south of the airfield. It seemed to Bill that they were just fishing for information, so he gave them the 'This is private enterprise and most of what we do is proprietary, but I'm cooperating routine' and sent them off on a tour. It was pretty clear to Bill that they were especially interested in the planned space colonies on the Moon and Mars."

"And he thinks that they will get around to us?" I asked.

"Without a doubt. Bill thinks they're going to hit everyone on Sand Flea and the worst part is he thought that he recognized a couple of them from the big engine test. That might be a problem for us when they see the new Voyager."

Phil said, "Don't show it to them. I will go and personally break all the Stardusters."

Alex laughed. "I appreciate the thought, Phil, but I don't think that would work. No, I've thought this could be a possibility and everything that we have here with the exception of the expanded Voyager, if anyone knows that its expanded, reinforces my monthly reports. We run a space tourist business and are still building a spaceship to send an exploratory mission to Mars."

Alex smiled at Dot who nodded, then Chet, Dot and Phil got up to leave. I started to follow when Alex waved me back to my chair. "Stay here, John. I have a special mission for you." Then she did some magical things with her many computers and her face was on every Vid screen in the complex and her voice on every speaker.

"Ladies and gentlemen, sorry to interrupt your morning, but a few minutes ago I was notified that we may have some nosy visitors. We want these visitors to leave here convinced that sending tourists up into near space in Stardusters is our primary occupation and if we are asked, yes VU still plans to send a survey team on Voyager to Mars to explore the possibility of establishing a colony. Please go about your normal work. If these people do show up in your work area be polite and answer any questions as honestly as you can, but there is no need to volunteer any additional information. Thank you. Have a good day."

Alex switched off the screen and sat back with her fingers steepled under her chin again. After a few minutes of quiet contemplation, she shrugged and gave me a smile. "Well, my sweet, my special mission for you is to be ready to dazzle any visitors that I send up to Voyager. I guess that's all we can do. We'll just have to wait and see how it all turns out."

"How do you keep nosy politicians from digging too deep?" I asked concerned, thinking of Gutman and his comment that the government always gets involved. Herr Professor was right again.

"Bafflegab, my sweet. We'll bore them with long briefings and Vid presentations. Phil can tie them up for a day and half looking at Stardusters and if they want to fly our home-made simulator and land on Mars, he can dazzle them even longer. Chet will show them all of our security arrangements—to the farthest corner of the airfield. And you should catch André and Cathy's presentation on how they are going to cook for the survey crew in low gravity."

"Sounds like a plan." I laughed, then I had a thought. "What about the kids? They wouldn't mean to, but they might say the wrong thing."

"They might, but they really don't know anything except Mars, but just to be on the safe side, Dot is taking them on a very long field trip up to Junction. We've had this planed for a long time and that head bob Dot gave me when she left here means that it's already underway. She'll bring them back when I say they've learned enough."

I shook my head in awe that she'd already had a plan in place for all this. "I've got to hand it to you, Luv. You seem to have covered all the bases."

"Well, we'll see. I do see one or two potential problems. Bill said that he thought he recognized a couple of them from the engine test."

"I didn't know for sure that we had any government people at the engine test."

"Neither did I, but who knows who some of the VU Directors may have invited? It could be awkward if someone who saw the original Voyager gets a look at the upgraded version. Even to someone as anti-science as the people in the present government with that rather large cylinder sitting on her back Voyager looks pretty large for just a survey mission."

Alex thought for a minute, shrugged and then went on, "We'll see what happens. They may not even want to go up, but if they do, I can't refuse them. What I want you to do is get on back up there and do what you can to get ready for a possible visit."

"Roger that, my lady."

Not only did I take the regular shuttle of space tourists up to Wisdom the very next day, I flew it simultaneously making me happy and Phil happy by filling yet another training square. Phil is right, though, you have to keep your hand in flying them. The Starduster may be advanced technology that puts VU way ahead of everyone else as far as near space travel goes, but they are not fun to fly. In my opinion, they have the aerodynamics of a brick. A brick that wants to fall out of the sky at the slightest provocation.

After I got back up to Wisdom and briefed the guys that we might have company and to remember that we were going to Mars to explore the possibility of establishing a colony living in the caverns, blah, blah, we just went back to work. There wasn't much else we could do. It would be kind of hard to hide the fact that Voyager now had a rather large growth on her back and that we were building a very large something, rather two separate somethings, in our space dock. Well, as Alex said we will see.

Nothing happened for the next two days and then Alex called and told us that the team had finally shown up in the Visions Unlimited area, or part of the team anyway. She said there were three military and two civilians, but had no idea where the rest of the team had gotten off to. For some reason they seemed particularly interested in the Stardusters. Then the next thing I heard was that the five civilians and the military jet just disappeared. Without a word they just took off and flew away. None of her contacts in the other companies knew where they were headed so she assumed that they went back to Washington.

But the three military guys *hadn't* left. I was out in the space dock in Sam working on one of the cryo cylinders when Alex called.

"Good evening, Madam Director," I said cheerfully. "And what can I do for you this fine evening?"

"And a good evening to you too, John," Alex said formally, though I was already clued in when she called me "John". "I have three military gentlemen in my office who we're going to send up to Wisdom for a visit tomorrow."

"Great! Always happy to show off our handiwork. Is there anything in particular that they are interested in and could I get their names?"

I could hear mumbling and Alex said, "A Colonel McPherson from the Pentagon, a Major Kennedy and a Major Rawls who say that they are computer experts on the White House Staff."

"Okay, boss. I don't know what we have that would interest computer people, the robots maybe, anyway we'll show them what we have."

"Thank you, John. Are Tony and Paul up?"

"Yes."

"Good. Have them take care of Major Rawls and Major Kennedy and I would appreciate it if you showed Colonel McPherson around personally."

"You got it, Boss."

When the Starduster docked the next day, the first one to float up into Wisdom was an Air Force Colonel and for a newbie to space, he was doing pretty good. A lot better than I did the first time I experienced weightlessness. He looked pretty fit for a Pentagon desk jockey, too. That suspicion was confirmed when I reached out to take his arm and guide him into Al's weather shop and I thought that I had grabbed an iron bar.

Paul and Tony guided the two Majors in and when everyone was anchored and not floating around, we gave them a few minutes to just look down at the awesome sight of Mother Earth.

Al had his presentations down pat. After he let his audience look for a few minutes he would start pointing out whatever obvious weather patterns were currently taking place, usually easy to spot events like hurricanes (there were two) and typhoons (three of them). Then Al would swing into his favorite subject Global Warming/Climate Change and how we humans were screwing up the earth.

The Colonel didn't say anything but the two Majors got all defensive and started arguing that Global Warming wasn't happening, it was all a hoax, fake news, etc. Al was loving it and started pulling out all kinds of data sheets, comparative videos and statistics. Of course, in a discussion with government flunkies committed to the idea that Climate Change wasn't happening, Al was doomed to lose; After all, all he had were facts. I looked over at the Colonel and nodded toward the hatch. He smiled and the two of us drifted out.

I took him to another window where he could see all of Voyager and the space dock. I gave him the standard Mars exploration spiel, but I could tell that he wasn't buying it. He didn't say much, but he asked me why we needed a bigger supply cylinder and what were we building in the space dock?

What could I do? I was sure that he already knew so I told him about the additional six hundred passengers. He didn't say anything, but just smiled.

There was nothing to do but press on and we went through the tube into Voyager. While he was very polite, attentive and asked intelligent questions, I couldn't shake the feeling that, not only did he know all the answers already, but he also knew something that I didn't.

He was wearing Command Pilots Wings so I wasn't surprised that he was interested in the Command Section with its dual controls for atmospheric flight and space flight. "Is Gutman's Drive going to work?"

"Yes, it is, sir," I said. "I'm afraid I don't know much about the physics of his engine, but every test indicated it will work perfectly."

McPherson didn't pursue the topic of the engines, but when we went back into the cryogenic section, he seemed to get really interested.

"How exactly do they work? Is there any risk?"

"Again, that's not my field, sir, but they've been rigorously tested. I'm not aware of any risks."

"I see. Do you know how long a person can stay in cryo-sleep?"

"To my knowledge, indefinitely as long as the pod is in good working order."

"And children? Could children survive in cryogenic stasis?"

What the hell?

I deflected that by telling him again that these questions were out of my line, but we did have experts around who could answer them. McPherson just smiled and said to never mind.

I took the Colonel back into Wisdom and out into R3 and he seemed to be really impressed with our little machine shop. Apparently, the tour had flipped his humor switch because he genuinely laughed when I told him about living there and he was absolutely fascinated by Sam. McPherson floated all around her and enjoyed it when I told him the grease story. And when I pointed to our pile of spare and broken robot arms, he just shook his head over that and the many other design flaws. He laughed again when he said that, in his opinion, we should never again deal with Ajax.

"Well, sir, that little problem has already been taken care of by an EF5 tornado."

He chuckled at that one.

Then we climbed into Sam and I flew him out into space. After we cleared R3, I just hovered and let him take in the various degrees of awesome.

Flying up to the bottom of space in a Starduster and experiencing weightlessness for the first time, that's awesome; Looking out Al's window and seeing all of Earth from space is beyond awesome. Sitting in a clear, plastic ball in space itself—well, awesome doesn't even begin to describe it.

I let McPherson have a good long look at the planet before we flew all around Voyager and the space dock.

I checked out his Command Pilots Wings and asked what he flew.

"Mostly heavies."

"Want to have a crack at Sam?" I smiled.

Oh, yeah, he wanted to! I showed him the controls and let him take over. He was a natural and flew around Wisdom like an experienced RJ. McPherson proved that his humor switch hadn't been turned off yet by giving the two Majors a scare when he floated Sam right up to the window they had their noses pressed against.

By now I am confused... I mean, more than usual. I couldn't help but like this guy even though I suspected that his purpose for being here was to shoot us down and turn us over to the Inquisition. On the other hand, I wasn't so sure. He already seemed to know a lot about us and after I had answered his questions, I was certain he knew everything... and I mean *everything*. I wondered if he knew about Sanctuary.

While I was wondering McPherson said quietly, "Mr. Marshal, let's just hover here for a moment."

"Sure, and by the way my name is John."

"Thank you. Alex."

"What?"

"Alex. My first name is Alexander, but Alex to my friends. And, yes, I did go through the Alex/Alex routine with your director."

"I bet she got a kick out of that," I laughed, "but to call you 'Alex' would be too confusing. If you don't mind, I'll stick to Colonel."

"You're on a first name basis with the director?"

"You might say that; She's my wife."

"Ah! I didn't know that. I will have to chastise Josh for not briefing me fully."

"Josh?"

"Josh Simmons."

That rang a few bells. I asked, "Josh Simmons, as in Dr. Joshua Simmons... the one that's on the Visions Unlimited

Board of Directors and is manufacturing half of this stuff?"

"The very same. Josh and I go way back. Before he got into cryogenics and became super rich, we built a couple of airfields together."

I took a minute or so to digest all that and said, "Well, Colonel, what can we do for you?"

He smiled. "First we can dispense with the cover story. It's pretty good, by the way, but I know all about Sanctuary. Secondly, I think it's more like what we can do for each other. I do want something, but for now let me tell you what I can do for you… what I have been doing for you."

That was both confusing and alarming.

McPherson explained, "To be blunt, the Pentagon and especially the regular Air Force doesn't want to be bothered by Moon Colonies or Mars exploration. They especially don't want to be bothered by nutty conspiracy theories about aliens or subversives or terrorists taking over our orbiting platforms, so they shuffled anything to do with space or space colonies off onto Space Force. It rolled downhill for a while until my boss dumped it on my desk. The uniforms are the same but I am in Space Force, used to be regular Air Force, but my office is in the Pentagon. For the last two years your Alex's reports and the reports of every other private company that has anything to do with space, have been coming to me and whenever the Administration or Congress asks a question, I'm the one who writes the answer or trots his little buns over to Capitol Hill or the White House and gives the briefing. They have already asked what you do here and to set your mind at ease, as far as Washington knows VU is a bunch of rich nut cases who think they can build a spaceship in space. They're much more interested in big outfits like Wendover and

Robertson."

I just shook my head. Here's a guy who had our backs and we never even knew it! "What about the two Majors and the civilian suits?"

"Don't worry about the Majors. Both are nothing more than Administration drones and are probably still trying to convince Dr. Wilson that what they can see happening isn't happening. The 'suits' as you call them are a different proposition. Hatchet men for the Vice President. True believers."

I was dazed. "Does Alex, my Alex, know any of this?"

"I don't think so," McPherson shook his head.

"Okay," I said, my mind racing ahead. "I'll take care of that. Now seeing as we owe you big time, what can we do for you?"

"John, my wife and I have a son and a daughter, a daughter-in-law and three grandchildren that we love dearly. If they want to take the chance on Sanctuary—a proposition I haven't even mentioned to them yet—I would like to give them an opportunity to get away from this mess that we have made of the Earth."

That was an easy promise. "No problem, Colonel. I could do that with a Vid call right now, but I think a better idea would be for me to ride back down to Sand Flea with you. I think you should tell Alex and maybe a couple of other people what you just told me."

Nodding his ascent, I commed Alex.

"Well, my sweet," she said, "and to what do I owe this call? You haven't lost the Colonel, have you?"

The Colonel and I laughed. "Not yet, Luv, but the Colonel is the reason I called. When's the next Starduster due up here?"

"On its way. Why?"

"We'll be on it. The Colonel has much to say and I suggest we let it wait until we get there." Turning to the Colonel, I asked, "What does your son do?"

"He's in the Army and my daughter-in-law is a nurse."

"Did you get that, Luv? Chet and one or both of the Docs should be there."

"Your daughter?"

"Dietitian."

This was just getting better and better! "And Cathy. Got it?"

"Got it. See you in a couple of hours."

That's my Alex! Cool as a summer's breeze and she didn't even ask why.

CHAPTER 19

Colonel McPherson and I talked for a little bit as I gave him a final tour around Voyager. We went back through the airlock into R3, put Sam in the rack and drifted over to Al's shop to wait for the shuttle. McPherson commed the Majors and told them that he had seen enough and was going down, but if they wanted more time, they could stay up overnight and come down tomorrow.

They were having the time of their lives flying around with Tony and Paul and answered with a very enthusiastic, "Oh, yessir, yessir, thank you very much, sir!"

The Colonel just shook his head and went back to talking with Al as they gazed down at the oceans and said, "My wife and I love seafood, but you just can't get it anymore. For a while seafood was available, scarce but available, but the prices seemed to climb every day until they were out of sight. Now you just can't find seafood, even shellfish, anywhere, at any price."

Give Al an opening on his subject and he was off, but his tone was far more muted with his new like-minded and sympathetic audience. "I know! We in the scientific community have been trying to tell people for years. The excessive carbon in the atmosphere not only warms the oceans, but the oceans can't absorb it. It kills the reefs which used to be the nursery for a quarter of all fish species. With too much carbon in the water baby shellfish can't form their shells; It turns the water acidic which also kills off many fish species. If this changing of the ocean's Ph. happened over a period of thousands of years, as it has historically done, most species would probably adapt, but it's all happening too fast. The sea creatures that form our food stocks can't change fast enough. When you add overfishing to all of that—there's no more seafood."

McPherson kind of nodded and gave that little smile of his, so I asked, "What about Washington, Colonel? Seems to me that I heard once that DC was built on some kind of swamp."

"It is, or it was. The southern part of the city was built on tidal marshlands. With the rising water levels, right now that area is flooded and we have tidewater all the way up to the Mall. Fort McNair has been abandoned, the Jefferson Memorial is only occasionally open and all the Japanese Cherry Trees are sitting in salt water and dying. On the other side of the river, the Pentagon side, they are fighting to keep Regan International Airport open with a sand bag wall and dozens of portable pumps, but if you ask me to put on my engineers' hat, I'd say that it was hopeless. Oh, and the subways quit running a couple of months ago."

"What about the Pentagon?"

McPherson shrugged. "So far so good. The east parking lots are unusable during a really high tide, but the real problem are the roads and highways on the west side of the Potomac. They are all just about always under water these days."

"Wow!" I said. "What about you? How do you get around or even get to work?"

"Come on, John!" he scoffed. "I'm an engineer and I didn't just fall off the turnip truck yesterday. When I got the Pentagon assignment, Joan and I only looked at houses out to the west and as far away as we could from DC and the Potomac. Found a nice one, too. While it's less than ten miles from work, it still takes me the better part of an hour to get there with the traffic. The only time I ever go into DC is when I'm sent over by my bosses to the Capital or the White House."

The Starduster showed up and the Colonel was in a quiet contemplative mood as we rode back down to Earth.

When the Stardusters are taxing, just like being in a commercial air liner, you can't see much out of the windows, but the Colonel noted the automatic security gate we passed through. As we came up to the hangar he said, "I meant to ask the ask the other day about the door and plastic arrangement for the hangars."

"Bugs," I answered. "Heat and Bugs. See that cloud? Nothing but bugs. It's probably 120 degrees out there right now, so we try as hard as we can to keep them out and the cool air in."

"Does it work?"

"Well, not completely, but it helps. To finish the job,

we have our Bug Brigade."

"Your what?" the Colonel asked and I pointed out the kids chasing down the few insects that managed to slip through the sheets of plastic.

"That's our pint-sized Bug Brigade. Everyone here at Sand Flea has a job and Alex gave the little kids the job of killing every bug in all six hangars. They take it seriously and are pretty good at it, too."

"What about the older kids?"

I couldn't help swell with pride as if they were my own. "They're all apprentices. They pick the trade they're interested in, carpenters, blacksmith, cooks, or whatever, and we put them in a training program. There are five up at Voyager learning to be robot jockeys. We have a big ceremony when a little kid graduates from the Bug Brigade to Apprentice."

McPherson smiled and kept looking around for bugs as we walked through the tube into Hangar 3 and laughed when I asked him if he saw any. I was looking around as well, saying hello to people I knew when I thought I caught a glimpse of a familiar face.

When I stopped to give a double take, McPherson asked, "Something the matter?"

"No, no. I just thought that I saw someone I knew." It left me with the feeling that I'd mossed something important again.

When we walked into Alex's office, I was surprised to see that it was empty as I expected Alex to have called in a few people to hear what the Colonel had to say. Alex got up from her desk and greeted the Colonel before nodding us toward the Conference Room.

Finally placing the face, I mentioned to Alex that I'd thought saw Brian Anders in Hangar 3 as we headed in.

"Yes, you probably did," she smiled slyly.

"What happened to his Nordic Sorceress?" I asked, miffed at being out of the loop yet again. "I thought his heart was with blond hair and blue eyes up at Junction."

Alex laughed. "Oh, Helen is here, too. She and Brian are very much together and they both say they want to go to Sanctuary."

"That's great! Now we not only have a blacksmith, but if we ever have cows, we will have a milkmaid."

"Kevin came back too."

"Don't tell me… with the girl."

"Yup! Turns out Olga's as big a nerd as Kevin is and she has joined the drone team."

"Hmm," I frowned. "Too bad. Junction could have used those drones."

"Oh, don't worry. Our Kevin is a bright boy. He trained a few of the local teenagers and left the drones up there."

"Well, good for him!" I exclaimed, happy again.

Alex laughed again and as we went into the Conference Room, I could see why her office had been empty: not only had she called in the whole staff, but it looked like a few extra people as well. The table was full except for the two empty chairs Alex waved us to before taking her place at the head of the table.

McPherson and I sat down and Alex said, "Ladies and gentlemen, I called this special staff meeting because I believe that the very distinguished looking Air Force gentleman at the other end of the table has information that we all need to hear, together. John, would you do the introductions please."

"Ladies and gentlemen," I said rising from my chair. After everything the Colonel had done for us, it felt rude not to. "It is my privilege to introduce Colonel Alexander McPherson. Although the uniforms are the same, Colonel McPherson is actually a member of the Space Force and as the name implies Space Force is charged with monitoring anything and everything that happens from the upper atmosphere to infinity. Colonel McPherson's current assignment is in the Pentagon in Washington and, before you hear what he has to say, let me tell you that he is the best friend that we never knew we had. Colonel."

I must have said that rather well because it sure got everyone's attention. McPherson started to get up, but Alex waved him down into his chair. Looking around the table, he gathered his thoughts before he began.

"Ladies and Gentlemen, as Mr. Marshal said my name is Alex McPherson. I am from the Pentagon and I am here to help you in any way I can. For your non-military people, when the inspector shows up and says 'We're here to help you' and the hapless inspectee responds 'We're glad to have you', well, those are probably the two oldest military lies in the world. But in this case, it's true. I am here to help you in any way I can."

McPherson was well used to briefing a crowd and paused a moment for his words to sink in. "If you wonder why that should be, let me tell you that Josh Simmons from the Visions Unlimited Board of Directors, and I go way back. More years ago, than I'd care to admit, when I was not only a brand-new civil engineer, but also a very green junior lieutenant, Director Simmons was a very senior Major and my boss. We built a couple of airfields together and, even after he left the

Air Force, went into cryogenics and became rich and famous, we stayed close.

"Because of our relationship, I have known everything about the Voyager Project from the beginning never dreaming that I would become so closely involved. Now, I can see how that raises many questions as to how I might be involved, so please bear with me for a little history. A few years ago, Congress passed a law that essentially said that any individual or organization that operates in space, if it's not directly under government control, will be under the government's observation and supervision. This was mainly for security concerns, but as Director Cummings will tell you, the government, being the government, has expanded that edict to cover space activities of any kind. Among other things, it requires strictly peaceful organizations like Wendover, Neilson, Robertson and you to submit what was originally a quarterly but is now monthly progress reports on whatever projects you are currently engaged in and to submit to inspections on demand."

In McPherson's next pause, I couldn't even hear the slight rustle of someone shifting position or clearing their throat. Everyone one of us was riveted to his words as he continued.

"Before there was a Space Force, that oversite kind of bounced around through several national Security and Air Force offices, but now that there that there *is* a Space Force, oversite is squarely in our lap and a space activities oversite office has been established in the Pentagon. Not to put too fine a point on it—my office. If a question concerning civilian space exploration or space colonies or even the activities of individual companies in space comes down from the

Administration or Capitol Hill, it lands on my desk and I'm the one who investigates, writes the reply or actually goes across the river to give the briefing."

That comment sent a ripple of apprehension around the room which McPherson had clearly anticipated. "Relax, people. I'm on your side. No one in the Pentagon is interested in your activities—yet. All of Director Cummings reports come directly to me. By the way, Dr. Cummings, I have to believe that somewhere in your collection of university degrees you must have one in Creative Writing. Never have I encountered so many imaginative ways of not actually telling the whole truth."

A laugh went around the room and I watched Alex blush right up to her hair roots. Smiling at our amusement at our boss' expense, the Colonel added, "I have been in my present position for almost two years now and have answered a thousand questions from the Administration and Capitol Hill. I've also been part of a team that has briefed Congress twice and the President once and, as far as anyone across the Potomac knows, you are a bunch of starry-eyed, bumbling dreamers. So far, I've convinced them that you only have a half-built spaceship whose engines don't work, who think you can live in the caverns of Mars and, as long as I can manage it, that's the way it will be."

Alex asked, "Is there any reason to think that the situation will change?"

"None that I know of at the moment, but remember that it's the government that we are dealing with. Washington is full of fairly ignorant, unstable, irrational people whose only conscious thought is to maintain or improve their current position. If they wake up one fine morning and decide for whatever reason—be it the environment, politics or even zombies—that they have to get out of town and going to Mars is a good idea, they *will* come here. They will not only demand to be taken up to Voyager, but demand that they be taken to Mars."

"What is your advice, Colonel McPherson?" Alex asked when the wave of mumbling outrage died down.

"To keep doing what you're doing, Dr. Cummings, but do it as fast as you can. My advice would be to get out of Dodge before it's too late." McPherson also waited for the next ripple to expend itself before he continued. "Now, I don't know how much you know about our current administration, so please bear with me. Our President, Jerimiah Rheingold, is a nice guy. Tall, courtly and distinguished, he rose up through the diplomatic ranks to become Secretary of State. For all of his professional career he was a gentleman representing the interests of the United States, whatever the administration said those interests were. That being said, if Jerimiah Rheingold ever had an original thought, he never let it show. Because his party was so hopelessly deadlocked, he was the compromise candidate in the last election and managed to squeak out his win. He doesn't have a clue about what to do to stop the country from falling apart and pretty much says and does whatever the Vice President tells him.

"And that brings me to my next point. The real power in Washington these days is Vice President Sam Collins. Make no mistake, this guy is flat out dangerous. He was and still is the CEO of Big Oil Inc. and he was put on the ticket to bring in the Rust Belt vote. It worked, but now that he is in power, the party has a tiger by the tail and they seem to be helpless. Sam

Collins doesn't believe in Climate Change and he will do everything in his power to protect and even advance the interests of the fossil fuel industries. The bottom line is that the United States will not be taking any steps to mitigate the impending global climate disaster."

I noticed a lot of us nodding grimly as we'd been fully aware of push backs on every positive action for years. I asked, "Colonel, what do we need to know about Collins and how he affects us?"

McPherson held my gaze before addressing his comments to the room. "As far as you're concerned, Collins is about as paranoid as they come and believes every conspiracy theory that was ever invented. Unfortunately, he is now thinking about space which was why my team was here. I can control what comes out of the Pentagon and have tried to reassure Collins that you're all a bunch of harmless dreamers, but I have no idea what that group that just left here is going to tell him. In my opinion, he is unstable and he is surrounded by a cadre of true believers."

There was dead silence around the table and finally Alex said, "All we can say is thank you, Colonel, for waging a war that we didn't even know was happening in our behalf. I do have two questions and one is why? I don't want to appear ungrateful, but why have you stuck your neck out for us for two years now? And the second is why tell us now?"

McPherson smiled that little smile of his and said, "In answer to your first question, Dr. Cummings, Josh Simmons is a friend of mine and a man to whom I owe much. When I fell into this job, quite by accident by the way, and he told me what Voyager was all about, it was a chance for me to at least partially repay many favors. The answer to your second question is because in the past I didn't desire anything."

"But you want something now?"

"I do."

Alex looked around the table. "Name it and if it's in our power, it's yours."

"Thank you, Dr. Cummings, I appreciate that, but it is a little complicated. If I may, I would like to speak to you in private." He patted me on the shoulder and added, "You and John."

Somehow getting patted on the shoulder by Colonel Alexander McPherson made me feel really good.

Alex looked around the table again and said, "Well, people, in light of what we just heard I guess we just press on and I don't think we need to share any of this with anyone outside of this room. Agreed? Good! And by the way—and check me if I'm wrong, Colonel—but the two Military people who are currently up at Wisdom are not privy to the information that the Colonel just gave us so circulate and quietly caution your people. Thank you"

The meeting broke up and everyone came over to shake McPherson's hand and thank him before they left. Alex gave the Docs, Chet and Cathy a nod and they came with us as McPherson, Alex and I moved into Alex's office.

As soon as we were settled, she asked, "How many?"

The Colonel smiled and said, "Six."

"Done."

"Don't you want to know anything about them?" McPherson laughed. "I did say that it was a bit complicated."

"Not unless you want to tell me," Alex shook her head.

McPherson thought for a minute as he looked around

at the slightly expanded group and decided that he did. "As I told John, I have a son and daughter, daughter-in-law and three grandchildren. My wife and I love them dearly and would miss them terribly, but I would like to see them have a chance at a better life on another world. Now, at the moment they know nothing about you and Sanctuary. So, if I do make the proposal and they choose not to go, there is always the risk that the secret will leak out."

Alex said, "Thank you for your concern, Colonel, but please don't worry yourself about that. That's a risk that we have been running ever since we expanded Voyager and the VU Board started nominating colonists. Many of the people here at Sand Flea and working to make Voyager a success don't know about Sanctuary."

I added, "Actually, I'm kind of surprised we haven't hit the Vid before now."

McPherson looked at us. "Are you sure?"

Alex smiled. "Sure Colonel? Never. But sure enough."

"Okay, thank you. I'll tell them. My son Andrew is an Army Captain. He went to West Point, was in the Infantry, did two tours in Africa and I know at least two generals who have their eye on him for higher command. Andy's stationed at Fort Benning in Georgia on the commander's staff and it would be difficult for him to just disappear without raising all kinds of questions."

Alex just said, "Noted. Chet?"

"We would certainly love to have a man with your son's credentials," Chet said, "but Link Lincoln is already designated as our security chief. When you make the proposal make sure that he understands that he wouldn't be top banana so to speak."

I jumped in. "If Captain McPherson came on board, I would recommend that he replace one of the two assistant chiefs."

Alex laughed and said, "Inside joke, Colonel. Mr. Innocent here has been trying to get out of that job for a year."

"I'm just a grunt, Colonel. I put four years in the Army and I was a buck-sergeant squad leader when I got out. That's good enough for me. When I'm not pushing junk around space or flying a Starduster, I'm happy to be just one of Chet's deputies."

McPherson laughed. "I sure that will not be a problem, but I will mention it. But now I have a question. Chief Barton, you said Mr. Lincoln is your Chief of Security, but I thought you were?"

Alex gave a little sigh. "Chet and his wife have decided not to go to Sanctuary. More than half of the people you see here have chosen not to go and will remain here. All of our facilities will be theirs when we leave and I am acquiring everything I can to help ensure their success and survival. Elections have already been held and Chet's wife Dot has been elected Mayor and Chet here will be Chief of Security."

I said, "That's also another possibility for your family, Colonel."

"Yes," McPherson said slowly as he gave it some thought.

Alex asked, "Your daughter-in-law?"

"Audrey. She's a nurse and a damn good one, too."

The Docs looked at each other and smiled. "We would love to have her. Right now, our medical team consists of two doctors, two nurses, two medical assistants and three apprentices."

Alex asked, "And their children?"

"Peter's eight and a real space nut and little Sally, four."

"And your daughter?"

"Erin and her girl, Judy, is seven." He sighed. "Erin had a bad marriage to a bad man; This was followed by a messy divorce which cost us a bundle—not that it wasn't worth every penny. Erin got custody, but that butt-hole wouldn't let go. Kept calling at odd hours, showing up here and there. Fortunately, that useless piece of humanity is no longer among the living."

I asked, "You didn't do anything rash did you, Colonel?"

"No—not that I didn't think about it! No, it was one of those road rage incidents and he was the rager. He was always yelling at everyone when he drove... waving a hand gun around. Stupid. Anyway, he got into an altercation with a guy with many gang tattoos and with even more felony convictions. Both cars stopped and when Darryl jumped out waving his pistol, the other guy shot him dead."

We all looked at each other—wow.

McPherson went on. "They've had a few tough years, but Erin is doing pretty good. As you can imagine men are not among her favorite animals at the moment. Joan and I hope that she meets a decent guy out there somewhere."

Alex smiled at me and said, "Well, we do have a few decent guys around. Does Erin work?"

"Yes. She's a Registered Dietitian."

We all burst out laughing.

"I said something funny?" McPherson asked.

"Forgive us Colonel," Alex said. "Just another inside joke. Let me introduce Cathy Jackson. Cathy manages our kitchen, runs the cafeteria, does all the menu planning and orders all the food, but she has a problem."

"André," I interjected.

"André," Alex agreed. "He's our French chef and let's just say that he and Cathy don't quite agree on what constitutes a healthy meal. Cathy makes our meals nutritious, but André makes them delicious... usually by adding butter, salt..."

"Fat, sugar and every other part of the food pyramid that should be avoided," Cathy finished.

"Alex," my Alex smiled slyly, "I would love to have Erin join us and watch her and Cathy gang up on André."

"Ooh, Luv! I never knew you had such a nasty streak in you."

When we finished laughing about how we could make a fortune by selling tickets to the three-way food fight, Alex asked about Erin's little girl.

"Judy. Well, as you can imagine, it's been hard on her. She's a lovely and very pleasant child, but quiet and withdrawn. I think an adventure like Voyager would great for her."

Alex said, "Thank you for sharing, Colonel, and I look forward to meeting your family."

"Well, they might not want to come."

As Alex and the Colonel started to get up, she said confidently, "They'll come."

"What about you, Colonel?" I asked. "I can think of a dozen ways that a man with your experience would be an asset on Sanctuary. What about Joan? What does she do and she would sure miss those grandbabies?"

He was thoughtful for a moment. "I hadn't thought about Joan and I going. As for your other question Joan is an artist—a potter and good one too, if I do say so myself. And your right we would miss those babies."

Alex perked up. "A potter as in hand thrown pottery and vases, jars?"

"Yes. She works in the old-fashioned style on a wooden foot peddle potter's wheel and turntable that I made for her."

I said, "You *made* a potter's wheel?"

"I did. Wood working and carpentry are hobbies of mine; In fact, I have quite a complete little shop in my basement."

Alex said, "Well, Colonel, where we are going the skills that you and your wife have would be invaluable. When we add that to the debt which we already owe you, I hope you will consider joining us."

The Colonel smiled his little smile and we could see that he was thinking and, maybe for the first time, actually considering the possibilities of going with us to Sanctuary. I looked at Alex and she gave me a nod, so I said, "Colonel, believe me we understand the conflict you are having between duty and your family, but also consider this: what do you think your personal chances of survival will be when Powers-That-Be find out that Voyager has sailed away into the void?"

"Well, I think I could cover myself . . ."

"Come on, Colonel. As you said, you didn't fall off the turnip truck yesterday. The bottom feeders on Capitol Hill will want someone to blame and you're the obvious candidate.

They will roast you slowly over a low fire and you know it."

With a sigh, McPherson shrugged, but his smile let me know that he knew that I was right.

"Well Colonel... Alex," my Alex said, "I for one look forward to a long association and I can't wait to meet your family. For right now, though, let's see if we can get you and your two associates back to Washington."

CHAPTER 20

Rita booked the Colonel and the two majors on a flight out of McCarren in Las Vegas for the next day, so McPherson called his two fledgling robot jockeys up at Voyager and told them to be on the first shuttle down in the morning. I had to admit, I was anxious to get back up there myself so I could continue to follow his advice on finishing Voyager so we could all sail away.

Alex and I, along with Chet and Dot, Phil, Cathy and a couple of others were sitting with the Colonel in the cafeteria having coffee and laughing our heads off over his tales of bureaucratic Washington when his phone rang. Giving us that little smile of his, McPherson put his finger to his lips to shush us before putting his call on speaker so we all could hear the conversation. "Hello, yes? Good evening, General."

"Good evening my ass! God Damn it, Alex, where the hell are you? The plane with those White House pukes got back yesterday."

"I'm still here at Sand Flea."

"What the hell are you doing there? I need you back here."

"Well, sir, the reason that I'm still here is that those 'White House pukes' as you call them decided that they were finished here and just took off leaving me and the two majors from the White House communications staff stranded. I'll get back as fast as I can. We are booked out of Vegas tomorrow."

"Damn it! I wish it was sooner, they're driving me nuts."

"Who? What's happening?"

"What's happening is that gang of idiots from the White House that were out there with you at Sand Flea are running all over Capitol Hill saying that Wendover is about to launch a spaceship to colonize Mars. And as for who, I've already had calls from four senators, five congressmen and the Vice President himself asking me what I know about this pending space launch."

We are cracking up and the Colonel kept gesturing to us to be quiet, but he was having a hard time keeping from laughing, too. "General, this is all crazy. Wendover has been working to send an exploration team to Mars; In fact, they've been working on it for several years. They do have plans to eventually establish a small colony, but they are probably a year or two away from actually launching anything."

"You know that, which is why I need you back here. You've gotta calm the morons down—especially the VP—before something else happens."

"Ah, sir, outside of them bugging you, has something else happened?"

Though General's gruff voice calmed slightly, he still sounded annoyed. "Gray called a few minutes ago and told me that he has been ordered by the President, by the President *personally*, to take military control of Sand Flea."

We stopped sniggering. As McPherson sat up straight in his chair, he managed to keep the alarm out of his voice. "Damn, General! Outside of that being illegal as hell, why would he want to do that?"

"Alex, I have no idea. They're scared and you know how paranoid the VP is. He's got half of Washington spooked and they're not very bright to begin with. The environment's going crazy; Law and order is breaking down, there are food shortages, water shortages, riots! Hell, there were several thousand people yelling outside of the White House today screaming that the space companies are going to fill the sky with missiles. I don't know."

Though McPherson looked at us and smiled, the thought of the military being stationed right here in Sand Flea had us looking pretty apprehensive. He just gave his head a little shake to dispel our fears. "Well, General, in my opinion they are all overreacting to nothing. What do you want me to do? Should I stay here and wait for the Army?"

There was an explosion on the other end of the line. "No! Damn it, you get your ass back here as fast as you can and get the goons from the Vice President's office off me. But, if you think that it's appropriate, you can give the people out there a heads up that the Army's coming."

"Sure thing, boss. Thanks. They seem like good people."

We could hear the general chuckling. "I'm serious, Alex. The meatheads across the river are driving me nuts. You get back here pronto. Hear?"

"Got it, General."

McPherson was about to hang up when the General stopped him. "Oh, you still there, Alex? I almost forgot that when Gray called, he passed along a bit of good news. Andy's on the promotion list to Major."

"That's great, Hawk. Thanks! And I'll get back to Washington as quick as I can."

McPherson hung up, looked at us and said, "As you probably guessed that was my boss, General Henry Hunter, but everyone calls him 'Hawk' which was his call sign when he was a fighter pilot—which he would dearly love to be again, but we don't have four-star generals as fighter pilots. He's the Air Force Vice Chief of Staff and he hates being a desk jockey; He hates the Pentagon, hates Washington and hates absolutely everything that goes with it. But for all his pissing and moaning, he does a hell of a good job."

I asked, "Who's Gray?"

"General Gray Harris. He's the Army Chief of Staff and another good guy. He and Hawk are old friends and I'm sure he has no more idea what's going on than Hawk does. However, if the President told him to send troops out here and take military control of Sand Flea, he may not know why, but he will do it."

"How will that affect us?" Alex asked.

McPherson thought for a minute, then gave his little smile and shrugged. "Can't say for sure. It depends on who they send and what their orders are. Damn, if I was back in Washington, I might be able to influence those orders." He shrugged again. "Well, all we can do is press on to Mars. My advice to you is the same: keep doing what you're doing and accelerate the time frame if you can."

I liked the 'we'.

Alex's smart phone vibrated. This was our evening for phone calls. "Hello, Al. What's up?"

Al Wilson laughed. "What's up, Madam Director, is going to stay up. We won't be sending your two Air Force boys down tomorrow."

That got our attention.

"Why not?"

"You should be feeling it any time now. Sorry I didn't give you the usual warning, but the mother of all Haboobs came out of nowhere. One minute nothing and then there it was."

Right on cue, we started to feel the hangar shake. The Colonel looked a question at me and I mouthed, "dust storm."

Alex said, "Thanks, Al. How long will it last do you think?"

"Well, in spite of my grandiose description, it doesn't look like one of the really big ones. Average size, so I'd say about three or four days maybe."

"Okay, Al. Thanks again. Is keeping the two Majors from catching on to what we're really doing going to be a problem?"

"Oh, I don't think so. They seem like just a couple of young dumb nerds. Everything is a computer game. Tony and Paul are making robot jockey's out of them and put them to work."

"To work? As in building rather large cylinders in space?"

"Yep, but don't worry about it. The last time I checked, our boys had them trying to fit a San Diego section into the Italian job. Tony's plan is to convince them that the factory is sending up inferior sections, so it will probably take us until the far side of forever to finish Voyager."

We all laughed. The Colonel hardest of all.

Al signed off and Dot said, "Well, Colonel, I don't suppose the idea of your being stuck here for three or four days is going to make Mr. General Hawk very happy."

With a sigh, McPherson said, "No, it sure won't."

"Are you going to tell him?" I asked with unmistakable glee. "We would all love to hear it."

He looked around in shock at our smiling faces. "I didn't realize until just now what a sadistic bunch you were." Which, of course made us laugh again. Shaking his head, McPherson said, "No, why spoil his evening even more? I'll call him tomorrow."

"Good thinking, Colonel!" I said, "His evening is already spoiled; Let's spoil his tomorrow, too."

With that, McPherson joined in the amusement. When the group started to break up, I said, "Come on, Colonel. Seeing as you're going to be with us for a few days, let's get you bedded down."

I took him through the beds and office paneling over to where the billeting ladies hung out. No one was there, so I just picked a bed, pushed some paneling around to make him a little cubicle and marked it up on their grease-board chart.

"How are you fixed for clothes?" I asked. "I don't think that you want to stay in that blue suit for three or four days."

He said that he had a couple of civilian suits in his bag, but something a little more comfortable would be nice. I walked him over to our supply section in Hangar 3. Again no one was around, so I went around the counter and got him a couple of flight suits which he said made him feel right at home. When we got back to the dormitory, we ran into one of the billeting ladies and I introduced the Colonel and told her what I had done to make him a sleeping area. She said that that was fine, but gave McPherson's uniform a visual once over before telling him to give it to her and she would get it freshened up for him.

"Thank you!" the Colonel said sincerely while patting her hand. "John, I sure like the service in this hotel of yours!"

The compliment made her blush a bright red.

I actually didn't see much of McPherson for the next couple of days as he kind of wandered around from shop to shop. It seemed that he met everyone, asked a ton of questions and seemed genuinely interested in everything. The overwhelming report from everyone regarding the Colonel was that he was "a real nice guy". He spent a lot of time around the Stardusters and after he took a turn in the simulator, Phil was ready to sign him up. With his experience of flying heavies for the Air Force, we might just have ourselves a new pilot to bring Voyager down from orbit at Sanctuary. To my own amusement, the Colonel also agreed with me—the Stardusters flew like a brick.

Like all storms, this one finally blew itself out and the two Majors came down from Wisdom happy to be on the ground and already missing being in orbit. When I loaded the three of them into my little PJ and we headed for Vegas, I had to laugh. Kennedy and Rawls were still dressed in their wrinkled (and rather ripe) uniforms that they'd been wearing for four days in space while their Colonel wore a sharply pressed fresh uniform looking all spic and span like he just stepped out of a recruiter's showroom window. I'm sure they wondered how he did that.

I was in for a surprise as we approached Vegas. The sky was still a bit smoggy, but nowhere near as bad as it had been when Alex I came up a couple of years ago. Another surprise was the air traffic at McCarren. It seemed that jets were landing and taking off one right after another just like the old days.

Apparently, my internal mumblings weren't as internal as I had intended them to be and McPherson asked me what was wrong. "Nothing's wrong," I answered. "I'm just confused. The last time I was here, Vegas was a very smoggy and almost ghost town."

McPherson laughed. "You've been out of touch. Ever since Collins got even more paranoid, if that's possible, the administration has been pouring money into the town. He's turned it into a second capital with the alternate White House out at Nellis, the big Air Force base just north of town."

The tower didn't seem too happy to hear me call in and asked me how I was on fuel. After telling them I was good for an hour, I wasn't happy when they put in a holding pattern down around the dam and said that they would try to fit me in. What the hell? When we finally did get clearance, they at least fit us in after a couple of prop jobs which was good. A little guy like my PJ doesn't take kindly landing too close behind those big jets; The engine turbulence would flip him in a heartbeat.

I was directed to taxi over to a small air service company and as we came up a hangar opened and we were waved right in. Well, that was neat, but I was confused when two guys ran over to the plane smiling and waving like we were expected.

The confusion was apparently mutual. When the four of us got climbed out, these guys stopped short and blurted out, "Where's Paul and Tony?"

The moment they asked was when I remembered that Paul and Tony had been using PJ to fly into Vegas on their down time. At the time, I didn't know that those two playboys had pilots' licenses (turns out they didn't), but I couldn't complain too much. It wasn't like I could take PJ with me to Sanctuary and, in the meantime, their Vegas friends were performing regular maintenance on my plane *and* we had gained André from their little excursions.

The guys brightened when I told them Paul and Tony would be back in a couple of days. All I could do after that was shrug and walk the Colonel and the Majors over to the terminal. As we shook hands and they headed for check-in, I wondered if I would ever see the Colonel again. I hoped so, but his journey with us still wasn't a done deal.

While there were a lot of people in the terminal, it wasn't crowded, but at least it was busy. Not like when I was here with Alex a few years ago. That emptiness then was just creepy. Since I was already here, I decided to take look around town. Stepping outside, I caught a cab and fortunately, got one with a cabbie who liked to talk.

I asked, "What's going on? A couple of years ago the town was all but dead."

The cabbie laughed, "Oh, lots of things. See this car?— electric. Look around, every car on the road is electric. Gasoline vehicles are not only not allowed in the city, but not allowed in the county either. Anything that burned fossil fuel is gone—small factories, power plants... everything."

Well I thought not quite everything—there were still

the airplanes going in and out of McCarren. I wondered if our fossil fuel happy Vice President knew about all this electric business, but why quibble? The air quality had certainly improved. Maybe not clear mountain air, but at least everyone wasn't wearing a gauze mask.

"What's the city doing for electric power?" I asked.

"Once the government moved in, the big money boys who ran the casinos came roaring back and got hold of the electricity and the water."

"Come again?"

"The dam and Lake Mead," the cabbie explained. "Somehow, Vegas now has first claim on all the power and water. People upstream or downstream might be doing without, but Vegas is doing fine. No more water restrictions in the hotel rooms, the fountains are on and look—we can't do anything about the heat but all the sidewalks are now covered walkways right down the strip with fans and mist sprays."

I had him drop me off around Caesars and he was right; It was at least thirty degrees cooler in the walkways. Still hot but at least survivable. Looking around, the lights were bright, the shows were on and the roulette wheels were turning. If anyone complained about the excess at the expense of the rest of the country, they were quickly discouraged by a police force that was the size of a small army and if need be, they would probably be augmented by the United States Army.

The power of government and money and gambling. I wondered how long it would last.

I called Alex. "Question, Luv: when was the last time we did active Starduster promotions here in Vegas?"

"I don't remember. It has been a while. Why?"

"You wouldn't believe it, Luv, but Vegas is up and running. Maybe we should start advertising again. It would help our cover."

Alex was quiet for a moment. "That's a good idea. I'll see if any of the charter companies that used to fly customers down to Sand Flea are still in business."

I asked her if there was anything that she needed me to do while I was here. When she said there wasn't, I wandered into a casino, lost a hundred bucks on a very unfriendly slot machine and headed back to McCarren.

It was a quiet and lonely flight back to Sand Flea. Once I got away from the hustle of Vegas, it looked like the country was deserted. Las Vegas was literally an oasis in a growing desert. The only things that moved seemed to be the occasional car on vast stretches of empty, dust covered roads. It was kind of spooky and again, I kept thinking about those old sci-fi movies.

As usual, I landed on the apron right by our hangars, taxied in, shut down and spent a half hour or so just puttering around PJ before I headed over to Alex's office. When I walked in, Alex was on her screen and she smiled and waved me to a seat. I wasn't paying much attention to Alex's side of the conversation, just a bunch "yeahs" and "uh-uhs" and "OK! I'll take care of that". When she hung up, she didn't say a word, but just flipped a couple of switches and she had Doc Nancy on the Vid.

"Nancy, we have the possibility of multiple heatstroke cases in Nielsen's area. Right. All the help you can send."

What the hell? I was bursting with curiosity but I kept my mouth shut.

Alex still didn't say anything. She sat there with her

hands steepled under her chin for a couple of minutes before giving herself one of those "I've just made a decision" shakes. Still without a word to me, she flipped a bunch of switches on her console and her face and voice were suddenly on every screen and speaker in the complex.

"Ladies and Gentlemen, may I have your attention please. A situation that we have talked about for the last few days seems to have happened. I'm afraid that we are about to receive some unwelcome visitors, probably a lot of unwelcome visitors and probably for an extended period of time. Just be aware that they may be around and carry on with business as usual. Thank you."

"Sorry, my sweet," Alex said as she switched off the screens and looked over at me. "When you came in, I had Amy Turner on the screen. She's Nils' secretary, receptionist, gate keeper and general girl Friday."

"Nils as in Nils Nielsen... as in Nielsen Enterprises?" I asked.

Alex nodded. "Amy doesn't know all the details, but shortly after you landed, an Air Force cargo plane also landed. They taxied into the Nielsen Enterprise area and what looked like about a hundred men in military uniforms got off. She says three men in civilian clothes seem to be in charge. Once they were off the plane, instead of getting inside out of the 130-degree heat and the bugs, the civilians had the military people fall in out on the parking apron by the airplane while *they* went inside the nearest building."

"Which just happened to be one belonging to Nielsen Enterprises."

"Yes. Amy thinks these idiots wandered into one of Nielsen's machine shops and collared the first person they could find, some poor mechanic probably who was certainly wondering what the hell was going on. They asked him who the owner was and, when he told them it was Mr. Nielsen and that he was probably in his office in the building next door. From what Amy heard, the civilian suits then ordered the mechanic to call him. By this time the mechanic had had enough, told them to go and see him themselves before throwing them out of his shop. He, of course called Amy and gave her a heads up."

"What actually happened gets a little fuzzy after that. The suits stormed into Nielsen's office, confronted Amy and demanded in very loud voices to see who ever was in charge. Before she could buzz him, Nils came out of his office to see what the noise was about. Now, Nils Nielsen is Norwegian, a self-taught engineer who started a little machine shop and built it into a really big machine shop."

"I've met him," I said. "If I remember correctly, he's about sixty-five, six-foot-two, two hundred ten pounds none of which is fat, and has probably the shortest fused temper in the known universe."

"That's him. He took in the situation at one glance and then lit into the suits wanting to know who in the hell they thought they were coming in and trying to imitate *his* people. When they told him that they were sent to establish a military oversite on all civilian activities on Sand Flea, Nils let them have it again by telling them that Gray had already called and told him all about it, that that wasn't what their orders were and whoever they were working for they had no right to overstep their authority."

"I bet those idiot suits didn't catch on when Nielsen mentioned Gray."

Alex sighed. "Nope. They went on to say that they were direct representatives of the Vice President and they had full authority. That was when Nielsen asked how many men, they had with them and was told there were a hundred fully armed soldiers and that they were standing in formation on the parking apron waiting for their, and they emphasized *their* orders. Amy said that Nielsen turned pale and asked how long have they been out there. The suits were still oblivious when they said it had been nearly an hour!"

"My God!" I exclaimed. "An hour in that heat?"

Grimly, Alex nodded. "Amy said the morons kept talking over him about their explicit orders from the VP while Nielsen was trying to explain the dangers of heat stroke. By the time Nils and Amy got through to them what idiots they thought they were, Nielsen's people were already pouring out of the shops and helping the soldiers inside. A half a dozen soldiers were on the ground and maybe a dozen more were about ready to collapse. You came in while Amy was calling me and anyone else with a medical facility and I notified the Docs."

We found out later that the Wendover medical people arrived first and went to work and Doc John and Doc Nancy showed up in a California Highway Patrol car. Doc John said that he told the rest of his staff to dig the ambulance out of the motor pool and follow them. Once they got everyone inside, cooled down and hydrated, the Docs think that with a little rest everyone will be okay.

Incredulous at the entire situation, Alex went on. "But even while all this was going on the suits were still blustering around saying that they were now in charge! The last thing that Amy said was that they said that they wanted a building to house all their personnel and they wanted a meeting with representatives of all the companies on Sand Flea at 1500. I have been 'summoned' to this meeting."

Stunned, all I could say was, "Wow. It looks like we have ourselves a very big problem."

At my comment, an idea clearly popped into my wife's head. Turning to me with a wickedly sly smile, she said, "Indeed we do. And I think that it would be a good idea if you came with me to the 1500 meeting."

Oh boy! That look meant someone was in trouble. I took great heart in that this time it wasn't me.

CHAPTER 21

Alex was hatching a plan. The wheels were turning in that clever mind of hers and, while I didn't know why she wanted me in this meeting, if she figured I'd be of assistance, I wasn't about to argue.

When we walked into the motor pool hangar, we thought the place was empty. It was almost echoey silent until Pedro slid out from under one of the police cars right near our feet and laughed at our startled expressions. He laughed again when Alex asked for a car to go over to Nielsen's complex. It was only a quarter mile away but no one walked outside in the heat and bugs if there was any way to avoid it. On days like this when a Haboob wasn't blowing through, the air was deathly still and the rising heat waves warped the tarmac into an out of focus shimmer. Alex had me drive and the refracting light made it look as if I were heading into an ocean, but each pool evaporated into the arid sand as we neared the mirage.

Alex was quiet and seemed distracted as we neared Nielsen's, so I asked, "Do we have a plan, Luv?"

If she did, it wasn't time for me to know about it. Giving me a wan smile, she said, "Let's wait and see what the Vice President's men have to say."

Yes, ma'am. In full chauffeur mode, I stopped right in front of the main entrance, got out, went around and opened Alex's door for her. It certinally looked classy, so maybe that was why she wanted me to come along, I thought as I drove off to park. If anyone was watching, Alex was clearly an impressive bigwig in these parts.

The way to the conference room was obviously through the main office because I could hear the raised voices of a couple dozen people trying to shout over each other the moment I entered the front doors. I assumed the middle-aged lady sitting with a bemused expression on her face was Amy and I asked what was going on.

Amy smiled. "Well, I guess if they ever stop yelling it's going to be a meeting. Or a pre-meeting anyway. The people from Washington ordered all the company heads to be here at three and Nils wanted to talk with them before they met with the Vice President's representatives."

"Doesn't sound like he's having much success," I quipped which made Amy laugh.

"No, it doesn't," she scoffed before giving me a scrutinizing frown. "I don't remember seeing you before; Are you here for the three o'clock?"

"Yes. John Marshal," I introduced myself. "I work for Alex Cummings who asked me to attend."

"Well, Mr. Marshal, I wish you luck. That way."

"Thanks, but I think if I just follow my ears, I can find it."

That made Amy laugh again.

When I walked into the conference room, the bedlam had simmered down a little. At least Nielsen had managed to get everyone seated around a rather large conference table. Nielsen frowned in my direction when I headed for a chair next to the wall behind Alex, but didn't say anything directly to me. Maybe he thought I was with the suits. As I seated myself, Nils began the meeting by recapping what had happened up to now: the military airplane, the troops, the suits from the Vice President's Office, leaving the troops out in the sun—everything that had led up to him ordering this meeting.

Once everyone was riled up with righteous indignation, he then dropped the big bombs. "According to the 'Gentlemen' from Washington," he snarled. "Sand Flea is now under military control and the Vice President's men are demanding buildings for their operations and personnel housing."

In the uproar that followed, I heard several people exclaim this was outrageous. Who the Hell did Collins think he was? Let 'em stay out in the sun. And so on... .

Nielsen made patting motions with his hands until some semblance of order returned. He told them that he agreed with them completely, but until things were straightened out, he wanted to at least keep the soldiers out of the heat. "Agnes," and he gestured to an older, silver haired lady at his side, "thinks that she has an old warehouse that she could make available that would probably do."

As a couple people smirked at that suggestion, I

thought that McPherson must be right and that I must be a sadist. While the warehouse would be suitable, it would still be uncomfortably warm for Collins' men and I found that I was really enjoying watching some of the high and mighty executives here at Sand Flea run in circles screaming and shouting. While the rest of the room was expressing their righteous indignation, Alex just sat there not saying anything.

The door opened and Amy poked her head in. "Mr. Nielsen, the gentlemen from Washington are here." She didn't give their names which I thought was a nice touch.

The room immediately simmered down; Nielsen composed himself and said, "Thank you, Ms. Turner. Would you show them in please?"

As the three suits walked into a room full of seriously pissed and fairly high-powered executives, I had to admit that I was loving it. It was like Daniel walking into the lion's den, but I soon released that, if Daniel had God on his side, these guys had the Vice-Presidential Seal of Approval. From the arrogant, ram-rod way in which they carried themselves, in their opinion they thought that was just as good.

I also thought it was also a nice touch that Nielsen made sure there were no chairs for the suits around the table. No one spoke or offered up their own seats, so they were forced to remain standing with a couple dozen people glaring at them.

Finally, Nielsen demanded, "Well, you called the meeting. What do you want?"

The short fat one, Hagen I think was his name, puffed up his chest and said, "We are here at the direction of the Vice President..."

Nielsen snapped, "We know that. What do you want?"

"The Administration believes that your activities pertaining to space here at Sand Flea airfield may be detrimental to National Security, so we are here to ensure that you do not engage in those activities. Effective today, we will be monitoring all your activities and your progress reports that you have been submitting to Washington will now be submitted here to me."

The room exploded. What the Hell are you talking about? What activities? We are private companies engaged in legitimate business. Did you ever hear of private enterprise, proprietary information and on and on?

Hagen and the other suits weren't interested. "Have you designated buildings for my men?"

Nielsen said, "The men you almost killed today? Yes. Ms. Turner in the outer office will see that you are escorted to Robertson Rockets where a building has been designated for your use. Good day."

It seemed that the boys from Washington might have had more to say, but as far as the executives around the table were concerned, Nielsen had dismissed them and their presence in the meeting was over. Fortunately, they took the cue and left.

Once the suits were gone, indignation again erupted around the table. With everyone talking at once, the consensus seemed to be that they were not going to cooperate. They were going to resist, call their congress people, refuse them entry and anything else they could think of.

Personally, I thought that was a bad strategy. These guys from Washington were little men who now had power... a lot of power. Drunk with it, I was certain open defiance would only make it worse.

In all of this, Alex just sat there with her hands steepled under her chin thinking, listening but not taking part in the conversation. After a few minutes, she gave herself that little decision-making shake of hers and very quietly said, "Actually, I plan to cooperate."

Despite all the noise that quiet statement was clearly heard. The room was so stunned by her announcement that you could have heard a pin drop.

"Well," Alex continued, using the riveted attention for her next words to carry even more weight, "to be clear, I plan to follow a course of what I call 'grudging cooperation'. I know we're all seriously offended by this high-handed abuse of authority by the administration, but in my opinion, open defiance will only bring more repression. As I see it, at least for the near future anyway, our best way forward is to politely cooperate. I had no intention of being what you would call friendly or volunteer any help or information, but if they want to inspect what we're doing at Visions Unlimited I won't try to stop them. I don't plan on helping them, but I won't stop them."

In the continuing silence, she smiled slyly to drive home her devious plan. "After all, every project that we are engaged in has been made public. I plan to show them anything that they want to see and if they want to pay me two-hundred and fifty thousand dollars for a ride in a Starduster, we can arrange that, too."

Though Alex was still getting some rather dark glares from several people at the table, a few of the executives began smiling as they caught on to her devious plan.

Grinning wickedly, Alex continued, "Think about it. It's

no secret what our various companies are doing. Hell, much of your work is under government contracts. As for Visions Unlimited, in addition to our Stardusters, we are building a spaceship to explore Mars. If the Administration wants to station people out here in the desert to watch us do it, it will probably be annoying as hell, but I don't intend to try to stop them."

Everyone around the table ate it up! Alex was right, they weren't engaging in illegal or secret activities and were only doing what they said they were doing. Like the deceptively sunny day at the eye of a hurricane, their mood changed drastically; No one here had a secret program masked by their normal work, so why should they care about the idiots in suits?

Well, nobody but us perhaps. If they only knew…

Nielsen said, "Food for thought, Alex, and as usual, you make a lot of sense. Is there anything else you can think of?"

"Two things, Mr. Nielsen, if I may. One, our distasteful friend will now receive our monthly reports, but I intend to continue to send a copy of my reports along the established channels as well. And two, if it's agreeable to all of you," and at this point she looked back at me, "the gentleman seated behind me is John Marshal. He is my senior construction engineer for the Voyager spacecraft and when he is not floating around in space, he is a senior deputy for Chief Barton. In light of what we have seen and heard today; I would like to hear if he has anything to add."

Nielsen said, "Of course. Mr. Marshal?"

Ooh, Alex was going to pay for that! Blindsided by her introduction, all eyes were now riveted on me and my little brain was racing to try to put my thoughts in order. Failing to come up with something spectacular on the spot, my thoughts just kind of tumbled out in a mental alphabet soup. Standing up to give myself another three seconds to try and sound intelligent, I cleared my throat and began.

"Ah, okay. First, I think the strategy of what Director Cummings called 'grudging cooperation' is the best option we have. Now, I know you're furious, but as an ex-soldier myself, I would urge you to please not take it out on the soldiers. They're here because they were told to be here. They will follow orders and do what the suits tell them, but I would bet anything that they don't have a clue as to why they're here or to what's going on."

Heads nodded around the table.

"Second, the demand for a building is not the last demand you will receive. Mr. Nielsen, did you see any vehicles downloaded with the military contingent? Did they bring any vehicles with them?"

"No, don't think so. I was busy trying to get them out of the sun to really notice, but no I don't think so."

"I don't think so, either. They're going to need them to move around out here in the desert and, unless I miss my guess, they're going to demand that you give them to them or get vehicles for them."

That brought more sputtering around the table. What am I? A used car dealership? They can go to hell. I won't do it. Etc.

"You can refuse, but what would happen then? They would probably just take them either from you or from a car dealership in town, if there are any left."

Another round of indignation.

"I suggest another strategy: if they ask, give them vehicles. You must all have some old junkers around and if you don't, the streets of Sand Flea City are full of them. Hide the good stuff and, ahem, 'cooperate'."

I gave the last word some finger air quotes which made everyone suddenly love the idea. Alex just smiled.

Nielsen also smiled. "I like the way you think, Mr. Marshal. Do you have anything else?"

"Yes sir. Our security forces."

That got their attention. Murmurs of what about them and I'm not giving up my security now swept around the room.

When they quieted down, Nielsen asked, "What about them, Mr. Marshal?"

"Sir, I think that the mere fact that they exist would be seen as a threat to them. To paranoid conspiracy believers like our current administration, our security arrangements would be seen as a threat to their control. I wouldn't be surprised if their knee-jerk reaction to seeing dozens of people walking around with weapons would be to confiscate them."

That brought another round of sputtering indignation. I won't do it. Second Amendment rights and we would fight.

I looked around the room and asked myself how I could get through to these people that open resistance was futile. I looked at Alex, she smiled and mouthed—'Indians'.

What? Ah! Got it. "Please, Ladies and Gentlemen, I know that you are seriously pissed, pardon my crude phraseology." That got a couple of smiles. "But think about it. Yes, you could fight them and you'd probably win, too. Altogether you have four or five times as many men as they do. But then what? Remember the Native Americans and the settlers. The first invaders were killed off by the Indians and what did the Indians get—more settlers and the Army, too. In this fight, we're the Indians."

Nielsen was pretty cool. "Do you have any recommendations, Mr. Marshal?"

"Well, sir, a couple of thoughts anyway."

"You're on a roll, son, let's hear 'em." That brought a titter around the table and I had trouble getting started again.

"Ah, yes, sir. I suggest that you erase any and all signs that you have organized security forces. Pull in all your deputies from perimeter security. Keep them close, of course... maybe give them other jobs around the work areas. Hide the weapons, abandon the outposts and no more roving patrols around the outer fence. While leaving maybe one or two guards on the main gate and your inner gates, make everything else look like the security fences were built and then abandoned. You know: dumb, naive civilians."

"How do we explain all the inner fences?" someone asked.

"Make it look like they were built to protect you from each other; Built to keep those VU bastards from stealing your secrets." That got a real laugh around the table. "If we're lucky, the suits will see that we have no security against insurgents, car bombers or roving bands of zombies and they will put the Army to work guarding our fences." Another laugh.

Nielsen looked around the table and said, "Thank you, Director Cummings, Mr. Marshal. I think you may have just kept us from doing something foolish. I, for one, intend to follow your advice."

Looking at the number of nods around the table, it

seemed like most were agreement and the meeting broke up.

When we got into the car Alex gave me a big kiss and said, "I knew I brought you along for a reason. Good work!"

"You rat!" I scolded. "You didn't tell me I was going to have a speaking part."

Alex laughed. "Sorry, my love, I didn't know, either. It just kind of seemed right. And it worked. You hit all the right notes, but I'm afraid you're not done talking yet. When we get back, I'm calling our own staff meeting. Among other things, you're going to present a full status report on Voyager."

"Yes Ma'am." Geeze! I hadn't talked this much since I tried to get Mary Lou Ferguson to go out behind the bleachers at the Junior Prom.

While Alex went off to organize her staff meeting, I gave Pedro a heads up on the possible vehicle grab. Pedro was ecstatic at the subterfuge. Right! He had just the vehicles. Don't worry the lemons would be all shiny in the front of the hangar if the suits showed up.

I hoped he wouldn't make it too obvious, but while I was giving Pedro a heads-up, Alex was alerting other people, too. As the staff gathered around the conference table, Alex waved me to a chair and when everyone was settled, she didn't waste any time. Standing up, she gave a summary of the events that had let up to the owners' meeting, the suits, the Army and the medical emergency. Doc John was present, so she had him report on the condition of the soldiers. He had two in the VU infirmary for observation, but he thought that the rest would be alright after a night's rest. They were staying in Nielsen's air-conditioned machine shop until the Robertson warehouse was cooled down and they found some beds.

Then Alex went over the main points of the owners' meeting while emphasizing grudging cooperation, security arrangements and where she thought we stood right now. My girl was in her element! She had a problem, saw solutions, made a plan and now it was time to execute the plan.

"Well, Ladies and Gentlemen," Alex smiled, "it would appear that the end of all our endeavors is upon us. A bit sooner than we may have liked, but on the other hand maybe we were lucky to have progressed this far before the wolves started sniffing at our door. As you know, during the last few days we were visited by members of the government and today a bunch of soldiers landed to place us under government control. So, here's what we are going to do to look as small and unthreatening as we can. Chet?"

"All underway, Alex. My deputies are coming in and once they get their weapons hidden, they'll be going to work for Pedro, Alice, Cathy or Phil."

"Good, very good. Pedro?"

"I have the boys pulling that old Hummer with the funky transmission and a couple of the police cars up front." He puffed himself up and went on, "Since I keep all my vehicles are in A-1 condition, these aren't bad, but they are the worst of what we have."

That brought a snicker, but none of us could deny that Pedro was pretty good. He wasn't sailing away on Voyager with us for only one reason: on Sanctuary, there would be no cars for him to work on. We didn't have room to bring them nor would we have materials to make them.

Alex looked around the table and asked, "Can anyone think of anything else?"

When no one did, she looked down the table at me.

"Okay, John. Let's have a progress report on Voyager."

"Okay," I said, standing up. "Pardon me if I tell you things that you may already know, but I don't know who knows what. Voyager, the original Voyager, is complete except for the dozen or so cryogenic pods we use as a dormitory which still need to be hooked up. Also, the supply and equipment sections are only about a third full. The Command and cryogenic sections are shirtsleeve environments, but for ease of loading, the supply and equipment sections are presently open to space."

I paused in order to run through my mental inventory and continued, "The first of the add-ons, the big supply cylinder, is attached to the roof of Voyager and I would say it's about half full. We load the supply cylinder and the supply and equipment sections of Voyager as fast as the supplies and equipment come up to us in the Stardusters and Grant and Maryanne tell us where they want them.

"Under the expansion plan, we're building two additional cylinders to hold the cryogenic pods. The original cryo section that is in Voyager had twenty-four individual pods which was later expanded to forty-six and each of the new cryogenic cylinders will have three hundred pods. One cylinder is being built in Milan, Italy—we call it the Italian Job—and the other is being built in San Diego. All the individual pods are being built in San Diego.

"For shipping, the large cylinders are sliced like a loaf of bread into twenty-five sections, then each loaf is again cut in half down the middle making fifty half sections in each cylinder. The Italian Job could be completed anytime; We have all the half sections, but have left it open because it's easier to fly the pods in with the robots. We plan to install all the pods and the servicing walkways, attach the cylinder to Voyager and provide a shirt-sleeve environment before the cryogenic technicians hook up the pods. I believe the Italian job still needs about fifty pods."

"And the San Diego Cylinder?" Alex asked.

"It's still short six half sections and has no pods."

Alex nodded and waved for me to go on.

"R3, the robot repair and storage facility, is still attached to Wisdom, but could be disconnected and attached to Voyager anytime. Wisdom itself is made up of five individual modules, three of which are still in use, two are packed for transit, but are still connected."

"Robots?"

"We have eleven working robots, but you should probably count on eight or nine being operational on any given day. And thirteen RJs counting our four apprentices."

"Thank you, John. How long to finish?"

I thought for a moment before answering. "Ah, hard to say. Don't mean to hedge, but it all depends on when we get the pieces. Three—four months maybe."

I took my seat as Alex stood up. "I wanted all of you to hear that so everyone knows where we stand. We still have a great deal of work to do before Voyager sails. Having said that, we have held off doing some work because it makes other things easier." She looked at me. "We may no longer have that luxury."

Alex was quiet for a minute, then she looked around at everyone gathered around us. "Okay, boys and girls, this is what I would like. Basically, I want Voyager to be ready to sail at a moment's notice—even if it is not fully complete. John, I want you to finish the Italian Job, attach it to Voyager and provide an environment so when the cryogenic technicians get here, they can start hooking up pods. I know that it will be a pain to maneuver the remaining pods in through Voyager but I think that that's the best way forward.

"John, Maryanne and Grant, the next priority is to get the supply and equipment sections in the original Voyager loaded and get Voyager sealed up. Grant, I would like either you or Maryanne to go up to direct the loading. I know that haste in loading here may give us some awkward moments at Sanctuary, but the clock is ticking."

When Maryanne and Grant nodded that they understood their tasks, Alex continued. "Alice and Phil, as soon as Voyager is loaded, send everything else up to finish loading the big supply cylinder.

"Phil, John tells me that Vegas is back in business, so to help our cover we are going to try to get Starduster flights increased. Every tourist flight gets a full load for Voyager in the cargo bay."

"On it," Phil assured her.

Alex stood there for a moment and asked, "Speaking of questions, does anyone have any? No? Okay, then! Remember: not a word about Sanctuary. We're a division of VU with three jobs: service Wisdom, run tourist space flights with the Stardusters and build a spaceship to explore Mars."

With a smile, Alex paused to catch the eye of our many comrades and friends. "Thank you, everyone and good luck to all of us."

CHAPTER 22

Right after the big meeting, Nielsen and the other company heads immediately pulled all their men and women off of the outer and inner fences, so except for the main gate and the gates that Wendover and Robertson used to get to their rocket pads, the airfield was wide open to anyone who wanted to climb over the fence or try to wade through the barb-wire tangles.

None of that seemed to worry Hagan who didn't waste any time in putting every private company on the airfield under 'surveillance'. He didn't replace any of the Sand Flea people who had been on guard around the airfield's perimeter; His concern was the companies themselves. As soon as the soldiers were back on their feet, Hagen split them up into small groups and stationed a group in each company area.

I was sitting with Alex in her office having a last cup of

Rita's excellent coffee before heading back up to Voyager when we were visited by a rather obnoxious snot of an Army Lieutenant named Schmidt. He pushed past Rita as if she wasn't there and it was obvious by his lack of reaction to what she was yelling at him that he didn't understand the Spanish language; However, one of his troopers did and was trying really hard to keep from busting out laughing.

When Schmidt barged in, Alex and I didn't even react, but just sat there looking at him. Schmidt was another character from the past. If Gutman was the middle-aged businessman from the 1930's, Schmidt was the Gestapo Lieutenant: short, a bit on the chunky side with wispy hair going prematurely bald. Adding to the image, he also wore a starched camouflaged fatigue uniform with the pant legs stuffed into highly polished black boots. I learned a long time ago to be wary of anyone wearing *starched* fatigues. His boots shone like mirrors and I was willing to bet he didn't polish them himself which meant he probably had a batman.

I was trying hard not to laugh at the sight of him, but I guess that it wasn't really funny. It was obvious from the way Schmidt carried himself that he was another True Believer; Whatever Collins said through Hagen, this man would make sure it was done. If he was ordered to have us lined up and shot, I had no doubt he'd do it in a heartbeat.

Following Alex's lead of grudging cooperation, I just sat there while Schmidt reeled of his orders: To guard against any subversive, anti-government or terrorist activity a military detachment consisting of (he looked at his notepad) a non-commissioned officer and five men (turned out that one of the men was a woman) would be billeted in our area. The sergeant and his men would be garrisoned in the (he looked at his pad again) Visions Unlimited Compound. Visions Unlimited would be responsible for their billeting and rations.

I was thinking how right Gutman was, the government will always interfere and take over, but Alex just smiled as Schmidt went on. "Also, to preclude any threats to the United States, you will not conduct any further activities in space."

I jumped at that one and started to say something, but Alex just smiled and quietly said, "Lieutenant Schmidt, those are not your orders."

That rocked him back on his heels—me, too, for that matter.

When he began a sputtering protest, Alex waved him to silence. "I have discussed the situation with my good friends in Washington and if this is what you have been telling the other companies here at Sand Flea, either you or Mr. Hagan have misinterpreted or exceeded your orders. Your orders are certainly to prevent any subversive activities in space, but not to prevent or impede any legitimate business activities. Our business is to take tourists up into space and we will continue to do so."

Schmidt was clearly taken back by her calm revelation of friends in Washington. Sputtering again like a car engine that refused to turn over, he recovered by barking at his Sergeant. "You have your orders, Daniels!"

With that, he spun on his heel and stalked passed the soldiers, one of whom was actively trying to put the make on Rita, and headed toward his car with a loud and angry tirade in Spanish following him all the way. This time the Spanish speaking soldier did burst out laughing.

Poor Daniels. If he knew what his orders were, he was way ahead of me. He kind of looked after the Lieutenant then turned and looked at Alex who just smiled and nodded to me.

"Come on, Sergeant Daniels," I said getting up. "I'm an old sergeant too. Let's go get your people bedded down."

"Hangar 4, I think." Alex said with her fingers steepled under her chin. "I'll give Alice and Pedro a call."

As we gathered up Daniel's squad and headed through Hangar 2 toward supply in Hangar 3, one of the soldiers, the one who had been putting the make on Rita, asked, "Where are we going?"

With a flash of inspiration, I answered smugly, "We're going to meet Rita's daddy so you can explain things."

The man stopped dead in his tracks while the rest of the squad almost fell down laughing. I desperately wanted to laugh at the terrified expression on his face as well, but that would have spoiled everything.

Grudging Cooperation. I got it when Alex said Hangar 4. We would provide accommodation and food, but they weren't going to eat or sleep with us and we certainly weren't going to be what you would call friendly. Alice smiled and nodded as we walked up. "Good to see you, John, and are these the lady and gentlemen that Director Cummings called me about?"

"Yes," I replied while silently chanting my new "Grudging Cooperation" mantra. It did help. "They'll be billeted in 4, so cots if you have them and rations for," I looked at Daniels who kind of shrugged. "let's say three days to start."

Alice nodded to a couple of her people and they started scurrying around collecting the stuff. Then, I swear she pulled out an old supply sign out note pad. I hadn't seen one of those in years; We never signed for anything.

Alice was beautiful! She must have stretched the sign out process for almost an hour. Meticulous, precise; One soldier at a time, by hand on a sign-out sheet, every line and square filled out. She made sure they put in their name, rank, serial number, unit, home station—everything except next of kin and blood type, but probably because there wasn't a slot on the form for that information. Then the items: cot, sleeping bag, rations. If the item had a lot or serial number, it was entered. Alice even checked their ID cards when she had them sign. And all this with a straight and very serious face.

Once I let the laughter out, my sides were going to hurt for a week.

With the soldiers carrying all their stuff, we finally headed toward Hangar 4. Either Rita or Alex or both had given her family—her very big family—a heads up about the soldier's amorous attempt because we were met not only by Pedro, but by three of Rita's brothers. Each of them made a big and obvious show in looking the squad over to identify the culprit who was by now trying to disappear inside his fatigues.

This was too much. I quickly left the Army guys with Pedro and his boys and headed for the Starduster so I could burst out laughing in the privacy of space. As I headed back up to Voyager, I kept running Alex's orders through my mind. I could see where she was coming from—get as much done and Voyager as buttoned up as we could if we had to make a fast get away. But would it really come to that? Was our own government so far gone, so scared... so *paranoid*... that they would confiscate privately funded endeavors to Mars or the Moon and turn them into what, military missions?

Of course, they would!

And what about us? If they found out we were really

planning to go to Sanctuary, would they stop us. Would they lock us up? *Kill* us? I couldn't think of any logical reason to do any of those things, but logic was rarely involved with these people. They were already here with every intention of taking everything away from us. Not only had they thrown out everyone with scientific training and experience, they'd replaced them with their own sycophants.

I rather enjoyed that last thought as it played in a loop in my head. Based on past performance, there might be a real possibility they'd blow themselves up in the process of hijacking our endeavors. But on the other hand, if they did that, they'd probably blame us for sabotage.

Well, at this stage of the game, anything was possible and Alex was clearly planning for the worst. My job was to get Voyager ready to fly.

After we unloaded the supplies out of the Stardusters storage bin and sent it on its way back down to Earth, I called everyone into R3 and briefed them on the recent events down below. The Robot Jockeys and even Al, Grant and the two scientists currently on Wisdom grumbled about having to maneuver the cryo pods through Voyager, but they understood the necessity. The scientists agreed to wrap up their experiments in the next couple of days so we could pack up, but not detach all of Wisdom—we still had to keep up appearances from Earth that there was nothing unusual to see up here. To maintain the illusion, three of Wisdom's tubes would remain, but two of them would be fully packed up ready to go. That would leave Al's weather station for last. In the meantime, he could mimic a whole space station.

We split the functional robots between the Italian Job and supplies and I put Grant with an RJ inside Voyager. A box or bag of something would be flown up to the door, Grant's robot would take in and Grant would direct its stowage. It was slow, but like a bunch of ants we were getting it done. Personally, I didn't care where the stuff went as long as there was food and water handy in Voyager's supply section behind cryo 1 for the flight crew. The big brains that designed Voyager had decided to have three people awake during the flight to handle any emergency whatever they might be should they arise. The flight crew would consist of a medic, a cryo technician and an RJ and they would be on duty for a year at a time. Seeing as it was a twenty-year flight and there were only nine fully qualified RJs, seven medical personnel including our only doctors John and Nancy, and so far only six cryogenic technicians who had volunteered to make the trip, some of us were going to spend more than one year-long shift watching space go by.

As I said before, I could understand why they would want medical and cryogenic people, but what the hell emergency was I supposed to take care of? If something did break or if we were pursued by Space Zombies, there was no way I could take Sam outside and fix whatever it was—up to and including fighting off zombies—while we were traveling at .98 the speed of light.

We were notified that Rocket 3 was sending up a container with thirty cryogenic pods which was great news. Once we got them inside the Italian Job, that would only leave twenty to squeeze in the hard way. We fudged a bit on Alex's orders and delayed finishing off the Cylinder while we waited for those thirty pods to come up. When they finally did, we flew the pods into the cylinder, fasten them down and the Italian Job was finished.

Fantastic! Now what?

I sat there in Sam looking at this... thing, this great hunk of metal floating in space. The Italian Job just sat there, three hundred feet long, fifty feet around, half in and half out of our space dock. I wondered if we'd be able to control it once we cut it loose and pulled it out.

Apparently, I wasn't the only one as I could see the other guys just sitting there staring right along with me. Finally, JJ said, "Why don't we go in, get some food and think about this."

We did and got nowhere until Billy said, "Piece of cake."

Come again?

"Tug boats and the Queen Mary. Four on a side, take her straight-out past Voyager, line her up and slide her in."

With eight robots working together and Billy in his robot standing off and directing the operation it, worked just like Billy said. Although I felt like a guppy trying to shove a whale around, it was yet another job done. Voyager now had a huge cylinder on its back and an even bigger one on its left side above the delta wings.

It made a nice show for our Starduster visitors. From Wisdom's view ports after they watched mother Earth for a while, they could watch the robots unloading the Starduster and flying the boxes or whatever for the Mars Mission into the supply cylinder.

If we had the time, we would take the paying customers into R3. They seemed to get a kick out of floating around among the robots, spare parts and the work benches. Good PR—tell all your friends about the Mars Mission.

By this time, I had been up for about four weeks and

was half-way through my rotation when, Alex called. "Guess who turned up today?"

"I give up. Who?"

"The McPhersons, well three of them anyway."

"Really?" I was delighted.

"Yup! The Colonel's wife Joan, their daughter Erin and her little Judy. They called from McCarren."

"Are they still there?"

Alex laughed. "No, I was going to send Phil or one of his pilots up in PJ, but it seems that PJ wasn't here."

"Paul and Tony?"

"Paul and Tony," Alex confirmed.

"Our poor little airplane's getting a workout. I assume you got hold of the boys and told them they had to bring back passengers."

Alex laughed. "Yes and it must have been quite a flight. In addition to their bags, the McPhersons had a fair-sized box containing Joan's potter's wheel."

"How the hell did they get all that into poor little PJ?"

Alex laughed again. "I guess it wasn't easy. I think they got the box in behind the seats and stuffed their bags where they could. Joan ended up holding one bag and Judy rode on Erin's lap. I don't think the FAA would have approved. But, my love, the real reason I called was to see how we are progressing."

I sighed. "Nothing you don't already know, I don't think. The Italian Job is attached and the next shipment should finish off the pods. About a hundred are completely installed. You could actually start doing the cryogenic installation if you wanted to. Why?"

"Oh, I don't know. Things are getting dicey around

here. Have you been watching the Vid?"

Of course, we had been watching the Vid—it was like a train wreck we couldn't tear our eyes away from. Whenever we weren't working or sleeping that's what we did and what we were seeing wasn't very pretty. The human race had been slowly dying for several years and now the pace was accelerating. The thirst and famine caused by the extreme weather had made refugees out of half the world's population, but without any place to go, most borders were sealed with the military forces guarding them. Many countries, especially in Africa, the Mid-East and Asia had already demonstrated a willingness to use lethal force to keep outsiders out and several nations were actually at war with each other—mostly over resources.

But even in the face of imminent environmental disaster, humans could still kill each other over nationality, race, tribe or religion. The national and international aid and relief agencies, or at least those that were still in operation, were completely overwhelmed and had been for a few years. Sadly, there was no help coming for stricken areas in East Africa, India, Australia and most of South America. Millions were dying and millions more were on the move.

From what we could see on the Vid, the European Nations were at least still semi-functional and surviving, but no one knew for how long. Millions of displaced humans were pushing on the European Union's southern and eastern borders. As far as it was reported, those refuges hadn't been fired on, except by the Russians, but it was just a matter of time. We even had reports of fairly large fire fights on our Mexican border.

The democratic governments of the world were

elected by the people and the people were demanding resources and protection and if the government didn't provide them there would be another government. Any politician that opened his or her mouth about charity or humanitarianism these days would be voted out in a heartbeat if they weren't run out of town on a rail first.

International trade which had been declining for years had for all practical purposes disappeared. Made in China was a thing of the past. The only items that people cared about these days was water, food, shelter and clothing. People were left to wander and it was one hundred percent guaranteed that wherever they went no one would let them in.

With a heavy sigh I said, "Yeah Luv, we've been watching. Anything in particular?"

"Well, the Colonel called and he thinks that Sand Flea Airfield might soon become a Walmart."

I caught the reference. With a supply of food and resources stored within the walls, a Walmart could become a fort with those inside willing to use deadly force to keep those outside out. Three Walmart's in different parts of the country had been taken over with those inside shooting anyone who came near. In the same sense, Sand Flea may become occupied and defended by the United States Army even more than it is now.

"You mean more troops?"

"Yes. McPherson hasn't heard anything for sure, but the Vice President has already talked the President into moving a whole Army division out to guard the Air Force Base just north of Las Vegas."

I groaned. "And he thinks we might be next?"

"Maybe."

"Well, I'd be the last one to doubt the Colonel's judgement. We'll concentrate on getting the rest of the Italian Job's pods installed."

"You read my mind, love."

The next four weeks went by quickly and fairly quietly. The remaining sections for the San Diego Cylinder came up and, except for leaving two sections open so we could fly the pods in, it was complete. I could see that we were nearing the finish line and I felt pretty good when I went down with Billy for our week on the ground.

Alex, myself and most of the old crew had a bunch of tables pushed together in the cafeteria when I met Joan and Erin McPherson. After introductions, I was listening to Cathy's hilarious tales of how she and Erin were ganging up on poor André when Billy walked up to the table.

It was a kind of unforgettable scene. Alex introduced him to Joan and they said some polite hellos, she then introduced Erin.

"Billy Wright, this is Erin McPherson," Alex said.

"Hi," Erin said and turned absolutely crimson.

Billy just stood there and didn't say a word. I swear, he looked like he had just been hit in the forehead with a mallet.

Billy finally managed a breathless, "Hi."

I could hear Alex say under her breath, "Oh my."

Erin smiled up at him and Billy said "Hi"

"You said that," I said and was rewarded by a kick from Alex under the table.

Billy got a chair and squeezed in next to Erin. Alex looked at Joan and they both smiled although Joan McPherson looked a little stunned. The conversation picked up around the table, but lost in their own little world, Billy and

Erin were oblivious to the rest of us.

Being the typical dumb male, maybe dumber than most, I whispered to Alex, "What just happened?"

Alex gave a little laugh, patted me on the cheek and said, "My sweet, if you didn't believe in love at first sight before, you surely would now."

For the next couple of days Billy didn't get ten feet from the kitchen. When Erin was busy, Billy was helping her and when she wasn't busy, they just sat and talked. Then Erin must have reached a decision point and one evening she brought Judy over to the evening gab fest so she could spend some time with grandma... and to meet Billy.

It was pretty obvious that men were not among Judy McPherson's favorite people, but she already knew about Voyager and robots and Robot Jockeys from her new classmates and her mother and grandmother knew a real-life Robot Jockey—well, two if you counted me.

Billy Wright was no dummy. He knew the family story, so he was cool. He and Judy talked as though there was no one else at the table. They talked about space and robots and what her new friends in school had told her. After a while Billy asked, "Well, how would you like to take a ride in a robot?"

I swear Judy's eyes got as big as dinner plates as she looked at Erin, her pleading gaze echoing how crushed she would be if the answer came back no.. "Could I? Could I, Mommy?"

Erin was as surprised as Judy and the rest of us, but before she could say anything Billy said, "Sure, why don't you and your Mommy meet me at the Starduster tomorrow morning and we'll take a little ride together."

What could Erin say... or Joan or even Alex?

The next morning, they were off and that evening we were all dying to hear the story of the day's events. They all had their own take, but it was probably best told by Judy herself as she bounced around the table with the words just tumbling out of her. She was so excited, she didn't even pause for breath, but just kept on talking as she sucked in more air to continue her tale.

"We got on a big airplane and we flew all around the world and then I could fly. I could really fly! I looked out of all the windows and then we kind of floated up to a big shiny thing in the sky and I floated into a round room that had all kinds of things in it and a very nice old man. He had white hair, but he was very nice. He let me sit in his lap and showed me the whole world. Then Mr. Wright took me to another window and there was the Voyager! It is ever so big and then we flew right into the Voyager and I sat in the driver's seat and then we went to what Mommy said was the pods. I'm not sure what they were, but there were a lot of them. They went as far as I could see and they were stacked all the way up to the celling. And then we flew through the tube again. I liked that.

"And then we went into a garage and that's where the robots were. Well, there was only one, Mr. Wright said the rest were out working. He said that this one was his and it had a name on it. My name... Judy! He asked if that was okay and I said yes. Then we got right inside. Mommy, Mr. Wright and me with a bunch of pillows and we flew right out into space. There was nothing around us and we could see the whole world and Voyager and everything! We flew all around. We even went over and waved at the nice old man. I even got to sit in Mr. Wright's lap and fly a little. Then it was time to go home and we got back into the airplane, but after a while I couldn't fly anymore. I liked to fly."

But Billy wasn't done yet. After Judy told her story Billy reached under his chair and pulled out a package and said that seeing as she had done so well as a Robot Jockey this was for her, but she had to take it back to her cubicle to open it.

Judy said thank you and went off. Two minutes later there was a delighted squeal that could be heard all over the hangar and two minutes after that Judy came running out wearing a bright blue flight suit with a Robot Jockey patch that said JUDY.

CHAPTER 23

Once again, Alex's phone rang just as I walked into her office, so with an apologetic smile, she waved me to a seat and flipped on the speaker. "Good evening, Colonel. And how are things in Washington this fine evening?"

McPherson chuckled. "Well, Madam Director, seeing as you asked, things are getting rather exciting in what's left of the Nation's Capital—and not necessarily in a good way."

"Oh?"

"First, I have a new job... well, not really a new job. I still work for Space Command and I'm still the point man for all things civilian space-wise, but I'm no longer in the Pentagon and I no longer work for Hawk Hunter."

I said, "Wow! What happened?"

"Hello, John. I didn't know you were there. What happened, what *is* happening, is that that idiot Hogan... "

Alex said, "Hagen."

The Colonel scowled, but his agitation wasn't at Alex's

correction. "Whatever. That idiot suit from the White House Staff who has been running around Sand Flea making an ass of himself for the last couple of months is now running around Washington spreading all kinds of ridiculous rumors about what you civilian companies are up to."

"Ah," I said knowingly. All of us expected this. "And just what are we up to?"

"Well, for starters you are all part of a 'Deep State' conspiracy that is planning on going to Mars to set up a rival government that is going to come back and invade Earth. And if you don't like that one, another theory is that you're not planning to go to Mars at all, but are going to place all kinds of weapons of mass destruction in orbit around Earth. Hogan actually has half the people in Washington convinced that you're planning on taking over the entire Earth!"

Alex and I cracked up thinking that people could actually believe that garbage.

"Go ahead and laugh!" McPherson wasn't nearly as amused. "You think it's funny, but there are plenty of paranoids in the White House and on Capitol Hill who will believe any conspiracy theory that comes along and they are believing this one or one of the ones. Yesterday I was called over to the White House to brief the President, the Vice President and the entire National Security Council on what you shifty, devious, anti-American, socialist, commie civilians out there in the desert at Sand Flea are up to. The briefing went pretty well, I think. I managed to calm everyone down and made Hogan…"

"Hagan"

"Out to be an idiot. That actually seemed to please several of the White house Staffers, but definitely not Collins. I think, I hope, I sent most everyone away with the thought that you are all a bunch of nut cases with looney ideas of space or Martian habitats with half-built space ships or rockets or whatever. Of course, I made sure to let them know that you at Voyager are the most pathetic of all."

Alex became more sober. "Thank you, Alex, but that doesn't explain why you are now in the White House."

McPherson ruefully shook his head. "All you have to know about that is how the mind of the typical ass-kissing political staffer works and the explanation follows. After I finished my briefing, the President said to no one in particular, 'McPherson seems to be the only one who knows what's going on. I don't like having him way over in the Pentagon.' Not a half an hour later I was re-assigned from the Vice Chief of Staff United States Air Force Office to the President's Chief of Staff's staff. I even have a desk right here in the White House. It's not much of a desk and it's shoved into a room with a lot of other desks, but it is here in the White House. I guess I should be kind of proud of that, but it's inconvenient as hell. Beside the fact that most of my contacts are in the Pentagon, I am still living in the house out in Virginia. Hell of a commute and unlike my old office I don't have a place here where I can rack out when I don't feel like going home."

McPherson paused to mentally digest the change before going on, "But we do have a potential problem. After the briefing, the Vice President asked me what I knew about something called Sanctuary. I played the dumb route and asked if he meant the Sanctuary Cities. He said that he didn't think so and that he had heard the term from a business associate of his; That it sounded more like a destination. I told him that I had no idea, that I hadn't heard the term used that way before, but that I would look into it. That's where we left it, but I'm afraid someone, probably someone from Visions Unlimited who was asked to join Voyager and declined, has been talking."

"Damn it!" I swore. "Well, Colonel, I guess we should consider ourselves lucky that the secret has been kept this long, but what about you? If they find out how you have been covering up for Sanctuary and us, you're a dead man. You better polish up that bug-out plan of yours and get out here."

"Thanks for the concern, John, but I don't think that it's that desperate yet. Anyway, with the move to the White House, my original bug-out plan is shot. While I could probably have dropped out of sight from the Pentagon, I now have a hundred political staffers watching me like a hawk just waiting for me to screw up so they can eliminate another rival. No, don't worry I'm working on a new plan. A better plan."

Alex frowned and asked, "Have you told Joan any of this?"

"Of course. I called her before I called you."

Alex just shook her head. "You said there were two things?"

"Yes, and this one may have a more significant impact on our plans."

That didn't sound good.

"Have you been watching the news feeds or what's left of them, lately?"

We looked at each other and I said, "Sure, when we can. Why?"

"Have you seen anything about the spread of infectious diseases?"

Alex said, "No. Most of the coverage that we've seen

has been on the demonstrations around the White House, the refugees piling up on the Mexican border, the North Coast of Africa and the dozen or more wars that are taking place around the world. I haven't heard anything in particular on disease."

I shook my head; I didn't know, either.

"That's what I thought. The reason you haven't seen it is because the administration is suppressing it. Earlier today, representatives from the Centers for Disease Control and the World Health Organization were in the White House briefing the President, VP and a half dozen of the senior staff. I wasn't in on the briefing, but from what I gather, there isn't just one pandemic building in various parts of the world, there are three. An Ebola strain that probably started from humans eating jungle animals in Central Africa, a particularly nasty coronavirus coming out of the mid-east and a return of the plague, if you can believe it. The original Black Death is moving west from Mongolia."

We were stunned. Alex asked, "What does the government plan to do?"

The Colonel snorted. "Outside of keeping their mouth shut and closing our borders that are effectively closed anyway to all international travel—nothing. Apparently, the Vice President blew up during the briefing said that it wasn't true, that it was all a political conspiracy to make him look bad and threw the medical professionals out."

I said, "Wow! What did Rheingold say?"

"As far as I know, not a damn thing."

"What do you think?" Alex asked the Colonel.

"Are you kidding?" McPherson could barely contain his outrage. "If the CDC and WHO say there's a pandemic out there, there's a goddamn pandemic out there! In normal times with international cooperation, pandemics would probably be contained, but these are far from normal times. With climate change knocking economic and political structures apart, there probably aren't a dozen functioning governments left in the world outside of Europe and North America, so there will be no organized response. In my opinion, those diseases are going to go through the hordes of refugees in Asia and Africa, maybe even Europe too, like a hot knife through butter."

Alex asked, "What about us—the United States or even the Western Hemisphere?"

"Hard to say. There certainly isn't a lot of international travel these days, so if air travel to the US is cut off maybe it won't jump the ocean. But if it does or if the paranoids in charge even think it has—I don't know. There are already mobs shouting for electric power and food around every state capitol in the country; Mobs around the White House and Capitol, too. There are protesters out there day and night—perfect breeding grounds for a virus or even rumors of a virus, to spread.

"The White House is hunkering down, or should I say becoming even more hunkered down, if that's possible. The only way in and out of the building is through the tunnels. The roads are all blocked with concrete barriers and there's a ten-foot metal fence around the perimeter. Guards are everywhere checking for passes and photo IDs. I have a designated parking space in a disused parking garage five blocks from the White House and I need three separate badges to get to my desk. I need one badge to get into one of the tunnels that lead to the White House, another badge and a finger print check to get into the basement of the White house, then one more to get into the West Wing. And to make it more paranoid, if that's even possible, the badges change every ten days, so I can see that I am going to spend half my time processing new badges."

I guess that it wasn't really funny, but Alex and I couldn't help laughing.

McPherson, however, was not amused. "Go ahead and laugh, but I guarantee you wouldn't think it was funny if you were here. In addition to the badges there are people with guns all over the place. Not soldiers or marines but people in civilian clothes."

Alex said, "Sorry, Colonel. I know it's a serious situation, but I can't help shaking my head. What about the Congress?"

"Still functioning after a fashion. Several Senators and Representatives went home and stayed there, but many didn't. Those who are left are mostly living in their offices. Even at that, there is still some semblance of order and government here and in most parts of the country, so I guess if sealing the borders works, the US might escape a pandemic. But if any one of these diseases gets loose in the country, anything can happen. The people that I see here in the White House and on Capitol Hill every day aren't wired too tight. Who knows what they may decide to do?"

Alex thanked McPherson again, told him to not take any unnecessary risks and rang off. I didn't say anything, but just sat there and watched as she steepled her hands under her chin in her typical thinking position.

She brains, me brawn; I continued to quietly wait.

After a few minutes, Alex shook herself and smiled. "John, would you please go and quietly round up Chet, Dot,

Phil, and the Docs and bring them here. Oh, and whoever the senior cryogenic expert is from that San Diego bunch who's been waiting to go up to Voyager."

I was off. It didn't take long, but I had to laugh when I got to the cryo engineers. According to them, no one was really in charge and none of them seemed to want the job. They finally settled on a guy named Dave Allen. From past experience, I figured that he must be the junior man.

We all trooped into Alex's office and while I introduced Allen around Alex waved us all to our seats. Perching on the edge of her desk, she got right to business. "Dot, Nancy, gentlemen... John and I just got off the phone with our good friend in Washington."

Nods and smiles around the room and a puzzled look from Dave Allen.

Alex smiled at him and said, "You don't need to know his name, Mr. Allen, but we do have a very good friend deep inside the Administration who keeps us informed on current developments and looks out for our interests. But before I go into the details of the conversation, I would like a status report from each of you so we all know where we stand. Phil, what's our shuttle status?"

"Knock on wood, all four are up and running," Phil answered.

"Good, very good. Spare parts for the Stardusters?"

"I've already received everything that the manufactures had and I don't think that there will be any more. From what my contacts tell me, the latest flood completely wiped out the plant in Kansas and they're not going to rebuild. Unless we get another manufacturer for Stardusters, the parts we have on hand are all we are ever going to see."

Alex thought for a moment and said, "Right. Chet, what's our security situation?"

"I have forty deputies here at Sand Flea and Link has eight running security for the pods from the factory in San Diego to the launch pad in Tucson. Since Colonel Blake came in with his big battalion or small regiment or whatever it is, the Army and *only* the Army are guarding the air field gates and patrolling the perimeter fence. We are strictly private security around our own facilities."

The arrival of Colonel Blake and about fifteen hundred soldiers happened while I was up at Voyager. One day Nils Nielsen got a call from a very apogeic Army Chief of Staff, one Gray Harris, (I never did get the exact connection but apparently Nielsen and Harris went way back) who told him that he and the rest of the executives on Sand Flea would be visited by a Colonel Blake who originally had orders directly from the VP to 'take over the airfield'. Apparently, a furious Harris had stepped in at that point and had revised the orders to where Blake was going to absorb the hundred or so soldiers that were already at Sand Flea and then Blake would be working directly for him and not the Vice President. Harris had also made it clear to Nielsen that Blake's orders were to secure the airfield and not harass the private businesses.

As far as Alex was concerned Blake was one of the good guys. When he flew in to Sand Flea, it was just himself and a couple of aids and, unlike Hagen, Blake's meeting with the Sand Flea executives was a very quiet affair that had been coordinated well in advance. Alex said that Hagen had been in the meeting and, though he hadn't said a word, she thought that he might self-combust at any moment.

Anyway, Blake told them and Nielsen confirmed from his conversation with Harris that he was definitely not there to pursue or confirm any nutty conspiracy theories, but to secure the airfield. He went on to assure Nils that he and his soldiers would not interfere in their legitimate business activities and to emphasize that the first thing he was going to do was to pull all the soldiers out of the private enterprises.

Alex said that Hagan was really ready to explode at that, but one look from Colonel Blake and he didn't say a word. I had never met Colonel Blake, but I liked him already.

I asked if Sergeant Daniels and his squad were still with us and Alex laughed and said that they had been pulled out, but before they left, Alice made Daniels and his squad turn everything that was issued back in and meticulously checked off each and every item.

Alex said another very amicable meeting with Colonel Blake followed. The soldiers were moved out of Agnes Robertson's rather warm warehouse and air-conditioned buildings were subsequently found for all of his men and women and a few days later they started flying in. According to Alex, she certainly approved of all the decisions but "just kept my small-fry company mouth shut".

"Geeze!" I said. "If this Colonel Blake has his soldiers all guarding the outer fence, they must be dying out there in the heat, sand and bugs."

Chet chuckled. "No, Blake has them all in some kind of vehicle. He commandeered, very politely, almost every vehicle he could find on the airfield and after that he scooped up everything that he could find that would run in town. Then he sent his engineers out to drain every drop of gas they could find from the abandoned gas stations and immobile cars all around Sand Flea. He even had one of those big flexible gasoline bladders flown in. His soldiers might have to get out of their vehicles if they have to shoot someone, but they can walk their posts in a car or truck or something."

"Good, very good," Alex said, though I was sure she already knew. She turned to the Docs. "Status on personnel for Voyager?"

"There are about three hundred men, women and children here in the hangars waiting to go up and more are flying in every day," Doc Nancy answered.

Alex nodded and then smiled at a completely baffled Dave Allen. "I guess that it's a bit over whelming, Mr. Allen, but bear with us. I understand that you have five technicians with you?"

"Yes, Ma'am."

Continuing to smile at him, Alex turned to me. "Okay, John, you're on. What's the status of Voyager?"

"As you all know, the large supply cylinder is attached to Voyager, but it is still open to space and I'd say about ninety percent full. The Italian Job is finished as far as we can go. The cryogenic pods are all installed and the service catwalks are finished. The rest is up to the cryogenic specialists and, I guess the doctors. The second large cryogenic cylinder, the San Diego Job, is still open to space, but we do have the sections to finish it and it is not yet attached to Voyager. The San Diego Job has two-hundred and thirteen cryogenic pods installed, but like the Italian Job, none are cryogenically ready. Link is currently escorting a convoy of thirty pods to Rocket 3 and he thinks that after that there might be one more shipment of thirty, but he's afraid that might be it. Two of Wisdom's five cylinders are attached to Voyager, two more have been packed, but are still attached to Wisdom."

"John, how long do you think it would take to close up the San Diego Job and get it attached to Voyager?"

"Not long, a week to ten days if everything fits."

"Thank you. Does anyone have any questions?"

We all looked around and Dave Allen kind of hesitantly held up his hand.

Alex smiled. "Yes, Mr. Allen, I think I know your question. You have over six hundred cryogenic pods to hook up; John didn't tell you about the dozen in the original Voyager that still need to be done. And you have to then put that many humans into cryogenic sleep *and* you only have six people. Anything else?"

"No, Ma'am," the poor man whispered. The poor man was operating well above his pay grade, so even if he did have any other questions, he probably was too overwhelmed to ask them.

"Thank you, Dave—may I call you Dave?"

"Yes, Ma'am."

"Alex, please," she said before going over McPherson's phone call with us. Grimly, she said, "The wolves aren't closing in on us quite yet, but they're getting close. I think that it's time to plan for the end game—maybe a very quick end game."

Giving us all another smile, she said, "Alright, people, this is what I would like: John, you, Dave and his men are to go up on the next Starduster and get with your merry men. The first priority is to get the cryogenic pods in the Italian Job ready to receive the colonists, then close up the San Diego Job, get it attached to Voyager and give it an environment so Dave and his people can get to work. And I don't want to hear any grumbling about how hard it is to move pods through R3 and Voyager."

"Yes, boss."

"Next, move AI into the cockpit of Voyager, pack up Wisdom—all of it—and attach it to Voyager. I don't know if AI can look like a space station once that's done, but after the last month or so, I sure know that he can sound like one."

The got a chuckle and Alex asked, "Is anyone else on Wisdom?"

"Entomologist Dan McIntyre and the botanist Tyler West; Both scheduled to go on Voyager."

"Good." Now Alex turned her attention to the very dazed Dave. "Dave, if you would get with your people, I want you to brief them on the situation and tell them to be ready to go up into space in the morning. If you think that it would be helpful to have any or all of them come in and talk to me, that would be fine. Also, put your heads together to see how we can help. There's the medical staff and all the robot jockeys are engineers. Of course, we will want one of our medical staff people on hand when people are put into cryogenic sleep."

Dave Allen gave kind of a dazed nod.

"Questions? No?" When the poor guy didn't move, Alex made shooing motions with her hands. "Then go."

It was a busy afternoon, but by the next morning we were ready to go. Once Dave Allen and his techs caught up on the situation, they were right in with the rest of us. Overnight they had loaded the Stardusters cargo bay with six hundred and fifty identical boxes. When I asked, I was told that each box contained a complete set of connections for a cryogenic pod.

I looked at Alex and said, "Three or four weeks?"

She smiled and nodded. "Yes, I think so. It will probably depend on when the Colonel can get here and when, where and how we can pick Link and his men up."

"Don't worry, Luv," I smiled. "We'll get them."

CHAPTER 24

I flew the Starduster up to Wisdom the next day with Dave Allen and his small team of Cryogenic specialists. Dave seemed like a nice guy; In fact, they all did and, if I understood correctly, they were all going to Sanctuary. But I could see that with so few people doing the final installation on the cryo pods that part of the operation had the potential of being a real bottleneck. Despite the fact that we were working as fast as we possibly could, the clock was now ticking which made every move we made in zero gravity feel like we were moving in slow motion.

With time now an unexpected enemy, the moment we docked at Wisdom, Dave and his crew were given a warp speed indoctrination on living in space before getting right down to business. While the work was relatively easy, it was slow and frustrating. Three hundred cryogenic pod instillation kits not only had to be retrieved from the Starduster storage bay and floated into the Italian Job the hard way through R3 and Voyager, but Dave and his people didn't have time to adjust to the pitfalls of being weightless before they had to get working. People had to enter through Wisdom, while everything else went through R3 and Voyager. I'm afraid that with four robots pulling the kits out of the shuttle bay and passing them out to the rest of us like a bucket brigade, it took a while before the cryo specialists were more help than hinderance.

I suppose that in reality, it really didn't take that long and the slow motion was just an illusion brought on by my anxiety of how short on time we were now.

However, we still had the three hundred pod kits that were for the San Diego Cylinder plus the last dozen cryo installation kits for our dormitory. Since Dave's gang wasn't ready for them yet, I just wanted to leave them in the Stardusters' cargo bay and pull them out as we needed them, but Alex nixed that. Since she needed that shuttle for other supplies, we had to move the kits one by one into the storage yard.

Once that was done and the cryo specialists were no longer needing our help maneuvering, we got going on the rest of Alex's orders. Al and the two scientists took care of packing up the last tube of Wisdom by carefully cushioning all the delicate items with dozens of rolls of toilet paper while Fred and JJ attached the other two sections of Wisdom to Voyager.

Another item we had to handle was scrap iron. Brian Anders, our resident blacksmith, managed to convince Alex that without some metal on hand, he wouldn't be able to produce anything once we got to Sanctuary. So, two big bundles of scrap were brought up and fastened to the outside of Voyager's hull in what we hoped were out of the way places. When we were finished, Voyager really began looking like a flying junk yard.

Dave Allen may have been a little hesitant in his first meeting with Alex and the staff, but once he got started, he proved that he really knew his stuff. Working with Tony and Paul along with our four apprentices and two of the Watson's medical staff, he soon had them organized into five teams and they were leap-frogging right down the aisle hooking up pods. By the end of the next day, we were happy to tell Alex that twenty pods were ready for space travelers.

Alex didn't waste any time. After a brief conference with Dave, the Docs and Josh Simmons to confirm that there were no safety issues with putting people into cryogenic sleep at one end of the Italian Job while we were still working on the other end, two Starduster loads of intrepid and very apprehensive space travelers arrived.

Talk about being Guinea Pigs!

I really felt sorry for these guys and gals and even recognized a few of them from the Voyager compound at Sand Flea, but whether they were old hands or newbies none of them had ever been into space or had actually ever seen Voyager. Their minds might have been more at ease if the ship that was going to ferry them to another star system actually looked like the sleek model they had been shown in Alex's office and not the piecemeal collection of parts we ended up with. To say that they were a little apprehensive as we hustled them through Wisdom and Voyager and into the huge cryogenic cylinder would be a gross understatement.

But, for the most, part they took it well, laughing and

joking as we floated them down the cylinder. Then we hit a show stopper. Human beings are funny critters. Flying out of Earth's atmosphere into space, no problem. Crawling into a torpedo tube naked and sleeping for twenty years, they were fine with that, too. They had been told in advance that they couldn't wear clothes or jewelry of any kind into the pods and a couple actually thought it was a little bit kinky.

But when it came to actually stripping naked in front of a couple dozen strangers—*that* was a problem.

Geeze!

The cryo team were professionals and managed to preserve as best they could the colonists' modesty. Eventually, it all got done with the travelers' tucking themselves into the pods for their long sleep while their clothes went into the storage bins at the head of each pod. As more colonists came up and saw the others already bedded down for their long sleep, their modest inhibitions became fewer. If their neighbors had stripped, so could they.

I must admit it felt kind of creepy working at one end of the cylinder while a growing number of people were in cryogenic sleep at the other end. Somehow afraid I might wake them up, I found myself whispering and trying to be quiet.

While Dave, the Docs and their teams were doing their thing, the rest of us worked on installing the last of the pods that we had into the San Diego Job. That gave us two hundred and forty-three pods with a possibility of maybe thirty more. Unfortunately, even if we received every pod that had been promised, we would still be twenty-seven pods short of the planned three hundred. That was a bummer. It would be a ballbuster if we didn't have enough pods and we had to leave someone behind.

No, stay positive, I told myself. That won't happen!

To ensure we were ready on our end, when we finished the San Diego Cylinder, we temporally pulled all the RJs off of pod installation and dealt with our second 'Queen Mary of the Space ways' by moving the second Cryogenic Cylinder out into the void and then attaching it to Voyager.

To our relief, we had no problems. Having already attached one, there was nothing like experience to make the next one easier. Two days later, the second Cryogenic Cylinder had a shirt sleeve environment and was ready for Dave and his crew.

We set up another bucket brigade and moved the last three hundred installation kits out of our scrap yard and into the San Diego Job.

Down on the ground the Visions Unlimited compound was just as busy getting the colonists and last of the supplies and equipment up to us under the noses of the ever-increasing military and government presence on Sand Flea. Alex said that she wasn't worried about the military people, Colonel Blake had been true to his word and kept his soldiers out of the civilian work spaces. I had a laugh when she told me that just about the only time, she saw any uniforms was when Colonel Blake and his staff showed up for one of André's excellent dinners. Of course, Voyager was always glad to oblige and André would come out of the kitchen and keep them laughing with his tales of being a chef in Vegas. It was great PR and we were sure that as far as the Army was concerned, VU was one of the good guys.

The government goons, i.e. the Vice Presidents goons, were another matter. Those paranoid morons wandered in and out of every companies' work spaces day and night knowing that eventually they would catch somebody doing something subversive. When Hagan was at Sand Flea and not creating havoc back in Washington, he seemed especially interested in our Starduster tourist flights. No wonder, with one or two flights almost every day, everyone must have thought that our business was booming. Alex said that once he came into her office and demanded a flight. Alex said sure—for a quarter of a million bucks. That hadn't happened yet.

Alex interviewed every one of the colonists and did the best she could to select the right specialists for her potential 'away teams' when we arrived at Sanctuary and, using all four shuttles, she sent them up just as fast as we were ready and the Stardusters could make the trip. Alex put out the word to the VU Board of Directors that now was the time and anyone who was on their "to go" list should get to Sand Flea now.

In short order, a flood of executive jets, both private and cooperate, were landing at the normally pretty sleepy Sand Flea Airfield; However, not all of those jets were taking off again. Most flew in, dropped their passengers and departed, but several didn't. In those aircraft, everyone on board was making the trip to Sanctuary and now Alex had a new problem on her hands of what to do with the dozen or so executive jets that were starting to pile up. She didn't want to leave them parked around the VU area because the neighbors might notice and start asking embarrassing questions.

Again, the brilliant Rocket Jockey, John Marshal, came through with an ideal solution. Seriously, I really should go on strike for more money! My idea, of course, was the boneyard.

When I first flew into Sand Flea three years ago, I noticed that on the southwest edge of the airfield there was a graveyard of airplanes, both large and small, being slowly sandblasted into oblivion by the unrelenting desert now that their commercial use was gone. All we had to do was taxi any leftover jets over to the boneyard and park them with the other hundred or so commercial air liners and they would blend right in.

Of course, despite that solution, everybody on Sand Flea was beginning to notice all our activity. The fact that something was going down around the Visions Unlimited area was pretty hard to miss. But at least for now, they, along with the Army and I guess the government goons, must have thought that we must be doing one hell of a business in space tourism because, surprisingly enough outside of wondering and speculating, no one said a word—not even the goons.

I was beginning to think that things were going too smoothly and, naturally, they were. And when they started to come unglued, it was with a vengeance.

First came the weather. Al called down to Alex to give her a heads up that yet another monster Haboob was moving in fast and as luck would have it, five business jets had just landed. Two of them wanted to risk taking off, but Phil recounted to them our unfortunate episode a couple of years ago and managed to talk them out of it. We had one Starduster up at Wisdom and he had three parked in the hangars, but he managed to cram three of the executive jets in with them. The other two were scheduled for the boneyard so they were left on their own outside between the two rows of hangars.

It was five days later that the Haboob finally blew through and people could get back outside. I was up at

Voyager so I didn't get the full story until Alex called.

And quite a story it was! Alex said that when they finally got outside to check the damage, one of the executive jets had every inch of paint sandblasted off its fuselage and was such a wreck that it had to be towed over to the boneyard. But as bad as that one was, it had fared better than the other one that was lying on a crumpled heap with one wing plastered against the door of Hangar 3. Alex wondered what to do with it, but Dot was in favor of just leaving it there. She said that it added to Visions Unlimited harmless pathetic refugee look.

So, that's where they left it and as far as I know it's still there.

The airfield itself was in such bad shape that it took three full days with every company on Sand Flea contributing. Surprisingly, even the army pitched in to clear the runway and taxiways to make the airfield operational again.

Of course, the weather didn't bother us up in space, but we were still affected by it. We had gone as far as we could go with the material that had been sent up. If nothing more could be sent up until the storm blew through, we had nothing to do except watch Planet Earth turn slowly through the void as it tumbled further into ruin. As we no longer had AI's big screen in Wisdom to look at, everyone sat well anchored around the dormitory and watched the world disaster play out on our own pads.

I was switching around from one disaster to another when Tony said, "My God! Go to International Channel 2."

Immediately switching over, it took me a few moments to understand what I was seeing. It must have been late evening wherever this was because the screen was almost dark. I couldn't even tell what country I was watching until I finally realized that the Vid wasn't showing land but water. What I was seeing was hundreds of boats and a reporter was giving a voiceover describing the scene.

"After the reported outbreak of the Ebola pandemic in both Tunis and Algiers, there are now close to a million refugees crowding into boats of all sizes and types all along the North African shoreline. Each and every one of these boats seems to be headed out into the Mediterranean Sea and straight toward the blockade of European Union naval vessels that have been in place for months."

The Vid was pretty dark, but I could see it now: two lines of ships facing each other. On one side, there were maybe fifty modern warships representing every maritime nation in the EU and on the other side there seemed to be anything that would float—everything from rubber rafts, row boats, fishing boats, ferries and even small cargo ships. All of them were crowded to overflowing with refugees who at first had been trying to get away from thirst and starvation, but now were trying desperately to get away from the suspected Ebola outbreak.

The EU flotilla was unempathetic and unyielding. If they were going to refuse the refugees entry into European Countries before, they for sure were not going to let a pandemic reach European shores.

Suddenly the camera zoomed in on one boat. It was one of those big rubber rafts that could probably safely carry about twenty people and now must have about fifty aboard. The reporter who was now speaking Italian, suddenly sounded panicked as people started jumping overboard.

"What happened?" Al asked.

Tony said, "The reporter thought that someone onboard had Ebola and everyone started bailing out to get away from them."

They were in the middle of the Mediterranean! Bailing out to where? Not one of the boats on either side, the Europeans or the refugees, made a move to help anyone in the water.

The camera pulled back just as a small fishing boat in the refugee flotilla tried to take advantage of the general confusion and make a run through the EU lines. A European Corvette charged up and just ran the little boat over—literally plowed him under. That seemed to be a signal and the entire fleet of refugee vessels charged toward the EU fleet and the supposed sanctuary of Europe.

The European Fleet didn't hesitate and every ship opened fire with everything they had. In the dim light of boat lamps and reporter's cameras, I saw ships being blown out of the water and the flashes of thousands of guns streaking across the night sky.

While I was trying to absorb that shocking massacre, someone else said, "Channel 1."

Switching channels, the time was about midday. I was looking at the White House and a mob of protesters numbering in the tens of thousands pressing up against the heavily fortified barriers protecting the executive mansion. The camera must have been on a drone because there was no way that a stand or tower could have stood in the wave of people that were surrounding the White House grounds. The Army units deployed around the White House were easily outnumbered a hundred to one.

I couldn't hear the reporter over the roar from the

mob shouting "Food, give us food!" "Let us in!" and sinister chants of "Rheingold!". The ugly scene was made even more so by the fact that in Washington it was like a sauna at nearly a one hundred and twenty degrees. The heat must be driving already angry people to even further fits of insanity.

There had been crowds, even mobs, outside the Sand Flea gates, but this one was far worse than anything we'd ever had here. It was a powder keg; One spark and it would blow turning this crazed gang into killers.

The spark came when the camera shifted to the mob and we could see a clear space opening up around someone lying on the ground and then the mob started yelling "Plague! Plague!"

As we watched, five big helicopters swept in and landed on the White House lawn. When they touched down, the mob went berserk. Ramps appeared against the fence that surrounded the White House and the rioters now panicked by the plague rumor quickly climbed over and poured onto the White House grounds. The soldiers opened fire and people began falling like ten pins. I guessed that in less than a minute at least a hundred were killed. The panic-stricken mob didn't even notice and swept over the soldiers without even breaking stride.

Four of the helicopters were already loaded with the people fleeing from the White House and were taking off as fast as possible while the fifth one was boarding its last passengers. One individual was starting to climb on, but then stopped. Turning, he started walking toward the on-rushing wave of humanity and I was willing to bet anything that it was Rheingold. Always the diplomat, he must have thought that he could reason with this pack of rabid dogs. The mob washed over him like a wave hits the shore and poured onto the helicopter. It didn't get off.

As the four helicopters escaped, the mob turned its wrath on the White House itself. We watched spellbound for over an hour while they rampaged through the White House with the drones zooming in recording the entire scene. They might have been shouting for water and food and relief from the pandemic outside, but once inside the White House they were just looting everything they could get their hands on from paintings, silverware… even furniture if they could carry it.

Then the White House was on fire.

I was aware of the announcer again as he reported that the helicopters had flown to Andrews Air Force Base and Air Force One and Two along with several other government aircraft had taken off.

Riveted by what was happening, I jumped as my Vid chimed and Alex asked, "Are you watching?"

"Yes, but I'm having a hard time believing what I'm seeing. I wonder where the Colonel is in all that. I hope he's okay."

"He is," Alex said. "McPherson just called and said that he was executing his new bug out plan. You will never guess where he is."

"I'm too stunned to take guesses, Luv."

"He's on Air Force One."

"He's where?" I was incredulous.

"That's what he said! Also, they're heading for the Air Force Base just outside of Las Vegas. Also, Rheingold is dead and Collins was just sworn in as President."

"Oh, joy. I thought that was Rheingold that went

down under the mob. So, what now?"

"We just keep going, John, as fast as we can. The Colonel doesn't think that the Collins' government is going to last too long at Vegas. Have you got all the pods installed?"

"Yes!" I couldn't keep the relief out of my voice. "All two hundred and forty-three of them and we buttoned up the Supply Cylinder."

"Good, because Link is on the road from San Diego to Rocket 3 with thirty more pods. Rocket 3 is closing down, but they are going to do this last lift for us. The bad news is that we will only have two hundred and seventy-three cryogenic pods—twenty-seven short."

"How many people do we have?"

"For the San Diego Cylinder, two hundred and fifty-six so far and as soon as this damn sand stops blowing, I'm going to send the rest of them up."

"Good—and you get up here, too!"

Alex smiled. "No, not yet, my sweet. There's still Link's people down in Tucson or San Diego or wherever they're going to be and the Colonel."

Damn! I knew she would say that. "Okay, send everyone up and all the Stardusters. When everything is ready to go up here, I'll bring a shuttle down and we'll wait together."

"Together is good. See you soon."

The next few days were a blur. The colonists and the last thirty cryo pods kind of arrived together so we had colonists floating around before we had all the pods fully installed. It had been hard enough moving seven-foot-long pods through R3 and Voyager; It was even harder with a couple of dozen colonists drifting by.

While they were trying to help, they actually ended up just getting in the way. Most of them were the ones who had been nominated by the VU Board who had just arrived at Sand Flea. These people hadn't been with us for the last three years watching this crazy dream grow, so to say that they were apprehensive would be an understatement. Having just left whatever hidey-hole they had been in, they had climbed aboard their very comfortable executive jets and flown out into the desert only to then be loaded on to a Starduster and flown up to a spaceship—without their belongings. I'm not sure what they were expecting to happen once they got here, but being told to strip and lie down in a torpedo hadn't been it.

Things got much better after Doc John and Doc Nancy took over and calmed everyone down and Dave's crew put everyone into the pods for the long sleep. I had to laugh when Billy came in to help put Erin and Judy into hibernation. Judy put up major a fuss—not about going into the pod, but because she didn't want to take off her cherished flight suit. Doc Nancy was all smiles and patience and in the end it all got done with Judy tucked in for her long nap with her flight suit folded neatly inside her own personal storage box.

No longer needed on Voyager, I immediately took the last Starduster down to Sand Flea… and Alex. I was very glad I did. The moment our new President Collins landed in Vegas, he started a purge of all organizations and individuals he deemed "subversive or disloyal" to him personally… especially all those space people. One of his first orders was that that there would be no more rocket launches or space flights. I was coming down anyway, but the only reason I was considered an authorized flight was that the Colonel convinced him to allow a flight to bring down the scientists from Wisdom and not leave them stranded in space.

Of course, there was no one on this Starduster flight except me.

CHAPTER 25

J ohn, where are you?"

It was almost dusk in Sand Flea when Alex screened me and the urgency in her voice could not be a good thing. "About twenty minutes out, why?"

"I've got the Colonel on the Vid. Go ahead, Colonel."

McPherson wasn't wasting any time with pleasantries, either. "Alex, John! Let me give this to you fast. At the moment I am with the rest of the administration staff loading on to Air Force One here at Nellis. There was a rumored report of a case of Plague in Vegas and then a case of Ebola right here on Nellis. Collins panicked and ordered everyone to take him to Sand Flea. I guess that outside of Area 51, Collins thinks that you're the only secure place in the country. My suggestion to you is to implement your own bug out plan immediately."

Before I could say it, Alex said, "Not without you,

Colonel. And we have a few other loose people to take care of, too."

Thinking fast, I asked, "Colonel, do you know where Collins is going once you land here at Sand Flea?"

"I'm not a hundred percent sure, but my guess would be over in the Wendover area."

"Okay. When you land, you get clear as quick as you can and then come and find me. I'll be between you and the VU area and I'll be in a California Highway Patrol car."

"No," the Colonel insisted. "I don't want to get you involved. Once Collins lands, that runway is going to be closed, so you had better get away now while you can. If I try to join you and Collins finds out that I have bolted, his minions will be after me in a heartbeat. I had better stay put."

I drew in breath to retort how bad an idea that was, but Alex beat me to it again. "Colonel, why don't you let us worry about the getaway plan and please follow John's instructions. Besides, I don't want to be the one who has to wake Joan up in twenty years and tell her that you're not with us."

McPherson clearly didn't like it. With Alex hitting that low blow, he sighed and said that he would do it. By this time, I was on final approach and the tower started screaming at me to abort and get out of the way because there was priority traffic behind me.

Ha! Fat chance of that. I went ahead and landed with the tower still frantically yelling in my ear to clear the runway. Just as I was turning off toward the VU area, a huge plane touched down right behind me followed closely by a second... both had United States of America painted boldly across the fuselage.

That was close! The moment I taxied into hangar 5 and exited my Starduster, Alex, Phil, Dot, Chet ran to meet me. Giving me a quick kiss on the cheek, Alex said, "Air force One just landed and is headed over to Wendover. Now, go and get our Colonel."

Pedro had the CHP car ready and waiting when I ran into the hangar and he handed me the keys. Grinning mischievously, he shook his finger at me and said that this was his best one and be sure to bring it back. Apparently, he'd just heard about the *Rocket Incident* and no longer trusted me with his vehicles.

I was still laughing as I drove out of the hangar.

Driving out onto the apron I could see that already a half dozen cars and trucks were pulling down the runway to park. Collins sure didn't waste any time! He was going to make sure that whatever pandemic was out there wasn't going to follow him here. It was tough luck for the other airplanes that had followed Air Force One and Two out of Vegas. I could see their lights circling overhead, but it was clear that no one else was going to land at Sand Flea.

Of course, there were six or seven hundred people that had packed into the two 747's that were already parked in the Wendover area. There was no way to know if anyone on board either one of them were already infected, but I'm sure Collins hadn't given that possibility a thought. As he was now the man in charge, I was certain he considered himself immune to anything that affected other people.

Picking a spot on the runway between the presidential planes in the Wendover area and VU, I hid in plain sight with the rest of the cars and trucks before calling Alex. "So, Luv, what can you see?"

Alex was in her office and with all her magic machines she could see just about everything on Sand Flea. "Not much. Air Force One taxied in and the doors opened. A bunch of people started exiting the rear of the airplane, but Collins just stood in the main doorway waiting for the stairs. When it became obvious that no stairs were going to materialize, he disappeared and finally exited out the rear with the rest. Now it looks like a crowd is going into Wendover's main administration building."

The passenger door of my squad car jerked open. I was so startled I almost jumped out of the car. "Geeze, Colonel! Don't scare me like that."

McPherson laughed and gave me an apologetic, "Sorry."

As I started driving back toward VU his phone rang. There is nothing like hearing one half of a conversation.

"Hello! Andy? Is that you? Where are you? Really? How—never mind. No, I don't think that that would be a good idea. Just a minute." Turning to me, he said, "I can't believe it! It's my son and he's here in Sand Flea with Audrey and the kids. I can't believe it! I haven't heard from him in weeks. He said that the minute he heard that the administration bugged out of Washington, he packed Audrey and the kids up headed out here. He hadn't called because he didn't want to be tracked. I can't believe it. I can't wait to tell Joan!"

I didn't think that anything could phase the cool, calm Colonel, but who could blame him? I wasn't about to crush his look of sheer joy by reminding him that Joan was already in cryogenic sleep and he wasn't going to tell her anything for twenty years. He'd remember on his own soon enough. Instead, I asked where his family was.

"Andy, where are you?" McPherson asked, quickly pulling himself together. "Okay, wait a moment... He says he's on the main road coming into town and he wants to know if he should try to get onto the airfield."

"No," I said, "definitely not! There are mobs at the gates and if they don't shoot him, Blake's soldiers surely will." I was trying to think fast and I had a flash. Ask him if when he was driving in if he saw a small state road going off to the right. State road 304."

McPherson passed the question on. "Yes, they just passed it."

"Perfect! Tell him to take that road north for at least five or six miles, find a straight stretch that's clear on both sides of the road with no trees, big rocks or anything like that. Tell him to sit tight and wait; We'll come and get him."

The Colonel looked at me like he thought I was nuts, but he passed on the instructions. Judging by the one side of the conversation I could hear, I'm guessing his son thought I was nuts, too.

I drove into the motor pool, parked and took the Colonel into hangar 5 and met Alex next to the Starduster. The next few minutes in the hangar were some of the hardest I'd ever endured as we had to rush our goodbyes. We'd never see Chet, Dot, Rita... all of these people whom we'd grown so close to over the last three years. I'd hoped to share one last meal with them as we talked about the good old days; They deserved much more than a hurried handshake and hug as we rushed past them to board the Starduster.

Sadly, it couldn't be helped and they understood. I could see that McPherson was wondering where the hell I thought I was going to go as Phil got a tug and pushed us out of the Hangar and left us sitting there on the apron with Hangar 6 in front of me and Hangar 3 with a crumpled up executive jet plastered against it behind me.

Yeah, I couldn't resist. Without a word, I just lifted the Starduster straight up like a helicopter and then turned west and moved out over the hangars, the perimeter fence and into the gathering darkness.

Dumbfounded, the Colonel said, "You sneaky devils! I never knew."

"Ha! Ha!" I laughed. "That's one little secret that Phil didn't put into the simulator. And let's hope that for the next three hours or so, no one around Collins knows that the Stardusters have a vertical lift capability, either."

I flew west before turning northeast. "Now, Colonel, let's get your family. With any kind of luck, they should be on the road to Junction."

He looked a question at me and Alex laughed. "Just another one of our secrets, Colonel. I'll tell you about it sometime."

"If you would, Colonel," I said, "get your son on the phone. Tell him to park in the middle of the road facing north and turn his bright lights on. And have him double check for trees on either side of the road."

Flying over Junction, Alex and I gave each other a look. Silently, we said goodbye to another group of wonderful people we would never see again before we turned south. I suddenly realized that this great idea of mine might not be so great after all. In my tiny brain I thought that all I had to do was line up on the road until I saw Andy McPhersons headlights up ahead and then just set down. But it was darker than I expected it to be. So dark, I wasn't even sure I was over the road. Oh, John, you idiot! What have you done now?

Fortunately, before I could really work myself into a full-blown panic, we saw the lights up ahead. I still couldn't see anything below me, so I just lined up on the lights and settled this pig of a Starduster down as gently as I could and, wonder of wonders, it worked and we were sitting in the middle of the road.

I couldn't help but imagine what the Colonel's family thought when our Starduster... this *alien* spaceship... suddenly materialized out of the darkness and landed right in front of their car!

"Okay, Colonel, you're up. Go and get your family. And while you're out there, would you please disable the car? I'd rather not have people using this road."

Just a minute later, a clearly baffled Audrey McPherson and two wide eyed kids climbed aboard the shuttle and Alex got them buckled in. In the headlights, I could see the Colonel and his son moving around the car. There was a small flash and as the men walked back toward the Starduster, the flash was followed by a big flame and then a huge explosion.

Wow! When the McPherson's disable a car, they disable a car!

Alex gave me the go ahead that everyone was settled on board. As I started to lift off, I felt a large presence behind me as a deep, rumbling voice that sounded like it came echoing right out of a mine shaft said thanks for coming to get us. Holy smokes! Andy McPherson was even bigger than JJ.

"No problem!" I said cheerfully, but my internal *no problem* had more of a *you, I'm going to stay on the right side of!* Slipping a hand back, I give Andy a handshake; His hand was the size of a Sunday ham and completely engulfed my own.

Alex came up and took the seat beside me and I asked, "Okay, Luv, where's Link and his merry men?"

"I'm not sure. Head for San Diego."

I flew southwest while she did magical things with the Stardusters Comm suite. It was an eerie feeling looking down at a featureless black Earth. Just a few months ago, this countryside would have been aglow with the lights of towns, small cities, and even the occasional lights from the local highways and backroads. All of this area would have been alive in the night, but now there was practically nothing. With the collapse of the western power grid, for most people in remote areas nighttime now meant almost total darkness. And the few who did have a source of electricity weren't going to advertise that fact to the wandering murdering gangs. In this day and age, out here in the lonely wilderness, it was safer to stay dark.

I was getting melancholy when Alex snapped me out of it. "I've got Link. I'm putting coordinates into the nav system, but he says that we might not be able to land."

"Why? What's up?"

To answer me, Alex flipped the speaker on and I heard popping sounds. Geeze! That was gunfire!

"Link says that the bright lights we're coming up on are Simmons manufacturing plant. There's a helicopter pad just to the west, but at the moment they are a little busy with a large group of migrants moving through the area."

The Simmons Complex was just ahead and I maneuvered the Starduster around to the south so I could pick out the helipad. The good news was that it looked big enough to get the Starduster down. The bad news was that I could see gun flashes all around the west side of the landing pad.

Ooh! This was going to be fun! I asked Alex to get me a connection with Link. "Good evening, Deputy Lincoln," I said. "You seem to have a bit of a situation here. I have a Starduster about a mile south of you. How do you want to handle it?"

"John, good to see you! Are you okay?"

"Yeah, I think so for now. I don't think anyone's noticed us yet."

"Good. Why don't you just stay put for a few. The mob seems to moving around the big building away from us. Be ready to come in fast when I call."

"Got it."

"Is one or both of the Docs with you?"

"No. Why?"

"I have one wounded. Kurt took one through the shoulder."

"Copy. We'll be ready."

Alex nodded and said that she and Audrey would take cake of Kurt and that she would send the two McPhersons up to talk to me. What a gal, always thinking two steps ahead. When the guys came into the cockpit I just pointed ahead where they could see the bright lights. By now there was only the occasional gun flash and I told them that we were going to pick up nine, one of whom was wounded. Not a flicker of emotion from either of them, but they were definitely happier when I told them that there were weapons in the panel by the passenger door.

I contacted Link again and told him we were ready anytime. We also had two guns on our end, so don't shoot the good guys.

Link laughed and said that it looked clear for us to come on in. I ghosted in at about a hundred feet over the southeast edge of the helipad. I still couldn't see anything right underneath me as I slowly, very slowly, settled this big pig to Earth. I had barely touched down when Alex pushed the door open and the McPherson boys piled out loaded for bear. Ducking behind some pipes for cover, Link sent a group of three over, two of them supporting the injured Kurt in the middle. When they were on board, Link then sent the rest over in three groups of two. Once everyone was inside the Starduster, the Colonel and Andy hopped back in.

Smooth. Not a shot fired.

Quietly, we lifted off and I turned the Starduster east into the darkness. Disappearing into the night, we made one circuit around Earth on our way to Wisdom and Voyager's position in orbit. What made me feel really good was that no one had been left behind. There were about twenty-seven empty cryo pods, but that was only because whoever was supposed to occupy those never showed up at Sand Flea. At least we had room for six more McPhersons.

Alex came up to inform us that Kurt would be okay. Audrey McPherson, who obviosity had seen more that a few violent injuries, said was a clean wound that hadn't hit anything critical. We took one last sad wistful look at our dying world as made our circuit around the Earth.

Just when I really needed something to cheer me up weightlessness kicked in and I could hear the kids squealing in the back. Good! Let them have some fun. It had been a pretty traumatic day for all of us, so far. As a big grin spread across Alex's face, it dawned on me that in the three years I'd been working in space, this was her first time up, as well.

Blowing me an excited air kiss, Alex suddenly leaned forward and started fiddling with the comms again. The screen winked on and then the image split with her office back at Sand Flea on one side and a view of the airfield on the other.

How does she do that?

"What are we looking for, Luv?" I asked.

With a wicked grin, Alex pointed to the screen and said, "This."

There suddenly seemed to be a lot of activity in the Wendover area and soon we could see strings of headlights zooming across the runway and heading straight towards the Visions Unlimited area. Several cars went out of our view around Hangar 1 and a few minutes later people burst into Alex's office with guns drawn. After they gave the office, bathroom and conference room a thorough sweep, one of them went to the door and said something. On the screen, we watched President Collins walked in.

With a frown, Alex fiddled with the comms a little more and we had audio. We also had a crowd as everyone tried to squeeze into the Starduster cockpit so they could also see and hear the excitement.

Collins walked up to Alex's desk and picked up her name plate. Glaring at his aids, he threw the plate down and demanded, "So where is this Dr. Cummings?"

Displaying various stages of confusion, his assembled flunkies scurried around looking for a person that they had never seen before. We were just cracking up; It was just too funny!

Collins walked around the huge desk and sat in Alex's

chair while he waited for his minions to produce her out of thin air.

By this time, we were coming up on Voyager and I had to run everyone out so I could dock. As soon as I said we had a good seal, the entire compliment of the Starduster disappeared up into R3 and Voyager as if by magic. There were lots of screens in Voyager and they wanted a good seat so they wouldn't miss the rest of the show.

I, on the other hand, still had work to do.

Billy and JJ were out in their robots and they towed me over to the last hard point on the wing where the Starduster would join her sisters for the long trip through space. I secured the shuttle and climbed into Billy's Judy robot with him and we followed JJ into R3. Giving everything one last look, we fastened everything down in R3.

We were ready to go.

Floating into the Command Section, I hoped that I hadn't missed anything exciting that was happening back in Alex's office. Apparently, I had because the gang was falling down laughing. Alex was sitting in the Command Seat, but she scooted up and I slid in and she settled herself on my lap. Buckling myself down and holding her tight so she wouldn't float away, I knew I had the best seat in the house, well the spaceship, anyway.

Everyone started talking at once to fill me in. Collins was in a frenzy. Not only could his men not find Alex, but now it seems they had lost the space shuttle. At the moment, Collins was sitting alone in Alex's office with his feet propped up on her desk waiting. Alex shushed everyone when Collins' flunkies of Keystone Cops started crashing into each other when none of them wanted to the be the first to enter and give their boss the news that they still couldn't find Alex or the shuttle.

Collins growled at his lackies. "You said it landed just ahead of us."

"Yes, sir!" they said, snapping to. That much they were sure of.

"And it didn't take off."

"No, sir." Though now they sounded less sure. No one had seen it take off, but it couldn't have as their cars and trucks were blocking the runway... but it clearly wasn't in any of the Hangars.

"Then where in the hell is it? And where is this Dr. Cummings? Does anyone here know what's going on?"

Dot Barton walked into the office.

Collins looked up. "Who are you?"

"Good evening, Mr. President, my name is Dorothy Barton. Your people said that you wanted to speak with me."

"No, no. I want to speak to the person who's in charge here... this Dr. Cummings."

"Seeing as Dr. Cummings is no longer here, I guess that I am the person in charge."

"Not here! What do you mean not here? Where is she?"

Dot waved around the room. "Mr. President, as all of these people know, Dr. Cummings is up at Voyager."

Oh, Dot. That was mean!

"What?" Collins exploded as his roomful of minions suddenly tried to become invisible. They were all denying any knowledge of anything. Collins was about to self-combust.

Dot said, "Mr. President, if I may sit at the console for a moment perhaps, I can clear this up." And she loomed over the chair that Collins was sitting in until Collins was forced to relinquish it. I had to admit, Dot Barton does a good loom. Punching a couple of buttons, her face suddenly appeared on every screen in Alex's old office and on our screen in Voyager.

"Good evening, Ms. Barton," Alex said all sweetness and light.

"Madam Director, the President of the United States is here and he would like to speak to you."

Dot got out of the chair and motioned for Collins to sit back down. Collins, however, was looking around the room as if he expected Alex to pop up from under a chair. Finally, he took his seat and peered into the Vid screen as if was looking for something behind it. Of course, he could see Alex, but with at least a dozen of us packed into the Command Section he couldn't help seeing several other faces, too.

Alex said, "Good evening, Mr. President."

Collins squinted into the Vid screen. I never noticed before that he had little squinty pigs' eyes. "Where are you?" he demanded.

"I'm about three hundred miles over your head on the spacecraft Voyager."

"No, you couldn't be there. You were just here."

"Mr. President, are you, all right?"

He began to self-combust again. "Can anyone of you idiots tell me what's going on?" Then he stopped as if he just had a thought. "McPherson! Where's McPherson? He's the only one who knows what's going on."

As the word went out, the minions and flunkies started running around looking for the Colonel. We are cracking up and even Alex was having trouble keeping a straight face looking at Collins and shushing us at the same time. It wasn't working so she killed the Vid. When she finally got us quieted down turned it back on, we caught Collins in mid rant. "You can't find Cummings…"

"We found Cummings, sir"

"Shut up! Then you can't find a space shuttle and now you can't find McPherson."

Alex hadn't said anything in a while, but she was still on Collins' screen. The Colonel pushed his way through the crowd up into the cockpit and motioned to Alex to move over. Still sitting on my lap, she couldn't move too far, but did manage to lean back enough to where McPherson's face replaced hers on Collins' screen.

"Good evening, Mr. President. How may I be of service?"

Collins looked at the screen. "Ah, good! There you are McPherson! Now maybe we can get this mess straightened out. Where… ." and he stopped looked at the screen again, then he looked around the room and I swear he looked behind the screen again.

He squinted at the screen with those piggy eyes again and asked, "McPherson, where the hell are you?"

"Why, I'm up on the Voyager spaceship, Mr. President."

"What? Good. As usual McPherson you're way ahead of the rest of these idiots I have around me. Good. You bring that Cummings woman down here immediately."

"Oh, I'm afraid I couldn't do that sir."

Grinning widely, the Colonel nodded to me and with the flip of a few switches, I activated Gutman's magic engine. Together, McPherson and I both took Alex's hand and placed it on the rheostat. As she slowly turned it, with an almost silent whisper, Gustav Gutman's magic engines came to life and started moving Voyager away from Planet Earth.

Collins was in full sputter. "What do you mean? You can't do that! That's an order, damn it!"

Alex motioned the Colonel back and took over on the screen. "No, Mr. President, I won't be coming back nor will the Colonel or any of the other six hundred human beings here on Voyager. Despite all the warnings, you and people like you have transformed a once beautiful and fruitful oasis, an oasis that had nurtured life for billions of years, into a toxic waste dump. I hope you can repair it, but because of people like you, I don't think you can so we are going to try our luck on another world. Good bye, Mr. President."

We left the Vid on with Collins sputtering his threats colorfully punctuated with all kinds of dire consequences upon our heads. We didn't hear him over our own joyous whoops as Voyager began her journey through space.

We were on our way!